Books by Abigail Hilton

ARCOVE'S BRIGHT SIDE

a Hunters Universe Novel

ABIGAIL HILTON

P

*Pavonine
Books*

Cover Art by Iben Krutt
Map and Design by Jeff McDowall
Some design elements by Sarah Cloutier
A product of Pavonine Books

Special thanks to the beta readers and patrons who read this book as I wrote it. An incomplete list: Chris, Romi, Orin, Blue, Jason, Stefni, Steve, Mike, Betsy, Dragonsmark, Guardian Lion, Sandra, Accalia, Amberly, and Rebeca.

Thanks also to the many people who drew inspring fan art on Tumblr. You have no idea how easy it is to bribe me with art. Probably an incomplete list: iKrutt, Elliejaybird, Karvolf, Tunagriff, Corvithearti, Weirdweirm, Peculiurperennial, Focshi, and Eisly.

Table of Contents

THE ISLAND OF LIDIAN

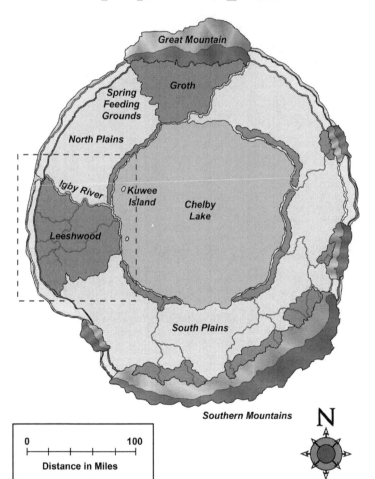

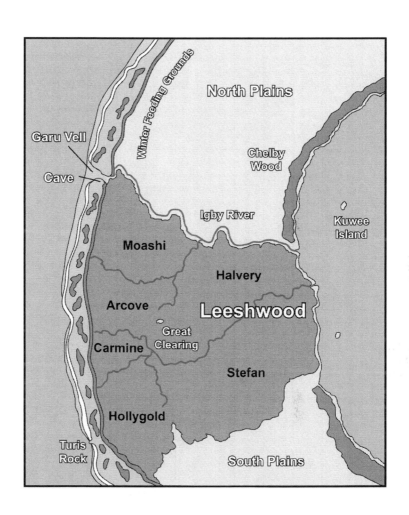

Regarding Chapter Notes

Dear Reader,

I originally wrote *Distraction* and *Arcove's Bright Side* for my Patreon donors. I included notes after some chapters, explaining my thoughts while writing them and giving some extra information that did not make it into the story.

For *Distraction*, I was able to work those notes into a single, coherent Author's Note at the end. For *Bright Side,* this just wasn't possible. I couldn't turn these notes into a single, coherent essay, but I still felt that some of you would enjoy them.

So instead of one long note after the story, I've created notes at the end of select chapters. You can either read each note after finishing the chapter, or you can read them back-to-back at the end of the book.

If you do read them after each chapter, be aware that you may get some small spoilers. I tried not to include major spoilers, but just reading my thoughts about what I wrote will give you some idea of what's coming next. Use this information in whatever way best enhances your enjoyment of the story.

Thanks for coming along,
Abigail Hilton
April, 2022

Part I

Summer

1

The Future to the Past

Halvery had spent all night on the border between his territory and Stefan's. They'd been mutually engaged in settling a dispute between dens on either side of the boundary. Halvery thought that, ten or twenty years ago, this would likely have been a very ugly dispute, since it involved cats from two different officers' territories and game poaching. There would have been dead animals, probably dead cubs. There would have been prolonged fighting. Halvery, Stefan, and their officers would have had to break it up by means of even more violence. If the instigators had escaped alive, they would have had to be killed or exiled from the territory.

That was how such a dispute would have gone twenty years ago. Now, though... *They just talk endlessly.*

It was obvious that the territory border had been muddled for a long time, going all the way back to Treace's demotion a decade ago and the reallocation of his territory that had occurred in the aftermath, a little before the rebellion. Both sides claimed the other den had contributed to the confusion. Stefan's cats had brought a very ancient den mother, nearly seventy, who claimed to know the entire history of this confusing patch of boundary markers.

Halvery's cats had given her a disdainful dismissal, claiming that she lived in the rival den and was not a disinterested party. They'd brought another elderly den mother, this one from an entirely different den within Halvery's territory. The newcomer proceeded to shout at the first female until Halvery feared that the only blood shed would be between two arthritic den mothers.

When Stefan's cats brought witnesses from a fourth den to join the argument, Halvery leaned over to Stefan and said, "Do you think we could get them to sort it out by single combat?"

Stefan had laughed. He was twenty-one years old and had taken over this clutter at nine, about a year after the rebellion. He was Treace's own blood, a cub from an early litter, but he'd had the good sense to join Arcove's creasia after the disastrous fight in the Great Clearing. Stefan had fought beside Arcove's cats that evening, come to Arcove's den that night, and made the journey with them to Kuwee Island. He'd stood beside them during the last, difficult battle.

After the violence ended, he'd been an ideal candidate to take over Treace's clutter. Those cats knew him and respected him because he was one of their own. However, his loyalty to Arcove was unquestionable. Still, the first five years had been difficult, with many challenge fights and complicated problems involving cats who'd fought on the wrong side. Things had slowly gotten better after that, but Halvery still had a sense that Stefan dealt with more complicated issues than any other officer in Leeshwood and rarely complained about it.

Stefan looked at the two groups, bringing their witnesses one by one, and said, "This is the way of the future. Surely it's better than a bloody melee."

Halvery made a face. He thought he had just about enough time to get back to his own den by dawn at this point. He raised his voice and thundered over the continuing discussion, "Listen up, you lot! I am going to make a ruling!"

"But we're not done talking," objected one cat.

"Oh, yes, you are," snapped Halvery. He marked the new boundary himself, following a route that he knew would give both sides a little of what they wanted and neither of them exactly what they wanted. Stefan saw what he was doing, adjusted it slightly, added his own scratch marks, and the two alphas parted cordially, while the two dens continued to whine around them.

The den's alphas should have just fought, thought Halvery. *That's the way this is supposed to work.* Granted, these sorts of disputes rarely worked the way they were supposed to. *But is this new way really better?*

Halvery couldn't help noticing that the dens themselves had been composed of a curious collection of animals. On Stefan's side, two adult sons of the den were living there with mates, side-by-side with their father and his mates. It was unusual to see more than one breeding male in a den unless he had some sort of partnership with another male.

Halvery had asked Stefan whether there was crowding in his territory. Perhaps Arcove needed to reinstate restrictions on the number of cubs. There had been few restrictions since the rebellion, since so many cats had died in the fighting or fled to the Southern Mountains.

"Oh, they're not crowded," Stefan had said. "They just like each other, and there's enough game in that area to support all of them. Feel free to come see for yourself."

Halvery believed Stefan, but he wasn't sure what to make of the rest. On his own side, the den had included three brothers, all with at least two female mates, along with one unrelated male who was den-mate to one of the brothers. Again, this many adult males in a single den was unusual. They seemed to be getting along.

I guess we don't fight about much of anything these days.

This was just Halvery's frustration showing and he knew it. Only last month, Stefan had had a very serious challenge fight. Halvery was glad Stefan had been the victor, because he didn't much like the challenger—one of Treace's old officers. The fellow had behaved impeccably since the rebellion, working hard to win back his status, and yet Halvery did not want him for a neighbor.

Halvery's own officers chattered behind him on the long walk back through his territory. They were nearly all of Stefan's generation, though he did have one left from before the ferryshaft wars. A couple of them tried to engage him on various topics, but Halvery just grunted. He was tired of talking. He picked up his pace until none of them had breath for it.

At last, his officers began to drift away in ones and twos. They went in search of their own dens or to visit friends or to hunt. Halvery had never encouraged the sort of familiarity that would have prompted them to tell him goodbye. *See yourselves out.*

By the time he reached the lake, he was alone. He surprised a hapless juvenile buck beside the water, ran it down, ate well, and felt an improvement in his mood.

The moon was setting as Halvery groomed the blood from his whiskers. He glanced at it critically. *Roup should be here in another few days. I wonder what absurd scheme he's orchestrating now. I wonder whether Arcove has made him go back to his own den.*

Roup had moved into Arcove's den during his convalescence last fall. And somehow he'd just…never left. Halvery had caught a couple of his own officers gossiping about what this meant. Stefan had come right out and asked, his manner polite, but probing.

Halvery had responded curtly, "Are you saying that you don't think Roup is an asset to the council?"

"No, of course not," said Stefan. "But does Roup have a clutter, or does Arcove? Are we letting kings have clutters now?"

"Lyndi doesn't have a clutter," objected Halvery, although he knew it was a weak argument. "Or her clutter is Roup's."

"Is Lyndi taking over Roup's clutter, then? I'd just like to know."

Halvery wasn't sure how to answer. *Arcove, you need to get out in front of this.* He really didn't want to bring it up to Roup. *It will ruin his visit.*

Halvery began encountering his own juvenile cubs and mates well before he reached his den. He accepted their cheerful greetings with half an ear. One of them said something about a visitor, but he wasn't really paying attention. When he came padding down the ridge into his own den, he was greeted to the unwelcome sight of Moashi sitting in the mouth of a cave, chatting away with Samathi.

Halvery rolled his eyes. "I assume you have come to visit Ilsa," he growled. "Please do me the courtesy of staying out of my sight so that I can pretend you're not here."

Moashi stood up. "Actually, I came to see you, sir."

Halvery gave him a look of exaggerated astonishment. "Has the future got something to say to the past? I feel like I've heard from the future quite enough already this evening."

Moashi laughed nervously. He was carrying his plume of a tail lower than usual. "Just a few minutes of your time, please?"

Ghosts of our fathers. Why me? "Alright, Ears, come on out to the beach. Samathi, did I see cubs swimming on my way in, or are my elderly eyes deceiving me?"

Samathi snorted. "Your eyes work just fine. And you can't call yourself elderly to a mate who is fifteen years your senior. It's insulting."

"Noted. Who's with those cubs?"

"Petra and Ieoli."

Halvery frowned. *That's not enough to watch ten cubs in the water.* "Well, me and Ears here will join them."

"I wish you'd stop calling me Ears," muttered Moashi as he followed Halvery in the direction of the lake.

"You'd prefer Runt?" asked Halvery cheerfully over his shoulder.

"I'd prefer Moashi."

"Yes, but I don't like you, so I'm disinclined to honor your preferences."

Moashi laughed as though he thought this was a joke.

Halvery stopped on the edge of the trees. The cubs weren't far out into the lake, just splashing around in shallow water. Two of them did look like they were deep enough to be swimming, but these were three-year-olds and big enough to take care of themselves. Petra and Ieoli were stretched out on the sand, chatting.

The breeze was at their backs this late in the evening. Halvery let it carry his scent to his mates. When they turned, he nodded at them. However, he remained far enough away that his conversation with Moashi could not be overheard. "Alright, what is it?"

Moashi swallowed. "Well, first off, Arcove has called a council meeting at sunset. I volunteered to come tell you."

Halvery peered at him incredulously. "You are going to give officers a bad name, Ears. We don't run our own errands."

Moashi screwed his eyes shut. "I know that, Halvery." He thought for a moment and added, "Sir."

Halvery gave a snort of laughter that made Moashi wince. "Please, just…listen for a moment."

He really did sound upset about something. Halvery waited.

"There is—was—this cat in my clutter named Vashon. He was about twenty, a pretty good fighter. He was one of those who sided with Dazzle. He didn't like the way I do things. He didn't think much of my fighting skills, even after I beat Dazzle. He said I won by accident. He didn't like me hanging around with Storm. He didn't like how I made a cave for writing and invited telshees to teach us. He didn't like me sparring with ferryshaft. He didn't like the way I take advice from my den mothers. He just…didn't like me."

"Well he has a point," drawled Halvery.

Moashi ignored him. "I knew he was going to challenge me. And I thought…I thought he had a large following among the other young males. I didn't think he would stop stirring them up, even if he lost the fight. He didn't stop after I beat Dazzle. Also, I'd had complaints from his neighbors. He may have killed a cub that wasn't his. It was…unclear. Anyway, I decided that if I won, I was going to kill him."

Halvery was listening closely now. He'd stopped making mocking noises. "Did you?"

Moashi shut his eyes. His voice came in a whisper. "Yes."

Halvery thought he would continue, but he didn't. Only the wind spoke in a whisper over the sand.

"So you won a second challenge fight," said Halvery at last, "against an opponent who had already seen you fight. That's not nothing, Moashi."

Moashi did not look proud of himself. He didn't even respond to his name. "I got him behind the head and crushed the back of his skull. Exactly how you showed me a thousand times. It was…

easier than I expected. Afterward, I thought I'd have some trouble from the rest of his friends. I thought I'd have some revenge fights. I was prepared for it. But then...nothing. I started asking around, and Halvery...nobody misses Vashon!"

Halvery laughed.

Moashi turned away as though he'd been slapped. He directed his next words at his paws. "The other young males seem almost relieved that he's gone. His den doesn't care. I...I think I made a terrible mistake."

Halvery cocked his head. "How's that?"

"I killed a friendless misfit!" exclaimed Moashi. "I imagined that he had all kinds of support against me, that he was a threat to my position, but now...I don't think that was ever true. I...I didn't need to kill him!" Moashi shut his eyes. "No one even wants to take him to the Ghost Wood. I've got his tail in the back of my den. Is that stupid? I'm sure you'll tell me it's stupid."

Halvery sighed. "I'm surprised you're not expressing these concerns to Roup."

Moashi looked miserable. "I can't bear to face Roup! I'll see him at the council meeting tomorrow, and I'm so afraid he'll ask about the fight. He gave me those skills, Halvery. I mean, you did, too, but Roup arranged it because he thought that I'd make a good alpha. And I took the skills he gave me and used them to murder someone! Someone who wasn't a threat to me." Moashi was actually rocking back and forth in his paroxysm of guilt. "Roup has never killed a challenger in his life! You have. Tell me how I'm supposed to think about this."

Halvery opened his mouth...shut it again. *How did I end up in this role?* He thought for a long moment. "Alright, first of all, Vashon was a bully. I've seen his type before. The fact that no one misses him should be your clue that you did the right thing. I guarantee you that he bullied everyone who knew him. But that doesn't mean they wouldn't have followed him under the right circumstances. It doesn't mean that he wasn't a threat to you. He was. You didn't make a mistake. Stop second-guessing yourself."

Moashi's eyes rose to Halvery's face, desperate with hope, seeking reassurance. Halvery wasn't sure he could stand that look for long, so he added, "And now I'm going to tell you some things about your hero that you may not know. Roup hasn't ever killed a challenger; that's true. He hasn't had many challengers, because cats are terrified of what Arcove would do to them if they hurt him.

"Roup exiles cats from his clutter when they misbehave. He doesn't fight with them, but they go to other clutters, and sometimes someone else has to kill them. Which is just lazy if you ask me. No, don't interrupt me, Ears! I am your superior officer; I am talking. Be quiet.

"Roup does many things well, but killing troublemakers is not one of them. It may surprise you, therefore, to learn that Roup wanted Arcove to kill Treace quite early in their acquaintance."

Moashi stopped trying to interrupt.

Halvery let his words sink in for a moment, then continued, "Roup knew that Treace was a threat to Arcove, and he knew that Treace would cheat. He figured those things out long before the rest of us. Arcove was exceedingly patient with Treace. He gave him second chances and third chances and fourth chances, and all the while, Roup wanted Treace dead.

"I think Roup would have been willing to bend the rules just to get rid of him. He actually suggested that Treace go attack the ferryshaft herd at one point, knowing the herd would turn and kill him. It would have resulted in a lot of dead ferryshaft, broken treaty laws, broken promises... It would have been the kind of mess Roup normally avoids at all costs. That's how badly he wanted Treace dead."

Moashi was silent, listening.

"Roup is not above using cunning to get rid of a dangerous enemy," said Halvery. "He's not above striking first. He's not even above breaking the rules. He's got a sweet temperament and he does not like to cause pain, but don't let him fool you. He's capable of ruthlessness, particularly when he thinks something is a threat to Arcove." *He's capable of watching Arcove fight and kill an animal*

9

whom he considered a brother. Halvery almost said it aloud, but decided he'd already said enough.

"You want to know how you should think about this?" continued Halvery. "Officers have to do hard things sometimes. You just did one of those. Now maybe the whole clutter will settle down, and you won't have to kill any more of them."

Moashi winced, but he did look calmer. "What about Vashon's tail?"

"You really should ask Roup about that," said Halvery.

When Moashi continued to stare at him pleadingly, he said, "Arcove used to take challengers to the Ghost Wood...if they didn't have family or friends to take them." *And I hope I am not betraying a confidence by saying so.*

Moashi's eyes went round. "He did?"

"Yes. But I don't think he talked about it much, so I'd appreciate it if you didn't, either."

To Halvery's dismay, Moashi stepped forward and butted his head against his shoulder. "Thank you. Thank you, thank you, thank you."

Halvery stepped back with a rumble. "Ghosts and little fishes! Have some dignity, Ears. I am not your mother. I still don't like you."

Moashi stepped away from him, smiling and looking relieved. "Oh, I know you're not my mother. But you're a very good commanding officer."

"I feel like you're not really listening to me."

"Roup said to listen to what you say and not the way you say it."

"Roup is not my interpreter."

This made Moashi laugh. His tail and ears came up. Finally, he glanced sidelong at Halvery with a mischievous expression. "There's one more thing I wanted to talk to you about. A female came to my den recently. Her name is Mitza. She's twelve years old—"

"I approve," said Halvery briskly. "Anything else?"

Moashi sighed. "She wants to join my den, yes, and I think I can defend her, so we have been talking."

"Less talking, more mating," said Halvery. "Now I'd like to go to sleep. Please leave."

Moashi looked unfazed. "Yes, well…about the mating…Ilsa says you do a thing that is remarkable, and I…"

Halvery had been in the act of walking away, but he stopped and turned slowly. "Oh, this is interesting. Is the future seriously asking the past how to mate?"

He'd hoped to embarrass Moashi, and he'd succeeded. *Maybe you'll shut up and go home now.* Moashi's ears flattened, but he didn't back down.

"I am familiar with the act of mating, thank you. But Ilsa says…"

"Let's leave Ilsa out of this. Look, here's the secret: your tongue feels better than your prick. Every young male thinks he is the exception to this rule, and every young male is a terrible mate until he realizes that he is wrong. Get over yourself. Use your tongue more. Every time you hear the females whispering that a male is 'very good at it,' that's what they mean. That's the secret. It's not complicated."

Moashi was clearly teetering between fascination and a desire to hide his head. "Yes, sir. I have grasped this as well, but…that's not what Ilsa was describing."

Halvery could feel a smirk curling the corners of his mouth. "Oh? Is it possible that the past does something better than the future?"

"Please, Halvery?"

"I hate to tell you this, cub, but there aren't any other short-cuts. The rest is just a lot of practice."

Moashi was practically vibrating now, mincing back and forth with his front paws. "Practice what?"

Halvery looked at him critically. *I should tell you to get lost.* Finally, he said. "Pulling out hurts. So do less of that."

"How?"

"I'm tired of looking at you. Goodnight."

"Halvery!"

"Goodnight, Ears!"

2

Generous

Halvery woke in the afternoon and promptly started for the cliffs. He arrived a little before sunset, intent upon finding Arcove in order to have a word before the council meeting started.

As he approached the den, he was surprised to catch the scent of ferryshaft and... *Curbs?* Other species attended the fall and spring conferences, but now it was midsummer. Moashi had called the meeting a "council," not a "conference," so Halvery had expected only creasia to be in attendance. As far as he knew, curbs had never attended a creasia council in any capacity.

But I bet I know why they're here now.

"Halvery?" It was Seeka, one of Arcove's older mates.

"Good evening, Seeka. Do you know where I might find Arcove?"

"He and Roup just came back from a hunt. I believe they carried a couple of sheep to the mouth of the den."

Halvery thanked her and continued on along the winding course of Smoky Branch, through the hazy warmth of the hot springs beneath the big trees, until he arrived at the packed earth caves among ancient roots. Arcove was lying in front of the main den, dozing a few paces from a mostly destroyed sheep carcass. The remains of the kill were surrounded by jostling cubs who were joyfully pulling it to pieces.

Halvery paused. It was the very picture of a successful hunt, and he regretted waking Arcove from what looked like a well-earned nap. As Halvery drew nearer, he caught a flash of gold further in the depths of the den—Roup, stretched out on his stomach, talking to someone. The other cat turned her head, and Halvery saw the bony silhouette of Nadine. She had been ill for several years—not the swift, sudden death that most cats hoped for, but a lingering illness that waxed and waned.

Arcove's ears twitched as the wind shifted. He sat up, turned, and caught sight of Halvery, hesitating on the edge of the trees. "Halvery... You're early." Arcove yawned, white teeth flashing against black fur. "I can offer you a sheep femur. There's not much else left."

Halvery smiled. He padded across the open space in front of the den and sat down beside Arcove. "Thank you, sir; I have eaten." Against his better judgment, he added, "Are those highland curbs I smelled on my way in?"

"Yes. They've offered to give us some details about the Southern Mountains. Or, more correctly, Storm has offered. Roup tells me this was your idea."

Halvery flicked his ears. "Can we pretend it was his?"

Arcove rumbled a laugh. He looked like he was about to call Roup over, and Halvery said, "I was hoping for a word in private, sir. Before everyone arrives."

Arcove gave him an assessing look, and the relaxed amusement fell away. He rose with a sigh and a flick of his tail. "Come on, then."

Halvery trailed him into the trees. They reached the banks of Smoky Branch, and Arcove said, "You're going to tell me that I need to send Roup back to his own den. I already know this. Anything else?"

Halvery took a deep breath. "With respect, sir, that is not what I was going to say."

Arcove turned to look at him in surprise.

Halvery steeled himself and continued, "I was going to say that if we lose you when we lose him...and our enemies know this...I don't think Roup's den is very safe."

Arcove's bright eyes narrowed.

Halvery knew he was treading close to impertinence, but... *Arcove, you disappeared into a telshee cave for ten days and by all accounts, you mostly stopped eating until Roup woke up. Dazzle may have been a sneaking rat's pizzle, but he wasn't wrong about how to destabilize Leeshwood.*

There was a long pause, during which Halvery wondered whether Arcove was going to tell him exactly how far beyond the scope of his authority he'd strayed and exactly how unwelcome his opinions of his king's private life might be. Then Arcove said, "Unsafe how?"

Halvery let out a breath. "Breeding females will protect a den and patrol its territory, sir. Cubs give alarms when they see or smell something they don't expect. Roup lives with neither at this point. It's just him and Caraca and Lyndi. Lyndi is frequently out on clutter business, and I'm told that Caraca has projects around the cliffs that keep her occupied more than half the time. I'm sure that grown cubs and friends come to visit, but I'm also sure that Roup's den is often empty. His personal territory borders the cliffs, so an intruder need not cross any other territory to reach it. He has always kept a small clutter, so the territory is sparsely populated. How difficult do you think it would be for a cat like Dazzle to find his way into Roup's den undetected?"

Arcove considered this. When he did not respond at once, Halvery continued, "You have room for all three of them if they—"

Arcove spoke at last, "Roup can't rule a clutter from my den."

"Does he want to?" *He's barely ruling it now!*

Silence.

"I suggest offering the clutter to Lyndi first," continued Halvery, "but I think she'll say no. I think she'll want to stay with Roup, although whoever takes over the clutter would be a fool not to consult her. Ultimately, I think you should give the clutter to Carmine."

Arcove's tail twitched. "You're suggesting I give Carmine a clutter and a place on the council without making him win a fight?"

Halvery flicked his ears. *That's the way of the future, isn't it?* "Yes. Although if he simply accepts those terms, he'll be the lowest ranking officer, and I doubt that will satisfy Carmine. He'll challenge Moashi and then Hollygold and so on. He'll fight his way up until he finds his proper rank. According to Roup, the only reason he hasn't challenged one of them so far is that he doesn't want to leave Roup's clutter or establish a new den. If he doesn't have to do those things, I think he'll find his place among your officers in short order."

Arcove considered this.

After a moment, Halvery added, "I think leaving Carmine off the council is dangerous, Arcove. He is well-disposed towards you, but he has a huge following among the young creasia in every clutter. Male and female—they all like him. Give their favorite a voice and some authority. They'll be more likely to remain loyal."

"Agreed," said Arcove at last. "Between Carmine and Moashi, I would have the perspective of the younger generation." Another pause. Arcove cocked his head and looked at Halvery narrowly. "Are you suggesting that I add Carmine as a seventh officer...or that he replace Roup?"

Of course you think I'm trying to get Roup off the council. "I am suggesting that you add a seventh officer, sir."

Another long moment. Then Arcove seemed to relax. He stretched, and his claws fanned. "Well, this will all be immaterial if Roup doesn't want to give up his clutter."

Halvery sighed. "He'll want to stay in your den, Arcove. He has always wanted that." *So have you.*

"If Lyndi follows him and remains on the council, it would mean two officers sharing my den..." Now Arcove sounded uncertain.

Halvery had an overwhelming instinct to change the subject. He could almost hear Roup saying, *"Let him show a little fear, Halvery."*

"May I be candid, sir?"

Arcove chuffed. "More candid than you are already being?"

"The fiercest opposition to this in the past would have come from me."

"And now it won't?"

Halvery shook his ears. "You and Roup have put aside your personal happiness for nearly forty years in service to Leeshwood. Sharing a den is not unusual. You can have this. The assembly will let you." Half under his breath, Halvery muttered, "They'd better."

Arcove smiled. For a moment, Halvery was afraid he might say something shockingly personal and blurted, "How is Nadine?"

Arcove became instantly sober. "Uncomfortable. She has good nights and bad nights. Roup spent a lot of time talking to her while he was healing from his injury this winter. It made her happy to have him there. That's one reason I haven't sent him home."

Halvery looked at him sidelong, and Arcove flicked his tail. "Of course it's not the only reason."

"Arcove, you don't need excuses. Just let him stay. Make it official, and give the gossips something else to talk about. Like Carmine's promotion."

"I have heard what you've said, Halvery, and I am thinking about it." He hesitated. "I appreciate what you are trying to do."

"Thank you, sir."

Arcove's mouth curled in a smile that was almost a smirk and he said, "My den is also a little closer to yours."

Halvery coughed. "It is."

"Still a long walk," observed Arcove in a tone that made Halvery think he was enjoying himself.

"Yes."

"And yet he always comes back in a good mood."

Halvery fixed his attention on a spot further downstream where the council was beginning to assemble. "I do my best."

Arcove laughed. "I distinctly remember you telling me once that Roup doesn't like anyone other than me."

"I'm sure I have said any number of foolish things over the last forty-odd years, sir."

"If something happens to us, the council will probably choose you..."

Us. It was as close as Arcove had ever come to acknowledging that he and Roup ruled Leeshwood cooperatively—an accusation that would have caused no end of trouble for him in the past.

Please don't trust me this much; I don't know what to do with it. Halvery forced himself not to react. "That has occurred to me. Please stay healthy, Arcove."

Arcove looked at him quizzically. "You used to have some interest in being king."

"I was young and stupid. These days, I often wonder whether being an officer is worth it. You should have heard the long-winded, never-ending squabble that Stefan and I had to sort out last night. Dens don't even fight anymore. They just *talk*. It's unbearable."

Arcove listened with amusement while Halvery gave him a colorful and highly abbreviated review of last night's dispute. Further downstream, Hollygold had come out of the trees, and Roup had joined him, along with Storm and two highland curbs. They were far enough away that Arcove and Halvery couldn't hear what they were saying.

Halvery finished his story, and they were both quiet a moment, watching the shifting body language of the group as Moashi appeared and then Stefan. Halvery didn't think any of them had seen him and Arcove, still sitting in deep shadow. He watched Roup pad over to Moashi and ask a question, saw Moashi's guarded response. *Roup is asking about the fight. Don't flinch, Moashi. Don't apologize.*

Roup said something, and Moashi's ears came up. Then Roup turned away. He was standing against summer green, the sunset light catching in his fur, haloed in gold.

"You know he's beautiful, right?" Halvery wondered at his own audacity, but Arcove didn't say anything. He cocked his head with a puzzled expression. Halvery thought he was sincerely trying to see Roup the way a stranger might see him…and failing.

Halvery hurried on. "It really is a shame that he's never managed to give that fur to any cubs. It's obvious that his color will never breed true with Caraca. If he's in your den, do you think he'd be willing to share one of your mates? I know he doesn't want the responsibility of another breeding female, but he might share…"

A long silence.

Halvery could feel his nerve slipping. *What on earth makes me think I can talk this way to Arcove?* "Sir, I realize that I am far outside the scope of my role, and if I am giving offense, I trust you'll—"

"I offered a long time ago," said Arcove quietly. "Roup really doesn't want…" Arcove didn't finish the thought, and after a moment continued, "At that time, he pointed out that if we were so unfortunate as to produce a litter with one black and one golden cub, we'd never hear the end of it. This would be forever presented as evidence that we really do share a den. Roup would lose his place on the council, and I would lose respect."

Halvery inclined his head. "That was a reasonable concern… twenty or thirty years ago."

Arcove shot him a quick, almost shy smile. "You think Roup *wants* to share a mate?"

Halvery frowned.

After a moment, Arcove continued, "Roup and Caraca shared a den for two years before they produced a litter of cubs."

Halvery blinked.

Arcove was talking so softly now that Halvery had to strain to hear him. "He doesn't like mating with anyone he doesn't know extremely well. He—"

Halvery laughed. "He doesn't like anyone who isn't you."

"That is demonstrably untrue."

"I'm joking. I see your point. But he knows your mates. He's friends with them."

Arcove rolled his eyes. "Some of them. Especially the older ones. I suppose if Nadine were in season, we could share a mate."

Halvery chuffed.

Arcove continued, "It only takes Roup thirty years or so to make friends." He gave Halvery a pointed look.

Halvery couldn't bring himself to follow that joke where it was leading. Instead, he said, "Roup has more friends than anyone I know!"

"Not friends he wants to mate with."

Lyndi had joined the gathering of officers. She was larger than most females, but still a little smaller than all the males in the group except for Moashi. She stopped to speak to him in what was clearly a friendly tone, probably congratulating him for winning another challenge fight. This time he showed no anxiety. He butted his head against her shoulder in that overly familiar way of his. Halvery frowned. *Don't let him do that, Lyndi.* But she only licked the top of his head.

Storm sat down beside Moashi, and the two began an animated discussion. *Might as well start calling him Storm Ela-creasia. Or perhaps Moashi Ela-ferry.*

Arcove cut into his thoughts. "You certainly did a good job with that cub. I confess, I did not think he'd make an officer, but now he seems well on his way to a long career."

"That really was Roup's doing from beginning to end," said Halvery.

Arcove shot him a look that said, *"You are not fooling anyone."*

Halvery hurried on, "Would you be offended if *I* offered to share a mate with Roup?"

Arcove looked at him in frank surprise. "That is…very generous."

It was almost unheard of for two males to share a mate when they were not sharing a den. Roup was not hunting for Halvery's mates and cubs, not patrolling their territory, not defending the den from challengers.

Arcove shook his ears. "It is a very generous gift…" He broke off and laughed helplessly, "that Roup will in no way appreciate." He thought a moment longer. Halvery didn't try to interrupt him.

At last, Arcove said, "I think Roup was a little disappointed that none of his cubs looked like him. But he believes it is a foolish thing to care about, so you'll have a hard time getting him to admit it. He'll tell you that his color is terrible for hunting."

"Only in summer," objected Halvery.

Arcove was still thinking. "If it's the color you want, you'd need to choose a female with the right blood. It's not a common color. I've never seen another solid gold; have you?"

"No," said Halvery, "but that color is around. There's Hollygold, obviously." Hollygold had the distinction of being able to trace his line to Arcove and nearly every officer in Leeshwood. He was mostly a brindled tan, but he had a golden blaze over his face and bright green eyes like Arcove's. The combination of gold and green had inspired his name.

"Roup won't mate with his own blood," said Arcove flatly. "He'll find the idea unsettling."

Halvery cocked his head. "Even a distant relative?"

"Hollygold isn't that distant. He's a great-grandcub. Roup will see his daughters as kin. He will also see them as much too young."

Halvery rolled his eyes. "He'll see every female who can still have cubs as 'much too young.' That objection is inevitable."

Arcove smiled.

Halvery plunged on. "I thought I might ask Nadine if any of the breeding females in my den or yours have the right blood. She knows the bloodlines of Leeshwood better than anyone."

Arcove looked at him narrowly. "How long have you been thinking about this?"

Halvery shifted his paws. "A while... But if you don't want me to—"

"Roup won't thank you."

Halvery couldn't repress a laugh. "He doesn't thank me for a lot of things."

He started to say something else, but Arcove spoke first. "If you want the best chance of getting Roup's color, it's not Nadine you should talk to. Or not *just* Nadine. It's Caraca."

Halvery was surprised. "Will she be offended?" Halvery had never heard of a female being offended that her mate sired cubs with another female, particularly after her own fertility had passed. *But Roup does have the oddest cats in his clutter.*

"Offended?" said Arcove with a laugh. "She'll be delighted."

Halvery was even more confused.

"Roup used to complain that Caraca wanted to breed him like one of her oories," said Arcove, and Halvery gave a surprised snort of laughter.

"She's curious about how color and other traits are inherited," continued Arcove, "but she's not one for visiting, and I doubt she knows the bloodlines of Leeshwood, so you might have to get her to put her head together with her mother."

Halvery quirked a smile. "Thank you for that information, sir."

The sun had just set behind the trees. Arcove got to his feet. "Time for me to go talk about developments in the Southern Mountains."

"I'll come around the other way," said Halvery. If he and Arcove walked into the council meeting together, it might provoke jealousy. It might make cats question whether Roup was still second in command. It was the sort of thing that Halvery would have been pleased to do twenty years ago.

Arcove shot him a look that Halvery couldn't quite interpret, but when he spoke, Halvery could tell that he'd won a little more trust. *As if I don't already have too much.*

"It really is a relief to have the two of you getting along... whatever form that takes."

Halvery nearly choked on a laugh. "Well, I hate to disappoint you, but I'm not sure we argue any less. You'll certainly listen to us arguing this evening if Roup is still trying to save Dazzle."

Arcove's look darkened. "Well, I'm with you there."

Halvery's teeth flashed. He couldn't help a trace of smugness. *Roup, you may not get your way.*

Arcove continued in a dangerous murmur. "If Dazzle is lucky, you killed him. If he's unlucky...*I'll* get hold of him."

3

Chaos and Council

Roup listened with interest as Storm introduced the high-land curbs to Moashi, who was positively radiating curiosity and goodwill. The curbs' names were Cohal and Maoli—one male, one female. They had grown up in the Southern Mountains. Cohal had come north about sixteen years ago as beta to Eyal's long patrol pack. Maoli had fled from the mountains two years later when their sheltered valley was overrun by lowland curbs. Their queen had been killed, their cubs and breeding females slaughtered, and their people scattered. None of the highland curbs from the small pack on the northern plains had ventured back into the mountains since. There were too few of them, and every animal was precious. Besides, it seemed unlikely that any of their kin had survived.

Roup gathered that Cohal and Maoli saw themselves as expendable to their struggling species, since Maoli was past her breeding years, and Cohal had recently given up leadership of his pack. There were now more than forty highland curbs living on the northern plains, most of them younger than this pair. Cohal and Maoli were therefore willing to risk a dangerous excursion into the mountains with Storm, based on the small chance that they might find another group of highland curbs surviving somewhere in those peaks.

Moashi, who'd always had an abiding curiosity about other species, was fascinated. He wanted to know about their pack structure, their denning arrangements, and their offspring. Was it true that the curbs had a new queen? Were they still living in telshee caves for part of the year? Did their cubs really hang from their bellies like ticks? Moashi lay down so that he was on eye-level to talk to them. He stretched, flopped onto his side, and then, absurdly, onto his back.

Roup watched with amusement as the curbs went from stiff distrust to mild bewilderment, and at last to guarded civility. By the time Arcove came gliding out of the shadows from further upstream, they seemed to have decided that Moashi was some sort of honorary ferryshaft.

Roup was watching this exchange so closely that he did not notice Halvery padding up behind him until he spoke in Roup's ear. "You're welcome," he whispered.

Roup glanced around with a smile. "For what?"

"Later."

"Councilors," began Arcove, "I've called you here this evening because there have been developments in the Southern Mountains that may eventually affect us."

The group went instantly quiet. Arcove sat down. His gaze fell to the highland curbs and then to Moashi, still upside down and looking extremely informal. Arcove gave an infinitesimal frown and Moashi turned over and scrambled to his feet. Halvery made a barely audible grumbling noise beside Roup. "Have some dignity, Ears."

Arcove continued, "As some of you know, the limits I placed upon the number and range of the ferryshaft over the sixteen years they were under treaty law had some unintended consequences. Ferryshaft repress lowland curbs. Without herds of ferryshaft scattered throughout the island, lowland curbs became more numerous. They advanced into new territory and eventually overwhelmed their rivals in the mountains."

"We were collateral damage of your war," snapped Cohal.

Arcove's gaze fell to the curbs, who were glaring up at him with undisguised dislike. "An unintended consequence," he repeated.

Cohal was standing in creasia territory, looking up at a creasia king easily ten times his size, yet he seemed unruffled. Roup had to admire his temerity. "You allowed our enemies to breed unopposed for nearly two decades," said Cohal. His head jerked around at Halvery. "Then, when we were desperately few, that one killed three of our packmates." His gaze returned to Arcove. "And you never apologized."

Arcove looked down at the curb, his face inscrutable. "Would that have helped?"

Cohal's whole body vibrated on a growl.

Behind him, Storm said, "I led Halvery's clutter into your pack, Cohal."

Cohal shot him a look that was equal parts fondness and irritation. "Yes, but you paid your debt. You saved our pack from Quinyl. You ran with us until Eyal called you a curb. You used your influence to hide us with telshees so that we could keep our pups safe. You owe us nothing, Storm Ela-ferry. The creasia, on the other hand, owe us a debt that I do not think they can possibly pay."

Arcove gave a flick of his ears. "And yet here you are."

"We are here because of the small chance that we might find kin in those mountains. We are not here to help you. We are here to collect a debt."

Well, that attitude will get you nowhere, thought Roup. He glanced at Arcove's face and was momentarily worried that he might tell the curbs to get out of his wood.

Then Storm stepped around Cohal, physically shielding the curb's body with his own. He spoke brightly, "*I,* however, am here to help. Cohal and Maoli cannot reach their valley without cooperating with larger predators. They know the canyons up there better than anyone. I'll vouch for them. I promise they will be of assistance."

Arcove's posture softened. His ears came up, but he still looked like he didn't care for the tone in which this meeting had begun. "In that case, Storm, keep your friends in check. This is not a fall conference. This is a creasia council."

"Yes, sir."

That got the barest flicker of a smile. In spite of the amount of time Storm had spent in Leeshwood over the last decade, Roup couldn't remember hearing many "sirs" out of him.

"You always bring chaos to my council," murmured Arcove, though without any heat.

Storm gave his most disarming grin. "But also useful information."

"That's debatable. Sit down."

Storm backed up, forcing Cohal to back up with him. Maoli had remained sitting beside Moashi during Cohal's outburst. Roup didn't think she'd been present for the run-in with Halvery. She didn't look friendly, but she didn't look ready to attack anyone, either. She began muttering to Cohal as soon as he rejoined her. Roup thought she was telling him to stop being a fool.

"Let's start with unfinished business from our last meeting," said Arcove. "Stefan, have you been able to determine how a spy from the Southern Mountains was able to pass himself off as a member of your clutter?"

Stefan stood up. "I have, sir."

Roup pricked up his ears. He'd tried to put this together himself and failed. *Granted, Treace's old dens don't trust me and would prefer not to talk to me.* He glanced at Halvery, who was friends with Stefan, but Halvery didn't look like he had any idea what Stefan was about to say, either.

"Dazzle came from a den on the eastern edge of my territory near the lake."

Stefan paused and Halvery spoke up. "That sounds like Treace and Moro's old den."

"Very near it," agreed Stefan. "Dazzle's mother was sister to one of Treace's mates. More relevant to the current situation: those dens are deep in that territory, quite far from any other officer's purview. Quite far from my own den, frankly. More than half of Dazzle's den went with Treace to the Southern Mountains, including Dazzle's mother and her cubs. He was three years old at that time, four by the time of the rebellion."

"Just old enough to make the walk," said Roup thoughtfully.

"Just old enough," agreed Stefan. "And by the time of the rebellion, he was just young enough not to be included. There's a rumor going round that he was on Kuwee Island, but everything I've learned indicates this is false."

There was a pause, during which Arcove looked hard at Moashi. Roup knew that Moashi had encouraged not just the rumor, but the unabashed lie from cats who were smarting over Dazzle's success.

"Do I need to point out that honesty is the bedrock of organized society and without it, there can be no trust and no cooperation?" murmured Arcove. He didn't say Moashi's name, but he was looking right at him.

Moashi swallowed. "No, sir."

"I am never in favor of encouraging cats to lie, even for a good cause."

"Yes, sir."

"Stefan, please continue."

"Dazzle left behind relatives and friends to whom he was attached," continued Stefan. "This attachment was sufficient to bring him back to Leeshwood two years after the rebellion. There was still a great deal of dissatisfaction, disorganization, and chaos within the territory at that time. Many cats had died or left. No outsider wanted to join my clutter, in spite of extra space and plentiful game. Cats who'd sided with Treace were the targets of unprovoked attacks, including the killing of cubs and even females. It was a difficult time to be in my clutter.

"Among Treace's old followers, sympathy for those who had died and those who'd been exiled was at its height. Dazzle found his way into his old den, and they were happy to see him. He brought news of their families and friends in the Southern Mountains."

"Ah…" Roup sat back. "That would get him a hearing."

"It absolutely did," agreed Stefan.

"So he started as a messenger?" asked Roup. "Bringing news between displaced, but related, dens?"

"Correct. He would come for a month at a time, occasionally a season. He rarely strayed outside the den's territory, but he hunted with them and defended their border. Neighbors came to recognize him as part of the den, or at least part of an attached clutter. In this way, he established a history in Leeshwood that spans years."

Halvery frowned. "In that case...are we only talking about *one* traitorous den?"

Stefan made a face. "Not...exactly. Word got around among Treace's old followers that they could send messages to their friends and family in the mountains if they talked to the right cats. It was apparently an open secret among a certain set. Few cats knew all the details, however. Dazzle still spent most of every year in the Southern Mountains. He's rumored to have mates and cubs there. Some say he's Thistle's beta, although there's disagreement on that point."

"Thistle would have been a fool not to use him," muttered Hollygold.

"Agreed," said Stefan, "but I can't tell you when that started. The picture seems to be, first, of a cat who began, at six years of age, to run personal messages back and forth between separated dens. He gradually shifted to the role of spy, but even his friends don't know when that happened. Cats involved will insist that they were only ever trying to contact loved ones and that if Dazzle was a spy, they knew nothing about it."

Arcove spoke at last. "I gather several of these cats talked to you?"

"I managed to get one den talking, yes," said Stefan. "The story spans almost the entire period since the rebellion, and they claim that the cats who originally welcomed Dazzle back into Leeshwood are dead. Many of those now living in those dens were quite young when they were first introduced to him. They will tell you that they didn't know they were doing anything wrong until they were deeply involved. Then they were afraid to come forward.

"Dazzle is a skilled fighter. He helped protect his old den from attacks, and he made it known that he would exact revenge on cats who attacked his friends while he was away. He tended to cripple rivals instead of killing them, which inspired fear. A crippled cat provided a daily reminder of what might happen to anyone who crossed Dazzle. Cats were afraid of him. But many of them were also the beneficiaries of his protection and intervention. They loved him, too. The situation was...*is*...complicated."

"I suppose you promised these cats immunity from punishment in exchange for information?" asked Arcove.

"I did," said Stefan quietly. "Many of Dazzle's closest associates had already fled. As far as I can tell, at least a dozen cats from my clutter left for the Southern Mountains as soon as they heard about events following Moashi's challenge fight. The rest are terrified.

"I would appreciate it if you would tell me what you want me to do, Arcove. If punishment needs to occur, it should be swift and final. The cats involved need to know that they will not be paying for this the rest of their lives. I am not trying to make excuses for them. But if you want their loyalty...this is what needs to happen."

"It doesn't sound like I have ever had their loyalty," growled Arcove.

Roup felt sorry for Stefan. He was clearly torn between genuine devotion to his clutter and loyalty to his king. "With respect, sir, these *are* your cats. They truly are. But they also love their family and friends. Some of those attachments have survived more than a decade of separation. Surely you can understand the sort of bonds that span time, distance, and even political disagreements." His eyes flicked infinitesimally towards Roup and away.

Arcove is not going to respond well to that, Stefan...even if you're right.

Before Arcove could speak, Stefan said quickly. "I didn't catch Dazzle, and I should have. Punish me, Arcove. I'm at least as much to blame as my clutter."

Now you have said the right thing, thought Roup.

Arcove sighed. "Councilor, I am not blaming you." A long pause. "You've done well with that clutter, Stefan. Halvery tells me that you have a harder job than anyone else in Leeshwood. Deal out punishment or mercy as you see fit. I trust your judgment regarding your own cats."

Stefan let out a breath. "Thank you, sir."

Moashi spoke up, "If Dazzle was content to run messages between Treace's old dens and the Southern Mountains for years, what changed? Why did he decide to fight his way into Halvery's territory last spring?"

"An excellent question," said Stefan, "and I don't think the answer lies in Leeshwood. I think that, following the events surrounding Charder's death two years ago, Sedaron's herd became steadily more aggressive towards the cats in the Southern Mountains. Sedaron couldn't gain support for attacks on Leeshwood, so he concentrated his attention there. Things were never easy for creasia in those mountains, but over the last three years, they've become intolerable. I think that Thistle asked Dazzle to use his unique position to investigate the possibility of returning to Leeshwood, hopefully in a position of dominance.

"Until recently, Dazzle had never spent any time in Leeshwood outside my territory. He needed to get a sense of the other clutters, so he fought his way into Halvery's. To the credit of this council, we identified him almost as soon as he began to act on a larger scale. I thought Dazzle was sneaking off to the Southern Mountains, though I couldn't prove it. So did Halvery. Roup arranged for him to be traded into Moashi's clutter precisely because he wanted a look at what Dazzle was doing. I don't think anyone can say that Leeshwood is easily breached, although we were perhaps a bit overconfident in our ability to manage or use Dazzle as opposed to simply killing him."

Roup could almost feel the whole group carefully *not* looking at him. He'd given them an account of his interactions with Dazzle during the time when he was convalescing in Arcove's den. The other council members were aware that Roup would prefer a peaceful return of the exiled creasia to Leeshwood. Halvery was, as usual, the strongest voice of opposition, although even he had not taken a hard stance against *all* cats from the Southern Mountains. But he didn't trust them, didn't like them, and expected abject submission before he would be willing to consider forgiveness or a place in his territory. Roup had the sense that Stefan and Hollygold were of the same opinion, though they were more circumspect.

Moashi and Lyndi wanted to side with Roup, but it was, ironically, their fondness for him that made it impossible for them to do so in this case. "Roup, please don't expect me to take your side in favor of a cat who tried to kill you while you were offering him kindness and mercy," Lyndi had told him flatly. "That's asking too much."

"Thank you for that report," said Arcove to Stefan. "Hollygold, I sent you on a bit of a covert journey recently. What did you learn?"

Hollygold sat up straight from where he'd been lounging beside the water. He was a big cat with a powerful build and an easy confidence. Halvery sometimes called him "lazy," although not too loudly because Halvery liked him. Roup would have described him as "unambitious."

Hollygold could have aimed very high if he'd wished. His storied bloodline put other cats in awe of him, and he had the gift of making others admire him without provoking jealousy. He was a natural leader and a natural fighter. He could have been a contender for kingship. Perhaps he still would be, though he showed no inclination in that direction. He was the third cat to take over Ariand's old clutter since the rebellion, and he'd somehow remained friends with all of his old rivals. Both of the previous alphas were now his officers. He didn't seem overly concerned with rank. He'd never challenged Stefan, and the only reason he outranked Moashi was that Moashi had arrived on the council more recently.

"I learned that Thistle's cats have moved from their dens in the foothills and gone deeper into the mountains," said Hollygold.

"You went to the Southern Mountains?" asked Roup in surprise. Arcove hadn't told him about this.

"As requested," said Hollygold. "We made contact with some of Thistle's cats and were attacked for our trouble."

Roup shot a glance at Arcove. *You should have told me. I would have liked to frame the message.*

Arcove kept his eyes on Hollygold. "Did they say anything to you?"

"They said we were in their territory and to get out," said Hollygold. "We hung around the area for a few days just to see whether Thistle would decide to send a different message after learning of our presence. He did not."

"And what did you think of the country you passed through in order to reach his cats?" continued Arcove.

Hollygold took a deep breath. "As others have pointed out, game is not plentiful on the dry, lower slopes of the mountains. However, as we went higher, the land became greener, wetter, and there was more to eat. We spotted large, shaggy, hoofed animals with horns. They seemed to travel in small herds. I'm sure they're edible, but they seemed difficult to kill, and we didn't try."

"Woolly ox," muttered Cohal. "Extremely dangerous."

"Sheep were in abundance," continued Hollygold, "though often guarded by curbs, who drove them away at our approach. We found heavily furred pigs with sharp tusks. They are fiercer and bigger than the little desert pigs, but they are at least not guarded by curbs. One member of my clutter was injured while hunting them, but ultimately we all made it back to Leeshwood alive. We encountered some small prey and small predators, none of much note. However, we did run across the tracks of...something larger." Hollygold hesitated.

"A predator?" prompted Stefan.

"Yes. I have no idea what it looks like, but the prints were larger than a creasia's and had very long claws."

The entire council turned to the curbs, who were looking smug. "Well?" asked Storm at last.

"Ice bear," said Cohal. "You'd better hope that you never find out what one looks like."

"They sleep in winter," said Maoli. "They eat both plants and animals. At this time of year, they are slow and lazy, but they are more aggressive in the fall and spring."

"We are giving you information about our old home," said Cohal to Arcove, "but so far, you have shared nothing of interest with us, creasia king."

Arcove's tail flicked. Roup could tell he was losing patience with Cohal's attitude. "Hollygold, please describe the location in the mountains where you located these creasia."

"They're living in a wooded valley with a long, deep lake at the bottom," said Hollygold. "On its eastern end, the valley rises into a series of steep slot canyons. We didn't try to get up into those canyons or the peaks beyond. It seemed like a good place to get trapped by curbs or killed by rockslides or floods. It's obvious that snowmelt rushes down the canyons to feed the lake."

Roup's ears pricked. *I remember this place.* It was as far as he, Arcove, and Coden had managed to penetrate during their expedition into the mountains one carefree summer. Arcove had been eight years old. Roup and Coden had been nine. Arcove had beaten Ketch the previous year, but he had not yet begun to escalate the ferryshaft wars, and the full weight of kingship had not yet descended. They'd spent fifteen days in the mountains exploring. The idea that Arcove and Coden would fight to the death six years later had been unthinkable.

We were trying to find the secret dens of the highland curbs, Roup remembered. *Coden wanted to meet their queen. But we couldn't find our way through the slots. We almost drowned and turned back.*

Cohal and Maoli had gone completely still. "Our valley..." whispered Maoli.

"Did you see curbs?" demanded Cohal.

"We saw plenty of curbs," said Hollygold, "but I don't think they were highland curbs."

Cohal opened his mouth, but Maoli spoke first, "Were they running on the cliffs with the sheep? Or on the walls of the canyons? Only highland curbs run on cliffs."

"I didn't see that," said Hollygold.

Arcove spoke. "I have received a report from an ely-ary who flew over the mountains. She said that beyond the slots lies a high, sheltered valley, green with summer foliage. A river at the bottom is fed by the mountain heights and exits through the canyons into the lower valley. The upper valley rises on all sides to icy peaks. It is accessible only through those canyons."

He paused. The curbs were listening with expressions of longing and sadness.

"*That* is your valley, isn't it?" asked Arcove. "The upper one?"

For a long moment, Roup thought the curbs would not answer. Finally, Maoli spoke. "Our people say that the slots were once closed by ice. For years without number, since a time before we began to speak, our valley was completely closed off. Our people still came and went over the peaks in order to keep watch on the outside world. But they made the journey only in summer and only with difficulty. We are bigger and have thicker coats than lowland curbs. We are more surefooted in the heights. They could not reach us.

"Then, in a time that is still so far in the past that we barely have stories, the ice began to melt. It became possible to come and go from our valley without crossing the frozen peaks. However, it was still very difficult. The canyons are a maze, with sudden floods and ice floes that block the way. If an enemy somehow navigated these dangers, it was easy for us to defend the narrow passes. We kept guards there, always.

"Our queens sent out long patrols to scout the mountains and the plains, to report on the doings of Lidian. We kept our dens and our vulnerable pups safe, and we still made our presence known in the rest of the island. Lowland curbs were not so numerous that we could not keep them out.

"Over time, however, there was less ice, and the summers became longer. More of the mountains became hospitable to lowland curbs. Conflicts with our rivals intensified. We tried again and again to establish new dens in other parts of the island, but they were always overrun."

Maoli fell silent. After a moment, Cohal looked at Arcove and said, "Then you began killing the ferryshaft. Lowland curbs were the only predators on the plains for nearly twenty years. They became very numerous, while we became fewer and fewer, and at last they breached our valley."

There was another uncomfortable silence, and then Arcove said, "There are several islands in the deep lake of the lower valley. When the ely-ary flew over, she saw curbs on some of those islands."

Moali's eyes narrowed.

Cohal cocked his head. "I know the islands you speak of. They are difficult to reach in summer."

"They are *impossible* to reach," said Moali. "The swim is too long. The water is too cold."

"Agreed," said Arcove. "However, in winter, ice would make them accessible. That is doubtless how the curbs got there to begin with."

A moment's silence while Cohal and Maoli considered this. "They are probably just lowland curbs," said Cohal at last.

Maoli shook her ears. "Why would they trap themselves out there for the summer, though?"

"Lowland curbs fight with each other," said Cohal.

"Or..." murmured Moali.

"Unlikely," said Cohal.

"Finding highland curbs in those mountains was always unlikely," she whispered.

"That is the best news I can give you," said Arcove. "I intend to send another expedition up there this fall before the snows. You are welcome to accompany them if you wish. I do not know whether there will be enough ice to reach the islands, but it is possible."

As the curbs began whispering to each other, he turned back to Hollygold and said, "What is your estimate of Thistle's numbers?"

Hollygold frowned. "I believe that most of his creasia are denning in the rugged crests on either side of the valley, where food and water are scarce and other animals leave them alone. The cats are coming down into the wooded section to hunt and drink at the lake. The creasia we saw were lean. They threatened us, but they didn't want to risk injury by fighting. Most of them stayed out of sight."

"Their numbers, Hollygold," said Arcove patiently. "Your best guess."

"Not more than two hundred adults." Hollygold hesitated. "And I didn't spot a single cub or juvenile under three—not by sight, scent, or tracks."

There was a long silence. At last, Roup spoke, "Two years ago, Sedaron began aggressively attacking their dens..."

"He can't have killed *all* their cubs," muttered Stefan.

"He wouldn't need to," said Roup. "Cubs have a high mortality rate even in Leeshwood. In the mountains...on the move...I doubt more than a third of the cubs would survive, even if they weren't being targeted by ferryshaft and lowland curbs."

"Moving dens and territories would require significant effort," said Arcove. "I think we must assume that Thistle's cats are being driven by intolerable conditions, else they'd never have taken the risk."

Storm spoke at last, "The curbs and I will go with the clutter you're sending in the fall, Arcove. We'll get up into those canyons where creasia have difficulty penetrating and look for highland curbs. If we see anything that sheds light on Thistle's cats, we'll let you know. If this is acceptable, of course."

"This is acceptable," said Arcove. "Are any other ferryshaft planning to go with you? I know Sauny and Valla have been as far into the mountains as—"

At that moment, there was a crackle of breaking branches, and a small animal fell out of the tree overhead, narrowly missing Arcove. Everyone stared as Storm's two-year-old foal picked herself up in the middle of the council circle. She'd grown a little since training with Moashi last summer, but she still looked tiny amid the cluster of adult creasia. Her dark baby fur had lightened to a dusky red. The gray blaze across her forehead had grown even more pronounced. She had a gray belly, too, and a fluff of gray tail-tip, flashing in the evening light. Her eyes were the color of Storm's and Coden's.

Storm let out an exasperated huff. "Costa Ela-ferry! What part of 'stay with your mother' did you not understand?"

"Like you always stay where you're put!" flashed Costa. She was backing away from Storm, ignoring the creasia.

"This is not a game. You cannot come to council meetings uninvited." Storm made a lunge for her, as though he intended to catch her behind the head and physically march her out of the council circle.

Costa dodged him as neatly as Halvery had taught her to last summer. "I know it's not a game; I want to go to the Southern Mountains."

"Maybe in a year or two. Not this fall."

"All the fighting will be over in a year or two!" exclaimed Costa. To Roup's amusement, she retreated behind Halvery, who looked mildly surprised. "What was the point of training me to dodge creasia strikes if I can't come with you to fight Thistle's cats?" she demanded. "What was the point of teaching me to get away from Moashi and Ilsa if I can't use it on lowland curbs?"

Storm ran around Halvery, but Costa kept the cat between them. "The point," snapped Storm, "was to keep you alive in the unlikely event that you have to defend yourself from bigger predators! It was never to set you up for that at two years old!"

Halvery looked like he wasn't sure whether to laugh or be offended that he was being treated like a rock formation. The ferry-shaft were running around him, first in one direction, then another. "*You* were challenging *Arcove* at my age!" exclaimed Costa.

"Nice try, my dear, but I was almost three." Storm jumped over Halvery and came down nose to nose with her. "You're not ready yet," he hissed. "You are not coming to the Southern Mountains, nor are you sparring with creasia again this summer, because you really cannot behave this way!"

Costa gave a thwarted wail of frustration and tore off through the trees.

Storm glanced at Arcove, who muttered, "Chaos, always."

"I'm sorry," said Storm and took off after his foal.

* * * *

This chapter inclues an author's note at the end of the book.

4

Legendary

Halvery was tempted to call after Storm—something along the lines of, "Good luck catching her!" or "It's so inconvenient when ferryshaft don't do as they're told, isn't it?" or perhaps, "Try not to cause a political incident!" But Storm already looked frustrated and Arcove looked annoyed. Halvery kept his mouth shut.

The meeting broke up soon afterward. Moashi was talking to the curbs about their valley and the slot canyons that guarded it. Stefan and Hollygold were talking to each other about Dazzle and Thistle's cats. Arcove jerked his head at Roup, who came to him at once, and they walked off upstream.

Halvery imagined that Roup was giving Arcove an earful about being left in the dark regarding recent communications with Thistle's cats. *But do you really suppose he's going to give you and Dazzle another chance to send messages back and forth, Roup? He's had enough of that.*

Halvery hoped that Arcove would raise the subject of Roup remaining in his den and the possible reassignment of his clutter. *That, at least, will make Roup happy.*

Aloud, Halvery said, "Lyndi, may I speak with you a moment?"

She'd been padding off towards her territory, but stopped in surprise. "Certainly."

Halvery fell into step beside her. "Let's walk and talk. I wanted an introduction to Caraca, too."

Lyndi gave him a longsuffering smile. "You just keep making yourself at home, don't you?"

"You'll tell me if I'm overstepping, I'm sure." In spite of the low-key antagonism between himself and Lyndi, Halvery suspected that he would always have gotten along with her if she hadn't felt duty-bound to defend Roup's many contrary positions and ideas.

He came straight to the point. "Do you want Roup's clutter, Lyndi?"

She stopped walking.

"Don't look at me like that. No one's going to take it away from him if he doesn't want to give it up. But Roup has been living in Arcove's den for almost a year, and I just told Arcove that he should keep him there. I believe I made a compelling argument. Arcove is thinking about it. I wanted to give you a chance to consider what you will do if that happens."

Lyndi stared at him for a long moment.

"You're already ruling the clutter," said Halvery gently, "and more, if truth be told. When Roup was hurt, Arcove vanished into Syriot. My wounds festered, and I was delirious with fever. You were the highest ranking officer for quite some time. The same thing happened when we took Charder to the Ghost Wood."

Lyndi maintained a neutral expression. "The council would have voted on a new king if Arcove hadn't come back."

Halvery flicked his ears. "And in the meantime, you were ruling Leeshwood." He could not help but add, "Also inviting yourself into my territory to solve disputes that were none of your business. And doing such a good job that I didn't have anything to complain about later."

Lyndi smiled.

"My point is that I don't think Roup has the slightest interest in ruling a clutter, although he definitely likes manipulating the political landscape to Arcove's advantage. He likes solving problems, and he's good at it. He'll be sorting out tricky situations for

Leeshwood until the day he dies. I'm not suggesting he leave the council or his role, but there's no reason he and Arcove can't share a den at this point. Or keep sharing one. Honestly, I'm not sure Roup will go back to his den no matter what happens. It's purely embarrassing to listen to them making excuses."

Lyndi snorted a laugh. She started walking again, thinking.

"I told Arcove that he should give the clutter to Carmine if you didn't want it," continued Halvery, "but if you prefer to stay, that makes things easy."

"Which council member is Carmine meant to replace?" asked Lyndi carefully.

"No one. With seven council members, Arcove won't have to break ties. He prefers an odd number, so that he doesn't appear to take sides. He used to have five. Now he's got six. Might as well make it seven."

Lyndi didn't say what Halvery was sure she was thinking. Right now, the council tended towards a split with Halvery, Stefan, and Hollygold taking a stance opposite Roup, Lyndi, and Moashi. Carmine had grown up in Roup's clutter. He was fond of Roup and considerate of his opinions. However, he was more aggressive in his thinking. He could not be counted upon to side with either faction, and this would make him a good tie-breaker.

"You've thought this through," murmured Lyndi.

"I would not suggest alterations in the council without thinking it through," said Halvery.

"And you're doing it to make Roup happy."

"Not all of it."

She grew quiet again. Halvery let her think. When they reached Roup's den, he saw that Tollee was there, stretched out on a flat rock in the dusky twilight, alongside her adult daughter, Myla. They were both talking to Caraca.

Halvery regarded Roup's mate from a distance. She was small, even for a female—not much bigger than a juvenile cub. Halvery had never spoken to her much, because Roup was his superior officer. It was the job of ranking creasia to familiarize themselves with the dens of cats downstream of them. However, the dens of their superiors were none of their business. Consequently, Roup knew Velta, Samathi, and many of Halvery's other mates. Halvery, however, had little personal knowledge of Roup's den. He knew Lyndi because she was his fellow officer, but not Caraca.

Lyndi walked right up to the group, interrupting a conversation that sounded like it was about telshee cave writing. "Caraca, Halvery. Halvery, Caraca."

Caraca looked at him in surprise. Halvery had no doubt that her feelings towards him were complicated and that she was at least as difficult to get to know as Roup. He wasn't sure he could make friends with her, so he just said what was on his mind. "I've got some questions about how color is inherited, Caraca. Arcove says you know more about that than anyone in Leeshwood."

A look of startled pleasure flashed across her face, instantly swallowed by wariness. "I'm not sure that's true…"

"It's true for oories, rabbits, and rock rats," said Lyndi with a twinkle.

At that moment, one of the tame oory cats came sidling up to Halvery, causing him to dance sideways. He found the animals and their behavior extremely unsettling. They looked so much like miniature creasia, and yet they were no more sentient than deer. Oories would scavenge creasia carcasses if given the opportunity, causing most creasia to associate them with ghosts and death. Most of them had spotted tan and black coats, which, at least, gave them un-creasia like coloring. This one, however, was white.

Caraca called to the oory, and it came to her at once, purring. "Are you interested in a kitten?" she asked with studied innocence. "There's a litter due soon."

"I'm certain you would never forgive me for what would befall such a creature in my den," said Halvery.

Caraca's expression grew cold. "You're probably right. Why did you want to speak to me?"

Halvery forced himself to hold still while another of the oories came over to sniff him. "Roup's color... Do you know how it's inherited?"

Caraca's gaze sharpened and she cocked her head. "I think so."

"Well, that's good news. I don't suppose you could figure out whether any of the breeding females in Arcove's den or mine have the right blood to produce a cub of that color with Roup?"

Caraca's eyes widened. "Arcove's den...or yours?"

"Yes. Arcove said that you might need to talk to your mother to figure it out, since you may not know the bloodlines of Leeshwood. But he said that you know about color."

Caraca was shaking her head. "Let me get this straight... You are offering to *share* a mate with Roup...in order to reproduce his *coat color?*"

Lyndi looked just as surprised as Caraca. They both stared at Halvery.

"Yes." Halvery wasn't sure what else to say. "But if one of Arcove's—"

Caraca gave a dismissive shake of her ears. "Yes, yes, Arcove, of course, but *you?*"

"Yes, me." Halvery was beginning to feel self-conscious, and that made him irritated. "I have more mates to choose from, for that matter. And if you identify some other female who has the right blood and is interested in my den, I might be able to arrange something."

Caraca and Lyndi shared a look that Halvery couldn't interpret. "Well, this sounds like one of your projects come to life," said Lyndi to Caraca.

"Roup will never do it," she muttered.

"Oh, I wouldn't be so sure." Lyndi shot a cheeky glance at Halvery and added, "He's done a few things lately that I never thought he'd do. Seems like he's feeling adventurous."

Caraca snickered.

Halvery's ears flattened. He hated being laughed at. He could feel his temper trying to rise up and swallow doubt, uncertainty, and humiliation.

But when has that ever gotten me anywhere with Roup? Thirty-odd years of him using my temper to manipulate me. And these are Roup's mates. What did I expect?

Halvery was still trying to formulate a response that didn't involve snarling when Storm came trotting out of the boulders with his ears back and his tail low. He headed straight for Tollee and Myla, who'd been watching the exchange between the three creasia.

"Is she here?" demanded Storm.

"Costa?" asked Tollee in surprise. "No..."

Halvery forgot his own troubles. He turned to Storm in delight. "Did she lose you?"

Storm growled something unintelligible.

Halvery was suddenly having a wonderful evening. "Oh, that is delicious..."

"I'm not accustomed to...*chasing!*" snapped Storm.

"Is it harder than it looks?"

"Shut up, Halvery. Tollee, she interrupted the creasia council! She thinks she's going to the Southern Mountains this fall. She isn't! But now she knows a lot more than I'd like her to know about those mountains and the situation with Thistle's cats. I thought you were watching her!"

Tollee's ears settled back. "Storm, Costa is downright cunning, and she does not respond well to arbitrary orders. In other words, she is *just like you!* More than either of our other foals, *this one* is yours to the bone. Do not expect me to perform feats that the entire ferryshaft herd and Arcove himself could not!"

"Did you at least ask where she was going?" flashed Storm.

"She said she was going to hunt," interjected Myla. "I'll go look for her."

Storm gave a derisive snort at her retreating back. "Good luck with that."

Tollee was clearly not appreciating his tone. "Storm, you're the one who taught her to spar with creasia last summer! You had her running chases every night; what did you expect?"

"I expected better judgment!"

Tollee started to respond to this and then stopped. Halvery considered making an observation regarding Storm's judgment at a similar age and then decided against it.

When no one offered a retort to his outburst, Storm deflated. He sat down and wrapped his tail around himself in a posture of uncharacteristic self-doubt. Tollee came down from the rock and approached him. When he didn't raise his head or meet her eyes, she started washing his face. She spoke so softly that Halvery barely heard her. "You want Costa to what…? Stop trying to take on the whole world? I said she's just like you."

Storm spoke in a whisper, "I came so close to not being here."

"I don't know what to tell you. I don't think you can stop her."

"I'm sorry, I just…" Storm's voice sank to a murmur. The two ferryshaft got up and walked slowly away towards the mouth of the den.

Halvery wondered how much time they spent in Roup's den and how many ferryshaft were living in his territory. *I suppose Carmine will keep letting them do it. He shares his den with Teek, who regards Storm as some kind of parent and Myla as…what? A sister? Ghosts, what a strange world we've created.*

Further down the slope, Halvery caught sight of Arcove and Roup coming through the trees. They stopped some distance away, out of earshot, to finish whatever they were saying to each other. They looked like they might be having an argument, although they were being so circumspect with their body language that it was difficult to tell.

They've always been circumspect, thought Halvery. *Always afraid cats would get the wrong idea. Or the right one. No wonder Roup is so cagey when he comes to my den.*

Twilight was deepening into full night, with a half moon rising over the trees. Halvery watched the flash and shine of Roup's coat. He was walking back and forth in front of Arcove, talking forcefully, clearly trying to make a point. Arcove's expression was invisible, his eyes just glints of reflected starlight.

Lyndi came up so quietly that Halvery didn't hear her approach. She sat down beside him.

"Are you and Caraca done laughing at me?" he asked stiffly.

Lyndi's voice was cheerful. "For now."

"If you think it's a terrible idea—"

"It's not a terrible idea. Caraca is going to talk to Nadine. Give her some time to think about it. She likes to mull things over."

Halvery relaxed. "Of course."

"Good luck getting Roup to actually do it," muttered Lyndi.

"Let me work on that," said Halvery sweetly.

Lyndi laughed.

Halvery was sorely tempted to ask how often she and Roup actually mated and how he behaved when he was on top. Females who no longer came into season did get the occasional urge to mate. It was a pale shadow of their frenzy when they were in heat, and most males considered such attention a poor consolation compared to the prize of a breeding female. *But that pace might actually be more to Roup's taste.*

On the distant edge of the trees, Roup had sat down right in front of Arcove, still talking. He leaned forward abruptly and tucked his head under Arcove's chin. His golden fur gleamed against night-black.

Halvery murmured, "Arcove doesn't know he's beautiful." He realized an instant later that he'd said it out loud.

To his surprise, Lyndi responded without a pause. "Arcove has no idea."

Halvery laughed. "Roup could look like anything, and Arcove would love him just as much. I can't decide whether that's charming or terrible!"

Lyndi gave him a conspiratorial side-eye. "When did *you* notice?"

"Always!" exclaimed Halvery. "I thought that was why Roup got away with things!"

Lyndi was laughing again.

"I have to fight for everything," grumbled Halvery, "but Roup just sits there and looks gorgeous and Arcove gives him whatever he wants." Halvery caught his breath. "Except…that was never what was happening. I didn't understand."

A long silence. Then Lyndi spoke in a near-whisper, "Arcove was three years old…the first time."

Halvery went very still. He turned to her slowly. *"Three?"*

"Roup was four. Keep your voice down, please."

Halvery opened his mouth, shut it again. "I thought I was precocious, fighting my way into a den at five, but *three?"*

"They were rogue cubs, Halvery. In Ketch's Leeshwood, which was a violent and bloody place. Roup behaved like a ferryshaft, which made him a target. And Arcove wouldn't bend his neck to anyone, even when that meant constant attacks. They were fighting for their lives most days, and they didn't think they'd grow up." She hesitated. "You grew up in a den, didn't you?"

"Officer's cub…" said Halvery faintly.

"No turn-over?" asked Lyndi.

"No." He'd been driven from the den under ugly circumstances when he was four, but there'd been no change of power while he was living there.

"Then you were lucky." Lyndi jerked her head at Arcove and Roup. "They weren't."

A long silence.

"Did Roup tell you this?" asked Halvery hesitantly.

"I asked him, yes. Years ago. He thought about it for two days before deciding to tell me."

Halvery felt cold. "Why are you telling *me?"*

"Because I think you actually want to be friends. I wasn't sure before, but…you'd give up breeding rights, Halvery? And raise Roup's cubs in your den, even though you're not sharing it?"

45

Halvery shifted his paws, aware of a new kind of embarrassment. He didn't know how to respond.

Lyndi looked at him levelly. "I misjudged you."

"Oh, don't apologize. You'll never forgive yourself."

She laughed. "You are trying so hard, it's almost painful to watch."

"Ghosts, don't I know it! Can I resume being an ill-tempered curmudgeon? It's much easier."

Lyndi actually butted her head against his shoulder. "You're not ill-tempered. Mostly. But you are *so* different from Roup. Which is the appeal, I suppose. When he first started going down to your den every month, I thought... Well, we all get a little strange if we live long enough, don't we? We crave some new challenge to make us feel young again. Something risky and ill-advised, but exciting. For you, that's taking a six-year-old female into your den. For Roup, that's...you."

Halvery burst out laughing. *"I'm* Roup's equivalent of a six-year-old female?"

Lyndi looked embarrassed. "Maybe I'm not saying it very well."

"Oh, you're saying it perfectly."

"Anyway, I thought you were...curious about him, but also enjoying the chance to...get him under you. I don't like seeing him make a fool of himself. I thought he was going to get hurt. I thought *you* were going to hurt him."

"Oh, he's not nearly as helpless as you imagine," said Halvery acidly.

Lyndi swallowed. "I know he's not. He can say things that cut so deep... And when he lets his instincts take over, he can fight almost as well as Arcove. Maybe better, because he's craftier. I wish I'd been there the night you two fought."

"I doubt you could have stopped it."

"I would have tried."

"That fight had to happen."

Lyndi sighed. "Maybe it did. Anyway, I don't think I ever properly thanked you for saving him from Dazzle. I couldn't have done it alone."

Halvery looked away. "Please do not thank me for that. It was my fault he couldn't defend himself."

Lyndi smiled at him sadly. "Roup is lovable and clever, but he is not always easy company. I know that."

"He is, though," objected Halvery. "It's just that I often feel like a mouse being nosed around in a mouse circle."

Lyndi snorted a laugh. "He told me you said that. Sounds about right." She hesitated. "He does it to everyone. Including everyone he loves. Does that help?"

"I suppose."

"Except Arcove," amended Lyndi. "Arcove sees right through Roup's 'spin' every time. The only way Roup can hide anything from Arcove is by not mentioning it at all."

"Which is why Arcove didn't know about Dazzle's cave," said Halvery thoughtfully.

"To be fair, Arcove can't hide anything from Roup, either," continued Lyndi, "not if he actually talks about it."

"Which is why Roup didn't know about Hollygold's trip to the Southern Mountains," finished Halvery.

She made a face. "He's going to be so upset about that. It's probably what he and Arcove are arguing about right now. Roup will insist that he needs to go with the expedition this fall. Arcove will insist that he doesn't."

Halvery's tail lashed. "Roup is out of his mind if he thinks Arcove is going to give Dazzle another swipe at him."

"You know that, and I know that, but Roup won't see it that way."

"What other way is there to see it?"

Lyndi shut her eyes as though dredging up her alpha's perspective from some deep place. "Dazzle didn't trust Roup to act in the best interests of himself, his family, and friends. Now that Roup spared his life, maybe he will."

"You've got to be joking."

"I'm only telling you how Roup will see it. He will say that he took a great personal risk and paid a high personal price to make a point. He will not appreciate interference with the message he's been trying to send."

Halvery frowned. "Does he still limp when he's tired?"

"At the end of a long night, if he's really worn out, yes."

Halvery gave a low growl. "I'd like to hamstring Dazzle and leave him choking in his own blood."

"I suspect Arcove would like to help you. Which is why he and Roup are standing down there arguing when they would rather be up here visiting with us."

Roup and Arcove had taken their discussion back under the trees. Halvery had completely lost sight of Arcove and caught only the occasional glint of Roup's fur.

Lyndi spoke again, her voice very low. "I actually think it's good that Roup and Arcove don't tell each other *everything*. Good for Leeshwood, I mean. Their methods are totally different, and they need some space between them. Considering the way they started, it's amazing that they've managed to separate their lives at all. If they share a den…"

Halvery frowned. "I see your point, Lyndi, but…they're *already* sharing one."

She smiled. "I suppose you're right."

"Arcove isn't rolling over for Roup, nor has Roup stopped his endless scheming."

Lyndi snickered. "True."

"Besides," said Halvery loftily, "he'll be back and forth to my den."

"Until you have another fight."

"Arguments, sure, but one fight was enough."

Arcove and Roup finally reappeared between the trees and started up the slope. Lyndi glanced at Halvery and spoke in a rush, her voice a near-whisper, "If Roup went into an otherway, Arcove would claw a hole in the world to reach him. He would follow him into fire…into the dark. Arcove wouldn't beg Keesha for his own life, but he'll beg for Roup's.

"And yet you're right: Arcove doesn't know he's beautiful. They don't always see each other clearly. And I think…I think it's impossible to understand Roup without understanding Arcove. Roup won't tell you this. He'll say that Arcove is none of your business, but if you want to be Roup's friend…if you want to get close to him, and he wants to let you…then Arcove *is* your business. It's impossible to understand either of them if you don't understand how they started and how young they were. I'm trusting you with that. Don't make me regret it."

Halvery shut his eyes. *There's that word again.* "Lyndi, I would never—"

At that moment, Myla came trotting out of the boulders. She called out merrily, "I found her!"

There was a clattering sound from the direction of the den. Storm and Tollee appeared at a run. "Where?" demanded Storm.

"Oh, she's not with me," said Myla in surprise. "She's at Carmine's den."

"Who's at Carmine's den?" asked Roup as he and Arcove reached the others.

"Costa," said Halvery with malevolent pleasure. "She gave Storm the slip and left him running in circles."

"I was *not* running in circles," snapped Storm.

"I'm sure he fell into a stream or something," continued Halvery airily.

"Why is she in Carmine's den?" asked Roup.

"I believe they are offering each other condolences regarding the many frustrations of having legendary fathers," said Myla.

Roup and Lyndi burst out laughing. Halvery tried not to laugh and failed.

Storm sputtered. "They're *what?*"

"I feel I am being unjustly included in this—" began Arcove.

Storm dared to interrupt him. "I would have *killed* to have a father who was alive to care whether I reached my third spring!"

"Whatever!" sang Myla. "I'm going back over there. We're all going to play hide-and-hunt with Wisteria's cubs. Goodnight, legends!"

There was an uncomfortable silence. Storm was obviously seething. "Teek *knew* she was over there and didn't tell me."

"He might not have known you were looking—" began Tollee.

"Oh, I went by the den! I spoke to him."

Tollee sighed. "You're right. Teek has clearly taken her side and is now your enemy. You should challenge him to single combat."

"Stop making fun of me. I am seriously concerned that Costa will follow us to the mountains and get herself killed."

Arcove spoke with studied calm. "Would you like to hunt, Storm?"

Storm looked at him quizzically, and Arcove gave a flash of teeth as he realized how that sounded. "Would you like to hunt deer with me?"

"Arcove, I don't think I can bear to listen to you lecture me about bringing chaos to your council right now."

"You already seem well aware of that issue," said Arcove smoothly. "I was going to say that we could offer each other condolences regarding the many frustrations of having stubborn and ungrateful offspring."

Storm laughed out loud.

"Killing something always makes me feel better," continued Arcove blandly. "Tollee, do you want to come?"

She gave him an assessing look, then an answering flash of teeth. "Coincidentally, killing something makes me feel better, too. Alright, Arcove, let's hunt."

"One thing first." Arcove turned back towards Halvery and Roup. "I would appreciate it if Moashi's father and mother would communicate with him regarding the decorum expected in council meetings."

Halvery rolled his eyes. "Ghosts, yes."

"There is a fine line between being friendly with guests and making a fool of oneself."

"Agreed."

Roup gave an innocent smile. "I'm sure Halvery doesn't appreciate being called Moashi's mother."

Halvery returned the expression. "Oh, he didn't, sweetheart."

Arcove continued to pursue his point. "Attitudes presented to guests in council carry more weight than those represented outside of council. They ultimately reflect *my* attitude, and I would not choose to treat hostile guests like cubs at playtime. Moashi would have lost his place on my council by now if it weren't for you two. You've managed to get him within a few lengths of a fully competent officer. Please take him the rest of the way."

"I'll talk to him," said Halvery.

"Moashi's method of dealing with hostile guests seems to have worked," said Roup. "The curbs are at his den right now, chatting away about their valley without any mention of debts owed."

"That's because he doesn't owe them any," said Arcove wearily. "Roup, he can be friendly without literally rolling over for them. Before an audience, no less."

Roup had the grace to wince. "I see your point. I'll talk to him."

"Thank you."

Halvery tried to read the look they gave each other, but Roup and Arcove were expert dissemblers when it came to their own feelings in public. If they were still in conflict, there was no clue in their voices or mannerisms.

However, as Arcove and the ferryshaft moved away, Roup's gaze clouded and grew vacant. He stared off into the forest beneath the rising moon, so lost in thought that he didn't seem aware of Lyndi and Halvery watching him. At last, Lyndi said, "Boss?"

"Hmm?"

"I am going to check on Carmine's den, just to make sure Costa is really there. I might have a word with her. I think she might actually listen to me. Do you want to come?"

A pause. Roup spoke without looking at her. "I'm not sure I'd be of much use this evening."

Lyndi gave him a nudge. "Then go for a run with Halvery."

That broke Roup out of his trance. He glanced around at them and some of the sharpness returned to his eyes. "Have the two of you been making friends? Ghosts and little fishes. I think I've been discussed. Should I be worried?"

Lyndi gave him a lick on the nose. "Halvery just talked about how shockingly beautiful you are, and I could do nothing but agree. Easiest conversation we've ever had."

Halvery kept a straight face. "That's exactly how I said it, too. Shockingly beautiful. We talked about your ears until the moon rose, and then we moved on to your whiskers."

"Well…" began Roup and stopped. He was so dexterous with words, and yet compliments always seemed to knock him flat. It made Halvery want to deliver them non-stop. "You're both awful," he continued weakly. "I'm going for a run. Nobody has to come with me."

"May I?" asked Halvery.

Roup shut his eyes, opened them again. "Yes."

He sounded so unenthusiastic that Halvery took a step back and said, "Or maybe I'll go have that conversation with Moashi. Ghosts know he's probably eroding the dignity of our council even as we speak. Talking to Cohal while flat on his back, no doubt, and promising him curb dens all over Leeshwood."

That got a smile out of Roup. "No, come with me. I've got a few things to say to you."

"Things I'll hate?"

"This time…probably not."

"Well, as it so happens," said Halvery playfully, "*I* have something that *you'll* hate."

"That's the truth," muttered Lyndi.

Roup glanced between them. Halvery could tell he was still distracted. When neither of them volunteered further information, he said, "I suppose I can't have everything my way every time, can I?"

Halvery butted his head against Roup's shoulder. "No, Roup, you really can't."

* * * *

This chapter includes an author's note at the end of the book.

5

Keep Up

Halvery thought Roup might head for the cliffs. The run and the view were exhilarating. The sense of being outside any established territory was freeing and provided privacy. *Although I'm not sure he wants to mate tonight.*

Roup, however, struck out through the woods along the edge of the boulders, going south. Halvery thought he might just want to patrol—to traverse the edge of his territory and renew scent and scratch marks. It was the sort of task that Halvery found soothing while he was mulling things over.

Roup was definitely mulling something over tonight. In spite of his comment about wanting to talk, he didn't say a word as they ran on and on through the moonlight, past the edge of Roup's territory, along the edge of Hollygold's. At last, Roup struck out east along a common way trail that took them all the way through Hollygold's territory, past the last of the big trees, and finally out onto the open plain. Halvery considered asking Roup where they were going, but then he decided that he didn't care.

The breeze was cool and pleasant, redolent with summer grasses and loamy earth. He could smell water in the distance. They ran on.

At last, Roup reached a modest stream and turned to follow it in the direction of the lake. The moon was high overhead when at last they came down a rocky section of grasslands, and encountered a bluff. The stream dropped sheer over the edge and created a little waterfall with a bowl at the bottom. The hollow around it was pleasant, with more brush and trees than one normally found on the plain. Halvery was sure that birds, small animals, and perhaps even a few deer lived and drank here. It would be a good place to hunt.

Roup skirted the waterfall and dropped lightly into the hollow. To Halvery's surprise, Roup wound his way along the bank, behind the waterfall, and out again. He did this so quickly and casually that it seemed like a habit—something he'd done many times before.

That spot would be a good food cache, thought Halvery, although why Roup would come this far from his territory to cache food, he couldn't imagine.

Halvery didn't follow him behind the waterfall, but sat looking at him from the other side of the pool. *I believe you have forgotten I am here.*

Roup spoke as though Halvery had said it aloud. "I'm not very good company this evening."

"It's alright." Halvery started around the edge of the pool. "It's a beautiful night to run. Do you…come here often?" Halvery tried to picture where they must be in relation to Leeshwood. He felt certain they had passed Hollygold's territory entirely and must be south of Stefan's.

"Not anymore." Roup stared into the water. After a long moment, he added, "This is where Coden left the Shable for me… behind the waterfall."

"Oh…" Halvery had a sudden uneasy feeling, as though old ghosts might be watching.

Roup continued, "Coden and I used to meet here. Before— and during—the war. It makes good neutral ground—too close to Leeshwood for the comfort of most ferryshaft, too far for most creasia. Arcove and I found it as cubs. Back then, we used it to cache food on the rare occasions when we killed more than we could eat.

The waterfall keeps meat fresh for a couple of days even in summer. In winter, meat freezes solid back there. It'll keep for a month or more. Coming here was a risk, of course. We were always dodging hostile ferryshaft and curbs while crossing the plain. But it was worth the danger sometimes."

Halvery came slowly around the pool to stand beside Roup. *Caching meat as a cub...* Halvery had never gone hungry as a cub. He'd had some good-natured fights with his siblings over choice morsels on the den's kills. He'd had some lean times during the year after he left his birth den and certainly during the war. But he'd never gone hungry when he was small enough to worry about being killed by a single ferryshaft or curb.

He said the first thing that came into his head. "I doubt there are any rogue cubs in Leeshwood anymore, Roup."

"I hope not," whispered Roup.

"I think you made a world without those." *Cheer up?*

Roup just kept staring at the water. At last, he shook himself and seemed to come out of his reverie. "I know I should be thanking you."

"For what?"

"For whatever you said to Arcove before the council meeting."

"Oh! So you're staying in his den?"

Roup shot him a crooked smile. "Don't play coy."

"Alright, yes, I told him you should stay. Did he tell you my other suggestions?"

"That Carmine should take my clutter and join the council?"

"Only if Lyndi doesn't want the clutter." He paused and added, "Only if you don't."

Roup didn't respond at once. His gaze returned to the water. "It took so long for me to get used to ruling a clutter, having a den, maintaining a territory. I didn't want any of it. But now..."

"If you don't want to give it up—" began Halvery.

Roup shut his eyes. "No, you're right. In my den...I missed him every day."

Halvery didn't bother to ask who he meant.

"I don't want to go back to that," continued Roup. "Lyndi has done most of the work of ruling the clutter all year. She consults me, but, truly, she's done all the hard work without recognition or complaining. I need to officially let it go. It's just…a little hard, that's all."

Halvery leaned over and gave Roup's head a friendly lick. "You know that all the officers will consult you with their problems. Carmine certainly will. You'll have more to do than you even want."

Roup smiled. "I'm sure you're right."

"All Leeshwood is Arcove's clutter. It'll be yours, too."

Roup turned to face him. "Thank you. Truly." His eyes searched Halvery's face. "What did you say to him exactly?"

That you're not safe in your den? Halvery wasn't about to tell Roup that part if Arcove hadn't. "I said he'd have my support instead of my active opposition."

Roup laughed.

Halvery smiled. "Surprised him, I think."

"Yes, I can see how that would." Roup stretched out beside the water. After a moment, Halvery joined him. The spray from the falls was pleasantly cool after their long run. Roup's glossy golden coat shone luminous under the bright moon, beaded with moisture. He put his head down across Halvery's paws and murmured, "Take my mind off my troubles?"

Halvery didn't answer at once. He began grooming Roup's ears. "You seem sad."

"I'm just thinking."

"About something sad."

Roup did not smell remotely like he wanted to mate. Halvery groomed his head, hoping he would fall asleep. Instead, he flattened out and put his tail over. His presentation was as flawless as always, and Halvery's body responded to the sight instinctively. But it was like catching the scent of a breeding female who didn't belong to him—frustrating, but not appealing.

"I don't do sad mating," he said aloud.

"No," Roup murmured, "you only do happy and angry mating."

Halvery felt as though someone had dropped him into the cold stream. He got up and backed away. He felt angry and thought he probably shouldn't. He should probably feel guilty. Terribly, crushingly guilty. *You said you forgave me.*

Roup followed Halvery to his feet, already making conciliatory noises, "No. No, Halvery, stop. Please, stop. I shouldn't have said that. I—"

"I shouldn't have come," grated Halvery. "I invited myself when you obviously wished to be alone. I'll see you next time you come to my den."

"Halvery!"

Halvery ignored the desperation in Roup's voice as he turned away. *I can't do this. He's too complicated for me. Lyndi knew that. She was trying to tell me. He's Arcove's mess. Let Arcove deal with him.*

Roup whipped around in front of him, head low, almost like he wanted to fight. His voice broke. "Please, I am begging you."

Halvery stopped in surprise.

Roup caught his breath. "If you are going to...to talk to me when I am not at my best, you are going to have to...hear me say things I shouldn't. *Please* forgive me. *Please.*" He was shaking.

Halvery felt awful. "I don't know what to do," he whispered.

Roup was still talking, "I can't have both of you angry with me. I can't stand it. Please..."

"Stop saying 'please.'" Halvery closed the distance between them and folded his head over Roup's. Roup promptly buried his face against Halvery's chest. He was still shaking. "It's alright," Halvery found himself saying. "I'm not angry at you. Surely Arcove isn't, either."

Roup drew a shuddering breath. "No, but he doesn't trust my judgment right now. It's hard to know that he doesn't trust me."

"Roup..." Halvery searched for words. "You scared him *so* badly last fall."

"I know," whispered Roup. "And he's going to keep punishing me for it."

Halvery gave an exasperated huff. "He's not letting you go to the Southern Mountains to talk to Dazzle and Thistle, right? That's what you mean by 'punish'?"

Roup gave a mirthless laugh.

"That is absurd, Roup! You are being absurd!"

Roup flinched.

I am so bad at this, thought Halvery. *I am so bad at you.*

Aloud, he said, "If I am not supposed to take unkind comments to heart—and ghosts, Roup, you do know exactly where to put your claws—can you do me the same courtesy? I am not trying to hurt you right now."

Roup raised his head and started licking Halvery's muzzle.

Halvery sighed. He pushed Roup's head down, got a hold of his scruff and dragged him off his feet.

Roup let him.

Halvery dragged him back to the water and let go. "I am going to groom you. No, not just your ears. Stay down."

Roup rolled over, throat and belly exposed. Halvery pushed him back onto his side. "Stop with the submissive displays. It's confusing when you say cruel things and then turn over onto your back."

Roup laughed. "I am made of contradictions."

"You are." Halvery started at his head and began methodically working his way down his back and sides, getting into the muscles around his shoulders. He was soon rewarded by an ease of tension. He figured Roup would start talking eventually.

He was halfway down his spine when Roup said, "I should have confronted Dazzle sooner. When he wasn't running for his life...when he didn't have his back against a wall. I should have said something else—"

Halvery had been determined to listen without interrupting, but his resolution died at once. "Roup, the only thing you did wrong with Dazzle was meeting with him alone. There isn't any better thing you could have said, no different approach that would have made him love you. He came here to win, and, frankly, he almost succeeded. He took advantage of your kindness and optimism. He took advantage of Arcove's attachment to you; that is all!"

Roup went silent.

Halvery sighed. *Well, I've messed up again.* "Please don't stop talking."

"You think everything I say is absurd."

"Yes, but please don't stop." He nibbled into the muscles of Roup's side, just below his ribs.

That tickled, and Roup laughed. At last, he continued, "I do actually think Dazzle is trying to save cats he loves and that he has the capacity for loyalty and friendship. I regret not finding better words or a better moment to talk to him. I know you think that's ridiculous."

"I'm sure he has the capacity for loyalty," said Halvery. "Just not to us."

"I think you're wrong."

Halvery raised his head suddenly. "*That's* why you came here this evening!"

"What?"

"Coden. He's on your mind because of Dazzle. You think that if you'd found the right words, you could have made Coden surrender, kept him alive, and gotten better terms for the ferryshaft after the war."

Silence.

"I know you and Arcove…regret him," said Halvery slowly. "All I ever saw was a cunning, vicious enemy. But I accept that, to you, he was something else."

Silence.

"But, Roup, if *you* couldn't talk Coden off the path he was walking, no one could!"

"I could have *heard* him!" snarled Roup. He sat up and looked at Halvery with an expression of such intense pain that Halvery lowered his head and dropped his ears. "He came here to meet with me that last time, and I didn't come!" said Roup, his voice cracking with the effort at civility. "You have no idea what it's like to live with that!"

Halvery put his chin on the ground.

Roup turned back to the pool. "Yes, I regret things. Things that happened with Coden. Things that happened with Dazzle. I think that a lot of those cats in the Southern Mountains are going to die within the next year. Maybe all of them. I think the ripples of that tragedy will touch us here more than you or Arcove imagine. And I feel I came very close to preventing it. Just not close enough. I feel that there might still be an opportunity to use the connection I built at great personal cost, but I am being thwarted."

"Well, you did say that Arcove holds your grudges for you," muttered Halvery.

Roup gave a broken laugh.

"That's what he's doing. Being angry on your behalf...the way you *should* be. Roup, Arcove is not ignoring your wishes. He's sending cats up there so that Thistle has an opportunity to ask for help. He's bringing highland curbs to council meetings and suffering through their insults to get details about the geography up there. Ghosts, he's making deals with Syriot and treating with ely-ary! He is doing everything he can!"

Roup shut his eyes. "Except let me talk."

"Except *risk* you, yes!"

"Letting me talk is not 'risking' me."

"Alright, he doesn't want you involved. Can you blame him?"

"I'm not blaming him. I'm blaming myself."

Halvery gave a frustrated growl and dropped his head onto Roup's back. "I can't beat you at words, Roup. You win."

Roup didn't respond.

"Arcove said something to me about you last year," continued Halvery. "When you were hurt and he visited my den. He was trying to tell me that if I was going to get involved in your schemes, I needed to look out for you. He said, 'You think that because Roup can do things that most cats *can't,* he can also do all the things that most cats *can.*'"

A moment's silence. Then Roup started to laugh.

Halvery smiled. "That busy little brain isn't very good at self-preservation."

Roup kept laughing for a moment. Halvery could feel him relax. At last, he said, "You are both incredibly condescending. I'll have you know that I don't need anyone's permission to get things done. I would simply prefer trust and cooperation. But in order to save me from myself, you'd first have to begin keeping up with me."

"There are your claws!" said Halvery cheerfully. "I knew they wouldn't stay sheathed for long."

Roup sat up on his stomach. He rearranged his paws, looking a little more settled. "What were you going to tell me that I'll hate?"

Halvery hesitated. "Not tonight."

"Oh, spit it out. If you're not going to take my mind off my troubles the other way."

"No, I'm not telling you anything you'll hate tonight. But I do have a problem for you. Here, pass me your paw, and I'll tell you."

Roup looked at him in surprise. Paw-grooming was not common, even between friends. For the groomer, there was the risk of putting one's vulnerable face and tongue so close to sharp claws. For the cat being groomed, there was the risk of damage to delicate skin. Paws were sensitive and personal in a way that other body parts were not. Some cats couldn't stand to have them touched, but... *Velta does this to me sometimes, and knowing what I know about you, I think you might like it.*

After a moment, Roup scooted his right paw over against Halvery's left one.

Halvery grinned. "No, the other paw."

The only way to conveniently pass Halvery his left front paw was to turn it over. For a moment, he thought Roup wouldn't do it. Then Roup turned his left paw up, and laid it across Halvery's. Halvery put one leg over Roup's to hold his paw in place. He stopped to admire all those petal-pink pads in golden fur. Then he began a very business-like nibbling. After a few moments, he said, "Moashi's beta. Who is he?"

Roup didn't answer at once. Halvery didn't think his hesitation had anything to do with the question. He thought it had everything to do with a warm tongue sliding between Roup's toes. "Cat named Tetry," said Roup at last. "He's only a few years older than Moashi; they're cousins."

"Similar attitudes?"

"Very similar."

"Well, that will never do. What about his other officers?"

Roup shifted minutely. Halvery's tongue glided past sensitive skin, where the smallest rock or even a grain of sand could cause discomfort. Roup's voice came out a little uneven. "There are... um...four of them, I think. Another young one, and then two who are in their fifties or sixties..."

Halvery nibbled into the space between his pads. He paused to say, "So, I'm guessing the young ones are of the same mind as Moashi, and the old ones are just grateful to be given a voice and some relevance."

"I...I'm not sure what you're getting at..." Roup sounded like he couldn't focus.

Halvery raised his eyes to look at Roup mischievously over his paw. He let his wet tongue slide between Roup toes again, past that exquisitely sensitive spot where they met.

Roup's eyes had dilated. He gave up pretending to care about Halvery's questions. "How," he demanded in a near-whisper, "do you know these things?!"

Halvery laughed.

"*I* didn't know that...that my paws... Alright, stop. If you're not going to get on top of me, stop, because that is driving me crazy."

"Oh, I didn't say I wouldn't get on top of you," crooned Halvery. "I said I don't mate with sad."

"I hardly know what I am feeling right now."

"Uncomfortably aroused?"

"That for sure."

Halvery buried his nose in the dense velvet between Roup's pads. A cat's paws exuded his personal scent. It was the reason they used scratches to mark territory borders. Such markings left a strong scent signature, as well as a visual sign.

Halvery could detect a change in Roup's scent in just the short time he'd been grooming his foot. "Well, you're certainly not sad anymore," he murmured. "So, Moashi's den…"

"Really, Halvery?"

"I remember you used to want to talk about Moashi's den at the strangest times."

"I apologize with all my heart."

"Roup, he needs some officers who are *not* like him. He particularly needs a beta who has some teeth. The cub is too softhearted, but it could be balanced. Same way Arcove balances you."

Roup had closed his eyes. "Yes, alright."

"Instant capitulation! I should only ever talk to you when you're uncomfortably aroused."

Roup snorted. "I actually agree with you. Did you have someone in mind?"

Halvery turned his attention to a different pair of toes, drawing another sharp breath from Roup. "It seems like you want to end this conversation quickly."

"It seems like you love to watch me suffer. What brought on this concern about Moashi's beta?"

"Oh, Moashi was down at my den yesterday evening, eating himself alive because he killed that bully who challenged him. Asking me for permission to feel good about winning a fight. It was an embarrassing display from an alpha, if you ask me."

"Well, I was rather surprised that Moashi *killed* him…"

"Roup, if Moashi, of all people, thought Vashon needed killing, he did. Don't make the cub second-guess himself. Also, he won another fight! He actually *can* fight! Look at what a good job we did!"

"Did you tell him you're proud of him?"

"No, I told him I don't like him and to go away."

"Halvery!"

Halvery nibbled—the barest brush of teeth against delicate skin.

Roup's breathing gave a hitch. "Why does that...feel so...? How do you think of these things?!"

"Because," murmured Halvery, "you like feeling like someone could hurt you, but they wouldn't. You like trusting someone. You like being trusted." He hesitated and then added, "Also, your pink pads are so cute. I just wanted to lick them."

Roup gave a jittery laugh. "I know I'm in trouble when the compliments start."

"They're pinker than your nose-leather. They're the same color as your tongue. Nobody has pads that color. They're like a flower."

"How is it you can say such saccharine things to me, but you can't even tell Moashi he did a good job?"

"Oh, I did tell him that! 'Good job killing Vashon,' I said, 'and stop beating yourself up about it. Also, I dislike you; go home.' He just laughs at me, though, when I tell him I dislike him. It's infuriating."

Roup was obviously having a supremely difficult time following along. Halvery was positive he was tipping his hips up and curling his tail over. *But I am not going to look until I finish this conversation.* "Moashi was terrified of what *you* would think of him," continued Halvery. "He was tearing his fur out more over your potential reaction than over killing his challenger—who, I will add, sounds like a cub-murdering troublemaker."

"I'll...accept your judgment there," breathed Roup.

"Anyway, my point is, Moashi needed reassurance that he'd done the right thing in a tough situation, and he obviously couldn't get it from his officers. He needs a sharper beta—someone who thinks more like me or Arcove than like you, preferably someone who can fight, someone with some loyalty to him. I don't have anyone in mind, but I thought you might."

"Not off the t-top of my head," managed Roup. "Halvery, if we are having some kind of contest right now, you win."

"Aw." Halvery let Roup's paw go and scooted right over against him. He let his eyes travel down the length of Roup's body. "Ghosts, you're pretty when you're asking for it."

"Am I asking nicely enough?"

"*So* nicely, Roup." He buried his nose in the fur of Roup's chest. "Now you smell like you want me."

Roup gave an impatient squirm. "You're obviously very astute at reading these oh-so-subtle signs."

Halvery laughed. He licked his way over Roup's throat, and that shut him up. He stood, nuzzling Roup's chin back as he did, and looked down into his eyes—so black in the moonlight, with only the thinnest ring of gold. Halvery leaned close to his ear and licked the inside. Roup laughed and jerked away, but Halvery followed him, still licking. He murmured, "I'm going to make you finish on your stomach until you're wobbly and then flip you over and get inside you when you're flat on your back. We're done when you can't keep your hips up anymore. How's that for taking your mind off your troubles?"

"Do it," hissed Roup.

Halvery licked down the back of his neck, pausing to nibble and groom that spot that Roup found particularly stimulating.

Roup whined low in his throat.

"You're going to climax the moment I touch you," murmured Halvery. "It's so hard not to finish with you when you do that."

"Then don't wait," breathed Roup.

Halvery pulled back in surprise. Roup leaned up to nuzzle his face. "Just do it the old-fashioned way and then give yourself a moment. I'm not going anywhere."

Halvery didn't argue with him. He got up and took one more look at the long, elegant curve of Roup's back, the perfect curl of his tail. Then he went around behind him.

He thought for a moment that Roup was going to finish as soon as he started licking. He gave that long, low caterwaul that

Halvery found so gratifying, because it was obviously unconscious. It was also unlike any sound Halvery had ever heard from a mate. It wasn't quite the noise the females made. It wasn't a noise he'd heard males make. *You truly are just yourself.*

When he slid inside, Roup's yowl intensified and then broke off as his ears and whiskers fluttered. His whole body clenched, and Halvery's world blurred with pleasure. *The old-fashioned way. Right.* He let himself grab Roup's scruff while Roup was still twitching. Halvery forced Roup's chin tightly against the ground. He buried himself deep inside and finished with a possessive snarl. He let himself think, *Mine.*

Halvery didn't let go until the aftershocks had completely passed. He'd found that withdrawal was less likely to be painful when he did that. Coincidentally, keeping his partner pinned against the ground was supremely satisfying, although too dominant and aggressive for some females. *But you love dominant and aggressive, don't you, Roup?*

Roup made no attempt to push him off. Even after Halvery finally let go of him, Roup just lay there with his eyes closed, panting. Halvery nuzzled his cheek. "Feel good?"

"Yes."

"You're the prettiest thing on four legs, Roup."

Roup snickered. He flipped over and stretched, back toes curling, front legs extending over his head. This was familiar behavior. Females never mated on their backs, but they often flipped over and sometimes rolled around afterwards in a sort of joyful exuberance. It always made Halvery feel like he'd done a good job.

Roup proceeded to knead the air with his paws like a cub. *You really are so odd.*

Halvery lay down, draped both front legs across him, and started to lick his throat. "I'm surprised you're out here moping about Arcove not giving you what you want. I'm surprised you aren't just working around him."

Halvery stopped. Something Roup had said earlier flashed through his head. *"I'll have you know that I don't need anyone's permission to get things done."*

"Unless you already are working around him..." *Ghosts, of course you are.*

Roup had gone still.

"In order to save me from myself, you'd first have to begin keeping up with me."

"You've already figured out a way to send messages to the Southern Mountains," said Halvery slowly. "Have you and Dazzle been sending messages back and forth all summer?"

Roup spoke with measured calm, betraying none of the emotion he'd shown earlier. "Now you're giving me too much credit. I don't even know whether Dazzle is alive."

A voice in Halvery's head whispered, *You can't out-think him. Stop trying.*

But if I can figure out how Roup wants to be licked, when he doesn't even know himself... "Arcove won't let you go with the expedition. He won't let you send a message with those cats. But—oh, Roup, this isn't actually hard—the curbs! You've got Moashi making friends with them right now. Did you put him up to it? Ghosts and little fishes, what idiots we all are. The curbs would have an easier time getting near Thistle's cats anyway, because they're less intimidating. The curbs don't like Arcove. They won't like Hollygold, because Arcove sent him. But they like Moashi and Storm, who are yours. *That's* how you're planning to send a message."

Roup shifted out from underneath Halvery and turned over. They both sat up. Roup's face was completely closed. Not unfriendly. Just unreadable.

"Roup, you can't expect me not to at least *try* to keep up with you. I'm sure you'll run circles around me in the end. But I'm right, aren't I? And to think I *helped* you put Moashi in a position to be your tool and accomplice—"

Roup buried his face abruptly under Halvery's chin, exactly the way he'd done with Arcove earlier. "Please stop."

"Stop what? Trying to get ahead of your machinations?"

"Stop making it sound as though I am using you and others in a cold and indifferent manner."

"Well, you are—"

"I am trying to protect people, including you. I love you and I want you to live for a long time."

Halvery opened his mouth, shut it again. *Don't let him change the subject.* But Roup always knew exactly where to put his claws. Halvery swallowed. He tried to formulate a gracious reply. Instead, he just choked out artlessly against Roup's ear, "I love you *so* much." *And you are using the fact to change the subject, you ice-cold weasel.* But he couldn't bear to say it.

Roup lifted his head without backing away, his chin sliding up until his throat was right against Halvery's mouth. Halvery could not resist the invitation. He started licking. Roup smelled like he wanted to mate again. His low voice vibrated under Halvery's tongue. "Please, Halvery. Please put me on my back…"

Halvery opened his mouth. He put his teeth around Roup's throat, carefully controlled, and pushed him down. Roup folded onto his side and then onto his back. He was all compliant curves, quivering muscles, and soft fur. He felt so good that Halvery almost finished before he'd intended to. He let go of Roup's throat and leaned back just a little to get control of himself, to get the angle right.

Roup was breathing quickly, his eyes glazed with pleasure.

You look so helpless. And yet you're so far from it. You could rule the world from your back, Roup. You can certainly rule me. How is that? I'm watching you do it, and I still can't quite get ahead of you. If we're having a contest, you win.

Aloud, he only said, "You are so lovely, Roup…with the stars in your eyes and the mist in your fur."

Roup laughed between pants. "You'd think I'd get used to your compliments…that I'd figure out how to respond, but…"

Halvery grinned. He kept his voice playful. "You'd think I'd get used to your schemes, that I'd figure out how to respond, but…"

Roup started to say something and Halvery found exactly the right angle to make him throw his head back and whimper instead. Halvery leaned forward and growled against Roup's ear. "Less talking, more mating. Let's see how many times I can make you finish before you can't hold your hips up anymore."

6

Good News and Bad News

"We have good news and bad news for you," said Caraca with more animation than Halvery had ever seen from anyone regarding the topic of coat color.

It had been over a month since Halvery's initial request for information. The leaves were starting to show the first signs of fall and he was becoming impatient. Caraca had visited his den several times with Lyndi and spoken with all his mates. She'd then tracked down their parents and siblings, then their grandparents and great-grandparents if possible, as far back as she could trace. The process seemed quite complicated. Halvery assumed she'd been doing the same thing with the breeding females in Arcove's den. She assured him that her mother was helping to fill in gaps in the various lineages. "But it's best to get eyes on them if I can."

Lyndi told him privately that she and Caraca had nearly been attacked several times, because Caraca would simply barge into territories and begin asking questions. "She hardly ever visits other dens apart from Arcove's," muttered Lyndi. "She's harmless, but a little odd."

"Everyone in your clutter is a little odd," returned Halvery.

"Yes, including me. I'm aware you think so."

"Oh, I've gotten used to *you*."

Caraca was positively chatty about her findings each time they met, but when Halvery said, "Just tell me which female," she would become evasive.

"It's complicated. Give me more time."

Roup knew something was going on. If Lyndi had been able to collect the necessary information alone, she might have passed it off as clutter business. But Caraca insisted upon seeing the cats in question for herself, and since she never left her territory under normal circumstances, Roup noticed.

"I'm making friends with your mates," Halvery told him sweetly. "You've made friends with mine."

Roup could have pointed out that Halvery had no right to familiarize himself with the mates of his superior officer, but saying so would have seemed unbelievably petty, given the circumstances. Instead, he said, "Caraca doesn't have friends!"

"I'm certain you're wrong."

"Caraca has fellow-investigators and experiments," continued Roup.

"And which are you?" asked Halvery.

Roup rolled his eyes. "The second thing, I'm sure."

Well, I'm certainly the first thing, Halvery thought, but did not say.

At last, Lyndi told him that Caraca wanted to meet with him and Nadine in Arcove's den at the quarter moon. When he arrived, Halvery learned that Arcove had been asked to take Roup hunting so that they could speak openly.

Nadine was sitting near the mouth of the den. She looked gaunt and smaller than he remembered, but she welcomed Halvery graciously. Nadine had been den mother to three kings, and as a result, her bloodline crossed half of Leeshwood's, including Halvery's. They were a similar color—dark brown, with black points around the mouth, ears, and paws. Nadine had a black tail tip. Halvery had had one, too, before he lost it. Nadine's muzzle was heavily flecked with white now and her eyes were cloudy. Halvery suspected that she identified him more by scent than sight.

Caraca came straight to the point. "We have good news and bad news, but mostly good, I think."

"Well, let's have the bad news first," said Halvery.

"I think it's important to tell you our limitations first," said Caraca.

"No," said Halvery, dreading another detailed discussion of oory coat color, "it really isn't."

Caraca ignored him. "The problem is that Roup won't mate downstream of his own blood. I'm sure of this. I've brought it up so many times. Even distant relatives. He just won't mate downstream of his color."

"Yes," said Halvery, "you're looking for a female who is not related to him. I knew that already."

"Golden color is a trait that hides in the population," said Caraca. "It's in our blood, but it doesn't show in our fur very often. When it does show, it's usually in males. I don't know why. Females carry it, but males show it. Solids, too. Solids of any color are most commonly male."

"Alright..." Halvery found Caraca's way of thinking about color hard to understand, but he knew that if he asked for a further explanation, they would be here all night. "So you need to identify a color that is hiding in the blood, but doesn't show in the coat very often. I knew that already—"

"And upstream," cut in Caraca. "Upstream of Roup, not down."

Halvery screwed up his face. "An example, please?"

"If Roup had siblings," said Caraca, "their descendants might have the color. Or a cousin's descendants. Or anyone from that clutter or territory."

"But," came Nadine's softer voice, "that's a problem, because we don't know where Roup came from. He was taken by raiding ferryshaft before he opened his eyes. It would be helpful to know who his parents, siblings, and grandparents were, but we don't."

"I'm with you so far," said Halvery.

"Those are our limitations," said Caraca. "That's what makes this hard. But Mother thinks she knows where Roup came from."

"Oh?" asked Halvery in surprise.

"There was a solid gold male in a den on the northern edge of what is now your territory during Masaran's reign," said Nadine. "I remember that male, because he was mate to a daughter from my first litter. He died before he reached twenty, but he ruled a den with half a dozen females for some seven or eight years. He sired a number of cubs, and he was striking. His blood would have been all through that den and the related clutter. I remember that a number of those cats had golden ears, bellies, or paws."

"Ferryshaft raided all over the wood during that time," said Caraca, "so Roup could have come from anywhere, but..."

"But they were more aggressive around the edges," finished Halvery, "and a den on the northern edge of my territory would be vulnerable."

"Precisely," said Nadine. "And even if Roup didn't come from that den, I think there's a good chance he could trace his blood there. For instance, one of the daughters of that den might have made her home on the other side of Leeshwood. Same blood."

"Alright," said Halvery, "but..." He thought about the birth dens of his mates. None of them were on the northern edge. "You said you have good news?"

Nadine shook her ears. "Caraca, just tell him."

Caraca rolled her eyes. "Alright, fine. Ilsa."

Halvery gaped at her. "What...?"

"I told you good news and bad."

"But... Oh, ghosts. Of all the possible females! Are you sure?"

"We can't be sure, no," said Caraca, "and it took a lot of digging to get this far. Ilsa comes from a den in the middle of your territory—"

"I know where she comes from. I know her parents!" objected Halvery. "Neither of them have golden fur."

Caraca cocked her head. "You know the den. So you know about Gensly?"

Halvery hesitated. "That was a while back…"

"Yes, eight years ago. Ilsa is eight years old."

Halvery shut his eyes. "Her father shared the den with another male, and they had a falling out. There was a fight. The other one left. I think he went to Hollygold's territory. Not sure after that."

"I found him," said Caraca. "He's not in a den anymore, just a clutter. He really didn't want to be found. He actually goes by a different name now. Anyway, he has a golden belly, and he was born in that den on the northern edge of your territory that once had a solid gold alpha."

Halvery cocked his head. "You think he's Ilsa's…"

"I can't prove it," said Caraca. "Her mother refused to admit the possibility. Apparently, the fight between the two males was ugly, and she felt it was in the best interests of her cubs to insist that they were the offspring of the winner. But the two males *were* sharing the den at the time Ilsa was conceived. After comparing her with her supposed father and his den-mate…I think she's Gensly's. The shape of her ears, eyes, and nose, together with certain brindling patterns in her coat all match him. Gensly is certainly carrying the golden color, and he would have given it to his daughters."

"Ilsa is your best chance," said Nadine gently, "but, Halvery, you need to understand that no match is certain to produce a golden cub."

"I know that," muttered Halvery. He sighed heavily. "Ilsa will happily lie down for Roup. No problems there. But, Roup… He gave me such grief about taking her into my den in the first place. And Ilsa wants to have a litter this spring. She already stopped eating bitterleaf. She'll be in season soon; there isn't much time."

"Your second-best chance would be Shazel in Arcove's den," continued Caraca. "One of her grandmothers birthed a golden cub, but it died before reaching adulthood. We couldn't find evidence of the fur anywhere in living relatives, but she does have the color in her lineage, so maybe."

"Shazel is still nursing her litter from last spring," put in Nadine. "She won't be ready to breed again for at least a year, probably two, so you'd have some time to get Roup used to the idea. She's twenty-eight, so he'd have fewer objections about her maturity. However, she's also getting near the end of her breeding years. She might not have another litter at all, although I suspect she'll have one more, possibly even two."

Halvery peered between Nadine and Caraca. "But you don't really think Roup is going to sire a golden cub with Shazel?"

Caraca and Nadine shared a glance. "No," said Caraca. "I could be wrong, but if you want my studied opinion, the only cat in either den likely to produce a golden cub is Ilsa. I did identify several females living in other dens who are probably carrying the blood and whom you might persuade to join your den. However, as someone who has lived with Roup most of his life, I'll tell you: he won't mate with a stranger. He won't mate with anyone he hasn't known for some time. He *does* know Ilsa after all that sparring last summer."

Halvery sighed again. "He calls her a cub."

Caraca flicked her ears in annoyance. "But she's not a cub, and Roup knows that. Frankly, it's a little insulting for him to say so. Insulting to *her,* not to you. You might point that out if you want to turn the tables on him."

Halvery barked a laugh. "When I play word games with Roup, I always lose, Caraca. I can tell that you're better at it."

Nadine spoke. "If he won't accept Ilsa, but is willing to consider sharing a different mate, that's still worth pursuing. There's always a chance that the right blood is hiding in another female. And even if that's not the case, color isn't everything, Halvery. Roup has many unique qualities that I would like to see perpetuated in Leeshwood. At this time, he has only five surviving offspring. Compared to other officers or even most den alphas, that is a tiny number. Arcove's blood will run through Leeshwood for generations to come. So will yours. But Roup's? Not so much. I appreciate what you're doing, and I don't think that you're wasting your time, even if the cubs aren't golden."

"I know," muttered Halvery, "but when I think about reproducing that scheming brain of his, I get nervous. Let me be a little shallow, and I'll get the job done."

Caraca cackled.

Nadine laughed and then started to cough—a wet, wheezing sound.

"You don't even like most of his 'unique qualities,'" said Caraca when she stopped laughing. "I still don't understand why you're doing this."

"Can we focus on the fact that his paw pads look like flowers?" said Halvery. "And he shines in low light like he's glowing. Like a firefly."

Caraca smirked. "Lyndi is right. You are precious. Alright, Halvery, we've done our bit. Go see if you can get him on Isla. I can't imagine how, but he does like going down to your den, so maybe."

Halvery looked between them. "Thank you, both. I know this was a lot of work. Nadine…" *How do I thank someone for spending what is likely her last year, possibly her last season, on my project?*

Nadine leaned forward, and Halvery bowed his head so that she could lick him between the ears like a cub. "This was a pleasant distraction," she whispered, her voice rough with illness, but not unhappy. "And Roup is worth reproducing, Halvery. He really is. I'm glad you see it."

He spoke automatically. "Thank you, sir. I mean—"

Caraca snorted. "No, you got it right. My mother is a legend."

Instead of correcting himself, Halvery butted his head against Nadine's shoulder. "If I can do anything at all for you, please let me know."

"Anything…?" she asked wistfully.

Halvery knew that look. He felt cold. *Something you don't want to ask of Arcove…* He swallowed. "Anything, Nadine."

* * * *

This chapter includes an author's note at the end of the book.

7

Beginning with No

"No."

"You haven't even heard the details yet, Roup."

"I don't need to."

"What did you tell me about beginning with no?"

"I don't always begin with no, only when a...how old is she now?"

"Eight! She's exactly the right age to have her first litter!"

"Her *first* litter. Ghosts, Halvery."

Halvery could feel his patience slipping. "She's been living in my den, eating bitterleaf for two years. I assure you this isn't her first heat! She's going about things exactly as she pleases; isn't that what you think females *should* do?"

Roup had his ears back. He didn't answer. Halvery could tell he was thinking about something else entirely. *I'm doing this all wrong.*

They were standing by Smoky Branch in the moonlight, waiting for the council to assemble. Halvery had intended to bring up this issue afterward, hopefully when Roup was relaxed and preferably flat on his back. But Roup had met him with an apologetic look and a quick, "I'm going to disappear after this. I'm sorry. I'll come down to your den in a few days."

Halvery didn't think the issue could wait a few days. Ilsa's season could begin at any moment. He'd been fretting since he spoke to Nadine and Caraca. *I should have talked to Roup that same night.*

But Roup and Arcove had not returned from hunting until near dawn, and Roup had not been in a receptive frame of mind. He hadn't been in a good mood since the last council meeting, truth be told. It was obvious to Halvery that Arcove was being intractable regarding the question of Roup going to the Southern Mountains or sending any message to Thistle's cats.

Arcove wasn't a fool, and he knew Roup like he knew his own whiskers. Halvery suspected that the possibility of Roup using the curbs as his messengers had occurred to him. "Arcove put his head together with Storm while they were out hunting that night," Lyndi told Halvery. "They came back very conspiratorial. I don't know what was said, but I think Storm agreed to keep Roup out of the mountains, and Arcove agreed to do the same with Costa."

No one had seen Storm, Tollee, or the highland curbs since the council meeting. Costa had apparently been told that since she liked Carmine's den so much, she could stay there until the fall conference. "She's been sparring with creasia as often as possible just to spite her father," said Lyndi, "but she won't know when the expedition leaves for the mountains, which was Storm's intent. I don't think she's so reckless as to try for the mountains on her own."

Meanwhile, Roup had been given no opportunity to speak to the highland curbs. Storm had made certain they were gone by the time Roup and Halvery returned from Roup's old food cache that night. Halvery wondered whether Roup resented him for taking his mind off his troubles during the one moment when Roup might have been able to get ahead of Arcove.

The summons to council this evening had seemed like a welcome opportunity to raise the issue of Ilsa. *The invitation to share a mate ought to be a fun and easy topic,* Halvery told himself. *It ought to be a welcome respite from the burdens of leadership. But this is Roup, so everything has to be difficult.*

Halvery had expected to have some time with Roup afterwards, but when that possibility had been rejected, he'd decided to broach the topic anyway. *Surely Roup suspects. Maybe he already knows. Maybe he'll just say yes and we'll all have some fun when he comes down to my den in a few days.*

From the look on Roup's face, however, he had *not* known. *He's been too focused on his own schemes to give any thought to mine.* "Caraca, Lyndi, and Nadine worked very hard—" began Halvery.

"I'm sure they did," snapped Roup.

"We investigated every breeding female in Arcove's den and mine! We did look closely at all of them, Roup. I'm sorry it's Ilsa—"

"Can we talk about this later, Halvery?"

Halvery shut his mouth.

The council meeting had been called for midnight, not sunset or sunrise, as Arcove usually preferred. Halvery suspected he'd received some urgent news. The messengers had gone out to the various officers in the afternoon, when most cats were still sleeping. Halvery considered asking Roup what they were meeting about. He'd probably been sleeping beside Arcove when the news arrived. The fact that he'd been standing on the riverbank alone was interesting, though not really telling. Roup frequently went off by himself to think.

Halvery had expected resistance to the notion of sharing a mate, but not unqualified refusal without even a hearing. *That's what I do! You always want to hear every side!*

Another part of his brain grumbled that if *any* other male in Leeshwood had been offered what he'd just offered Roup, they would be falling over themselves to accept. They would be flattered beyond words, humbled by the compliment.

Not Roup. Oh, no. He just snaps at me and lectures about her age. Like he didn't start lying down for Arcove at four. Better not say that out loud. I'll get myself into even worse trouble.

Other council members were beginning to arrive. Arcove walked in talking to Hollygold. They had two ferryshaft with them—Sauny and Valla. *They'll be the ones who brought the news that woke us all up,* thought Halvery.

Stefan arrived looking sleepy. His den was far from Arcove's, and Halvery suspected he'd left on short notice almost as soon as he got the summons. Lyndi trotted up and sat down beside Roup. She gave him a lick on the ear, but Roup didn't respond. Curiously, Moashi arrived last, and he was bristling. He sat down on the opposite side of the circle as far as he could get from Roup, looking guilty.

Well, this is interesting. Did you kill another challenger, Ears?

It was a foggy night, and steam from Smoky Branch made it even foggier. Arcove was just a shadow and a glint of green eyes as he said, "Thank you all for arriving so quickly. As you've probably guessed, I've had unwelcome news. Sedaron's herd has moved from their territory in the north. They've traveled south to a portion of the plain on the far edge of the Southern Mountains. This bodes ill for Thistle's cats, but more significantly, Sedaron's ferryshaft have begun attacking herds of ferryshaft who are our allies."

Sauny spoke up. "They completely obliterated a small herd composed mostly of Charder's old friends. A group of them attacked my herd, but we outran them."

Roup was listening closely now, all hint of distraction vanished. "What about Kelsy's herd?"

Sauny let out a long, frustrated breath. "Kelsy is Sedaron's son, as you know, and their herds are friendly. Or they have been in the past. Sedaron's herd ran past Kelsy's in the night during their migration and made no move to attack. This could be because Kelsy's herd is only a little smaller than Sedaron's. Sedaron may simply not want to risk a bloody altercation with them, but…"

"There's also a rumor that he's considering Kelsy neutral in this conflict," put in Valla. "Nobody knows whether it's true, because now Sedaron's herd is between most of the other herds and Kelsy's. Sedaron is not letting messengers pass. We don't know what Kelsy is thinking, but so far, he hasn't given us any reason to believe he's *not* neutral."

"Which means the remaining ferryshaft are badly outnumbered," muttered Roup.

"Yes," said Sauny. "We're mostly little herds, as you know. Sedaron is still allied with lowland curbs. They seem to be locating groups of ferryshaft and reporting back to Sedaron, who then organizes raiding parties large enough to overcome them. Some of the ferryshaft he's attacked seem to have joined his herd. It's hard to say exactly what happened, but I would guess they were offered the choice of joining or dying."

Halvery growled. "Well, it sounds like the next ferryshaft war is right around the corner. This is what happens when they breed out of control—"

"Halvery, Sedaron is killing ferryshaft because they are allied with *you*," snarled Valla.

Halvery tried to moderate his tone. "I know that, Valla, and I am in no way hostile towards those ferryshaft. But it seems to me that whenever ferryshaft multiply wildly, a majority of them decide that all creasia must die."

Sauny rolled her eyes. "You're wrong. This isn't happening because our two species are incapable of living peacefully. This is spill-over from the last war. At least half the ferryshaft on Lidian still remember your culls, Halvery. Some of them just can't forgive that. Some days, I'm amazed that I can."

"Well, I remember *their* culls," flashed Halvery. "I remember finding half-eaten cubs—"

"Enough," growled Arcove. "The only thing worse than reproducing the ferryshaft wars would be refighting them in council with friends."

Halvery looked away. He was bristling. *Don't make a fool of yourself.* He felt, more than saw, Roup glance at him. *Twenty years ago, you would have said something right about now to* really *make me lose my temper.*

But Roup said nothing.

"I do have some good news," continued Sauny, "or at least... interesting news. I spoke with Kelsy just last month, before his herd got cut off. At that time, he told me that his father is ailing."

"It's about time!" muttered Stefan. "Why do the mean ones always live forever?"

That made Halvery laugh.

"He's got a young lieutenant named Macex who doesn't always see eye-to-eye with him," said Sauny. "They might fight, especially now that Sedaron's judgment could be called into question by illness. In that case, the herd could be thrown into chaos. They might split up. They might lose their single-minded focus."

"Well, that *is* good news," said Stefan. "I don't suppose we could speed Sedaron on his way to the Ghost Wood? Perhaps Storm can exercise his preternatural skills to slip in there and kill him."

Sauny laughed uneasily. "I'm not sure that Sedaron dying would be to our advantage. I think that if he and Macex fought, that would be ideal. It might split the herd. But if Sedaron simply died…"

"You're saying that Macex is not our friend," said Roup dryly.

"He is not," agreed Sauny. "His ideas are different from Sedaron's, but probably not in the ways you'd prefer. For instance, Sedaron is opposed to any treaty with creasia. His goal is to eradicate creasia from Lidian. Macex, on the other hand, is rumored to be willing to parley with cats under the right circumstances. Just not Arcove."

Roup got there just a little ahead of everyone else. "So Macex might be willing to unite with Thistle's cats to take Leeshwood."

"That is a remote possibility," admitted Sauny, "but I've met Thistle, and—"

"Don't say he wouldn't do it, Sauny," hissed Valla. "He was perfectly willing to make common cause with *you* to catch two of his own cats who'd crossed him. Thistle *will* parley with ferryshaft."

"Yes, but he wouldn't roll over!" objected Sauny. "He was too proud for that. And Sedaron's officers think that creasia belong on their bellies at their feet. Thistle wouldn't grovel!"

"He might with his back against a wall." Valla hesitated. "He might if someone offered him Leeshwood."

"Maybe," admitted Sauny. "Anyway, this is what we came to tell you. I also wanted to ask…"

"You want us to offer sanctuary to ferryshaft fleeing from Sedaron," said Arcove in a neutral voice.

"Yes," said Sauny. "They're being attacked because they are your allies."

Halvery made a face. *We've already got too many ferryshaft living in Leeshwood.* But he didn't say it.

After a moment, Arcove asked, "If I welcome ferryshaft into my wood and allow them to move off the common way trails, what is to prevent Sedaron from sending his own spies? The relationships and loyalties between these various herds sound complex. I assume that many of these fleeing ferryshaft will be strangers to me and my officers?"

"Send them to my territory," said Roup immediately. "I'll make a place for them."

No one said what they were surely thinking—that it was questionable whether Roup even had a territory anymore, although Arcove had not officially made a decision about Carmine's promotion.

Lyndi chimed in. "We already have a small herd of ferryshaft living there, led by So-fet. Might she be able to identify which ferryshaft are truly our allies?"

Sauny looked relieved. "Yes. Maybe not all of them, but… Mother was Charder's mate for nine years. He had a lot of friends in all the herds. She met them. I think she could tell friend from foe."

"Even if you have a question about some of them, putting them all in one place will limit what they see and hear," added Roup. "Additionally, most clutters are unaccustomed to ferryshaft wandering far from common way trails and might attack them. My clutter is accustomed to ferryshaft; put them there."

"Very well," said Arcove.

"Thank you," said Sauny.

Arcove looked around at his officers. "In the meantime, I'd like all of you to decide which cats you would take with you if we need to get involved in a fight in the Southern Mountains. Make sure they're ready to move on short notice."

"A war clutter?" asked Halvery. "Or just a raiding party?"

Arcove hesitated. "We'll say ten animals each for now. I'm not ready to call it a war."

But that's a big *raiding party,* thought Halvery.

"The fall conference will meet in less than a month," continued Arcove. "Hopefully by then, we will have a more accurate idea of what we're dealing with."

The meeting broke up in a low hum of talk. Stefan and Hollygold both had questions for the ferryshaft. Their territories adjoined the southern plains and they were the most likely to encounter animals fleeing from Sedaron's herd. Halvery turned to ask Lyndi whether she needed help organizing a raiding party out of Roup's territory.

When he looked up, he noticed that both Roup and Moashi had vanished. Halvery was surprised. He'd expected Roup to want to talk to Sauny and Valla. Especially since he'd just volunteered his territory to host fleeing ferryshaft.

Roup's words came back to him suddenly. *I'm going to disappear after this.* Halvery scowled. *And Moashi looked guilty about something...* He broke off what he'd been saying to Lyndi. "I'm sorry; I have to go."

He headed towards Moashi's territory and picked up Roup and Moashi's scents almost immediately. They'd probably skirted the council circle so as not to be seen leaving together, but they'd joined up soon afterward.

Moashi wasn't feeling guilty because he did something Roup wouldn't approve of, thought Halvery. *He was feeling guilty because he's helping Roup do something* Arcove *wouldn't approve of!*

They weren't headed for Moashi's den. Their trail skirted the edge of his territory, angling towards the cliffs. Halvery glided through the fog, thinking furiously. *Sauny's news will spur Arcove to get that fall expedition into the mountains as quickly as possible. He'll be worried that Sedaron's herd might tighten their hold on the area. If hostile ferryshaft proceed up into the mountains, it could become difficult to get near Thistle's cats.*

The more Halvery thought about it, the more certain he felt that he was right. *Arcove will send the expedition now. Hollygold and his cats could meet Storm and the highland curbs anywhere between here and the Southern Mountains. But maybe Storm and the curbs were never far away. Maybe they've been in Syriot, just under the Garu Vell...where Roup couldn't find them.*

Halvery came around a little stand of trees and caught sight of Moashi and Roup. They were above him, a short distance up a cliff trail, easily spotted because they were higher than the drifting fog. For an instant, he thought they were alone. Then something moved against the dark rock of the cliff—a striped shape the size of a two-year-old cub. Another emerged from behind Roup.

Halvery scowled. *Cohal and Maoli. Where's Storm?*

Storm's silver-gray fur should have stood out against the red rock of the cliff in the moonlight, but Halvery saw no sign of him. *So Lyndi was right. Storm has been assisting Arcove in keeping Roup away from the curbs. Moashi is the one who facilitated this meeting.*

Halvery bounded through the last of the boulders, briefly foiled by a thicket. All four animals were still talking when he flashed up the trail out of the mist. He began snarling at them before the surprised group could decide how to greet him. "Moashi, you little fool, are you *trying* to get him killed?"

Moashi flinched. He stammered something and Halvery talked over him, "You think you're more clever than Arcove, is that it? Think you know his beta better? Do you want to give Dazzle another swipe at him? Maybe next time Roup will just bleed to death right in front of you. Would that make you happy?"

Moashi had tucked his tail and turned his head to the side.

Roup's voice cracked out, "Halvery, that's enough!"

Halvery rounded on him. "And you—!"

"Be quiet; that's an order."

Halvery barely checked himself.

Roup glared at Halvery just long enough to be certain that Halvery was going to respond to rank. Then he returned his attention to his junior officer. "Moashi, go home. I'll deal with this."

Moashi cut his eyes miserably sideways. "Roup..."

"Don't worry about it. Go home."

Moashi turned away, slinking like a beaten cub. He paused beside Halvery, started to look at him, and then seemed to lose his nerve. He darted on down the trail.

"That's right; run away, you little coward—!"

"I said enough!" hissed Roup. He turned to the curbs, "Well, you two had better get going if you're to meet Storm where he expects."

Cohal cocked his head. "He may not like what you're doing."

Roup's teeth flashed in the dimness. "Oh, but he will. And if he doesn't, it's low risk. I don't think he'll object. Go on, before Halvery loses his battle with his self-control."

"This is his version of self-control?" asked Cohal doubtfully.

Halvery was emitting a low, sustained growl that fairly vibrated the rock.

Maoli looked worried. "Will you be alright, Roup?"

"I am perfectly safe," Roup assured her. "Go on."

8

Breaking Your Heart

The curbs turned and trotted up the trail, which merged with a sheep trail a little farther on. Halvery expected Roup to begin some absurd excuse or explanation, but he only sighed and looked up at the stars.

"Am I allowed to talk yet?" snarled Halvery when he could contain himself no longer.

"No…" Roup shut his eyes. After an interminable pause, he said, "You want me to sire cubs…with Ilsa?"

Halvery felt as though he'd been running hard in one direction and then jerked violently in another. "What? No."

Roup finally looked at him, his expression quizzical. "I thought you said—"

"You can't just change the subject like that! You can't just... make me forget what I saw by saying—"

"The cubs won't look like me," continued Roup blandly, "which is a good thing, because I'm a terrible color for hunting. There's a reason I fish more often than I stalk deer. And besides, fathering cubs for the sake of a color is the vainest undertaking I can imagine—"

"Color isn't the only reason," snapped Halvery, "but you're not going to throw me off the scent like this—"

"I like lying down. Is that a trait you think needs to be replicated in males?"

"Yes."

Roup peered at Halvery doubtfully. "No, you don't."

"Yes, I do! What kind of a hypocrite do you take me for? But you're not going to send me off after that rabbit when you still haven't—"

"Oh," said Roup brightly. "So you're hoping to replicate the way I *think?*"

Halvery opened his mouth and stopped.

Roup gave him a slow, sad smile. It was a look that said, *"Say 'yes' to that right now. I dare you."*

Halvery felt like a mouse in a circle. Roup had put a paw on him, and now he couldn't breathe.

Halvery's attention was jerked away from Roup's face by movement further up the trail. An animal of modest size slithered down the rockface, landed lightly, and turned in the direction the curbs had taken. Halvery caught a flash of pale belly.

"Ghosts of our fathers!" He jumped over Roup and bounded down the path just in time to land on top of Costa before she reached the sheep trail.

The young ferryshaft gave a yelp. She struggled madly. Halvery could have held her with his claws, but he didn't want to use them, so he just lay down on top of her, with Costa's head between his front legs.

Costa's snarls turned to pleading whines. "Halvery, let me up! I'm just going to follow them for a bit. I want to talk to my father. I'll be careful. Please!"

"Not a chance."

Roup arrived in a hurry. "Costa Ela-ferry! You really are just like him."

"No, I'm not," she said miserably. "Storm never got pinned by Halvery."

"I feel that you are implying some insult," said Halvery. "You do know that I actually have claws, right? Just because I've never used them on you doesn't mean I can't."

"Storm got pinned by *me*," said Roup amiably. "There were definitely claws involved. Why do you want to go to the Southern Mountains so badly?"

Costa glared at him and said nothing.

Roup gave a disarming smile. He sat down facing her and then stretched out on his belly, matching Halvery's posture, but keeping his attention on Costa. "Let's play a game."

"Be careful, Costa," muttered Halvery between her ears. "He never loses." In spite of the fact that she was a ferryshaft, he couldn't help thinking of her primarily as his student. She'd been an enthusiastic yearling last summer, but not chatty, which suited Halvery just fine. She'd been far less whiny than Moashi. He'd knocked her down innumerable times as she learned to dodge his strikes, and she'd always bounced to her feet without complaints.

Costa had been sidelined as the focus of the group turned to attacking and grappling, which she simply could not do as a yearling foal. Halvery had let her charge at him, however, and jump around him, pretending to bite and kick. She'd been hardly more than a baby. He'd called her "cub," and neither she nor Storm had ever corrected him. Now he was reminded that she was not a cub and her legs were getting long, and she didn't seem even slightly afraid of him. It was a bit disconcerting.

Costa's ears pricked at Roup. "What game?"

"You can ask me a question. I'll answer honestly. Then you have to do the same."

Halvery felt her tail try to wave under his chest. "You played this game with my father once."

"I did."

Halvery frowned. *When?*

Roup was keeping his eyes on Costa. "You go first."

She thought for a moment. "Do *you* think I'd be useless in the Southern Mountains?"

Roup considered. "Useless, no. Fragile, yes."

"Storm was fragile. He's smaller than most ferryshaft; I bet he wasn't any bigger than I am when he was running from you."

"No, I don't suppose he was," said Roup.

Halvery was surprised. *Was he really this small?*

"My turn," said Roup. "Why do you want to go to the Southern Mountains?"

"Because that's where all the interesting things are happening!" exclaimed Costa. "And it's all going to affect the ferryshaft; everyone says so." She caught her breath and added darkly, "Storm would let me go if it weren't for Paeden. He took my siblings all the way around the island when they were my age. He let them follow him anywhere! Not me. I have to stay in Leeshwood where it's *safe*."

The assertion that Leeshwood was a safe place for ferryshaft made Halvery want to either swear or laugh. He was distracted by the unfamiliar name. *Who is Paeden?*

Roup's eyes flicked up as though he'd heard the question. "The one who died," he murmured.

Oh... Halvery remembered, then. Storm and Tollee had lost a foal several years ago. It hadn't happened in Leeshwood. Halvery couldn't remember the details. Until last summer, he'd rarely seen Storm outside of council meetings. While they weren't hostile, they certainly hadn't been checking in on each other's offspring. *Paeden must have been the foal before Costa. Ghosts, how do ferryshaft manage to outbreed us when they have babies one at a time?*

"You think Storm has lost his nerve?" asked Halvery with a hint of cheerful malevolence.

Costa answered him seriously. "Not when he's on his own. But he won't let me do things with him. Things he let the others do. Even though he made sure I could fight and run and walk on cliff trails… He won't let me *use* any of it! And before you say it's Mother, no, it isn't. She'd let me. It's him!"

"Maybe he'd just like you to be a bit older first," hazarded Roup.

"I don't think so," said Costa miserably. "I think he'll keep making excuses until I'm grown, and then he'll tell me I can take *myself* on adventures. But I want to go with *him!* I want to go *now!* And anyway, when I'm older, all the spying and fighting will be finished!"

"Don't be so certain of that," said Roup in a tired voice.

"My turn," said Costa. "Why do *you* want to go to the Southern Mountains?"

Roup opened his mouth…shut it again.

Halvery rumbled a laugh. "Oh, she's good at this game. Answer honestly, Roup; let's hear it."

"Because I would like to save Thistle's creasia from Sedaron's herd."

"Why?" asked Costa. "Dazzle almost killed you."

"Nevertheless."

Halvery whispered in her ear, "That's not an answer."

Roup's eyes flicked up at him in annoyance.

"That's not an answer," echoed Costa gleefully and tried to wag her tail again.

They were interrupted by Arcove, who whisked soundlessly out of the fog at the foot of the trail, head low to the ground, tracking. He looked up, saw them, and arrived in an instant. "Costa Ela-ferry!"

Costa put her ears back. "You can't keep me here— "

"Oh, but I can!" snarled Arcove. "Halvery, let her up."

Halvery stood. Costa sprang to her feet. She stood there hemmed in by three creasia, looking around defiantly.

Arcove bent, so that he was nose to nose with her. His jaws could easily have encompassed her head. He spoke in a dangerous murmur, "Creasia have territories, Costa. You have been made an honorary member of Carmine's den to share its territory this summer and fall. You are currently far from the shelter of that territory and therefore not under its protection. Do you know what cats do, even to each other, when they stray, uninvited, into another's territory?"

"Moashi doesn't care—" began Costa.

"And furthermore, all of Leeshwood is *my* territory," continued Arcove. "This is my wood, Costa. You are making trouble in it. Have you spent any time in the Cave of Histories *at all?*"

Costa was beginning to show signs of discomfort in the face of Arcove's relentless displeasure. Halvery thought she considered making another excuse, but wisely swallowed it.

"I promised Storm I'd keep you here," growled Arcove. "I didn't say I wouldn't do it by breaking your legs."

"You wouldn't hurt me," said Costa, though she sounded less certain than she had a moment ago.

Arcove stood up. "No? Well, how's this: I'll keep you confined to a cave for the rest of the season. I'll assign someone to guard you and bring you food. Maybe we'll just bury the entrance to make it easier. Shove food through a tiny hole. Is that how you'd like to spend your fall?"

Costa looked worried now. She was only two years old, after all. Halvery had seen adult creasia wet themselves in fear of Arcove's anger.

"Furthermore," continued Arcove, "respect and trust are precious things, as you'll come to know as you get older. Right now, you aren't winning any of mine. You seem to despise my hospitality. You are well on your way to becoming someone I would not consider a friend to Leeshwood."

That got to her. Costa's ears and tail drooped. "I'm sorry!" She lowered her head. There was real distress in her voice. "I'm sorry, Arcove. Please don't… I'm a friend to Leeshwood. I'll always be a friend to Leeshwood!"

"Then act like it!" he thundered.

Costa tucked her tail and turned her head. Then, as if that wasn't enough, she went down to her belly. She had seemed wily beyond her years a moment ago. Now she looked entirely her age and out of her depth. Halvery had an absurd urge to get between Costa and Arcove. *She's just a baby! You've won. Give it a rest.*

Arcove's ears came up. With Costa no longer looking at him, his expression changed. Halvery thought he was worried that he'd overdone it. He kept his tone stern, however, as he said, "Teek is tearing his fur out because he thinks he's lost you and Storm will blame him if something happens to you. Teek has been nothing but kind to you, and this is how you repay him?"

"I'm sorry," repeated Costa in a tiny voice. "Please don't bury me in a cave."

"Will you remain in your territory unless invited to leave it?" growled Arcove.

"Yes," she whispered.

"You know that promises are very important to me, don't you?"

Costa raised her head, eyes desperate. "I wouldn't break a promise to you, Arcove. I wouldn't. And I *am* a friend to Leeshwood!"

"He knows that," muttered Halvery.

Arcove shot him a look that contained a hint of displeasure, but mostly surprise.

Halvery looked away.

Arcove's gaze returned to Costa. His voice was kinder when he said, "I did not ask you for a promise earlier. Perhaps I should have. I thought you might be too young to understand such things."

"I understand," whispered Costa. She still had her tail tucked although she'd stood up a little. She was watching Arcove's face, clearly desperate for some hint that she'd been forgiven.

Halvery almost said, "Come stay in my den, Costa. We'll spar and you can play with a dozen cubs. You'll forget all about whatever idiotic thing Storm is doing."

Arcove made her wait for a long, agonizing moment before he said, in neutral tones, "Would you like to visit Keesha this evening?"

Costa's ears came up. "Is he coming to talk to you?"

"As it happens, *I* am going to talk to *him*…in an interesting place that you probably haven't been before. If I were to *invite* you to leave your territory and join me for the evening, would you behave like a member of my clutter with some discipline? Would you follow orders?"

Costa knew forgiveness when she saw it. Her tail waved wildly. "Yes, yes, I'll be a perfect creasia. Where are we going?"

"Oh, no," said Arcove. "First, you are going to find Teek and apologize. Then I will meet you at Carmine's den, which is where you live. Do you understand?"

"Yes, sir."

Arcove moved out of her way, and Costa trotted down the trail at speed.

When she'd disappeared, Roup said, "'You can't make me' to 'Yes, sir' in one conversation! I take it back; she's not Storm."

Arcove shook himself and his hackles settled. "Well, Storm never cared what I thought of him, so there's that."

"Did she leave Teek running in circles?" asked Halvery.

"Yes."

"But no one leaves you running in circles," said Roup with a smile.

Arcove looked at him sidelong. "Almost no one."

There was an uncomfortable pause. Halvery felt certain that Arcove had smelled the curbs. It was telling that he had not asked Roup and Halvery what they were doing out here on a path that went nowhere, far from either of their territories. His eyes tracked the sheep trail. In the extreme distance, Halvery caught a hint of movement near the top of the cliff and a flash of silver-gray—Storm, meeting the highland curbs.

Halvery glanced at Roup and saw that he was watching, too. He wondered whether Arcove was about to give Roup the sort of dressing-down that he'd given Costa. He wondered whether he should leave.

But when Arcove spoke, his voice was quiet, "Am I breaking your heart, Roup?"

A pause, and then Roup answered with a hint of mischief. "Always."

"What did you say to them?"

"I asked them to find out whether Dazzle is alive. If they can."

Arcove scowled. "I said no contact—"

"I didn't ask them to speak to any of those cats. Just keep an eye out." He shot the flicker of a smile at Halvery. "Dazzle should have a distinctive scar."

Arcove shut his eyes. Halvery could sympathize with his frustration. At the same time, he thought, *This is how Arcove and Roup talk when they're alone. They're not moderating their tone for me.* He felt oddly touched by that.

"I didn't go with them," said Roup. "I didn't countermand your stipulations about not speaking to Thistle's cats."

"If those cats want to ask for help, they can," growled Arcove. "I have made my messengers available. But we are not *begging* for their goodwill, Roup. They've shown nothing but contempt for yours—"

"I told you: I didn't."

Arcove looked at him narrowly. "What are you *not* telling me?"

Roup thought for a moment. "You remember that time when I was five and you were four, and we got trapped on the plain during a snowstorm? You asked if I was afraid, and I said no—"

Arcove spoke in a low growl, "Roup..."

Roup continued brightly, "Well, I lied."

He does it to Arcove, too! thought Halvery in wonder. *Turning every conversation in circles. How does Arcove handle it?*

"Also, that time we split up to hunt after the Volontaro," continued Roup. "You asked me if I'd caught anything, and I said yes, but it wasn't true. I didn't want you to give me any of your kill, because you're bigger, and you were going to have to fight..."

Arcove advanced on him. "Roup..."

Roup lowered his head and ears, but he didn't back away. "Also, I followed you when you took Treace to the Ghost Wood. I didn't tell you that."

Arcove let out an exasperated breath. He looked down at Roup, almost as though he meant to give him a pop on the nose.

Roup looked up at him, his expression coy. "Am I breaking your heart?"

Arcove wavered for a moment and then seemed to give up. His voice came out soft and low, with a gentleness that belied his posture. "Always."

You're not going to make him tell you, thought Halvery in amazement.

Arcove turned away. He looked at Halvery. "Well, I *thought* I preferred the two of you getting along. Should I be concerned that Roup now has you keeping secrets and running his errands, Halvery?"

Halvery sputtered.

Roup answered for him, "No, Halvery was doing his best to save me from myself. He showed up and shouted at everyone. Then he pinned Costa just before she managed to follow the curbs. You really should be thanking him."

"And why was Moashi here?" continued Arcove relentlessly.

Roup hesitated.

"Roup, don't make that cub choose between you and me."

"He didn't do anything you told him not to."

"Do I need to get very specific with him in the future? Does he need a lecture on what I consider treason?"

Roup turned his head to the side. "If you need to box some-one's ears, Arcove, box mine."

Arcove shut his eyes as though to collect himself. When he opened them, he said, "Don't work at cross-purposes with me, Roup."

"I'm not," said Roup immediately. "I promise you. I am not."

Halvery was afraid to speak or move. He'd never seen them talk like this, like peers, with Arcove willing to let Roup keep a secret and take "no" for an answer. He'd always suspected they treated each other differently in private; he'd just never seen it. *And here you are letting me see, and, ghosts, I am out of my depth.*

Arcove and Roup looked at each other for a long moment. Then Arcove got up and shook himself. When he spoke, his tone was lighter, "Since you are both here, I'll ask you to accompany me on my errand this evening. Ghosts know I could use some perspective."

"To see Keesha?" asked Roup. "What is this mysterious loca-tion you were teasing Costa about?"

"The Great Cave," said Arcove.

"Ah…"

"He wants a place for telshees there during the Volontaro, as they used to have before the war."

Halvery frowned. He'd experienced several Volontaros with telshees in the Great Cave before their involvement in the ferryshaft wars prompted Arcove to make them unwelcome. They'd mostly remained out of sight, although the threat of their presence had hung like a shadow over that refuge. Even now, the section of the cave that had once sheltered telshees felt haunted.

"I suppose he wants to reestablish the old boundary line that put most of the stream on the ferryshaft side as well?" asked Halv-ery with distaste.

"I don't know," said Arcove. "We're going up there to talk about it."

"This is what you traded in order to speak to the ely-ary?" guessed Roup.

"Correct."

"Do we get ongoing information from those birds?" asked Halvery. "Because this sounds like an ongoing obligation..."

"He hasn't put any limitations on what he will translate for us," said Arcove. "But beyond that—"

"Beyond that, you would have given him a place in the Great Cave anyway," said Roup. "Keesha is only calling it a trade for the look of the thing."

Arcove said nothing.

Roup's voice held a smile. "He loves it when you ask him for things, Arcove. If you asked him to sing to you every day, he'd be delighted."

"He'd be delighted by Leeshwood in his debt," said Halvery sourly.

"No," said Roup. "I mean, yes, he would. But mostly he just loves to hear Arcove ask."

"I am his favorite chew toy," muttered Arcove. "Are you coming or not?"

* * * *

This chapter includes an author's note at the end of the book.

9

Civilized

The negotiation in the Great Cave kept Arcove and his officers busy until dawn. Halvery felt they could have gotten it done faster without Costa running around asking endless questions. Keesha clearly liked her and would stop to explain obscure writing at tedious length. *But that's why Arcove let her come,* thought

Halvery. *Bring one of Coden's foals, get better terms from Coden's old friend.*

Although, maybe Roup was right, and Keesha really did have a soft spot for Arcove. While he frequently spoke with a sort of cheerful malevolence, Halvery noticed that Keesha did not attempt to put the creasia at a disadvantage in terms of the boundary line. He suggested a new line that split resources in the cave more or less evenly.

I do believe Roup is right and you have made, not just an ally, but an actual friend there, Arcove. Did he even ask for anything after saving Roup's life? If so, Halvery hadn't heard about it. *But maybe Keesha would have considered that a favor to Coden.*

Arcove, for his part, was not being sly or aggressive in his dealings with Keesha, either. Their negotiation of the boundary line was so straightforward that Halvery was inspired to compare it unflatteringly with his last den dispute. "How is it that an interspecies boundary with untold years of conflict behind it can be resolved faster than a territory line between two clutters who share blood?"

Arcove chuffed. "Are they still bringing witnesses?"

"Yes! Both dens. Stefan and I have been back twice. The point of contention is an unbelievably average tract of thickets."

"Your quarreling dens are bringing witnesses to their disputes?" asked Keesha with interest.

"Yes," said Halvery. "If they had any sense, the alphas would have fought, and it would all have been decided in a matter of moments. All of this talking is absurd. It wouldn't have happened two decades ago. I don't understand it."

Keesha looked pleased, which Halvery found irritating. "Oh, this is progress. You are developing lawyers."

"We're what?" asked Halvery suspiciously.

"All sufficiently advanced societies develop lawyers," said Keesha. "It is a sign of civilization."

"I have no idea what you just said."

Roup spoke up, "What are lawyers?"

Keesha thought for a moment. "People whose job it is to argue for you, instead of fight."

"How appalling," said Halvery. "I hope I die before we get *that* civilized."

They arrived back at Arcove's den just as the sun was beginning to make the mist glow. Halvery was invited to remain for the day, which he gratefully accepted. He fell asleep in a corner, lulled by the sound of Shazel's litter of cubs purring as they nursed, while their mother murmured and gossiped with her den-mates over their heads.

Halvery was jostled awake in the late afternoon as someone lay down against him. He'd been deeply asleep and didn't open his eyes. He thought for a confused moment it was Velta. Then he caught Roup's scent and remembered where he was. He had a groggy sense of surprise, but didn't question the clear invitation to cuddle. Halvery was lying on his stomach, while Roup was lying on his side, their faces very close in the cool shadows of the cave. Halvery put his head and one paw across Roup's neck and was almost asleep again when Roup murmured, "I know I'm being dreadfully ungrateful."

Halvery grunted. "Roup, I'm barely awake."

"Does it have to be Ilsa?"

Halvery opened his eyes a sliver. It really was broad daylight outside. *Ghosts, Roup.* "No," he said aloud. He stretched, careful to avoid kicking any of the cats sleeping around them. "It...it doesn't have to be anyone." He tucked his face against Roup's shoulder. *Can we talk about this when I'm not half asleep?*

"Who else?" asked Roup.

"Shazel. Or anyone in my den or Arcove's, but if you hate the idea..."

"You ran this by Arcove?"

"Of course I did."

Silence.

"Everyone told me you wouldn't thank me," muttered Halvery. "I should have listened."

Roup gave a silent laugh. "Everyone?"

"Arcove, Lyndi, Caraca, Nadine… No, actually, Nadine didn't say that. She talked about how unique you are and how much she wishes you'd put more of your blood into Leeshwood."

Roup snorted. "Yes, I'm very unique."

Halvery woke up enough to give him a lick. "Is it the mounting you don't like?"

Roup hesitated. "It always feels like my body is doing things without my permission."

Now Halvery was laughing.

Roup squirmed. Halvery pinned his head down and started grooming his cheeks. "Does that mean you don't enjoy it?"

"I enjoy some of it."

"But you don't like Ilsa?"

"I feel that I would be a massive hypocrite if I got on top of Ilsa!"

Halvery laughed harder. "That's what this is about? Your pride won't let you?"

"Oh, I'm not that proud."

"Oh, yes, you are."

Roup spoke in such a soft voice that Halvery barely heard him. "I think you'll be disappointed."

"What?"

"They *won't* look like me."

"Roup!" Halvery nuzzled his head up, blinking at him in the low light. "I will *not* be disappointed. Ghosts and little fishes. Color isn't everything. As shallow as I am, I do know that."

Roup gave an uneasy laugh. "I might not even have any cubs in the litter. I'm certain I can't keep up with you—"

He broke off as Halvery started washing his face.

"I think you'll be disappointed," repeated Roup.

"I think you're worried that *you'll* be," murmured Halvery. "But regardless, it sounds like mating with Ilsa would make you feel bad, and that's not what I'm after. Share a mate with Arcove if you like. I'll be just as happy that I set it in motion."

Roup looked at him searchingly.

I really did surprise you with all this.

"Can I think about it for a while?"

Halvery yawned. "Think about it for as long as you like. A year or two if you choose Shazel. Ilsa will be in season any day now, but it sounds like she's a definite no, so take your time." He hesitated. "Who would you choose in my den?"

Roup thought for a moment. He smirked. "Velta."

Halvery laughed and nearly woke a nearby sleeper. When the cats around them had settled back down, he said, "Velta hasn't had a litter in twenty years, but she loves you. I'm sure she'd lie down for you if you caught her in the right mood."

Roup snorted. "I'm sure she wouldn't. She loves *you.*"

"Oh, she knows I wouldn't mind."

Roup looked at him in disbelief. "You are treating me as though we're sharing a den, even though we're not. What you're doing... Ghosts, Halvery, nobody does that. Are you sure you're not ill?"

Halvery gave him a lick on the top of the head.

Roup settled back down. "I'll think about it," he murmured. "Thank you."

Halvery wanted to put his head back down across Roup's shoulders and drift off, but... *You're feeling a little guilty, a little generous. Maybe if I was a better person I wouldn't take advantage of that, but...*

"Roup, what did you ask the curbs to do?"

A moment's silence. When Roup spoke, he sounded more like himself—a mild and calculated neutrality, with no hint of emotion. "Exactly what I said. I asked them to keep an eye out for Dazzle."

"I heard you talking to them. You asked them to do more than that."

Roup rolled away from him and stood up. Halvery raised his eyes pleadingly. *You almost died. I can still see you lying there. The blood looked so bright on your fur. Please don't be angry with me for trying to stop that from happening again.*

Roup's face was closed and neutral. For a moment, Halvery thought he would stalk off without another word. Then he bent and gave Halvery a long, slow lick from his nose to the crown of his head. It was an oddly possessive gesture, and it certainly implied no anger. Roup didn't say anything else, though. He just turned and padded quietly away.

10

Creative

By the time Halvery woke again, Roup and Arcove had gone out to hunt. He didn't have anything else he needed to say to them, so he left for his own den in the early evening, pausing briefly to catch a fish from Smoky Branch. The air definitely had the nip of fall now, the breeze cutting lines through his thickening coat.

Halvery told himself he'd achieved a partial victory. *Not Ilsa, but he sounded like he might come around to someone else. At least he's not angry with me about it. I don't think he is, anyway.*

The many events and revelations of last night jostled for the focus of his thoughts:

The troubling situation with Sedaron's herd on the southern plains.

Costa's wiry little body between his front paws. *"I bet Storm wasn't any bigger than I am when he was running from you."*

The expression on Moashi's face as Halvery had snarled at him.

Cohal: *"This is his version of self-control?"*

Roup: *"Am I breaking your heart?"*

Arcove, with all the affection he never showed in council: "*Always.*"

Halvery ran faster until he couldn't think about anything except not missing a step on the riverbank—on and on, until he reached his den only a little after midnight.

It was record speed and completely unnecessary. Halvery paused to collect himself before entering the area where he was likely to encounter mates and cubs. He was more winded than he should have been and embarrassed for having pushed himself hard for no reason. *One would think I had something to be upset about. I don't.*

He encountered Petra and one of her four-year-old daughters on the banks of the estuary. They called a greeting to him, and Petra said, "I believe you have a visitor at the den, Halvery."

Halvery stared at her blankly. "Who?"

"Moashi."

There was a moment when he could not quite process what she'd said. Then, "You have got to be joking!"

"Not unless there's another cloud-gray, fluffy-coated, pink-nosed, big-eared..."

"Alright, alright," grumbled Halvery. "Thank you for warning me."

He felt more than ready to run again now and flashed along the beach in the moonlight. He stormed into his den, shouting, "Ears!"

Moashi's pale face appeared like a ghost in the mouth of one of the caves. Velta came up hurriedly. "Halvery, I'm glad to see you're back. I thought—"

"Things happened last night, Velta. I will handle this." He stalked towards Moashi, his voice rising. "Ears, you've got some nerve. Some considerable nerve showing your face here! I hope that fight with Vashon gave you a few new tricks, because you are about to need them."

He reached the mouth of the cave. Moashi stood in the entrance, crouching and bristling, but not backing away. He shut his eyes, turned his head, and tucked his tail.

Halvery snarled down at him. "You *knew* you were doing something wrong! You looked as guilty as a cub caught poaching at the council meeting, and it's easy to see why. You're the one who told Roup about Dazzle's cave last time. Do you never learn from your mistakes?" He caught his breath and added, "Arcove used your name and the word 'treason' in the same sentence. If you think *I'm* unpleasant when I'm angry, wait until you get a visit from *him*."

Moashi flinched as though Halvery had struck him.

"Why are you here?!" thundered Halvery.

Moashi looked up, his blue eyes almost completely black, his hackles as high as his ears. He was breathing like a rabbit. Still, he said nothing.

"Answer me!"

Velta spoke at Halvery's shoulder. "Halvery..."

Halvery gave a low, warning growl. *This is not your business, Velta.*

"He said he came here so that you could shout at him," she said patiently. "I think that's been accomplished. Perhaps you could move on to something else."

There was a long silence, punctuated only by his own quick breaths and Moashi's. Then Halvery grated, "Beach. Now."

He turned without waiting for Moashi. Velta walked beside him for a short distance, looking worried. "Please don't kill him—"

"I don't kill cubs," snapped Halvery.

He walked out to a spot just short of the lapping shoreline and took a deep, steadying breath. The cold breeze off the lake ruffled his fur. The moon created a silver track across the water. He focused on that.

Halvery refused to turn as Moashi's hesitant footfalls came nearer. The smaller cat sat down several lengths away.

"Well?" demanded Halvery.

Moashi swallowed. His voice came out in a near-whisper, "I thought…if you had a chance to shout at me as much as you liked…maybe you'd forgive me."

"Well, it doesn't work like that!" shot Halvery. "You made a mistake, and now I've lost faith in your judgment!"

Moashi gave a low, guttural whine of distress. "Then tell me what to do! I don't know how to say 'no' to him, Halvery! Roup is my superior officer and my mentor and my friend! He's the very best of us. I truly believe that. I know you're angry with me because you love him and you're afraid he'll get hurt again. But I don't know how to say 'no' to him. How do *you* do it?"

Halvery started to respond and then stopped. He'd told Roup 'no' when Roup asked for that bend in Crooked Tail…and when he asked Halvery to train Moashi…and on numerous other occasions, and yet somehow…

Moashi looked up at him, eyes desperate. "I *did* tell him that I wasn't sure Arcove would like what we were doing, and that *you* certainly wouldn't. I told him that I didn't want to contribute to putting him in danger again, but he just kept saying, 'Don't worry about it. I'll deal with it. Trust me.'"

Halvery sighed. He could feel his anger draining away. *Do I really expect Moashi to outmaneuver Roup when I can't? When even Arcove can't?*

Nevertheless, he couldn't quite bring himself to offer forgiveness so soon, so he growled, "Tell me *exactly* what happened."

Moashi shut his eyes and looked away. For a moment, Halvery thought his loyalty to Roup would not allow him answer. Then he said, very softly, "He wanted me to make friends with the curbs. And I was planning to do that anyway. I think it's good to learn about other species and have alliances with them. So I did my best to make friends, even though I guess I'm not supposed to roll over onto my back in council meetings—"

Halvery made a face. "Do you have any natural instincts, Ears? Any common sense at all?"

Moashi ignored this. "They told me they were staying out of sight in the Garu Vell until the expedition. Storm said that I wasn't to tell Roup where they were. Which I didn't. But Roup never asked. He's too clever to ask, when he knows the answer. I guess he knew I was still talking to them, although he never asked about that, either. Then, two days ago, Roup woke me up ahead of Arcove's messenger to say that the expedition to the Southern Mountains was leaving after the council meeting, and might I know where he could cross paths with the highland curbs on their way out."

"Why did you tell him?" demanded Halvery.

Moashi squirmed. "Storm only told me that Roup wasn't supposed to know where they were *staying*. Arcove never spoke to me about it directly—"

"Some advice, Moashi: do not get sly with Arcove. He has no patience with cats who obey his words, but not his meaning. Perhaps Roup gets away with it now and then, but you won't."

Moashi trembled. "Did he really call me a traitor?" He looked like he might be sick.

Halvery sighed. "Not exactly."

Moashi did not look reassured and Halvery grudgingly added, "He was trying to make a point to Roup. He's not going to attack you, although you might get an unpleasant visit. Just say 'yes, sir,' and look terrified; that should come naturally."

Moashi looked like he might wet himself.

Halvery made a face. "Roup is your superior officer. Arcove knows that. Roup should not have put you in that position. He did stand up to Arcove for you. You're not in real trouble...this time." Halvery realized, belatedly, that Moashi's visit might be the best thing that could have happened. "What did he ask the highland curbs to do? I know he asked them to look for Dazzle. What else?"

Moashi looked away and his breathing sped up again. He bristled with distress. Halvery wondered whether Roup had made him promise not to tell. *I am also his superior officer. If it wasn't fair to put him between Arcove and Roup, surely adding me to the mix can only make it worse.*

"Alright, stop thinking about that," said Halvery. He allowed some gentle mockery to creep into his voice. "Is ruling a clutter and sitting on the council turning out to be harder than you expected?"

"Oh, ghosts, Halvery." Moashi interpreted Halvery's softening tone with entirely too much precision. He sidled gratefully over to sit right beside Halvery, ears and tail still low. Halvery thought for one appalled moment that Moashi was about to tuck his face against Halvery's shoulder. Then he spoke in a low rush, "Maybe you were right, and I'm just a placeholder for someone who can handle all this better. Maybe I'm not old enough. I'll *never* be big enough. Maybe I'm not—"

"Don't you dare!" snapped Halvery.

Moashi stopped in surprise.

"Do *not* make all that time I spent training you into a wasted summer," Halvery continued. "Why is the future so whiny? I was telling Roup: you need a sharper beta. Someone who can fight, who is older than you, who has a more aggressive perspective."

Moashi smiled. "You just want me to stop coming down here and bothering you."

"Yes! That is absolutely what I want. I have mentioned that I don't like you."

"Did you have someone in mind?"

"No. I take it you're not entirely opposed to the idea?"

Moashi flicked his ears. "My beta, Tetry, is a good friend. He can fight, but he's not…what you're describing."

"No, he clearly isn't. Otherwise, you wouldn't have been down here tearing your fur out over Vashon."

Moashi cut his eyes up at Halvery. "No one is going to give me advice the way you do, sir."

"By insulting you every other sentence? I should hope not. Did you manage to figure out which end of your new mate to stick it in?"

Moashi blinked at the change of topic and then burst out laughing. "I…um…yes."

"Go alright?"

Moashi's ears flattened in embarrassment. "She's not looking for a new den, so…"

"Well, that's a ringing endorsement."

Moashi dared to give him an aggrieved look. "She seems pleased and keeps speculating about whether the cubs will have my eyes. But it's…so different with a female in season! A lot…*more*. And I do see what you mean. Pulling out hurts her. Sometimes a little, sometimes a lot. I can see how…um…staying in longer would be better for her, but…ghosts, it's difficult. I don't know how you manage to do what Ilsa was describing."

Halvery smirked. "Decades of practice. Anyway, more licking, less mounting."

"Yes, the licking definitely helped."

Halvery watched him. *I am just handing out advice as though it costs nothing, aren't I?* "Would you lick her with the back of your tongue?"

Moashi gave him an odd look. "Of course not. I wouldn't lick *myself* down there with the back of my tongue."

"Exactly. Well, your prick is like a smaller version of your tongue."

Moashi looked at Halvery as though he'd begun speaking Ely-ary.

"It's smooth in the front and rough in the back," continued Halvery patiently. "The back of your prick is exactly like the back of your tongue. Now consider where your sheath ends up when you're mating. Consider what it covers and when. Think about that for a while."

A long silence. Then Moashi turned to stare at Halvery. "Until last summer, I thought you were the most traditional alpha in Leeshwood. Conservative, inflexible, hostile to new ideas—"

"I believe I am. Your point?"

"But you're not…" whispered Moashi. "I mean, in some ways, yes, but I think…I think everyone is creative somewhere. Everyone tries, in some way, to rise above their limitations and instincts…to do something better or different from the past—"

Halvery yawned. "You're rambling, Ears."

"I am trying to give you a compliment!"

"The future is terrible at compliments."

"What I mean is...*this* is how you're creative! Mating! You are stunningly untraditional in this one way. You've thought and thought and thought about how you can make things better for your mates, and then...ghosts...*retrained* your body. It's impressive and compassionate and..."

Halvery was actually starting to feel embarrassed. "Alright, alright, that's laying it on a little thick, Ears."

"Anyway, I don't think anyone could give me the kind of advice you do, and it would kill me if I thought you truly hated me."

Halvery groaned. "Ears..."

"Yes, yes, I know you don't like me. I'm going home now."

"You *can't* care whether I hate you," said Halvery wearily. "You'll never survive as a den alpha, let alone a council member, if you care about things like that!"

"But I do care!" said Moashi earnestly. "I can't pretend I don't, Halvery; it's not in my nature. Anyway, *caring* isn't what's been getting me into trouble lately. It's not knowing how to handle Roup."

Halvery sighed. "Roup gets us all into trouble. Fortunately, he also gets us out."

Moashi hesitated for a long moment and then blurted, "He told them to write something."

Halvery went still. "Write something...?"

"Yes. He...he told the curbs to write something somewhere that Thistle's cats would find it."

Halvery shut his eyes. "Of course..." *He and Dazzle were writing messages back and forth in the cave. Arcove told the expedition not to speak to Thistle's cats unless they were approached. But he didn't say anything about writing.* "What was the message?"

Moashi shook his elegant ears. "By itself, it doesn't make sense."

"What?" repeated Halvery.

"He told them to write: 'I still mean what I said.'"

11

Scheming

Roup sat on the clifftop alone, watching the sunset. *We're going into another winter…with Sedaron's herd even more aggressive and no resolution in the Southern Mountains.* There'd been talk last winter of ferryshaft raiding in Leeshwood during that season when telshees were in torpor. *All of Keesha's goodwill can't save us then.*

Ferryshaft would target young cubs if they raided, but Roup was worried about something else, too. *Sedaron made a comment when he cornered us by the lake. He said, "We'll kill your deer until you starve fighting each other."* It had been one of many threats and insults delivered in quick succession. The threat might have been impulsive, immediately forgotten. Roup hoped so, but he doubted it.

Our overpopulation problems during Treace's rebellion probably got Sedaron thinking. Leeshwood never had problems with overpopulation before Arcove gave us a decade of peace. But without breeding restrictions, success has its own penalty. Surely it has occurred to Sedaron that he could produce the same effect by simply killing does. In the winter, he could get two for one…because the does are pregnant.

Roup scowled. *Cubs and pregnant does. That's who and what he'll target. Sedaron's ferryshaft have had a couple of years to practice on creasia in the Southern Mountains. Annihilating those cats will give them the last bit of practice and confidence they need before coming after us.*

"They won't attack you this winter," Sauny had said when she visited last month. "They're too focused on Thistle's cats and on eliminating dissent from other ferryshaft. Next winter, maybe."

Fleeing ferryshaft had begun to trickle into Leeshwood. They were given the option of sanctuary in Roup's territory, but only a few of them accepted. The rest chose to pass on to the northern plains—the area where Arcove had confined them after the war, an area most ferryshaft had avoided since then. In a stroke of irony, they fled there now, putting Leeshwood between themselves and Sedaron's herd.

Roup watched the track of the sunset—bright colors that mirrored the leaves. Up here, the winds blew colder, and the leaves had started to change in earnest. They spiraled down around him—a rain of red and gold. He didn't bother to shake them off his back.

Hollygold's expedition should return any day now. Arcove will want to share their news at the fall conference. Ghosts, I wish I knew what they were going to say. The uncertainty roiled inside him. *I should be out there, using my words and the thread of trust I built. Instead I'm here, where I can do nothing.*

He was startled when someone lay down beside him. Roup hadn't heard the approach. He turned, expecting Arcove or Lyndi. Instead, he saw Ilsa, her expressive brown eyes mischievous, her honey-brindled coat looking dense and soft with winter velvet. "Hello, Roup."

Roup gave an exasperated sigh. "Did Halvery send you all the way up here? Ghosts and little fishes, I thought he understood—"

"Halvery did not send me," said Ilsa primly. "I came myself—"

Roup screwed his eyes shut. "To talk me into something. Ilsa, you are very pretty and you fight very well for someone of your size, and I mean no insult to you when I say—"

"I came to talk to Wisteria," interrupted Ilsa with a trace of affronted dignity. "She's thinking about challenging Carmine, so that she can be den alpha and sit on the council instead."

Roup gaped at her. "I'm sorry, what did you say?"

Ilsa gave him a smug look. "No, please reject me again first, and then I'll tell you my news."

"I humbly apologize for my assumptions. Did you say that Wisteria is considering attacking her mate?"

Ilsa rolled her eyes. "Not *attacking* him. Formally challenging him before witnesses, so that she can sit on the council instead."

Roup was not easily startled by social innovations, but he found himself at a loss this time. "She can't... Most cats will not consider such a challenge legitimate! It won't even make sense to them! Besides, won't that destroy her den? She and Carmine are close. Won't her attack hurt him terribly? Is Teek supposed to take sides?"

"She's worried about those things, yes."

"I'm not sure she'll win," said Roup with growing alarm. Wisteria was Arcove's blood, as well as Roup's. She was bigger than most females, but still smaller than Carmine, who was nearly the size of his father. "It would be an ugly fight. I think they'd both be injured. They might even both die!" Roup got to his feet. "I have to go talk to her. Does Teek know?"

"Sit down, O my clever leader. There is no need to talk her out of it; I already have."

Roup sat back down, staring at Ilsa.

"The thing is," continued Ilsa, "females and males have different perspectives about what is best for Leeshwood. Broadly, we want the same things, but our priorities are different. Arcove's council is a male thing. I told Wisteria that we need our own council. A den council. Right now, there is no organized voice for females in Leeshwood. We don't even have an organized communication system—just rumors that run between dens when we visit each other. Nadine should have had a council of her own. She's more than competent to lead it. Or she was, in her prime."

Ilsa stopped as though to see whether Roup was going to argue. Instead, he sank slowly back down on his stomach. "Keep talking."

Ilsa grew more animated. "If a female council had existed during Treace's rebellion, he never would have gotten so powerful! Because how did he build his army? By abusing the females in his dens, destroying bitterleaf, keeping them pregnant all the time, hiding the cubs, overpopulating. If representatives from those dens had been coming to council meetings, speaking to other den mothers about their concerns, this would never have happened. Or it would have been caught much earlier."

"You make a good point," said Roup. He thought for a moment. "But do you really think we need a separate den council? I've always advocated for females on Arcove's council. Lyndi is already on the council. I was hoping she would set a precedent and others would follow."

Ilsa gave him a longsuffering smile. "Lyndi functions as a male, Roup. I love her, but she is not part of den life. She has never been able to have cubs, so she doesn't know what that's like. She's been your beta for decades, which is a role that most females know nothing about. She leads clutters composed mostly of males, rules your territory whenever you don't feel like doing it, and may one day rule Leeshwood. But Lyndi thinks like a male because that is the world she knows."

Roup considered this.

"I mean no insult to Lyndi," added Ilsa quickly.

"I know that."

A moment of silence. Then Ilsa continued, "Wisteria still isn't sure about the den council. Her instinct is to…blur the roles of males and females. So that females can do male things and males can do female things. I see the value in that. But I think females could have more power in our *own* role and in our own way."

"Would you send a representative from this den council to the…the king's council?" asked Roup.

"That was what I had in mind, yes. Do you think Arcove would listen to us?"

"I think so. Let me talk to him. Although I'm not sure you need me to soften the ground. You make compelling arguments."

Ilsa did not manage to hide her pleasure at this flattery. Her ears came forward and she blinked happily.

"How long have you been thinking about this?" asked Roup.

"Oh…for a year or so. I always knew I wanted to be one of the people who…who makes things happen, who…turns history, maybe." She shot a worried glance at Roup. "Is that terribly vain?"

Roup laughed. He rearranged his paws. "I could not stomach my own hypocrisy if I said so."

Ilsa cackled and leaned against him. "You've got the whole web in your head, don't you? You always know what's really going on and why."

"No," said Roup with a sigh. "I wish that were true, but it's not." *I don't know what that expedition has done or discovered, for instance, and not knowing is killing me.*

"When I was six, I thought the only chance of getting near real power was to have a high-ranking mate, and cubs with amazing blood," continued Ilsa. "And I still think I was right about that. Only I didn't expect Halvery to be such a sweetheart. He let me learn to fight, and then I got to meet Lyndi and Moashi. And Moashi is a little like me. I got Wisteria's attention, coming up here to the cliffs. And I even met Storm and Sauny." She hesitated a long beat. "And you."

Roup smiled. "You're getting quite the collection of officers in your social circle."

"I know!" Ilsa giggled. "Wisteria says I'm trying to get under as many of them as possible."

Roup barked a laugh.

"To which I say," continued Ilsa, "that I will have the most amazing cubs in Leeshwood."

"Are you still planning to go to Moashi's den after your first litter?" asked Roup.

"I think so. Although I'll miss Halvery. I'm learning a lot from the females in his den, particularly Velta. Things I'll need to know if I'm going to be an alpha den mother one day. If I stayed in Halvery's den, I wouldn't be an alpha for a long time, but I think in Moashi's den I can get to the top quickly, without making too many enemies."

Roup shook his ears. "You know that Moashi has already taken a breeding female into his den, right? He'll likely take others in the next two or three years. Are you sure you want to wait to begin establishing yourself there?"

Ilsa gave him a sidelong look. "Well, yes. I don't want to be his *first* breeding mate. Ghosts. It'll take him a while to figure out what he's doing, won't it? I got him to ask Halvery some questions."

Roup laughed and couldn't stop for a moment. "You got Moashi...to ask Halvery...how to mate?"

"Well, yes."

Roup tried to picture this and failed. "You are a rascal."

"Wisteria says I'm a scheming politician." Ilsa caught her breath, as though gathering her courage, and added, "She also said to tell you that the cubs would be clever, not just pretty."

Roup looked at her. He wanted to be irritated, but he couldn't. She'd set him up so neatly.

Before he could respond, she continued, "When Arcove was my age, he'd been ruling Leeshwood for a year."

It was a parallel that Roup would never have thought to draw, but she was right. *He was your age when we went to the Southern Mountains.* "I apologize for calling you a cub," he said quietly. "You are clearly a very wily adult."

"So make babies with me," she whispered and rubbed her cheek against his chin. "What are you worried about? That they won't be golden? I don't care. That you like lying down? I know that. Halvery will make up for anything you don't want to do; you know he will."

Roup laughed. *I believe I have been outmaneuvered.*

"Is it that you don't want to share Halvery with anyone else?" asked Ilsa playfully.

That made him laugh harder.

"I'll share so nicely, Roup." She leaned close to his ear and murmured, "I promise to be a useful person to know. You won't regret sharing a blood-tie with me."

"I have no doubt."

Ilsa sighed. "But?"

"Alright."

She stared at him for a moment, as though she hadn't fully anticipated her own victory. Then she jumped up and leapt back and forth across him before tearing around him in circles through the leaves. "Alright," repeated Roup, laughing. He got up and shook himself, "And your season is starting, so you really shouldn't be out here so far from your den."

"I know. I thought the scent might make you interested, but you act like you can't smell it."

"I can ignore it," said Roup quietly. "This…really might not be what you expect."

"I have no expectations, except cubs with the best blood in Leeshwood." The twilight was deepening into full night and Ilsa was giddy with her victory and with the beginnings of her first heat without bitterleaf. She wanted to run. She wanted to be chased.

So Roup chased her…all the way down the cliffs, and then winding through the forest, stopping once to hunt and to talk breathlessly about politics and the Southern Mountains and Sedaron's herd and the upcoming fall conference.

"I'm afraid that cubs born next spring will be directly in harm's way," Roup admitted.

"Cubs are always in harm's way," said Ilsa. "The future is always uncertain. Surely that's no reason not to plan it."

They reached the lake at last and surprised Halvery in his den, where he was supervising sparring matches between his three and four-year-olds. He stared at Roup and Ilsa as they came loping into the clearing in front of the caves. Even after they stopped in front of him, Ilsa smirking, he just looked confused. "Did I miss a messenger, Roup? I didn't know you were—"

Ilsa interrupted him, her voice a sweet singsong that reminded Roup of the way Halvery talked when he was teasing, "'Thank you, Ilsa, for getting me exactly what I wanted. Now I owe you a favor to be collected at some point in the future.'"

Roup snorted a laugh. "I see she's learned to speak your language."

"That is not my language," said Halvery, although an amazed grin was spreading across his face.

He turned to Roup, who refused to meet his eyes. The juvenile cubs were watching with interest. After a moment, Halvery returned his attention to his offspring and said, "Alright, you lot, you are exceedingly fortunate this evening in that two officers are going to watch you spar. Roup spars with Arcove; he knows how it's done. You can proceed as though it's a tournament, youngest to oldest, winner fights next in line. Go on; we'll give you a few pointers."

The cubs began enthusiastically throwing themselves at each other. Roup felt far too distracted to give pointers, but presently he saw a clear example of a missed opportunity and said so. Halvery delivered his usual brand of advice. "Was that a grapple or a premature attempt at surrender, Tashiki? I couldn't tell," and, "Recall that in a real fight, your brother wouldn't care if he blinded you, Raz," and, "Is your left hind limb under your conscious control, Vesenya, or does it just move on its own?"

Halvery's cubs knew him too well to be intimidated by any of this. They shouted their own insults, advice, and encouragement at each other. The tournament moved quickly through its predetermined pairings to a winner, after which point it dissolved into a melee of wrestling, pouncing, and chasing.

Ilsa had disappeared into the caves. Roup caught a glimpse of her talking to Velta. He glanced sidelong at Halvery, caught him doing the same, and looked away. "I don't believe I've ever seen you gloat so quietly," muttered Roup.

"I'm not gloating," said Halvery, but Roup could hear the grin in his voice. "Dare I ask what she said to change your mind?"

Roup thought about it. "She convinced me that…" he laughed. "That we might, in fact, have amazing cubs. Although I still don't think they'll look like me. And I still think I'm likely to disap—"

"Don't you dare say anyone is going to be disappointed!" flashed Halvery. He proceeded to rub his face all over Roup's in a cub-like display of affection that made Roup laugh and finally back away.

"We've got about a day before she's ready," said Roup. "Do you want me to do anything while I'm here? Take a look at that territory border that keeps causing problems, perhaps?"

Halvery rolled his eyes. "I would not dream of wasting your time on that. You just ran all the way from the cliffs; you must be hungry. Ilsa, too. There's a buck we killed in the woods. It's a nice walk along the river. Come eat and tell me the gossip from northern Leeshwood. I'll tell you about Caraca's very convoluted search for Ilsa's father. Also, I now know a staggering amount of useless information about oories."

12

You Win

Five days later, Arcove sat in a bend of Smoky Branch and considered what he'd recently learned and how he should frame it at the fall conference. The moon had set. It was well past midnight, but still some while before dawn, a time when even creasia often napped and the whole world slept.

Arcove heard a splash and looked up. Something was swimming towards him from downstream. A moment later, a ghost-pale shape materialized out of the mist. He was half-swimming, half-walking against the current. Arcove called softly, "Roup?"

His head swiveled and he struck out in Arcove's direction, until at last he came dripping up the bank. Roup shook himself, and then came forward with an uneven gait that caused Arcove to get to his feet in alarm. "Are you injured?"

"No," said Roup with something between a smile and a grimace. "No, I am just completely exhausted." He flopped down, and Arcove started to laugh.

"It occurs to me," said Roup with a yawn, "that we have created a world in which we are free to do truly silly things. If we were fighting a war, there'd be no time to figure out how to produce some utterly useless feature like golden fur and then scour the wood for the most likely candidates. If we were fighting for our lives with threats on every side, no alpha male would lower his guard enough to behave as though he's sharing a den with someone who is not, in fact, sharing it."

Arcove stretched out beside Roup on the bank. "Are you sorry we created this world?"

"No, of course not."

"Are you sorry you agreed to share a mate with Halvery?"

"No, but…ghosts of our fathers! I don't remember it being this much work last time I made a litter of cubs! How does he satisfy her all by himself? I felt like we could barely keep up with her together. And he's got *seven* breeding females in that den? Why would anyone do that to themselves? How does he have any energy left over to rule a clutter or attend council meetings or argue with *me?*"

Arcove tucked his head against Roup's side and shook with laughter. When he got himself under control, he said, "Most of his mates are well over ten, so less…energetic. And they only come into season for a few days at a time…"

"Four days! It was four days of constant mating!"

"Most males do not consider this a hardship," said Arcove with excessive tact.

"Yes, I know I am dreadfully odd and ungrateful. You should have told Halvery, 'This is why *I* don't want to share a mate with him: because I'll have to listen to him whine about it later.'"

"I would share a mate with you if I thought you wanted to."

"Well, at this point, I'm sure I will never mate again. I've used up every bit of interest in that activity for the rest of my life."

Arcove nibbled into his cheeks and along the line of his jaw. "I'm certain you will feel differently in a few days. A month at most."

"I'm certain I will not."

"Have you ever been with an eight-year-old?"

"Yes, you."

Arcove rolled his eyes. "An eight-year old female in season."

Roup thought about it. "No. Caraca was ten. And so was I."

"Well…"

"Four days!" exclaimed Roup. "And there was some hunting and some swimming and some talking in there, but mostly mating. I'm not saying it wasn't fun at first. But then you think, 'That's enough. Time for something else,' except your body won't let you stop. That smell gets into your nose. It feels like it worms its way inside your skull. It won't let you sleep and you barely eat and you can't think clearly. Or I can't. Maybe only I can't." He shook his ears. "I feel like I still smell like Ilsa and Halvery even though I've been swimming in the river. Do I?"

"A little."

Roup flopped his head over onto Arcove's paws. "Groom me? Until I only smell like you?"

Arcove smiled. He worked his way over Roup's head and shoulders, using the back of his tongue to comb the fur into place. After a moment, he stopped to murmur, "This world we've created seems fragile. Cubs born this spring…"

"Will be the youngest creasia in the wood next winter," finished Roup. "The thought had crossed my mind." He opened one eye and tilted his head to look up at Arcove. "Did the expedition from the Southern Mountains return?"

"Did you somehow read that in the angle of my whiskers?"

"No, but why else would you be out here at this hour staring into the river? Is Dazzle still alive?"

Arcove hesitated. *Let's not do this right now, Roup.*

Whatever Roup saw on his face made him lower his head. "Never mind. It's not worth it. I'll just be your den-mate. Give Wisteria my council seat and Carmine my clutter. No more politics. I'll keep your mates company and raise your cubs and help raise that litter of Ilsa's, although it's probably all Halvery's, but that's fine. I won't try to shape history, or keep secrets, or poke my head out of Leeshwood ever again."

Arcove felt as though something sharp had lodged in his chest. He buried his face in Roup's fur that smelled of *safe* and *comfort* and *trust*. "You are breaking my heart."

"I don't want to," whispered Roup. "I hate feeling as though you don't trust me."

"I just want to keep you safe."

"My sentiment exactly."

"Have we both lost our nerve?"

"Maybe a little."

"Dazzle is alive." Arcove felt Roup go still, felt his heartbeat quicken through his wet fur. "The curbs got close enough to identify him," continued Arcove. "As you probably predicted, Hollygold's cats did not. However, they noticed an interesting development. Thistle's cats have found routes into the high valley through the slot canyons. They seem to be retreating there, harried by lowland curbs. The curbs are making it difficult to hunt in the lower valley, but the higher valley has plenty of game. Also, better caves with more defensible openings."

"Of course it does," murmured Roup. "It was the birthing sanctuary of the highland curbs. Did Cohal and Maoli get up there?"

"They did," said Arcove. "They and Storm got into the valley and out again, though with some difficulty. Thistle's cats are trying to control the narrow entrances through the canyons. We think they're trying to cleanse the high valley of curbs and then keep them out in preparation for birthing their cubs in those caves in spring."

"Well, this is all sounding familiar," said Roup. "They want the valley for the same reasons the highland curbs wanted it. Does their situation seem likely to end the same way?"

"If their only enemies were lowland curbs and bears, then no. They would probably form a thriving population and never come down to trouble us again."

"But?" prompted Roup.

"But if Sedaron's ferryshaft make their way into the mountains, they could lay siege to the valley's entrance. If they managed to breach it, the valley could become a death trap."

"Do they seem likely to do that?"

"Not with winter coming on. I guess we'll see what they do this spring. Alternatively, they might give up on Thistle's cats and attack *us*." He looked down at Roup in frustration. "And I promise you, Dazzle is not tearing his fur out trying to figure out how to help us if that happens."

"Well, we do have a few more friends than he does. I'm sure Keesha would let us hide in Syriot." Roup spoke playfully, but Arcove growled.

"I am not hiding in Syriot! Besides, the ferryshaft hid in Syriot, and they lost the war. Telshees make good allies, but they are not the deciding factor in conflicts between land animals. *I* proved that thirty years ago."

"I was joking. I'm sorry to add to your worries, but I'm concerned that Sedaron might try to kill pregnant does this winter or next."

Arcove screwed his eyes shut. "That comment by the lake..."

"So you remember it, too."

"He made his point quite vividly."

"Attacking does would be low risk for Sedaron's ferryshaft. They'd avoid dangerous altercations with us. We can't guard the deer the way we guard our cubs, but we'll certainly be in trouble if enough deer are killed."

Arcove growled. "I need to deal with Sedaron's herd *soon*. I believe we could still win a pitched battle at this point, but..."

"It would cost so many lives," muttered Roup.

"It would, but maybe it would save more in the end. If I wait too long, those ferryshaft will grow so numerous that we can't win a battle at all. Each year, we'll be more severely outnumbered. We can't outbreed them. Even if I encouraged all the females to stop eating bitterleaf, we'd quickly outstrip our food supply. Meanwhile, ferryshaft can eat practically anything."

Roup sat up and started washing Arcove's face. "Thank you for talking to me."

"I always talk to you."

"You haven't lately."

I suppose I haven't. Please don't make me get into that right now. "Anyway, I definitely don't want a situation where ferryshaft are raiding in Leeshwood, killing does every winter and cubs every spring, ambushing us on our way to the Ghost Wood, killing all the ferryshaft who are our allies, chewing us away little by little until we're as rare as highland curbs. I'd rather fight a bloody battle now, while we can still win."

Roup started grooming his ears. "I'd rather not fight a battle at all. Sedaron's ferryshaft have set themselves a tricky task before they come to us. I'd like to see that they fail."

Arcove hesitated. *Don't make me talk about this, Roup. Not when you're happy and relaxed and just come home...*

Roup was watching him, as though he knew that Arcove was trying to decide whether to speak his mind. The other information he'd learned this evening curled inside him like a poisonous snake. *You want trust? Alright, I guess we're doing this.* "I see," growled Arcove at last, "and that's why you asked the curbs to take a message to your *friend?*"

Roup didn't quite flinch, but his ears flattened. "Ah."

"Surely you didn't think I wouldn't make the curbs tell me what you asked them to do? You didn't think Storm would keep that secret? 'I still mean what I said.' You told Dazzle you were a friend, and you said it again right before he tried to kill you."

Roup shut his eyes. "I should have told you."

"Yes, you should have."

"I thought you might call them back."

"Roup—"

"Arcove, I set something in motion at great personal cost. I made a mistake with my timing, but I still believe in what I was trying to do. Furthermore, I didn't tell Dazzle that *you* regard him as a friend. I didn't put words in your mouth or make promises that you are obliged to keep. I sent a message that only Dazzle would understand—a message that could only have come from me. Not from you. Not from Leeshwood. Just me."

Arcove gritted his teeth. He swallowed the first reply that came to mind and said, "Do you remember how many second chances I gave Treace? Because I thought he was a little like me."

Roup's lip curled. "Treace was *nothing* like you."

"You don't see me clearly," growled Arcove. "He was."

"You were never that cruel. You just wanted people to think so."

Arcove started to reply, and then laughed. "I think it would depend on who was telling the story...how cruel they'd say I am or was. Anyway, cruelty is not the similarity to which I'm referring. I made mistakes with Treace because I saw a little of myself in his ambition. He was willing to sacrifice personal happiness and a long life for the power to shape his world in the way that seemed best to him. That's rare."

"Alright," said Roup grudgingly. "I can see that."

"Dazzle," said Arcove quietly, "is a little like *you*."

Roup went still. Arcove let his words sink in for a moment and then continued, "Roup, you are basing assumptions about his character on such limited interactions! You have no idea whether he is actually a good or trustworthy cat, but you *do* know that he thinks a bit like you, that he is cunning and clever in a way that you also are. These are not necessarily the traits of a good cat, but they are *rare* traits that you happen to share. That sense of kinship is making you want to give Dazzle second chances that he hasn't earned."

Roup didn't reply at once. Arcove could tell that his words had penetrated.

"I spared Treace when I shouldn't have," whispered Arcove, "and as a result, I had to bite through the back of Ariand's skull."

"Arcove..."

"Let me finish. A lot of cats died in the rebellion, a lot of cats I regret, but there's nothing like having to kill a friend with your own teeth to help you remember not to make the same mistake twice. Can you imagine having to put down Halvery...or Lyndi... or Moashi because you made a mistake with Dazzle?"

A long beat, and then Roup gave a full-body shudder. He whispered, "You win."

"I know you are trying to be compassionate and see every side—"

"I said you win." Roup's voice had a brittle, defeated quality that made Arcove's heart hurt.

I don't want to win like this. But he was relieved that Roup was finally seeing sense.

"Do you want me to leave the council?" asked Roup in a small voice. "I'll step down; I mean it. I'll confine myself to den politics—"

Arcove gave a low, frustrated growl. "No, of course not. You and Halvery are the most senior and the most effective members of the council. You frequently have opposing views; you balance each other. I don't want you to...to stop..."

Roup looked up. He was squinting a little, as though in pain. Arcove wished he hadn't made his point so graphically. "Then what do you want me to do, Arcove? Not be myself?"

"I want you to *not* keep dangerous secrets from me! I don't want to have to *make* you tell me! I don't want to play games with you!"

"Alright."

"Roup..."

"I said alright."

"Stop rolling over so fast; it's making me nervous."

Roup gave a jittery laugh.

Arcove thought for a moment. In a softer voice, he said, "The next time you put yourself in harm's way, take me with you."

Roup glanced at his face. Next moment, he was pushing his nose under Arcove's chin, burrowing up against his chest so hard that Arcove nearly fell over backwards. Arcove got his balance and pushed back, folding his neck around Roup, licking his ears, his nape, his shoulders.

"Trust me," murmured Arcove, and it came out more like a plea.

Roup raised his head and said, "I trust you. Take me with you when you go, and I'll try to do the same."

Arcove started washing his face.

After a moment, Roup said, in a more normal voice, "Also, Halvery will feel so much better if he doesn't think it's his job to keep one of us alive."

Arcove laughed. "He'd share his den with you."

"I know. I just can't imagine living without you. I don't even want to think about it."

"Then let's stop thinking about it. Let's think about how you have a litter of cubs due this spring. When's the last time that happened?"

"Oh… Around ten years ago, I suppose. But they're probably all Halvery's."

"They're probably not," said Arcove sweetly.

"They won't look like me."

"You're very focused on that for someone who doesn't care about color."

"It's an absurd thing to care about."

"Well, Caraca and Nadine are speculating about it wildly. Nadine told me that she's determined not to die this winter so that she can see them."

"Oh…" Roup's ears drooped. "I suppose I should thank her for helping Halvery and Caraca with this misguided experiment."

"You should."

"Except now I feel certain that I am going to disappoint *even more* cats when the cubs don't—"

"Roup!"

"Alright, fine. The litter will definitely contain nothing but cubs the color of honeybees, who think in loops, don't like to fight, and prefer lying down. Ideal additions to Leeshwood."

"That's better."

Roup snorted a laugh. "Since when did you become the optimistic one?"

"Well, as you pointed out, we've created a world full of improbable things. For instance, Nadine seems to think that Halvery has completely lost his head over you."

Roup made a face. "Don't even start—"

"Your paws are flowers? Your eyes are stars?"

"I really can't take this from you, too."

"I might have to take a closer look at your paws."

Roup rubbed his face against Arcove's. In spite of their teasing words, the gesture carried a hint of bone-deep relief. Arcove could feel it, too—something that had been twisted inside him, uncoiling. *I am not going to lose you to Dazzle. You will stop making baseless assumptions about his character and taking foolish risks to protect him. And I can trust you again.*

Part II

Spring

1

Bargain

Roup and Lyndi trotted side by side along the banks of Chelby River, returning home after a visit to Halvery's den. The river was running high with snowmelt. Traces of ice still lingered in the shadowed hollows of the forest, but flowers were filling the sunny places. The air smelled of running sap and green shoots and thawing earth.

In the thickets, the does were birthing their earliest fawns. In creasia dens, births had started as well. They would continue throughout the season and into early summer. While cubs did sometimes arrive outside of spring or summer, they were less likely to survive. Most females now living in Leeshwood ate bitterleaf to avoid out-of-season pregnancies. Spring and summer were the most bountiful seasons, with plenty of time for cubs to grow bigger and develop survival skills before their first winter.

"I suppose we have to deliver the sad news to Nadine that your cubs are not born yet," said Lyndi. "Caraca, too."

Roup smiled. "You know Halvery would have sent someone if they'd been born. He wouldn't just wait for me to show up."

"He might. If he thought you'd be disappointed."

"*I* don't care. Everyone else does."

"Liar," said Lyndi sweetly.

She'd come with Roup on this visit for reasons apart from checking on Ilsa. It was the time of year when juvenile creasia began making enquiries about joining their first adult dens and clutters. Males typically left their birth dens a bit younger than females, at four or five, whereas females often waited until six to eight. Lyndi had come to talk to a few of Halvery's young adult offspring who'd expressed interest in dens and associated clutters in Roup's territory. She'd also spoken with Halvery, Velta, and

Samathi about a number of juveniles in Roup's territory who were interested in joining dens in Halvery's.

This sort of pre-evaluation by officers was not always done, but it was growing more common. Lyndi said that it decreased the number of fights and gave young creasia their best chance to survive and thrive as adults. Roup was inclined to agree with her. Halvery had grumbled something about fights being perfectly natural ways to meet your future clutter-mates, but he answered Lyndi's questions and told her who to speak with in various dens and clutters across his territory.

Afterward, Lyndi had spent some time visiting with the rest of the den, while Roup and Halvery went for a long run along the beach. They'd patrolled the entire eastern edge of Halvery's territory, talking all the while about the upcoming spring conference and whether Arcove would announce Carmine's promotion and perhaps Wisteria's new den council.

"He will definitely invite Carmine to the meeting," said Roup. "I'll officially let the clutter go, and the whole situation will stop confusing everyone."

"Will *Lyndi* be able to let the clutter go?" asked Halvery doubtfully. "She's putting in a lot of work for the young adults. In my day, youngsters just showed up and challenged someone."

Roup rolled his eyes. "Yes, in *our* day, youngsters just showed up and killed someone. I can't imagine why officers would want to avoid that."

"Not killed!" objected Halvery. "Not necessarily. Didn't you and Arcove fight when you met? Perfectly normal."

"Nothing about me is perfectly normal," said Roup quietly.

"Well, that's because you were raised by ferryshaft," said Halvery. "Not because you fought with the first cub you met. Or got under him later."

Roup refused to pursue this. "Lyndi just wants to leave our territory in good shape, with all the young cats off to as smooth a start as possible. She still says she wants to come with me to Arcove's den. I told her she'll get bored, but she says I'll need someone to watch my back while I'm scheming."

Halvery barked a laugh. "Remind me to give Lyndi a lick on the head every time I see her."

Roup rolled his eyes. "I am not going to do anything more stealthy than solve den disputes for the rest of my life."

"I don't believe you."

Roup felt certain that Halvery had become aware, over the course of the winter, of his change in attitude. Roup had barely mentioned the Southern Mountains, and when Halvery brought it up, Roup changed the subject. Roup had confined himself to Leeshwood's business, and hadn't even bothered to ask Storm or Sauny their news when they came to talk to Arcove. He could tell that Halvery was a little confused, but not unhappy.

At sunrise, he dragged Roup into a clearing full of spring green, and pressed him down among the flowers. Afterwards, he was at pains to point out which ones were the color of Roup's fur, nose-leather, and paw pads. "It's like you're made for spring," he purred in Roup's ear.

"You think I'm made for you to get on top of," breathed Roup.

"That, too."

Of course, the ostensible reason for Lyndi and Roup's visit was to check on Ilsa, whose belly was growing heavy with cubs. Creasia litters were usually no more than four, as they had only four teats. It was common to have only two or three cubs, or even singletons. First litters were often small. Nevertheless, Velta believed that Ilsa was carrying at least three cubs, possibly four. She did not think they would be born until mid-spring. "Tell Nadine that she will just have to stay alive a little longer," she quipped.

Nadine had, in truth, been miserable throughout the coldest months of winter, although she tried to hide the fact. Her joints were so stiff that she could barely get to her feet some days. She would lie beside the hot springs, the heat her only solace, though she didn't dare swim because being wet was too miserable afterward.

She was too stiff to groom herself, a fact she found humiliating. Her den-mates assisted when she would permit it. Arcove and Roup took turns, and then Caraca had joined in. Around midwinter Carmine had begun coming by every few days to check on his mother and groom her without being asked. Several of her other adult cubs had begun showing up, as well. It was clear that her appetite had fled, but she made an attempt to consume the gifts of food they brought her.

"I am so lucky," she told Roup one dim winter day, squinting through the headache that often plagued her.

Roup tried to smile. "You are loved, Nadine."

"I am loved, and I *have* loved. I've had such an interesting life, and I get to choose how I leave it. I've watched countless cats come and go who deserved those things just as much as I do and didn't get them. A little suffering is well worth such luck."

Roup had whispered, "Please don't suffer for me."

Nadine's eyes crinkled. "Oh, I'm not, dear heart. I'm suffering for me! One more look at the future before I leave."

"They probably won't be anything special."

"All cubs are special, Roup."

He'd sighed. *There's another reason you're holding on. You think your body will keep fighting, that you won't be allowed to step out of this world gracefully, and you want to ask Arcove to end it. Only you can't bear to leave him with that memory. I suppose I should offer.* But the idea made him sick. *Halvery is right. I couldn't do it.*

Roup was still thinking about Nadine as he and Lyndi reached Smoky Branch and Arcove's territory. It was near dawn, when creasia were active. They passed two juvenile cubs, who watched them, but said nothing. It took Roup a long beat to register that the cubs appeared to be standing guard. At the same time, Lyndi said, "Roup..."

It was too quiet. This close to the den, at such a busy hour, they should have heard the sounds of cubs quarreling or sparring, cats visiting, even guests like ferryshaft talking and laughing. Arcove's den was not as rambunctious as Halvery's, but it was still a busy place, particularly at dawn and dusk.

Roup's heart sank. "Nadine…"

Lyndi looked at him with sympathy. "Maybe not."

But Roup couldn't think of any other reason for the den to be so quiet and for cubs to be standing guard. The watchers were probably meant to keep all but the den's members out while Arcove took a moment to pull himself together. *I should be there.* Roup picked up his pace. He and Lyndi soon reached the caves among the roots of enormous trees, all bathed in the steam of the hot springs.

He was relieved and confused to see the matriarch of the den sitting in the entrance of the cave where she'd been sleeping. Roup loped up to her, a little breathless. "Nadine…"

She leaned out to touch noses with him, mistaking his anxiety for excitement. "Are your cubs born, dear?"

Roup laughed shakily. "Not yet. Velta thinks there are three or four of them, though. Why is the den so quiet? Why are cubs standing watch?"

"We have a visitor. Arcove doesn't want the news circulating. You need to go talk to him. They're on the Tail Tip."

Roup left her, his alarm replaced by baffled curiosity. Lyndi had caught up with him and asked, "What's happened? I see Nadine, so she's alright. But, in that case, why…?"

"She says we have a secret visitor. I have no idea what's going on. They're with Arcove on the Tail Tip."

The Tail Tip was a little island in the broadest section of Smoky Branch. It was so named because a tributary left the Branch at this point on its way to Crooked Tail. The island contained about a dozen trees scattered around a rocky hillock. It was too small for a den, but it made an ideal spot for cubs to play king of the hill. Many a king's cub had been knocked from the peak into the waters of the Branch by laughing siblings. Swimming was easy in the wide open section, the water just deep enough to cushion a fall. The Tail Tip was also a place that could provide privacy. Arcove and Roup had gone out there to be alone on numerous occasions.

Roup and Lyndi encountered another guard on the bank—one of Arcove's mates. "Roup." She looked relieved. "He said that if you came, I was to send you straight over. Lyndi, I'm sorry, but I'm not supposed to let anyone else pass."

"It's alright," said Lyndi. "Roup, I'll just go talk to Nadine about some of Velta's news. It doesn't sound like there's any danger here."

Roup agreed, although he felt even more confused. He swam across the Branch to the shore of the Tail Tip. He saw no one among the island's nearly leafless trees, but he was quite familiar with privacy options on the Tip and he walked around the hillock until he encountered the spot where the rock formed a little alcove, completely hidden from view of the shore.

Here at last was Arcove. He had Storm with him. They were talking to a cat that Roup did not recognize. At a glance, he was a juvenile male, probably four years old, with paws and head that looked too big for the rest of him. His coat was a very pale tan, with a dusting of white guard hairs and patches of white around his face, paws, and belly. He was lanky and underfed despite his thick fur, with sunken sides and clear signs of stress in the way he twitched and startled at the smallest movement. Roup's heartbeat quickened. He knew that look. It was how Kavi and Ruffle had looked when they'd first arrived in his clutter.

Roup spoke while he was still some distance away. He didn't want to startle them or to eavesdrop. "Arcove."

Arcove's head snapped around. He looked agitated. "Roup. I'm glad you're here."

Roup came forward. "Nadine said we have a secret visitor."

"For the moment. He's come from the Southern Mountains, from Thistle specifically, and he won't be a secret for long. I'll be calling the spring conference as soon as we're done here, but I wanted some time with his news before it starts spreading all over the wood. Also, he won't tell us his whole message without you present." Arcove hesitated. "His name is Flurry."

It was an appropriate name for a cat who looked dusted with snow. Roup sat down slowly. "Hello, Flurry."

Flurry's bright hazel eyes regarded him with wary intensity. Roup stifled the urge to insist that they feed him before interrogating him. "I have come from Thistle Ela-creasia," said Flurry, "with a message for Arcove Ela-creasia and Roup. I was advised not to give my message in its entirety to anyone else."

"Tell him the part that you're willing to share with everyone first," said Arcove.

Flurry shut his eyes as though recalling something he'd painstakingly memorized. "We creasia of the Southern Mountains are beset by enemies, Arcove. We believe they are also your enemies. We recognize that the relationship between our two Leeshwoods has not always been friendly. In the past, we rejected overtures of reconciliation, and we now regret those decisions. We humbly beg for your aid."

Roup let out a long breath. It was exactly the message he'd wanted to receive from these cats for two years. Even better, it was framed in such a way as to rouse Arcove's sympathy, with no excuses or demands. But there was something missing. Roup would have expected a gift offered in exchange for aid, probably reciprocity. Arcove's original offer to Treace had included the idea that their two kingdoms would come to each other's aid if needed. The message should have ended with, "We will do the same for you when and if the time comes." Instead, Flurry had stopped speaking.

Roup glanced at Storm. *Why are you here, friend?* Costa had returned to her parents that winter, which they'd spent in the area just south of Leeshwood, near the Ferryshaft Cave of Histories. It was an area that also contained hot springs that Charder had loved. Roup knew there'd been concern among the ferryshaft that Sedaron's followers might try to deface the caves. Specifically, they'd threatened to obliterate creasia writing there. However, as far as he knew, nothing of the kind had happened.

Sedaron's herd had remained at the foot of the mountains over the winter, neither pushing deeper into the hills, nor picking more fights with other ferryshaft. Storm had visited Leeshwood only a few times over the course of the winter, and his interactions with Roup had consisted entirely of happy chatter about Teek's cubs, Costa's improved attitude after spending two seasons in a creasia den, and the latest cave writing. If Storm had spoken to Arcove about more serious matters, Roup had not been privy to the details.

"Flurry approached me in the Cave of Histories," said Storm. "He was afraid to walk into Leeshwood without an introduction."

Flurry's gaze skipped to Storm and away. Roup read caution and distrust in that look, but also curiosity. *He's probably never had a friendly interaction with ferryshaft in his life until now. And yet he got up his nerve to approach Storm for help. Interesting.*

"There's more?" asked Roup.

"Yes," said Arcove. "Flurry, tell him what you told us about the situation up there."

"The ferryshaft have come to the lower valley in large numbers," said Flurry, his eyes skipping between their faces. "Right now, they're being held back by snowmelt that keeps water running in the slot canyons. However, as the water disappears, it may become impossible to keep them out of the upper valley, where we're preparing to have our cubs. The ferryshaft seem determined to kill us all. There are over a thousand of them, along with a few lowland curbs they've brought from the plain."

Roup stared at him. "A thousand?" he said faintly. "Did Sedaron take his spring foals up there?"

"No," said Storm acidly. "He left the young foals and their mothers with Kelsy's herd."

Roup made a face. "So Kelsy has taken Sedaron's side."

"He claims he's neutral," said Storm. Roup could tell he was seething about it. "Kelsy is coming to the spring conference, so he can explain it to you himself."

"Well, at least he's still talking to us," said Roup. "But, in that case…Sedaron's herd must be close to three thousand animals, all told."

He did not say the rest, but Arcove was watching him with eyes that said, *"See?"*

You were right, thought Roup. *We could barely win a pitched battle right now, and that's only if Kelsy's herd doesn't take sides against us.* The creasia would be outnumbered as it was, but creasia in groups were more dangerous than ferryshaft, and could usually win with a smaller army.

Roup could see another ugly possibility. *Sedaron has put a lot of trust in Kelsy by leaving females and foals with him. That's a weakness that Arcove would have exploited during the last war, but…those wounds are still festering. If we go that route, we'll leave a new generation of ferryshaft with grudges that only death can extinguish.*

Roup was so lost in thought that he almost forgot that Flurry had more to say. "I cannot finish my message with the ferryshaft present," he said stiffly. "I was told to deliver it only to Arcove and Roup."

Storm glanced at Arcove, who inclined his head.

"I'll be at your den," said Storm and disappeared through the rocks and trees.

Only after they heard the soft splash of Storm swimming away did Flurry continue, "Thistle instructed me to say this: 'We will render you whatever assistance our smaller numbers can provide in exchange for your help, Arcove. However, I understand that some appeasement will be required, given past events. My officer, Dazzle, attacked you on a personal level. I therefore offer you his life in exchange for your help.'"

Roup hadn't seen it coming. He stared at Flurry, who glanced between Arcove and Roup as though expecting some reaction, possibly delight. Neither of them moved or said anything. At last, Flurry continued, "Thistle says: 'Dazzle is a cunning animal who has many friends in Leeshwood and beyond, even now. He does not yet know his fate, nor am I in a position to kill him without endangering many other cats. I will see that you have him at your mercy when you come, but until then, I advise you share this information with no one.'"

Flurry took a deep breath and visibly relaxed. He blinked and said, in a more normal voice, "I am to lead you into the mountains if you are inclined to go, sir."

"And if I don't go?" asked Arcove heavily.

Flurry looked a little worried. He crouched down and said in a small voice, "Then I am yours to do with as you wish."

"Peace," murmured Arcove. "You are in no danger unless you do some mischief to me or mine. Go back to my den, and tell my mates that I said to find you something to eat."

The youngster's ears pricked up. Roup supposed he must think of food almost constantly. "Yes, sir. Thank you, sir."

When he was gone, Arcove said, "Well?"

"Well, what?" Roup's thoughts were tumbling.

Arcove just watched him.

I told Dazzle I was a friend. I told him there was a place for him here. I've reinforced that idea with my written message this fall. How could I participate in luring him to his death?

At the same time, Arcove's words battered at him: *"Roup, you are basing assumptions about his character on such limited interactions! That sense of kinship is making you want to give Dazzle second chances that he hasn't earned. Can you imagine having to put down Halvery or Lyndi or Moashi because you made a mistake with Dazzle?"*

Roup felt hollow, unsure of everything. He met Arcove's eyes. "I'm sure you'll do what you think is best."

Arcove looked away. Roup was certain that he didn't like this bargain. Even if Dazzle had been proven a thoroughly despicable creature, treachery wasn't how Arcove liked to dispatch his enemies. *But he tried to kill me. And you'll bend a lot of your personal rules to avenge that.*

"When are you calling for the spring conference?" asked Roup.

Arcove stood up. "As fast as everyone can get here. I suppose that'll be at least three days if I want to talk to Kelsy. And I certainly want to talk to him."

* * * *

This chapter includes an author's note at the end of the book.

2

Chaos Always

"You agreed to babysit his foals, Kelsy?!"

It had been three days since Thistle's messenger arrived. The swiftly assembled spring conference had gathered in the Great Cave at sunset. Arcove wanted to discuss the newly proposed boundary line and telshee territory in the cave in addition to more pressing topics.

Keesha was in attendance, blinking and yawning because he'd recently emerged from his winter torpor. Kelsy had just arrived, along with a small contingent of ferryshaft that he'd left near the mouth of the cave. Sauny and Valla had reached Leeshwood the day before, and their herd of some fifty animals was currently mingling with the ferryshaft residing in Roup's territory. Storm was still present, along with Cohal and Maoli. All the creasia officers were in attendance, in addition to Carmine and, after some debate, Wisteria. Arcove had *not* chosen to include Flurry, who'd been staying in Arcove's den under close observation.

Roup had assumed that the conference would begin with the relatively easy topic of the new boundary line and telshee territory in the cave. However, within moments of the meeting's opening, it had devolved into a shouting match between Storm and Kelsy.

"We share blood with my father's herd!" shot Kelsy. "One of my mates is sister to one of his officers' mates. You expect me to tell her, 'No, we won't offer shelter to your sister and her foal?' There are numerous such ties across our herds!"

"So you really are *neutral?*" spat Storm. "You're staying out of this while your father kills other ferryshaft or threatens them into submission so that he can try to annihilate the creasia? You're fine with him murdering mourners on their way to Groth?"

Kelsy rolled his eyes. "I told him what I thought of attacks near Groth, and those attacks have ceased! Now he's attacking Arcove's *enemies*, Storm! He has killed very few ferryshaft, and those he has killed had quarrels with him that go further back than disagreements about creasia. Yes, he absorbed some small herds under questionable circumstances. Yes, his scouts picked fights. I don't agree with it, but I am not ready to ask members of my herd to die because of it! You understand what that battle would look like, don't you? Hundreds of dead ferryshaft!"

"Your father is sharpening his teeth to come *here*," snarled Storm. "You know it as well as anyone. You are being willfully stupid in order to keep your nose clean."

"Keep my nose clean?!" thundered Kelsy. "What part of 'hundreds of dead ferryshaft' do you not understand?" He caught his breath and spat, "Oh, but I forgot. I'm talking to Storm Ela-curb. Or Storm Ela-telshee. Or perhaps even Storm Ela-creasia. It's never Storm Ela-ferry, is it?" He jerked his head at Arcove. "You care about what happens to *them* more than you care what happens to *us!* You've raised three foals, but you raised one cub, and that's all you can remember!"

"How dare you!" hissed Storm. "I risked my life for the herd when you were hiding behind elders and rolling over for creasia as fast as you could get your feet out from under you—!"

Arcove looked like he had a headache. He opened his mouth, but Sauny got there ahead of him, "Stop it, both of you!" she barked. "Kelsy, show some respect. You're alive because of what Storm did when he was not even three years old." Storm started to say something and she rounded on him. "Storm, you don't lead a herd. It *is* difficult to choose to put them at risk when you know that some of them will die." She caught her breath and added, "It's a little like choosing to put your foal at risk."

Storm's mouth snapped shut as though she'd kicked him.

Kelsy started to say something and then seemed to think better of it.

Silence descended over the cave. Arcove glanced at Storm. "Chaos, always," he murmured.

Storm laughed and seemed to relax a little.

"If you are all done posturing," continued Arcove, "I would like to update you on the situation in the Southern Mountains. Thistle has asked for my help, and I intend to give it." He let that sink in for a moment, then continued, "So there's clarity for you. I don't share council with enemies. Kelsy, whose side are you on?"

Kelsy screwed his eyes shut. "If you are asking me to threaten his foals and their mothers, Arcove, then the answer is no."

"I didn't ask that. I asked whose side you are on."

"I won't kill my own father!"

"One more time, Kelsy."

Kelsy looked at him levelly. "I like you, Arcove. Personally, I like you. If I can help you without causing harm to my own people, I will do so. If that makes me an enemy, I'll leave."

Arcove watched him, letting the silence stretch.

Kelsy made a noise of exasperation. "If I *order* my herd to attack my father's, there will be a rift. Because I will be ordering many of them to attack their friends, adult foals, siblings, and parents. Some of my ferryshaft will join my father's herd rather than do that."

"You're afraid of losing your power," murmured Storm.

Kelsy's eyes snapped to him again. "And *you* are a legend, not a leader. You don't even *live* in a herd, Storm, much less lead one." His eyes narrowed, and he added, "You never knew your father, but if someone told you to attack your mother, I think you'd hesitate."

"My mother is not a bully who murders those who've done her no harm."

"You're joking, right? When you say that creasia have done my father 'no harm'?"

"Enough," growled Arcove. "Kelsy, I accept that you are in a unique position in which your choice to take a firm stance could have adverse consequences. However, you may not be able to avoid taking a side forever. Will your position change if Sedaron begins raiding in Leeshwood or if there is a pitched battle between his herd and my cats?"

Kelsy shut his eyes. "With respect, Arcove, I will deal with the future when it arrives and not before."

Roup felt they were at an impasse. *I wonder if I might be able to guide us to a little common ground.* "What do you think of Macex, Kelsy?"

Kelsy's gaze flicked to Roup. "I don't like him."

"Why? Is he unfriendly to you?"

"No, he's *too* friendly. It was my impression a couple of years ago, that he was trying to get my support for an attempt to oust my father from herd leadership by force. Everyone knows that my father and I do not always get along, but I will not be part of a violent strike against him in a herd that isn't even my own. Macex can present his case to his elders and let them decide. That is how we have always chosen leaders. Or he can take his friends and go start a new herd."

"How did he hope to succeed in taking over Sedaron's herd if the elders aren't with him?" asked Roup.

"Well, I never heard his plans," said Kelsy. "It was all smiles and hints. But I'm guessing he would like to upend the entire leadership and replace it with his own cronies. The leaders of my father's herd are the oldest on Lidian. They are quite insular and old-fashioned in their thinking. I don't deny it. Macex and his friends are all less than twenty. A few of them remember growing up in Charder's herd, but most of them were born after the rebellion."

Arcove spoke again, "Why is Sedaron tolerating this threat to his leadership?"

Kelsy rolled his eyes. "Oh, Macex settled down after my father promoted him. They're cozy now. From my father's point-of-view, Macex has brought the younger ferryshaft to heel and is representing their interests in council. Maybe he is…or maybe Macex is just biding his time. Anyway, I think he's a sneak and I don't like him."

Halvery spoke up, sounding bored. "Let's not forget that both Macex and Sedaron want Arcove dead. They probably want every creasia at this conference dead. There is no material difference between them from Leeshwood's point-of-view. Can we move on to how we are going to deal with them?"

"There *is* a difference," said Roup quietly. "One of them is willing to unite with Thistle against us and one is not."

"Yes, but Thistle has apparently chosen *us*," said Halvery sourly, "though I can't say I'm excited about being chosen." He looked at Arcove. "Sir, are you simply planning to help those cats win a fight so that they can stay in their own territory? Or do you intend to return them to Leeshwood?"

"I have not yet made a decision about what form our assistance will take," said Arcove, "but the situation in the mountains has deteriorated. Thistle's messenger says that Sedaron's herd is laying siege to the upper valley and will likely break through as soon as the last of the snowmelt stops blocking the canyons. There are some thousand ferryshaft up there and curb allies—enough to easily overwhelm a few hundred cats."

Keesha spoke up. "*You* are going to break a siege?"

Arcove did not quite meet his eyes. "Yes, I thought you might find that amusing. Any advice?"

Keesha did not, in fact, look amused. "Don't run out of water," he said darkly.

"I'm afraid we'll have more water than we want," said Arcove. "Are there entrances to Syriot under those mountains?"

"None that we can access," said Keesha. "Telshees cannot swim through solid ice."

"I was not suggesting..." began Arcove and paused to collect his thoughts. "I meant that we may need a way to take those cats around Sedaron's herd. At this time of year, Thistle's dens will include pregnant females and spring cubs. Taking them through a battle will be as good as killing them."

Keesha looked surprised. "You intend to bring them out by stealth?"

Arcove looked annoyed. "What else would you expect me to do?"

"Based on past experience, I would expect you to engage in a bloody confrontation with Sedaron's herd."

Arcove shook his ears. "That would result in tremendous loss of life and leave Leeshwood unprotected. I'm not taking eight hundred cats up there so that half of them can die. We'll take a smaller group and attempt to intervene with some precision. If we fail, we fail. I don't owe Thistle more than that. I don't owe him anything."

"If we don't reduce Sedaron's numbers, what's to stop his herd from coming after us later?" asked Halvery.

"I don't think they'll have the stomach for it if they are foiled in the mountains," said Roup. "If they can't kill a couple hundred cats with a thousand ferryshaft, I think they will doubt their leaders and their own abilities."

"Possibly," said Arcove. "At any rate, a pitched battle in known territory would be less risky for us. I'll deal with Sedaron on the plain if I have to. In the mountains, there's also the issue of feeding a large number of cats. Dazzle told Roup it couldn't be done. Flurry says the same thing. Game is small and scarce on the lower slopes, large and dangerous in the high passes."

"Yes, but apparently there are plenty of ferryshaft to eat," said Halvery brightly and Stefan laughed.

Arcove started to say something and then he laughed, too. "I would say that I'd prefer not to offend our ferryshaft allies, but I'm not sure we have any."

"Of course you do," said Sauny. "Arcove, how stealthy do you mean to be? Are you trying to whisk those cats out from under Sedaron's nose?"

Arcove hesitated. "That depends on the attitude of Thistle and his creasia."

"Some kind of diversion seems easiest," said Roup, "an attack that lures Sedaron's herd away from the mouth of the valley long enough for Thistle's cats to escape." He shot a quick smile at Storm. "Lead them a chase?"

"This is sounding more and more like bringing Thistle's cats back to Leeshwood," grumbled Halvery. "If we pry them out of their valley, they have to go somewhere—"

"They had dens on the lower slopes in years past, Halvery," said Roup. "Surely they could return there if the threat of Sedaron's herd is eliminated."

"Yes, they had dens that were closer to Leeshwood, so that a spy could come and go undetected."

"He didn't go undetected—" began Roup, but then Arcove gave him an exasperated look and he subsided.

Arcove turned to look at Halvery with the same expression, and he wisely chose not to pursue his point. After a moment, Arcove turned to the curbs. "Cohal and Maoli, I heard from Storm that you were unable to reach those islands in the center of the lake last fall. Not enough ice. There may be sufficient ice this spring, particularly if we leave soon. Are you still interested in accompanying us?"

"You want us to guide you through the slot canyons?" asked Cohal with distaste.

Arcove flicked his ears. "I have no doubt Storm can do that without you."

"Oh, have some doubt," said Storm. "Those canyons are tricky."

Maoli spoke up, "Will you assist us in reaching the islands?"

"As much as I'm able," said Arcove, "but curbs are lighter than creasia, and if the ice won't hold you, it certainly won't hold me. I think the best assistance I can give you is my presence. Lowland curbs are numerous in the mountains now. I don't see how you'll even get close to the islands if you're not traveling with larger predators."

"What Maoli means," growled Cohal, "is: will you send another expedition this winter if we are unable to reach the islands this spring? In winter, the ice is certain."

"I will not risk creasia lives by sending them into the mountains at the most dangerous time of year," said Arcove.

"Then you are no true friend to us."

"You keep saying that," interjected Halvery, "and yet you seem to think that maybe if you keep spitting on our assistance, we'll come around."

"I have nothing to say to you, Halvery Ela-creasia," snapped Cohal.

"Then stop saying it," returned Halvery.

"Enough," growled Arcove. "Cohal and Maoli, you can come into the mountains with us and see whether the ice is thick enough, or you can stay behind. I've told you what I will and will not do for you. Storm, are you coming with us?"

"I'm coming," said Storm quietly.

Arcove's gaze shifted to the rest of his officers—an assessing look. At last, he settled on Carmine and Wisteria, who'd made the interesting choice to sit beside Keesha for the meeting. Lyndi had joined them. She'd been their immediate commanding officer their entire lives, and they were fond of her. The rest of the officers were clearly waiting to hear what Arcove had to say before deciding how to treat these two.

"You all know why Carmine is here," said Arcove. "He'll be taking over Roup and Lyndi's clutter."

A look passed between Hollygold and Stefan. Moashi shot a questioning glance at Halvery, who did not return it.

Roup watched their guarded expressions. No council member had ever been promoted in this way before—without a fight. *Will they allow it?* If any of the officers objected, Arcove wouldn't have any precedent to fall back on. He could easily be accused of giving special favors to his own cub. Having Halvery on their side would make a smooth transition possible, but it was far from a foregone conclusion.

Then Moashi spoke, "Can we just pretend that Carmine and I fought and he won? He can move straight on to Hollygold and save us all some time."

Halvery rolled his eyes. "Have some dignity, Ears…"

But Carmine laughed and said, "I don't know why anyone would assume I'd win that fight. Roup and Halvery didn't train *me.*"

"That's because you didn't need them to," said Moashi cheerfully, "but we can go a round if you like. Just don't rip the ears, please? That will make it impossible for Halvery to insult me in his preferred manner."

That got a laugh out of everyone, even Halvery.

Roup grinned at Moashi. *Good cub.* His outburst had reminded them all that Carmine's bloodless promotion was far from the only new thing they were trying lately and that the old ways might, in fact, be a little silly.

"I'm told that only amateurs rip someone's ears when they don't intend to," said Carmine. It was the sort of thing Halvery was fond of saying, and everyone chuckled again.

Arcove spoke, sounding relieved. "Carmine will begin as my most junior officer, and we can settle the matter of challenges later. Roup and Lyndi will both be in my den, though they will continue to serve on the council. If anyone feels this gives their views unfair weight, I will hear you afterward, but that is beyond the scope of a spring conference."

No one said anything.

After an infinitesimal pause, Arcove continued, "Wisteria is here because she would like to form a den council. She proposes to represent its interests at conferences and at…" He hesitated and then chose Roup's term, "At the king's council. Word about this has traveled, and I'm sure you have opinions. I would like to hear them now."

"We cannot have dens behaving like a law unto themselves, Arcove," said Stefan at once. "It would prevent alphas from solving difficult disputes. It would cause chaos."

Wisteria spoke for the first time, her voice low and even. "Do you think Treace's dens would have caused 'chaos' if they'd been allowed a voice on the council twelve years ago, Stefan? I don't. I think they would have prevented a war."

Stefan's hackles rose. Roup could tell he was trying to figure out whether to treat Wisteria as a subordinate or with the deference he would have reserved for another officer's mate. Wisteria's place in the hierarchy was confusing to everyone, and confusion produced short tempers.

Wisteria read these signs with as much precision as Roup. She cocked her head and gave Stefan a toothy smile. "Shall we fight, Stefan? What if I just challenged you? Would that make this easier?"

It actually might, thought Roup, but Stefan only lashed his tail and looked away.

In a quiet voice, he continued, "You are proposing to become a separate, *competing* authority over my territory, Wisteria—a territory that I've worked very hard to win and hold. If your den council is at odds with me in settling a dispute, who wins? Who outranks whom?"

Arcove was listening closely, but he didn't interrupt. Roup was sure he had the same reservations as Stefan. He felt it was Wisteria's job to respond to them.

Wisteria was ready. "I am not proposing to become an authority, certainly not a competing one. I am proposing to become a voice—someone who listens to the unique perspectives of den mothers, consolidates those perspectives, and presents them in council. I will, at any officer's request, help to settle disputes, but only if you ask."

Roup repressed a smile. *Very good, my dear. Wait until he asks nicely.*

A pause while Stefan considered this. Wisteria had sidestepped all of his objections. He wasn't convinced, but he didn't know what else to say.

Hollygold spoke up, "Exactly who would sit on your council, Wisteria? Alpha den mothers are often elderly and don't like to leave their territories. Also, it sounds like you want to hear from *all* dens, which is impractical."

"To start, I'd like representatives from the officers' dens," said Wisteria. "Alpha den mothers can come if they like, or they can assign a representative. In addition, I'd like to make it clear that other females are welcome to attend as they see fit in order to make sure their interests are heard."

"Well, that will certainly attract all the troublemakers," said Hollygold. "Enjoy listening to them argue."

"It will be difficult to match the unity and perfect peace of the king's council, I'm sure," said Wisteria with a bit too much cheek.

Keesha laughed.

"I meant," said Hollygold with a trace of bluster, "that females with a long history of petty squabbles will show up at your den. They will argue endlessly and possibly fight."

"Like we're doing right now?" asked Wisteria blandly. "I don't mind having an actual fight if it'll make you feel better, Hollygold."

He looked at her with a hint of exasperation. There would be no glory in winning a fight with a female and considerable shame in losing.

"Don't play word games with her, Hollygold," said Halvery dryly. "She's too much like her grandfather."

"Which one?" muttered Hollygold, and that made everyone laugh.

Arcove looked like he was ready to move on. "I am willing to let Wisteria try her den council as long as it solves more problems than it creates. Regarding the Southern Mountains, I mean to leave in the next three days. I want my officers to meet me at my den with clutters of ten cats each." He paused and added, "My officers who lead clutters, at any rate."

Roup could see them all adding up the numbers in their heads. The party would include about sixty cats total. They would be able to give a good account of themselves, especially considering the group would include some of the best fighters in Leeshwood. They might even be able to beat a much larger number of ferryshaft with a little luck and the element of surprise. But sixty animals was not the kind of army that would be necessary to win a crushing victory in a pitched battle. Arcove wasn't joking when he said that he intended a "precision intervention."

Moashi looked a little worried. "What happens if we don't come back, sir?"

"Well, then I hope you're leaving someone competent in charge," said Arcove.

"Yes, but...should *all* the officers—"

Halvery interrupted with a touch of pique. "You're a king's officer, Moashi. What did you suppose that meant?"

Moashi looked a little hurt.

Roup felt certain that this bickering and confusion about roles was precisely why Arcove wanted to take all his officers on this expedition. This group had never worked together under pressure before. Now, with war on the horizon and threats mounting, Arcove felt they needed seasoning, much as Sedaron must feel his ferryshaft needed it. There was risk, of course. If they were all killed, Leeshwood would be left scrambling to fill important leadership roles. *Wisteria might get more responsibility than she bargained for.*

But Arcove had never been one to avoid calculated risks. He'd never been one to shield his officers from danger or fights. "Officers are like claws," Roup had often heard him say. "If you don't use them, they don't stay sharp."

"Sauny," continued Arcove, "are you and your herd proposing to come with us?"

Sauny hesitated.

Storm gave her an incredulous look from between the curbs.

Sauny refused to return his gaze. "Here's the thing, Arcove. My herd is not large. I have maybe a dozen good fighters who do not *also* have young foals at the moment. If we go with you into the mountains…what am I asking them to do, exactly? Risk their lives for Thistle's cats?"

Storm burst out, "Sauny!"

She refused to look at him and addressed herself to Arcove. "If we were defending Leeshwood, yes, I would risk my life and theirs, but Thistle's cats aren't Leeshwood. And, yes, I know Sedaron is sharpening his teeth to come here, but I'm not convinced that rescuing those cats will make any difference in that regard. I think he'll *still* come here, and when he does, I think you'll need all of your allies at your side. I think we'll be more help here than dead in the Southern Mountains."

Roup expected another outburst from Storm, but he'd gone quiet.

Arcove didn't look angry or surprised. "Will you be remaining in Leeshwood, then?"

"We'll come with you around the lake if that's alright," said Sauny. "We'll bring as many ferryshaft as want to come from Roup's—" She checked herself. "Carmine's territory. If you come running out of those mountains with Sedaron's ferryshaft on your tail, we'll reinforce you and cover your retreat. If your creasia come limping out of the mountains wounded, we'll help them get home alive."

"That's valuable," said Roup quietly. "Thank you."

"I want to help," said Sauny, "but there are limits to the risks I'm willing to take."

Storm got up without another word and left the cave. Roup had a vivid memory of him stalking out of a conference in the Great Cave as a three year old, trailed by a cub he'd been threatening to eat.

Arcove glanced after Storm, looked back at Sauny's strained expression and Kelsy's stony one, and sighed. "I suppose we don't need Storm present in order to discuss the new boundary line."

3

Near-Misses

Halvery could tell that something was bothering Roup. He didn't think it had anything to do with their low-grade bickering in council. *Surely that just counts as friendly sparring at this point. The ferryshaft were snipping at each other worse than anything we said.*

Nevertheless, he stopped to give Roup a lick on the ear on his way towards the mouth of the cave. Roup was staring into the little stream, obviously thinking about something else. Arcove, Keesha, Sauny, and Kelsy were still wandering along the new boundary line, chatting about Volontaros. The rest of the creasia officers and guests had excused themselves. The officers, particularly, needed to select their clutters and prepare for an extended absence.

Halvery was already turning over the problem of which cats to bring on the expedition. He expected Roup to ignore his parting gesture, but Roup roused himself and said, "How is Ilsa?"

"Ready to have those cubs," said Halvery with a laugh. "She informs me that she enjoys mating a great deal more than being pregnant and would like to know whether one of us would be so kind as to carry the next litter."

Roup gave a startled snort of laughter. "Next?"

"I told her it's not fair in the slightest," continued Halvery, "but no one will ever try to kill her for the right to mate with *me,* so that part of being female is better at least."

Roup hesitated. "I suppose we won't get to see them before we leave."

"I doubt it," said Halvery. He kept his tone light. "So we'd better come back alive, hadn't we?"

"I suppose we'd better."

"Wouldn't it be funny if Nadine survived to see them and we didn't?"

"At least Caraca will get to see them," said Roup, matching Halvery's levity. "I feel it would be a great tragedy if she did not."

"*She* certainly thinks so," agreed Halvery. "She was telling me on her last visit about her long-haired oories and how she finally got a tricolor one. And ghosts help me, Roup, I *understood* what she was talking about."

Roup was laughing now.

"She explained it so many times," continued Halvery, "when we were trying to find the right female to get your coat color, and it must have sunk in at last, because I have an *opinion* about Munchy's pairing with Brindlefluff. The things I have done for you, Roup!"

Roup shook with laughter. "You're going to end up with kittens in your den."

"Blood and gristle! No. I'm sure I can't call myself an alpha anymore if I have abominations wandering around my den. I'm sure my cubs would kill them."

"She wants to do more pairings than she has time to supervise," continued Roup, "and she says it's good for the kittens to play with cubs."

"No!"

"She also says your den is interesting because you have so many cubs, and she'd like to study your point markings."

"Well, I've surely given her plenty of material for that already." Halvery adopted a beatific expression and added, "But she can breed me like one of her oories if she has a willing female in mind. Unlike some cats, I do not consider this a trial."

Roup smiled. Halvery could tell that his mind was already wandering back to whatever problem he'd been chewing on. "Caraca should have chosen you for a mate," he said absently.

"Nonsense; we'd never have made friends without you in common. Roup, what's wrong?"

Roup shot him an uneasy look. "You read me too well these days."

"I don't. Is it something I said?"

Roup got up and shook himself. "It's nothing to do with you, Halvery."

"Are you and Arcove arguing again?"

Roup hesitated. "No." He looked towards the mouth of the cave. "I need to help Carmine get his clutter sorted. His leadership is going to be put to the test immediately. Lyndi can manage the transition, but I would be a truly terrible commanding officer if I didn't help them. I'm sure you've got things to do as well."

Halvery had plenty to do, and he would only have a couple of nights in which to do it. Still, he hesitated. "You would tell me if it was something I could help with, wouldn't you?"

Roup met his eyes and seemed to *really* see him for the first time in their conversation. He leaned forward and rubbed his cheek hard against Halvery's in a gesture that was as affectionate as it was intimate. He finished by burying his nose under Halvery's jaw for a moment. Then Roup walked away. Halvery was at the bottom of the cliff before he realized that Roup hadn't actually answered the question.

Roup's odd behavior returned to him fleetingly over the two busy nights that followed. *He's been so content since we made that litter. Ghosts, what a chore it was to get him to do it! But now he seems genuinely excited about the cubs, although he pretends not to care. He and Arcove have obviously been getting along, and he chatters away to Ilsa and Velta every time he comes to my den. He hasn't even mentioned Dazzle all spring. Is he just worried that we'll get into trouble up there with a thousand ferryshaft and ghosts only know how many curbs?*

It was an obvious reason for concern, but Roup had been through fights with worse odds. Halvery had seen the way he behaved before battles. Roup didn't get nervous about that sort of thing. Halvery would have thought he'd be looking forward to the opportunity to finally get up into the Southern Mountains and save Thistle's cats, especially since Arcove apparently intended to do it by cunning instead of a blood bath.

Isn't this exactly what you wanted, Roup?

Roup wasn't any more forthcoming when they all met at Arcove's den three nights later. He greeted Halvery warmly, but then he went off with Storm, who was still sulking as far as Halvery could tell. He wasn't running with his sister or the rest of the ferryshaft, although that probably had something to do with the fact that Kelsy was accompanying them. Storm and Roup stayed with the highland curbs, who struck out across the plain instead of following the lake. The group soon disappeared from sight.

Halvery stayed with Arcove at the beginning, listening as he talked to Hollygold about what they could expect on the way into the mountains. Arcove and Hollygold were walking on either side of Thistle's juvenile messenger, Flurry.

Halvery had gotten his first look at the fellow this evening. He wasn't impressed—a twitchy youngster, with ears that looked ragged with frostbite, rather than fights. *But I suppose they sent him because he's expendable.*

Some part of Halvery's brain argued that, if Thistle's cry for help was so critical, he should not have entrusted it to an expendable four-year-old. True, Thistle's cats would feel the loss of an experienced fighter, but if their message did not reach Leeshwood, they were all dead anyway. Halvery had expected a cat like Dazzle. *Not* Dazzle, of course, but someone like him—a wily adult in his prime, who could fight his way through an ambush, trick Sedaron's scouts, and bring their message halfway across the island. Halvery would have expected someone old enough to have negotiating experience, who could get a hearing with Arcove in spite of Dazzle's treachery.

What did *Flurry say to him exactly?* The cub didn't look old enough to be trusted to frame Thistle's request. He must have delivered a memorized speech.

Everything about this suddenly seemed odd to Halvery, particularly Arcove's immediate capitulation. *They tried to kill Roup. It look him decades to forgive Charder for hurting Roup, and Arcove liked Charder.*

Halvery frowned. *Thistle sent a half-grown cub to do a warrior's job, and Arcove agreed to help Roup's would-be killers without a moment's hesitation. Nothing about this makes sense.*

Halvery fell back a few paces and let other cats crowd into the coveted space around Arcove. *Roup is upset, but he's not actually arguing with Arcove. He's...resigned? To what?*

Halvery was startled out of his reverie by a cheerful voice from somewhere near his flank. "Hello, Halvery."

He looked down. "Costa. Does your father know you're here?"

She grinned at him. "He does." She was three years old now—a leggy juvenile, not quite at her adult height, but getting close. The gray blaze across her face shone in the moonlight. "Do you want to chase him? We could see where he's gone with the curbs."

Halvery snorted. "I don't think Storm would appreciate that right now." *I'm certain the curbs wouldn't.* "Are you going into the mountains with us, Costa?"

She sighed. "I'm supposed to stay with Mother and Auntie Sauny and the other ferryshaft by the lake. I'm supposed to drag you home if you come down from the mountains limping and covered in blood."

"I don't think you could drag me," said Halvery critically.

"I might need help," agreed Costa. She pranced back and forth beside him, light on her feet, in a way that reminded Halvery of Storm. "Do you want to chase *me?*" Her gray eyes were all mischief. Halvery thought she was going to say something about the river, but she didn't. "It'll make the walk more interesting."

"Alright," he heard himself say, "but if I catch you, I'm going to carry you like a fawn I intend to eat, and you're not going to like it much."

Costa's eyes crinkled with amusement. "And if I get away, you have to tell me how you met Roup."

Halvery was surprised. *I would have told you that anyway.* Aloud, he said, "I suppose, but it's not very interesting."

"Everyone says you don't get along," said Costa, still with that wicked twinkle, "but it seems like you get along *really* well to me."

Halvery rolled his eyes. "That's because you've only barely come into existence."

Costa made an outraged noise, but Halvery continued, "We get along *now*. We didn't for a long time."

"Why?"

"Lots of reasons. Mostly because he liked ferryshaft."

"And you don't?"

Halvery almost made a joke about how they tasted better on grass, but instead, he said, "This is going to be a short chase if you keep talking. Shall I begin carrying you like a fawn right now?"

She leapt away from him and dashed out across the plain. "Count to ten first!"

"I don't remember agreeing to that!" he shouted after her.

Hunting Costa *did* make the long night's run more interesting. She obviously had some familiarity with the southern plains, whereas Halvery had almost none. She used the dips and hollows to her advantage and gained a substantial amount of ground before he started to catch up. To Halvery's amusement, she tried to lead him into a head-on collision with Storm and the curbs, but he caught their scent and gave them a wide berth. *Cohal and I will get into an actual fight if I jump on him out of the grass. If that prevents us from saving Thistle's cats, Roup may never forgive me.*

The main company of ferryshaft and creasia had spread out as they traveled, but they were mostly staying within sight of the lake. Costa and Halvery left them far behind over the course of the night.

Halvery finally lost her at a little pond surrounded by small trees. He snuffled around the water for a while, but eventually got bored and went off to rest and drink and to hunt small game. Only after he randomly crossed her muddy hoofprints sometime later did he realize that she must have been crouching in the tall watergrass watching him the entire time.

She would have surely escaped altogether if he hadn't known where she was headed. But Halvery knew she would turn back towards the lake at some point, and after a while, he left off following her twisting trail. Halvery scanned the eastern horizon and spotted a grove of tall nut-bearing trees that conveniently marked the edge of the water from a distance. They were also likely to provide cover that would seem attractive to a hunted animal. Halvery was careful to approach the lake at a spot well south of the grove, leaving no scent near the trees in the direction of the plain.

He swam a short distance, came ashore at the grove, identified Costa's likely route, and hopped onto a branch. Sure enough, Costa came slipping through the tall grass just before dawn, looking tired, and doubtless having left a confounding trail of tricks behind her. Halvery dropped out of the tree—a silent, deadly shadow—and knocked her off her feet.

Costa gave a startled squawk, and Halvery laughed to make sure she knew it was him. He didn't let her up, though. He got hold of her just above her bony shoulders, and proceeded to carry her towards the lake. It wasn't actually how he would have carried a fawn. He would have gotten a fawn by the throat to suffocate it, but her dangling legs were satisfying in the same way.

Costa went limp for a moment. Then he felt her stiffen all over. He thought, *She's about to panic. Good. Then she'll be a little afraid of us. She should be afraid of us.*

Afraid of me.

He set her down. Halvery didn't actually think about it. He just found that he was suddenly setting her on her feet as gently as though she'd been one of his own cubs. Costa kicked once before he let go of her. He thought she might take off running, but she didn't. She mastered herself and groaned, "I was so close!"

"Yes, well, I knew where you were going. The trees were too obvious. You should have known I'd think of that."

Costa's ears drooped.

Halvery gave her a nudge. "Come on, it's nice by the water."

Costa trailed him to the lake and then proceeded to drink desperately.

"Didn't you drink at the pond?" asked Halvery.

"I was afraid that water in my stomach would slow me down," muttered Costa between gulps.

"Well, you're not slow," said Halvery. "Slow's not your problem."

Costa didn't look at him. "Then what is? Why am I not as good as Storm?"

Halvery stretched out on his belly on the cool sand. "Same reason Carmine isn't as good as Arcove, I expect."

Costa raised her dripping muzzle to look at him. She'd been living in Carmine's den all fall and winter. Halvery was certain she'd seen him and Arcove spar. According to Roup, they sparred fairly often these days.

"Well, Carmine does win sometimes," she said, "but never the first round. Carmine tries and tries, but he doesn't start winning until Arcove starts to get tired." She cocked her head at Halvery. "Do you think Carmine just isn't as...as talented?" He could hear her unspoken follow-up: *"Am I not as talented as my father?"*

Halvery shook his ears. "No, I think Carmine has about as much talent as Arcove had at that age. He just doesn't have as much experience. He doesn't have the *right* experience. Arcove was fighting for his life from the time he was two years old. He had a lot of near-misses. If you survive fights that almost kill you, you take those experiences with you into the next fight and the next. You get smarter. Your reflexes get better. But each near-miss is also a chance to die. For every one of us who had all those near-misses, there are hundreds of cats who just died. My brother was one of them."

He stopped, surprised at himself. *When was the last time I talked about him?* Costa stood perfectly still, tail up, waiting.

Halvery told the story in brief. "He and I wandered away from our den when we were a year old. We were learning to hunt rabbits. A couple of ferryshaft found us, and we went up a tree to get away. He was just a tiny bit slower."

When Halvery did not continue, Costa came sloshing out of the shallows. To Halvery's surprise, she flopped down against his shoulder. She stared up seriously into his face with her wide, gray eyes. "They killed him?"

"One of them caught his tail. They pulled him down, and then pulled him apart. Ate him right there in front of me." Halvery spoke without emotion. He was not trying to elicit sympathy, but Costa's eyes went round.

She was silent for a long moment. "That's why you didn't like ferryshaft."

Halvery snorted. "My first litter was also eaten, but that's… just a thing that happens. Happened, I mean."

Costa was staring at him as though he'd told her that randomly bursting into flame was "just a thing that happens."

Halvery hurried on. "Anyway, my point is that my brother was just as good of a climber as I was. He probably would have been just as good of a fighter, just as good of an alpha. But he had a near-miss that wasn't a miss. He was unlucky for one moment when he was small and inexperienced. I got a second chance. And you'd better believe I was more careful next time I went hunting. I got smarter because of what happened to us, but he just got dead.

"Arcove had plenty of near-misses. He got lucky sometimes, and he got smarter. But now we've made this…gentler world. A world where ferryshaft don't eat cubs, and males don't fight to the death nearly so often. Carmine hasn't had all those near-misses. He hasn't had those ugly fights to season him, to make him quick, to make him wary. I promise you that somewhere in Arcove's head, he's fighting for his life every single time. But not Carmine. It makes a difference."

Costa was hanging on his every word. Halvery was beginning to feel self-conscious, so he stopped talking.

"Kelsy nearly killed Storm when he was a foal," said Costa thoughtfully. "I guess Storm had a lot of near-misses."

Halvery snorted. "Storm had *so* many! With me, for sure. With Roup, with Arcove, with all of us. He was running for his life from the time he was little. He got good because he had to. Because otherwise, he'd be dead. You, though." Halvery gave her a playful nudge. "You know that if I pin you, the worst I'm going to do is carry you down to the water and dump you in the lake."

Costa giggled.

"You were tired at the end of a long night," continued Halvery. "You were thirsty, and you got careless…because you knew that there was no real risk. Animals who succeed at difficult tasks do it because they *have to*. Because the only thing worse than what they have to do in order to win is what will happen to them if they *don't* win."

"Do you think we're weak?" asked Costa. "My generation?" She didn't sound defensive, just curious.

Halvery flicked his short tail. He thought about Moashi and his particular brand of politicking. *"You are the past. I am the future."*

"I don't know, Costa. Maybe the future needs different skills."

"Do you miss your brother?"

He shot her a suspicious look. "Of course not. It was a long time ago." Even as he said it, he remembered with shocking clarity that first night alone. They'd been the only cubs in the litter, and while Halvery had half-siblings in the den, there were no others of the same age. The absence of his brother's heartbeat had seemed like the loudest sound in the world.

Halvery had been a precocious cub and mostly weaned at that point, but after his brother's death, he'd stopped eating. After three days, his mother had invited him to nurse again. That was a hazy period in his memory, full of the low throb of her purring—a sound that was equal parts comfort for Halvery and grief for her dead cub. He'd been weaned a second time almost a year later, with none of the fanfare of the first. It had taken him many years to form another close bond with a companion.

Costa was watching him, as though she didn't believe what he'd just said. "What was his name?"

I am not sharing that with a ferryshaft. Halvery ignored her question. "I know you don't like the way Storm is treating you. You want to have those near-misses and get better. But just remember: you could just as easily be my brother instead of me. In the beginning, there's only the smallest difference between the ones who get better and the ones who get dead. Sometimes it's just luck."

A long silence. At last, Costa sighed and said, "I guess you're not going to tell me how you met Roup."

Halvery yawned. "Oh, I barely remember meeting him. I was much more interested in meeting Arcove. I was four and I'd been expelled from my den. I'd heard about this amazing cub my age who was leading a clutter and had killed a king's officer when he was only two. I went to see him fight, and I was so impressed, I asked to join. Arcove had a pretty, golden beta with him. I tried to make friends, but Roup wouldn't even speak to me at first. I found out years later that he was afraid I'd notice that he sounded like a ferryshaft. At the time, I figured he didn't think much of me. Roup didn't think much of anyone. Except Arcove. To be fair, no one ever compares favorably against Arcove."

Costa smiled. "Teek says you and Roup are going to have a litter of cubs with Ilsa."

"Any day now," said Halvery. "I wish we'd gotten to see them before we left."

"Are you worried that Sedaron's ferryshaft will—?"

Halvery growled. He hadn't meant to. It just came out—a bone-rattling snarl that made Costa jump.

"I'm sorry, I'm sorry." She leaned up and licked his muzzle, making him flinch away in surprise. "They wouldn't. Not in your den. They wouldn't dare."

Don't be so sure.

A long silence.

Then Costa piped up again, "Roup seems so nice. And he is. But he's hard to get to know. Wisteria is like that, too. You think at first she's easy to make friends with, because she's kind to you. But after a while, you realize that she thinks about everything she says five times before she says it, and she's rearranged all her words to show you exactly what she wants to show you and nothing else. I wonder sometimes what her first thoughts are, whether she tells them to anyone. Teek, probably, and Carmine sometimes. Trying to get to know her is like following one of Storm's trails—with all the backtracking and misdirection."

Halvery laughed. "That's Roup, too."

Costa grinned at him. "But you're a straight line. Whatever you're thinking comes right out your mouth."

Halvery's ears settled back. "Well, I've never been accused of clever—"

"You're my favorite."

Halvery blinked at her.

"But don't tell anyone I said so," whispered Costa.

Halvery gave her a lick across the top of the head. "Well, you are my favorite ferryshaft foal, although that's not saying much."

After a moment, Costa continued softly, "I know about the war and the culls and the rebellion. I've heard all the stories and read the Cave of Histories. But it's still so hard for me to understand why anyone would want to hurt you or Roup or Lyndi or Wisteria or any creasia. I think you're wonderful."

Halvery was saved from trying to formulate a response to this when Storm came gliding out of the trees, walking so softly that not a leaf crunched. "Well, this is interesting. Costa, you were supposed to be traveling with Sauny. Why are you out here bothering Halvery?"

"I'm not bothering him. He likes me."

Storm snorted. "He *tolerates* you."

"No, he likes me." Costa got up. "Are we really that far ahead of others?"

"Not too far," said Storm. "They'll start arriving any moment. I'm sure they'll sleep here."

Costa jumped up. "I have to tell Jaden that I found walking fish in a pond out on the plain. He thinks they're interesting."

"Who is Jaden?" asked Halvery as Costa trotted away.

"Valla's foal by Kelsy," said Storm with a hint of displeasure.

"Ah, so she does have some ferryshaft friends," said Halvery.

Storm sat down with a grumbling noise. "*Was* she bothering you?"

"No. She gave me a fairly entertaining night's run."

"Really? How'd she do?"

"Very well until the end, when she got tired and careless."

Storm grunted. "She is *not* ready."

Halvery chose his words carefully. "I don't think she would have made that mistake if she'd thought I was going to kill her."

Storm didn't react, which made Halvery think he'd heard this argument before.

"You've got to let her have some near-misses, Storm."

"Why?" he snapped. "Why does she need to do anything dangerous?"

Because she's just like you.

Storm was looking at him suspiciously and Halvery decided he was sticking his nose where it didn't belong. "How are your curbs?"

Storm smiled again. "They're not *my* curbs."

"Well, they're certainly not Leeshwood's."

"You know, you could just apologize to Cohal."

"For what? Defending myself? Chasing you? I stopped that fight as fast as I could, but you knew what you were doing when you led us into them, and it had exactly the effect you intended." Halvery bit down on the words, feeling absurd. Storm hadn't been quite as old as Costa during that chase.

But Storm didn't make excuses. Instead, he said, "If Eyal and his pack hadn't helped Sauny free the ferryshaft from Moro, you would have died on Kuwee Island, along with Arcove and Roup and all the rest of us out there. Eyal was killed in that fight. He was my friend. He was Cohal's friend and his alpha. Cohal doesn't feel like Leeshwood ever properly acknowledged the curbs' assistance or their sacrifice. I have to agree with him."

Halvery flicked his tail in exasperation. "You know Arcove doesn't *say* things. He *does* things. He really is doing everything he can to help them find any lost kin who may be lurking in those mountains, but the odds are poor. Arcove can't create highland curbs where none exist."

Storm sighed. "I know." He hesitated. "Thank you for tolerating Costa and giving her some pointers."

"She is my favorite foal," said Halvery cheerfully.

"I believe she is the only foal you know."

"Also true."

Storm was about to walk away when Halvery called after him, "Did Roup stay with you all night?"

"No, he struck off on his own after a while. Said he wanted to think."

Halvery frowned. "Do you know what he's brooding about?"

"I thought it must be that litter you two left behind."

Halvery frowned. "No. It's something else."

* * * *

This chapter includes an author's note at the end of the book.

4

Cozy

About fifty ferryshaft had come south with Arcove's party. They were a mixture of Sauny's herd, long-time residents of Roup's territory, and ferryshaft who'd fled into Leeshwood when Sedaron began attacking them. The delegation from Kelsy's herd was also accompanying them as far as the foothills. The ferryshaft had switched themselves to a creasia's nighttime schedule for this expedition, but most of them were not accustomed to it, and they were clearly feeling the strain.

Halvery remained by the water as the sky turned from gray to gold to pale blue. He watched as the grove filled with sleepy ferryshaft, who picked nuts off the ground and the lower branches of the trees, and then lay down in small groups.

The creasia had settled down mostly at the northern end of the grove, where tall grass mingled with the trees and a bit of underbrush. Unlike ferryshaft, creasia sometimes went without a substantial meal for two or three days, and none of them had expected to find much to eat between Leeshwood and the foothills. Still, Halvery had managed to catch some small game on his way across the plain, and he felt sure that many others had done the same or would by tomorrow night.

The creasia were resting in groups, mostly according to their clutters. Cats from the same territory had a similar scent, and creasia found this comforting in unfamiliar terrain. Halvery passed Moashi's clutter bedding down in the leaves, and was disgusted to see Moashi flopped over onto his back between a couple of his officers, exactly as though he'd been the runt of the litter instead of their alpha. *Have some dignity, Ears.* They looked content, though. They were all grooming each other.

Stefan and his clutter had gone off together to hunt on the plain. Hollygold's were curled up in a defensive ring—doubtless a habit from all the patrolling they'd done out here last summer and fall. Flurry was in the center. Halvery suspected they'd been told to keep an eye on him.

He spotted his own cats settling down together. The ten he'd chosen were males in their twenties and early thirties—excellent fighters with good common sense. He'd left his beta behind as his most suitable successor if he did not return, but his acting beta was one of his favorites—a quick-witted den alpha who often won their friendly tournaments and who'd stood with Arcove's supporters on Kuwee Island during the rebellion. Halvery liked this group. They would follow orders unquestioningly.

But as he spotted them settling down to sleep, talking and laughing, it occurred to him that they all knew each other better than they knew him. Not one of them had been alive during Ketch's reign. Not one of them had fought in the ferryshaft wars or watched

Arcove beat Coden on Turis Rock. They would have been just as horrified as Costa by Halvery's casual description of his brother's brutal death between ferryshaft teeth. These cats had grown up thinking of ferryshaft as beaten cowards. Later they'd come to think of them as allies and even friends, but never as merciless predators. The thought came to Halvery unbidden: *I am from another world.*

"You are the past. I am the future."

He watched them grooming each other, telling jokes, and thought, *If I go over there, they'll stop.* He'd never encouraged familiarity from his subordinates. It suddenly seemed unkind to burden them with his presence. *There was a nice crook in that tree by the water. I'll just hop up there, try to keep one eye open for danger. We really ought to put some sentries in the trees...*

"Looking for a place to sleep, Halvery?" He turned to see Lyndi at his shoulder. She was giving him a sad smile, as though she knew what he'd been thinking.

Halvery considered saying something curt, but then he only muttered, "Surely we need a sentry."

"Arcove already assigned a rotation."

"Oh." He felt guilty for not knowing this. *I suppose I disappeared all night without an explanation.* He wondered whether he was in trouble.

"You weren't on that rotation," said Lyndi patiently. "None of the officers were...or any of the older cats."

He sputtered and she butted her head against his shoulder. "Come on, come sleep with us."

He started to ask who she meant by "us," and then just followed her through the grove into the dense, tall grass on the edge of the plain. Carmine's clutter was resting there. Carmine and Teek were curled up back-to-back in the middle with the others nestled around them. Halvery recognized two of these cats as his contemporaries—Roup's officers from before the war. *Wise of Carmine if he decides to keep them. They're experienced, but about as gentle as you could expect in an officer of that era—Roup's picks.*

He expected Lyndi to lie down beside them, but she didn't. She went a little further into the tall grass, which was almost head-height to an adult creasia. They came abruptly upon Arcove and Roup, lying against each other with their heads pointed in opposite directions, the way they usually slept when they were far from home. Roup glanced up and Lyndi said, "I told you he wasn't with his clutter. He was getting ready to curl up alone."

Halvery made a grumbling sound. "I was getting ready to climb a tree and keep watch; somebody should."

"Somebody already is," said Roup. "Come lie down. Storm said you played hide-and-hunt with Costa all night."

Arcove had his head up, too, now. "Are the ferryshaft still getting along with each other? I was concerned that Storm and Kelsy might have a fight."

Halvery rolled his eyes. "No fights that I saw. I apologize for disappearing all night."

"Nothing important happened," said Arcove, "but I would appreciate it if you kept a little closer as we approach the mountains."

"Yes, sir." After a moment's consideration, Halvery stretched out beside Roup.

He lay down *beside* him, not *against* him, but Lyndi flopped down practically on top of Halvery, forcing him to slide over against Roup, which made both of them laugh. "Do only the youngsters get to be cozy?" complained Lyndi cheerfully. "Halvery, you're muddy. You smell like a pond." She started grooming his back and then nibbled into his ribs.

Halvery laughed. He stretched out on his stomach and said, "That's because Costa led me through one."

"Did she dump you in it? Were there curbs involved?"

"No, but not for lack of her trying."

To Halvery's embarrassment, Roup started grooming his chest and forepaws. *Am I really so muddy that I need two of you to clean me up?* But it felt comforting. His eyes were already sliding shut. After a moment, he put his head down across Roup's paws and let him nibble over his ears and shoulders. He realized a moment later that Arcove was grooming Roup. By the time they were done, they all smelled more-or-less like they'd come from the same clutter. Halvery felt relaxed and dozy.

Roup rolled onto his side with Arcove's head across his stomach and flank. Halvery had his head against Roup's chest. Lyndi was snug against his side with her head over his back, and he felt… safe…like he belonged here, with cats who understood him, even if they didn't always agree with him.

Halvery found himself thinking about his brother again. He remembered that time before he'd ever been alone. He and his brother had slept in a pile with the spring cubs and a few two-year-olds, sometimes with his mother, sometimes with one of the other den mothers. The composition of the pile had changed from night to night, but Halvery and his brother had always stayed together. His brother's heartbeat had been a constant—something Halvery had taken for granted every day of his life, until that terrible night when it stopped forever.

He pressed the side of his face against Roup's chest, listening to the steady thump of his heart. Roup's voice murmured sleepily near his ear. "Halvery, is something wrong?"

I don't know. "You're the one who went off alone all night."

Roup took a breath as though to respond, and then just gave his ear a lick. Halvery drifted off to sleep, listening to that steady thump, thump, thump.

5

Into the Mountains

They were traveling again by sunset and reached the foothills by the following dawn. There was plenty of small game near the water, and the creasia all took advantage of the opportunity to hunt as much as possible. Kelsy's party was planning to rest and then strike out in the direction of his herd in the late afternoon.

Halvery got the impression that some kind of resolution had been achieved between Storm and the others. He seemed to be talking to his sister again, and Halvery caught sight of Storm and Kelsy watching the sunrise on the edge of the lake. He heard Kelsy say, "I hate fighting with you."

Storm's teeth flashed. "Because you always lose?"

Halvery walked with Arcove, Roup, and Lyndi for most of the night, talking about the relative strengths and weaknesses of the current set of officers and their clutters. "Stefan's cats are very skilled, but he brought one of Treace's old officers," Halvery confided. "I know that fellow can fight, but I'm not sure it was a good decision. Stefan seems convinced that he doesn't have any attachments to Thistle's cats or to Dazzle. I believe that Stefan believes that, but…"

They talked about Moashi's relatively inexperienced clutter, all of them less than fifteen. "It was that or bring sixty-year-olds, Halvery," argued Roup. "He doesn't have many in between who are both loyal to him and reasonably skilled. I think he was wise to leave his best twenty and thirty-year-olds behind. The clutter will need them if he doesn't come back."

"Well, I won't deny that the clutter will barely miss the ones he brought," said Halvery with exaggerated malice.

"They'll come back better fighters if they come back at all," said Arcove. "Is Carmine's clutter accepting his leadership? Lyndi, are they asking you to verify his orders?"

"They seem content to follow him," said Lyndi. "I haven't spoken to any of them since we left."

Roup stifled a laugh. To Arcove, he said, "I notice that you're not wondering whether they're asking *me* to verify his orders."

"That's because Lyndi has been leading your clutter for over a year," said Halvery sweetly. "Really, I don't know why she hasn't challenged you."

Lyndi responded in the same lighthearted tone, "You suppose I can beat him if you can't, Halvery?"

"Oh, he doesn't dislike you enough to beat you."

Roup gave Halvery's shoulder a shove. "By what convoluted logic could anybody argue that I dislike you?"

Halvery almost made some remark about how Roup had been avoiding him the entire journey, but it would have sounded absurd. Roup curled up beside him again that night, and Arcove lay down with his head over Halvery's back, which made Halvery feel quite welcome. Lyndi cuddled up on the other side of Roup and gave a brief, contented purr. It was more companionable than Halvery would have imagined possible outside his own den.

And yet, Roup made sure that he and Halvery were never alone. If the group split up, even to do something as minor as get a drink of water, Roup went with Arcove or Lyndi, never with Halvery. It was starting to make Halvery feel as though he was being punished for something.

That's not it, he told himself. *Roup is just afraid I'll ask him what's wrong.*

He was drifting off to sleep that night, when it occurred to him to ask another question—one so obvious that he felt he should have thought of it sooner. "Arcove, if I run into Dazzle up there, what would you like me to do? Tell me now, because I'm going to want to rip the rest of his face off."

Halvery felt Roup's breathing still. It was one of his few tells. Arcove didn't have any tells as far as Halvery had ever been able to discern. He murmured, "What I want you to do is follow orders."

Halvery was confused. *I'm asking you what those orders are.* But Arcove didn't sound like he wanted to talk about it, and Halvery had already learned what he really wanted to know. *This is what Roup is upset about. But if Arcove is committed to killing Dazzle, why didn't he just say so? And if he's not committed to killing him, why is Roup unhappy?*

Halvery woke at evening to find Costa folded into the crook of his neck against his shoulder, hemmed in by one of Arcove's hind legs and Roup's tail. "Do you have *any* sense of self-preservation?" whispered Halvery. "Any natural instincts *at all*, Costa?"

She yawned. "You think I shouldn't lie down with the elderly?" Halvery put a paw on top of her, but she continued with a giggle, "Your hearing is deteriorating, and you need a sentry."

"I am going to carry you to the lake like a fawn, and I don't care if you panic."

Arcove and Roup were both stirring. Lyndi had already gone off somewhere. Arcove yawned, white teeth flashing against black fur. "Costa, I would say that I'm sorry you are not going into the mountains with us, but I try not to tell lies."

"Because you're worried I'll get hurt?"

Halvery chimed in, "No, because you are annoying."

She sighed. "I was *supposed* to come get you, but you looked so cozy that I lay down with you instead."

"Come get us why?" asked Roup. He sounded tired. Halvery didn't think he'd been sleeping well, cozy or not.

"Keesha is here," said Costa.

That made Roup sit up. He looked at Arcove and laughed. "I told you."

Arcove rose with a grumbling sound, but then he laughed, too. "I really doubt he has come to tell me good-bye, Roup."

"No, he'll have invented some excuse."

"He says the ely-ary brought him more news," interjected Costa.

"See?" said Arcove to Roup.

Roup just smiled. He and Halvery trailed Arcove out of the tall grass, through the trees to the edge of the lake, where Keesha was waiting in the glassy dawn glow of the water. His coils created furry hummocks, scattered about in the shallows. Storm and Sauny were already talking to him. He'd brought his head down level with theirs, but he raised it when he saw the creasia.

"Arcove. An ely-ary came to visit me this morning."

"Have Thistle's cats solved their own problems?" asked Arcove with weary sarcasm. "Are they coming down out of the mountains to meet us?"

"Unfortunately not," said Keesha. "There has been fighting around the entrance to the upper valley. The ely-ary described it as a battle. She says that there are still creasia in the upper valley and still many ferryshaft in the lower, but there was confusion for several days with bodies on the ground, and ferryshaft milling about."

Arcove frowned. "Could she tell who won?"

"I am afraid that was unclear."

Roup looked thoughtful. "I would guess that the creasia tried to escape from the valley."

"Or the ferryshaft tried to breach it," put in Halvery.

"It sounds like neither succeeded," muttered Arcove.

"I wanted you to know that fighting had already begun," continued Keesha. "By the time you arrive, those cats may all be dead."

Arcove was silent a moment, thinking. At last, he glanced at Roup and Halvery. "Your advice, councilors?"

"You know what I think," said Roup. "They're not dead yet."

"Halvery?" said Arcove.

Halvery hesitated. "I would expect Thistle's cats to give a good account of themselves, sir. Dazzle certainly did. If Sedaron manages to kill them, it will cost him. His numbers will be reduced. He'll have injured animals. His ferryshaft will be tired, but also giddy with victory. I can't think of a better time to ambush them.

Even with our smaller party, we could take them by surprise and do considerable damage. We'll be fresh and they won't. We could harry them all the way out of the mountains."

"If they've won, something like that will be necessary," said Roup, "because after they rest and regroup, we're next."

Halvery and Roup glanced at each other sidelong. *Apparently we agree about this.*

Arcove relaxed. "Then we're still going up there."

Halvery thought that Keesha looked disappointed. "I will try to send another eagle, Arcove, but there have been storms up there recently—rain and snow. It is dangerous at this time of year in the canyons. Be careful."

They said their farewells to the ferryshaft soon afterwards and struck off into the dry foothills, following a stream that Hollygold told them had not been running in summer or fall. "This is the easy time of year," Moali said. She and Cohal were anxious to get up into the mountains as soon as possible. This stream was running because of snowmelt. Every day that passed would mean thinner ice.

Storm and the curbs led the way as scouts, with Hollygold and his clutter not far behind them. Flurry wasn't saying much. As far as Halvery could tell, Arcove wasn't consulting him, which was a relief. *I don't trust Thistle's cats. I don't trust their message or their odd messenger.*

As expected, this was difficult country with little to eat, although spring had brought unwary baby ground squirrels and diminutive desert pigs into the world. Small fish, frogs, and crustaceans were zipping around in the shallow, muddy streams. Birds and rabbits could be caught, but they were fast and small. An adult creasia would have had to spend all night hunting to fill his belly. Arcove's party didn't try. They grabbed whatever prey they could manage and pushed on, through the scrublands and the jagged canyons of the lower peaks, up and up, where the winds blew colder.

Halvery was not surprised when their officers' clutter disintegrated on the third night out from the lake. "Carmine's cats say they miss me," said Lyndi apologetically. "I suppose I've been so anxious to support his authority that I've been rather cold with them. Teek asked if they'd done something to offend me."

Roup laughed. "For them, you're a den mother and a commanding officer rolled into one."

Lyndi harrumphed. "I am nobody's den mother."

"Go sleep with them," said Roup. "You won't undermine Carmine's authority in the slightest."

That left Halvery with Arcove and Roup, which felt awkward. Arcove and Roup had always gone off by themselves to sleep when they were on campaigns far from their territory. Halvery had assumed they mated sometimes, although maybe not. Creasia needed a sense of safety in order to be in an amorous frame of mind. Cats pursuing enemies far from home rarely felt safe.

Halvery found that he wanted to groom Roup simply for the comfort of it, but he didn't dare groom Arcove. Arcove had never encouraged familiarity from his subordinates any more than Halvery had. He didn't usually let Roup behave in an affectionate manner when other officers were present. Halvery was aware that Arcove's willingness to let Roup wash his face and lick his ears in Halvery's presence was, in itself, a compliment and a sign of trust.

And yet he couldn't help wondering whether Arcove really *liked* seeing Halvery grooming his den-mate. Male creasia were not normally jealous of each other. They were instinctively jealous and possessive of female mates, but not males. What would be the point? There were no cubs whose paternity could be questioned, and males did not have brief windows of sexual receptivity in the same way as females. There was no reason to be possessive of another male.

And yet... *Arcove and Roup have an unusually close bond. Arcove wants Roup to be happy, and I guess sometimes I make him happy. But there's a difference between sanctioning something you can't see and watching it happen right under your nose.*

Halvery knew that Ilsa intended to leave his den for Moashi's at some point. He'd made jokes about it and given Moashi advice.

And yet Halvery had no interest in actually watching them flirt or mate. *Maybe Arcove feels the same way about Roup.*

He wished he knew how to ask. *"I would not hurt you for the world, sir. I certainly wouldn't anger you. Please tell me whether you like seeing me draped across the person you love most in the world."* But he couldn't imagine saying such a thing to Arcove.

Instead, he simply excused himself. "My clutter needs a bit of guidance now that we're getting into difficult country, sir."

No one called him back. In truth, Halvery wasn't sure Roup really wanted him around right now, either. He was still avoiding being alone with Halvery, although he spoke to him warmly in company and seemed perfectly happy to have Halvery draped across his shoulders. *Maybe with me gone, you and Arcove will talk about whatever it is that's bothering you. Maybe Arcove doesn't care one bit whether I groom your ears, but he* does *need to say things to his beta that his number three doesn't need to hear.*

There'd been a time when Halvery had wanted so badly to be part of those conversations. He'd been terribly jealous of Arcove's trust and attention. Now Halvery was content with his role. He visited with his clutter, who seemed relieved to have him in their midst again. He watched with amusement as they jockeyed delicately for his favor. He tried to make their order of rank extremely clear, so that no one would question the chain of command during a crisis.

"Let's get something straight," he told them on the fifth night out from the lake. "If I die up there in a bad place, I want no heroics. No one else dies trying to get what's left of my tail; understand? I'll make my way to the Ghost Wood the old-fashioned way."

"If we can get it easily, sir, who do you want us to give it to?" asked his acting beta.

Halvery hesitated. "Velta. Although…let Roup take it to her."

Then they were all whispering to each other, voicing their own preferences in the event that their tails must be carried home. Halvery let the somber mood stretch. *You're a little scared now. Good. Take this seriously. We are doing something serious.*

When he decided that the fatalism had gone on long enough, he said, "But if you get hold of Dazzle's tail, I expect you to fling it off the nearest cliff straight away. Preferably with the rest of him attached."

Yowls of laughter.

"Before or after he's dead, sir?"

"Oh, I don't care. I expect he'll be dead when he hits the bottom in any case."

Halvery let them spar a little, although not enough to waste precious energy. He spent several nights pointing out likely-looking ambush spots if they needed to lie in wait for Sedaron's returning herd. He discussed the advantages and disadvantages of the terrain, and he hunted with them at dawn and dusk, bringing down one large pig on the sixth night, which they all shared with desperate relish. They were starting to feel the strain of physical exertion on small meals.

After the first day of steep climbing, both the curbs and Hollygold's cats advised two nights of rest. "The air is thin. You get used to it, but if you try to push too fast, you get sick."

It certainly felt like running was harder than it ought to be. Halvery's right shoulder hurt by the time they stopped to rest among the first tall trees they'd seen since the lake. He hadn't noticed the pain for most of a year, but he didn't usually spend all day climbing, either. He couldn't help noticing that Roup was favoring his left hind leg. *Ghosts take you, Dazzle. I really do hope someone tosses you off a cliff. I hope Sedaron has already done it, so that Roup doesn't have to watch.*

6

Above the Clouds

They rested for two nights, hunting aggressively, but not climbing higher. The game was still mostly small, so they split up. Nobody asked anyone else what they'd caught. Halvery managed a few birds and tree-climbing rodents, but he went to sleep hungrier each night, as he suspected everyone else did.

They moved on and spent three grueling days climbing over broken ground, with the occasional respite in scrubby clearings under cold stars. They came upon waterfalls and an increasing number of streams. They encountered more underbrush.

At last, they surprised some shaggy, horned creatures at a waterfall's bowl, and the clutters went after them en masse. They spent an inordinate amount of energy in pursuit, but managed to run down the herd. They cut out three animals and killed them with only one serious injury. Naturally, the cat who'd gotten kicked was one of Moashi's. The unfortunate nine-year-old was gasping with pain and probably had a broken rib.

"What do I do?" whispered Moashi to Halvery when they'd eaten. The entire company was red with gore, but pleasantly sated, panting clouds of steam in the chilly air.

"Haven't you thought about what you will do with injured clutter members?" asked Halvery severely. "Did you expect all of them to walk through this unscathed, Ears? As green as they are?"

Moashi shut his eyes. "Please don't lecture me; I'm worried. I'm not sure he can keep up."

Halvery relented. "Of course he can't keep up. You'll need to either leave him here or send him back to the lake. He'll have a hard time finding enough food either way, especially since he's in no shape to hunt. But if you force him to try to keep up with the rest of us, he'll almost certainly die."

Moashi winced. "I was afraid you'd say that. There's nothing else to do?"

"There's nothing else."

Halvery watched him going off to talk to his trembling subordinate. The rest of Moashi's clutter had made certain that the injured cat got something to eat. They were obviously bonded to each other and distressed about the fate of their companion. *Bonds like that can work for and against you,* thought Halvery. He couldn't help thinking of Arcove, disappearing into a telshee cave for ten days with Roup hovering between life and death. *What on earth am I going to do if something happens to one of them?*

Storm and the curbs did not attempt to share in the feast. Storm was finding plenty of forage as the woods grew greener, and the curbs were smaller than creasia and more able to feed themselves on small game. They'd been ranging far out ahead of the clutters, but were sticking closer as they got higher into the mountains.

"We passed the scat of lowland curbs," said Cohal.

"It was at least a month old," put in Storm, "probably some of the ones who accompanied Sedaron's herd into the mountains."

"I suppose they are not the same as the packs who live here?" asked Roup.

"Correct," said Storm. "In fact, there is likely to be conflict between the curbs Sedaron brought and those who usually live in the mountains. We'll start encountering curbs soon—or, at least, they'll spot us—but with any luck, they will not report our presence to Sedaron. His curbs are probably not ranging far from the ferryshaft herd, on account of being invaders in other packs' territories."

"Did the ferryshaft come into the mountains this way?" asked Halvery doubtfully. "I'm surprised we haven't passed evidence of their foraging."

"No," said Storm. "They took an easier, more easterly route. We are taking a more difficult, more direct route that will get us into the valley faster. However, we will soon encounter their trail, and then I think we need to be more careful. If Sedaron's curbs spot us, we'll lose the advantage of surprise."

Water was everywhere now, and the land was lush with greenery. Large trees towered overhead, their branches constantly murmuring in the high winds. Occasionally, the thorny underbrush was so thick that the creasia had to struggle to find their way higher.

They stopped again for a full night in order to adjust to the thin air. Halvery was hunting alone when he encountered hoofprints near a shallow stream. He stared for a long moment. The hoof was definitely solid, not split, and the prints were a little too small to be Storm's. The animal had only left the water for a moment, and no distinctive scent lingered.

Have Sedaron's scouts found us? But Halvery already knew the print was too small for that. Sedaron would never send juveniles after them.

Costa. It had to be. *Should I tell Storm?* Halvery thought of that suspicious look on Storm's face when he'd tried to talk to him about his daughter beside the lake. *Maybe he already knows. In any case, she's a young adult. If she's determined to have those near-misses, well… She'll either be me or she'll be my brother. Nothing anyone can do about it.*

On the ninth day, they came to a high pass between jagged peaks. Sedaron's ferryshaft had definitely been this way. Evidence of their foraging was everywhere, and the trampled underbrush made the narrow pass a little easier to navigate.

Halvery paused to stare down the slopes from which they'd come. Clouds lay like clumps of fur over the forest, obscuring the view. However, as he watched, the wind blew an opening, and he glimpsed the entire island laid out below in shades of green and blue and umber. Halvery had always thought the view from the Red Cliffs was spectacular, but he'd never been this high before and it took his breath away.

He was suddenly aware of Roup beside him. "I remember that," he whispered, "from the last time I was up here. I remember I felt like a bird."

Halvery looked sidelong at him. His experience of that incident had been very different. Roup and Arcove had disappeared for most of a month the first summer after Arcove became king, leaving Halvery in charge of Leeshwood. He'd felt flattered, but also confused and excluded. They'd never told him where they'd gone. They certainly hadn't told him they'd visited the Southern Mountains with Coden.

They'd come back happy. He remembered that. He'd kept waiting for some explanation, or at least an acknowledgement that he'd held things together in their absence without taking advantage of the opportunity to further his own agenda. But Arcove and Roup had returned to Leeshwood happy and carefree and completely uninterested in explaining themselves to their third in command. Halvery had felt bitter about it for a while, bewildered, but he'd never been one to brood and had eventually forgotten about it.

Not until years later, during Treace's rebellion, had Halvery learned where his king and commanding officer had vanished to during his brief reign. Roup had finally explained himself with Arcove dying at his feet. By that point, Halvery's jealousy and hurt feelings had seemed like a petty, juvenile complaint. He would have been embarrassed to even mention it.

Now, though, he had a dizzy sense of the past and future running together—to be up here with Roup, sharing this view. Arcove completed the sense of unreality by coming up behind them. The wind was gusting, and he spoke in Halvery's ear so that he didn't have to shout. "We'll follow the ridge even higher for a while beyond this canyon. It's uncomfortable, but by the end of the day, we'll descend into greener places. Tell your cats, and send one of them to tell the other officers: we'll have good hunting tonight, but don't try to hunt on the ridge."

"Yes, sir."

Halvery saw what he meant as they came out of the canyon. The ground dropped off in a long sweep of green to a river valley far below, but this was not their destination. Instead, Storm and the curbs led them up a steep ascent, along a spine of rock that wound ever higher, past the line of greenery, to the barren gray of desolate shale. They traveled above the tree line for most of the day with inviting valleys on either side. "These valleys are not where we are going," said Moali.

They glimpsed herds of sheep in the hazy distance, and sometimes the darting shapes of curbs, who guarded them. The lowland curbs were appearing more and more frequently now, sometimes outlined against the distant sky upon a ridge. *But they wouldn't dare attack such a large group of creasia,* thought Halvery. He glanced at Cohal and Maoli, who were sticking close to the group now. *You two can walk safely only because of us. I'd better not hear any more nonsense about how we're no real friends to highland curbs.*

He thought of Costa. A lone, three-year-old ferryshaft would be easy prey for a pack of curbs. *She'd better follow closely or not at all. If she's wise, she went back to the lake. But, she's Storm's foal, so probably not.*

Dawn broke in stunning shades of pink and gold over the sea of clouds. "We shouldn't stop to rest up here," Maoli told them. "We'll be down among the trees again soon enough." It was broad daylight by the time they began to descend from the ridge into a high, green valley. All the creasia were blinking. They were exhausted, thirsty, and hungry. There'd been no water on the ridge, and the rocks were sharp and crusted with ice.

Storm and the curbs brought them to a pretty spot beside a waterfall that cascaded in dripping icicles down a steep ridge. The waterfall's bowl formed a small lake at the bottom, before running away into several streams in varying states of thaw. The water of the lake was frozen in the center, though thawing at the edges. There were drifts of snow on the ground around it. Spring green showed everywhere, sticking up through the crust of ice.

The creasia lapped the chilly water on the edge of the lake or gulped mouthfuls of snow. They panted clouds of steam and stretched out in the sunny places beside the water, too exhausted to hunt.

Arcove went among them, talking quietly to his officers, and trying to ascertain which cats might have enough energy left to keep watch. At last, he called them all to sit in a crescent around him. "Our destination is just over that ridge," he said quietly. "The lower valley is long with a deep lake at the bottom. We are at the western end. Sedaron's ferryshaft will be clustered at the eastern end, around the entrance to the slot canyons that lead to the upper valley. That is where Thistle's cats are cornered. We will need to make contact with those cats before deciding what to do next. In the meantime, Sedaron must not learn that we are here."

He hesitated, and Hollygold spoke up. "My clutter has been up here recently, and I can tell you that the valley and the lake beyond that ridge are substantial. Even a thousand ferryshaft will have plenty to eat down there and no reason to come in this direction unless we give them one. If we stay quiet over here, I don't think they'll find us. Not unless we get unlucky with a scout. There is game in this area. Just don't be drawn into chasing something over the ridge. Keep close to this little lake, and we should be able to stay out of sight, at least for a few days."

Arcove assigned a rotation of sentries. "As soon as we've all had a rest, I'll send out scouts to look for herds of ice oxen or boar," he told them. "There's enough of us that we should be able to kill a few large animals, rather than hunting small game all night long. I want no excuse for anybody wandering over that ridge and giving alarm to the ferryshaft."

"Sir?" It was Flurry. Halvery had hardly heard two sentences out of him the entire journey. "I'd like permission to make contact with my people this evening. After I've rested, I'm sure I can do it. I've gotten in and out of those canyons before. Sedaron's cats will simply see one of Thistle's scouts if they see me at all."

"No," said Arcove flatly.

Flurry looked surprised and then apprehensive. "With respect, Arcove, you will have great difficulty making contact with Thistle if he doesn't come out to meet you. I know that Storm and the highland curbs can run on canyon walls, but—"

"I realize that someone will have to alert Thistle to my presence," said Arcove, "but an ely-ary reported a battle up here a few days ago. It sounded serious. Who would be in charge of your group if Thistle is dead?"

A long silence. Flurry's eyes darted everywhere except Arcove's face. "I...I don't know, sir."

Liar, thought Halvery. *It's probably Dazzle. Ghosts. No wonder Arcove doesn't want to commit to a course of action.*

Arcove didn't press Flurry for an answer, which made Halvery feel certain that he was thinking the same thing. "I want to have a look around," said Arcove quietly. "I want to count the surviving ferryshaft and see how they're positioned. I want a workable plan for how we might extract Thistle's cats. *Then* we will make contact. You will not leave this valley until I say so, Flurry. Is that clear?"

Flurry swallowed and looked at his paws. "Yes, sir."

7

A Job No One Wants

Halvery woke just after sunset with something tickling his whiskers. He opened his eyes to see Lyndi. She was clearly trying to wake him without waking the rest of his exhausted clutter, who were still sound asleep in spite of the evening light.

Halvery extracted himself from the group and followed her towards the lake. "What is it?" he whispered when they reached the edge of the water. He bent to lap at the ice.

"I was sent to tell you that Arcove and Roup have gone to do reconnaissance, and you're in charge," returned Lyndi. She did not sound happy about it.

Halvery raised his head to look at her in surprise. "Reconnaissance?"

"Yes."

He tried to clear his sleep-fogged brain. "They actually said I'm in charge?"

"Yes." Lyndi was watching his face, as if she wanted him to see something that she didn't want to say aloud.

Halvery screwed his eyes shut. "Are you sure they didn't just want some time alone?"

"Anything is possible." She clearly didn't think it likely.

Halvery frowned. Arcove and Roup didn't usually employ the clutter's resources for their personal pleasure. If they'd wanted to talk or mate, they would have done it within earshot of the clutter. They wouldn't have woken Lyndi and then Halvery from well-earned sleep. *So they didn't go off to do anything personal. They went on Leeshwood's business, and that means...* "They went to do something dangerous," he said aloud, "and they went together, because they want to come back together or not at all."

Lyndi let out her breath, as though she'd been worried he wouldn't figure it out.

"Did they say where they were going?"

She looked away. "No."

Halvery cocked his head. "But you have an idea." When she didn't answer, he continued, "Lyndi, do you know why Roup is unhappy? He's been chewing on something this entire journey, and maybe if I was more clever, I could figure it out, but—"

Lyndi's eyes flicked to his face with a miserable expression. "Yes, but I can't tell you. I'm sorry, Halvery. I overheard something I shouldn't have. Roup didn't tell me on purpose. I can't repeat it."

Halvery almost laughed. It was the sort of thing Roup would say. *If you pick a beta who thinks like you, my sneaky friend, don't be surprised that she keeps secrets.* Aloud, he said, "Well, I don't want this job. I'm going after them."

Lyndi gave a mirthless laugh, but she looked relieved. "I don't want this job, either, so you'd better come back."

"I'm not hearing: 'Halvery, that's a terrible idea. Arcove told you to stay here.'"

"Well, he didn't…exactly."

Again, like Roup. "You'd make a good king."

"I wouldn't, though. I'd immediately give it to Carmine."

"Carmine is the lowest ranking officer."

"Yes, but you know Stefan doesn't want it. Neither does Hollygold, and I hope to all the friendly ghosts that Moashi doesn't think he does."

"Surely not," agreed Halvery. "It ought to be you."

Lyndi rolled her eyes. "I cannot believe we're having this conversation."

"Me neither."

"Do you remember that time when Keesha called Arcove into Syriot during the rebellion, and nobody knew who was in charge? I thought you were going to attack Roup, and I thought I was going to have to attack *you*—"

Halvery grimaced. "Stop."

"Sharmel talked you out of it."

"Sharmel just helped me see reason."

Lyndi shook her ears. "Back then, it felt like everybody wanted to be king. Is it better or worse that now nobody does?"

Halvery snorted. "I think we're just old enough to know better." He hesitated and then butted his head against Lyndi's. "I'm sorry."

"Oh, I was not in search of apologies—"

But he rubbed his face against her shoulder until she backed away laughing. "I'll show you where to find their trail."

"*Do* you think this is a bad idea, Lyndi? They always seem to leave me behind without an explanation, and I don't like it, but I guess it's worked out so far..."

She trotted along the edge of the water and then started winding up the ridge. "Neither of them think as clearly when they're not in agreement. Go watch their backs, Halvery. I'll manage things here."

"I really wish you'd tell me what they're arguing about."

"It's not my place to tell."

He caught Roup's scent and then Arcove's. Their trail headed up the ridge towards the lower valley. Lyndi stopped and turned to him. "I'll give Carmine the leadership if none of you come back, because I'll be crippled with grief and in no fit state to lead."

Halvery turned and licked the top of her head. "We'll come back. Arcove will probably send me back the moment he sees me. I'll be lucky if he doesn't box my ears."

Lyndi didn't look convinced. "Watch their backs, Halvery. Don't you dare die."

8

A Little Meaner

Halvery followed Arcove and Roup's trail up the densely wooded ridge. Their scent was very fresh, and they weren't running. Still, he didn't catch sight of them until he reached the top.

Halvery had known the valley was large, but that knowledge hadn't prepared him for the true scope of it. An inviting world stretched beneath his feet—a patchwork of dense trees and open clearings around an immense frozen lake, the ice gleaming black in the light of the rising moon. "The lake is deep," he remembered Maoli saying, "and cold even in summer. It doesn't thaw as fast as the smaller streams."

Halvery spotted the islands that Storm and the curbs would be trying to reach. The wooded dots of land lay like steppingstones from the center of the lake towards the eastern end. Beyond, he glimpsed the narrow opening in the cliffs, which must lead to the upper valley. The bottom of the pass was a jumble of rock, with crisscrossing dark fissures. They looked like hair-line cracks at this distance, but they must, in fact, be the slot canyons through which water gushed into the lower lake. Halvery didn't see the ferryshaft, but there was more than enough cover and space down there for the herd to disappear.

Arcove and Roup's trail did not go down into the valley, but remained on the ridge, running east. Halvery turned to follow it and finally caught a flash of gold through the trees ahead—Roup, winding in and out of the trunks. A shadow moved beside him, and that was Arcove. Halvery ran on, faster now that he was tracking them by sight. He made no attempt to disguise the crunch of his footfalls, and they both turned as he came through the trees. "Halvery…" began Roup in surprise.

He'd been running hard, and he paused to catch his breath.

Arcove spoke with a hint of alarm. "Has something happened? Has there been an attack?"

"No, sir." Halvery realized that he hadn't considered what he would say at this moment. He'd always been one to follow orders, even implied orders, and the implication had surely been to stay with the others.

Arcove frowned, and his green eyes narrowed. After a moment's silence, he said, "Go back to your clutter, councilor."

Halvery found his voice. "Sir, with respect, I would like to accompany you."

"Why?"

It was a reasonable question and invited more of a dialogue than Halvery knew he deserved, yet he could not seem to find his words. He glanced at Roup desperately.

He didn't really expect help, but Roup said, "Let him come, Arcove."

"Why?" repeated Arcove, impatient now.

Halvery opened his mouth to say, "In case you need an extra set of claws," but what actually came out was, "You're doing it again! You leave me in charge without explanations and keep all the secrets and expect me to pick up the pieces if something happens to you!"

Arcove and Roup both stared at him as though he'd grown an extra eyeball.

Halvery could hear his own blood pounding in his ears. *What am I doing? He is going to kill me.* But instead of tucking his tail and apologizing, he continued, "Maybe I don't want to outlive the two of you! Ever think of that? Maybe I don't want to come back if you don't!"

Halvery shut his eyes. *Kill me if you like.*

He flinched when Roup began licking his muzzle. To his embarrassment, he heard himself whisper, "Please don't leave me behind again. Please…"

And then Arcove's broad tongue ran over the top of his head. "Alright, Halvery. Calm down."

Halvery remembered to breathe. He opened his eyes, but couldn't bear to look at their faces. Roup was licking him hard enough to shove his head to one side.

After a moment, Arcove said, "I thought you *liked* being left in charge. You…do a good job."

Halvery felt so embarrassed. *Why did I say those things out loud?* "I appreciate the compliment, sir. I know you would not leave me in charge if you didn't…didn't trust me—" Halvery could almost hear Roup say, *"He trusted you with me."*

Halvery forced his way onward, through the mire of thoughts and feelings that he struggled to articulate. "But we have all lived longer than any alpha creasia in memory. We're in unfamiliar territory, literally and historically, and I…I'd rather just…let the next generation have their turn, sir…if you're gone."

"Well, then I suppose we'd better go get Lyndi, too," said Roup with a smile.

Halvery gave an uneasy chuckle. "She told me that we'd better come back alive or else."

Arcove sighed. Halvery felt certain that he'd added a layer of complexity to Arcove's already complex set of problems. He felt guilty, but also desperately relieved that he wasn't about to be sent back to his clutter. "We're not going to do anything *that* dangerous," said Arcove. "*I* only want to have a look around and count ferryshaft. Roup, however, is determined to locate the cave where he asked Storm and the curbs to leave a message for Dazzle."

Oh... thought Halvery and then acidly, *Of course...* "'I still mean what I said'?" he quoted.

Roup glanced at him in surprise.

"Moashi told me."

Roup looked a little annoyed. "You really are his mother."

Halvery sputtered.

Arcove started trotting east along the ridge again. "Roup told Dazzle that he still wants to be friends. He'd like to see whether Dazzle replied. Roup's message was left last fall. Since then, Thistle's cats have been driven into the upper valley, making it difficult to reach the cave in question. It seems unlikely that a reply survived, even if Dazzle left one, but we are going to find out."

"How could you trust anything he says, Roup?" demanded Halvery. "What could he possibly say at this point that would matter?"

"An excellent question," growled Arcove.

Roup said nothing.

They loped along the ridge as the moon rose higher. There were clouds off to the east. Halvery had already seen how the weather could change quickly up here, but right at this moment, it was clear and splendid, with the smell of pines and thawing earth blowing through their fur.

At last, Arcove said, "I really would like to know what Dazzle could say that would make a difference, Roup."

Roup looked like he had a million responses in mind and was determined not to voice any of them.

Arcove continued as though Roup had replied. "*Nothing* has changed. You don't know any more about him than you did before. No, I take that back. *Now* you know that his own leader wants him dead, which does not speak well of him, Roup."

Halvery missed a step. *What?*

"Have you noticed that I'm not arguing with you?" snapped Roup. Halvery had never heard him use that tone with Arcove. He realized, belatedly, that his arrival had interrupted a disagreement that had already been in progress.

"Yes, and I've never seen you keep your mouth shut with such bad grace," growled Arcove. "You're not sleeping, not talking to me, and barely eating. You kicked me last night—"

Roup rounded on him. "If *you* complain about *me* waking you with nightmares, I may choke on the irony." They all came to an abrupt halt. Halvery wasn't sure what to do.

"Then argue with me!" snarled Arcove. "If you've got something to say to me, say it!"

Roup screwed his eyes shut. Halvery could see him losing his battle with his determination to keep his mouth shut. "Dazzle was *my* project!" he exploded.

"Yes, I left you to it," said Arcove in a voice like brooding thunder. "I thought you had that situation managed, and then you nearly died. And now you and Dazzle have my undivided attention!"

"You took my work away from me—!"

"After spending ten days in a telshee cave and then all winter watching you learn to walk again, yes, I took it away from you! What's more, you accepted that. I distinctly remember hearing, 'You win.'"

Roup's voice dropped to a deadly hiss. "That was *before* we got involved in an ugly, treacherous bargain that you are going to regret."

"I haven't *done* anything yet!" exclaimed Arcove. "But you left this situation between my paws, and I would appreciate it if you would stop sulking and trust that I am not going to do something stupid or unreasonably cruel!"

"What exactly constitutes unreasonable cruelty?"

"That's my decision! Do you want to fight me for him? Is that it?"

They went at each other in the blink of an eye and flipped over in a spray of earth. Arcove came up in a perfect cross-pin, but Roup twisted at the last moment, so that Arcove got hold of his chest fur, rather than his throat. Roup curled up, kicked Arcove in the head, and bounced to his feet. Golden fluff whipped across the ridge and away into the night.

"Did I tell you what to do with Treace?" shot Roup.

"Over and over," grated Arcove.

"But I didn't take the decision away from you—"

"You didn't have that right."

"Well, maybe I should have."

"Exactly what do you mean by that, Roup?"

Arcove went at him again, but Roup shot straight up into the air—Storm's trick from two summers ago—and landed on top of Arcove, forcing his head to the ground. For one breathless moment, Halvery thought he'd pinned him, but Arcove flipped Roup over his shoulders and they were nose to nose again, circling.

Halvery got a glimpse of Roup's face, at the wild look in his dilated eyes. *Don't say it,* thought Halvery, *whatever you're thinking, Roup, don't say it...*

"Maybe if I *had* taken it away from you, Ariand wouldn't be dead."

Halvery saw those words hit Arcove like a blow. The flawless rhythm of his movements faltered. Roup hit him hard, flipped him, and came up with Arcove pinned on his side. Arcove's long, dark legs lashed once, but Roup was out of reach. Roup was straddling him, his teeth in Arcove's throat, and Halvery thought numbly, *Don't choke him.*

Then Arcove stopped struggling.

Roup let go of him and stumbled backwards, eyes dark with horror.

Arcove stayed where he was, eyes shut, breathing in long, slow pants. "Well," he said in a ragged voice, "I suppose that's one way to take it away from me."

"Arcove..." whispered Roup.

Arcove got to his feet, his movements a little uncoordinated. He did not look at Roup.

Halvery remembered exactly how that felt. *But please don't respond the way I did.*

Arcove continued in a flat voice, "We have a witness and everything. I suppose you can take the clutters straight up into the valley tonight if you like."

"Arcove..." Roup sounded like he was disintegrating. He had his tail tucked, ears flat, belly almost in the dirt. He looked like a cat who'd just lost a fight, rather than one who'd just beaten a legend. He came around in front of Arcove, who didn't turn away from him, but didn't meet his gaze, either.

Arcove continued in that same emotionless tone, "Maybe if you'd done this thirty years ago, Coden would still be alive. I remember watching him go flying across that lake—"

"I didn't mean it!" wailed Roup. He was suddenly purring on every breath—loud and rough—a sound of pain. He was bristling with nerves, shaking.

Halvery didn't think he could stand to watch. *What made me think I belonged here?*

Then Arcove was washing Roup's face, and Roup was crowding against his chest, his desperate purr fading into something merely miserable. "I'm sorry!" he whimpered, voice muffled under Arcove's chin. "I shouldn't have said it! I didn't mean it! It's not true! I'm sorry, I'm so sorry..."

Arcove didn't say anything, but his rigid posture loosened. He raised his eyes to Halvery with a weary expression.

Halvery wasn't sure what to do, but Arcove was still looking at him, and after a moment, he screwed up his courage. "You could rule the world, Roup...if you were just a little meaner."

He meant to lighten the mood, and he was relieved when they both laughed. Arcove's shoulders relaxed. Halvery realized that Arcove had been worried that Halvery might make an issue of what he'd just seen. *But you two spar often, and surely Roup wins now and then. He knows all your tricks. This is why alphas don't spar with potential challengers. They spar with friends, who will let them lose gracefully on occasion.*

Roup was still muttering, "I didn't mean it. It's not true."

Halvery realized, then, that Arcove wasn't distressed about losing the fight, or not very. He was distressed because he was deeply afraid that what Roup had said *was* true. *And Arcove followed it up with something else he's afraid is true.*

Halvery finally knew what to say. "Arcove, can we stop saying that you killed Coden?"

Arcove glanced at him in surprise. Roup raised his head and turned to look at Halvery, eyes still huge and dark.

"Because I was there," continued Halvery, "and you didn't. Coden killed himself. And I'm pretty sure he did it because he was afraid that you were going to take him down off Turis Rock *alive* and make him do things he didn't want to do. We creasia say that you killed Coden because we are trying to give you a compliment, but the truth is more complicated. You stopped the war; that's what we *should* say. The ferryshaft were absolute monsters to most of us who were alive at that time, and we honor you for beating their hero. But if that is distressing to you…maybe we should just tell the truth. Which is that you didn't kill him."

Arcove was staring at Halvery with an expression that Halvery couldn't quite interpret. Roup began licking Arcove's muzzle, his pink tongue stark against Arcove's fur. "He's right, and you certainly did not kill Ariand. *I* am the monster here if anyone—"

Halvery burst out laughing. "Roup, you are as far from a monster as anyone could be, but, ghosts, you do know exactly where to put your claws."

Roup winced, but Arcove smiled. He finally spoke, his voice so soft and so gentle that it was barely recognizable. "If you were just a little meaner…"

Roup whined, but Arcove looked like he was teasing now. He stepped away, and Roup nearly fell over. He scampered after Arcove, who was clearly done cuddling.

Halvery decided that if Arcove could tease, so could he. "You could rule the world…if you didn't apologize for winning fights.

Really, Roup, I have never seen anyone fight so well and win so poorly."

That got a flare of annoyance. "Do *you* want to go again, Halvery?"

"Only if you don't talk."

"Alright."

In spite of their banter, Halvery was startled when Roup pounced on him and they went over in a blur. They came up in a confused tangle in no clear pinning conformation.

Halvery was further astonished when Roup bit him on the ear hard enough to make him bellow. Roup darted away, and Halvery tore after him. They raced pell-mell along the bluff. Halvery resisted the urge to shout insults. *We are more-or-less in enemy territory.*

Arcove passed him and tried to pounce on Roup, but Roup dodged. They were all running flat out now. Halvery couldn't remember the last time he'd run this hard. It felt exhilarating, like being a cub again. He put on a burst of speed that made his shoulder twinge, but he had the satisfaction of flying over Arcove's head to land right on top of Roup. They flipped over and Halvery came up with his teeth around Roup's throat—not quite a side-pin, but out of the way of Roup's back claws.

He let go, and Roup lay there gasping and still laughing.

Halvery was too winded to speak for a moment. At last, he managed, "You're...letting me win, I'm sure."

Roup got his breath. "No, that was as fair as it gets. Arcove wore me out."

"Well, I should only ever try to pin you after he's worn you out."

Roup's laughter changed to something closer to a snicker.

Halvery reviewed what he had just said and felt his ears prickle. He glanced up to see Arcove stretched out on his belly, with his face between his paws, breathless and also laughing.

Roup got himself under control and managed, "We're not laughing at you, Halvery; we're laughing at me."

"Are we?" asked Halvery doubtfully, but he forced himself to smile.

"Because I have a few things in common with Ilsa," said Roup.

Before Halvery could formulate a response to this, Arcove said, "Well, since we appear to be having a tournament, do you want to go a round, Halvery?"

Halvery was up in a heartbeat. He loved sparring with Arcove, although Arcove didn't invite it very often. Halvery always learned something, and this time was no exception. They grappled a few times, neither coming up with a good grip, and then Arcove switched up his circling pattern in a surprise lunge. He caught one of Halvery's back legs and pulled it out from under him. The resulting loss of balance was all it took for Arcove to catch him behind the head and force his chin to the ground.

"I have never seen that before," said Halvery in some admiration.

"Carmine's move," panted Arcove. "He tried it on me the other day. I thought it was clever."

"It is. Thank you, sir."

Arcove gave him a wry look. "I feel that we are beyond the scope of 'sirs' this evening."

Halvery laughed.

"Besides," said Roup brightly, "I'm not even sure who's king now. I beat Arcove, you beat me, Arcove beat you. It's very confusing."

"I am in no doubt as to my rank in present company," said Halvery quietly.

Roup gave him a nudge on the shoulder. "Your rank is friend."

"I can't think of anywhere I'd rather rank with you."

Arcove yawned. "Maybe we should just hunt tonight. Go to the cave tomorrow."

Roup started east again. "No."

Arcove sighed and loped after him.

* * * *

This chapter includes an author's note at the end of the book.

9

The Price You Paid

They moved along in silence for a while. Finally, Halvery said, "Am I allowed to know the details of this bargain you made with Thistle? It sounds like he traded Dazzle's life for our assistance."

"Correct," said Arcove.

"Flurry wouldn't deliver that part of the message to anyone except Arcove and me," said Roup. "He claimed Dazzle had friends who might warn him. It sounds like Thistle is afraid to kill Dazzle and wants us to do it. He's certain that Arcove will be blinded by the desire for revenge and will therefore do this ugly, treacherous job for him."

Arcove rolled his eyes. "*Or* Thistle knows his agent grievously offended me, and there's not much he could do or say to get me up into these mountains to help Dazzle. He's trying to distance himself from Dazzle's actions and allow me to assist these cats without *also* assisting your would-be killer, Roup. None of this strikes me as particularly cruel or unreasonable."

Halvery listened in silence. When he didn't volunteer a comment, even to sneer at Roup, Arcove said, "What are you thinking, Halvery?"

Halvery shook himself. "Well, sir, you know I haven't been excited about helping these cats from the beginning. I don't trust Dazzle and I'd love to finish him off. But I don't trust Thistle, either. I find Flurry a very odd choice of messengers. I expected someone with experience who could fight his way through a siege and argue persuasively with you in spite of what they did to Roup. Instead, they've sent this half-grown cub."

Arcove slowed down a little, clearly thinking. Halvery realized that Arcove had been so focused on the quandary of Thistle's bargain and the resulting rift with Roup that he hadn't really considered the messenger himself. Lyndi's words: *"Neither of them think as clearly when they're not in agreement."*

"Surely Thistle sent Flurry because he's expendable..." began Roup.

Halvery scoffed. "If their cry for help is so critical to their survival, that doesn't make sense, Roup. Getting down out of these mountains past hostile ferryshaft, and then all the way across the island, is a hard job. Getting a hearing with Arcove after what they did to you should have been the work of an extraordinary politician. It should have required negotiating skills."

"Flurry approached Storm at the ferryshaft writing caves," said Roup slowly.

"And yet Flurry has supposedly never had a friendly interaction with ferryshaft in his life!" returned Halvery. "Doesn't his behavior seem odd to you?"

Roup frowned. Finally, he said, as though thinking aloud, "Someone must have told him what Storm looks like and where to find him..."

"Yes," said Halvery, "and as far as we know, the only one of Thistle's cats who could do that is Dazzle. He's the only one who's been in Leeshwood since the writing caves were excavated, the only one who's seen Storm since he was a foal!"

"Storm does have a distinctive appearance..." began Arcove, but he sounded uncertain now.

Halvery sighed. "I agree with Roup that Thistle's bargain is suspect. Dazzle was the bait to get us out here. I'm just not convinced that Dazzle's life is actually on offer. I'm not convinced that he isn't orchestrating this. He thinks like Roup, and I guess I've gotten used to watching Roup turn me and everyone else in circles. This is the kind of thing *he* would do."

Roup gave an uneasy chuff, but he didn't argue.

A long silence. "You make good points, councilor," said Arcove at last. "I probably should have spoken to you about this earlier."

Halvery flicked his tail. He could easily imagine why Arcove had kept this news quiet. He didn't want to commit to a course of action until he better understood what was going on, and yet every cat in Leeshwood would have an opinion about Thistle's bargain from the moment they heard it. *Arcove doesn't want that kind of dissent splitting the clutters.*

Halvery supposed that Arcove was also trying to protect Roup. Plenty of cats would have no patience with Roup's continued determination to give Dazzle the benefit of the doubt. Roup's place on the council was more unconventional than ever now that he didn't have a clutter, and some cats might call for his removal. *Maybe Arcove thought I would do something like that.*

They all trotted in silence for a while. They were halfway down the valley, and Halvery still hadn't seen any ferryshaft. He finally spotted movement near the northern edge of the lake, where a long arm of water created a little peninsula. At first, he thought it was part of the ferryshaft herd, but after staring and squinting, they all decided that it was Storm and the highland curbs testing the ice.

"Did you tell them they could go out tonight?" asked Halvery with a frown. "I thought you told everyone to stay by the waterfall."

Arcove sighed. "I didn't say anything to them directly. I'm not sure it would matter. They're our allies, not our subordinates."

"Their attitude leaves a lot to be desired," grumbled Halvery.

"Yes, well, their situation leaves a lot to be desired. I don't think they're going to be able to reach those islands. Hollygold thinks the ice on the edges will be rotten, even if the ice in the center of the lake never melts. Twenty lengths of freezing water and rotten ice is all it would take to prevent them from ever reaching the middle."

Roup glanced sidelong at Arcove. "Coden got out there."

Arcove laughed. "Coden was careless with his life."

"You followed him."

"I was eight years old and fresh off beating Ketch."

Roup smirked. "Didn't we play tag along this ridge back then, too?"

Arcove hesitated. "You and I did. I think Coden was asleep." He glanced at Roup sidelong. "Do you remember what you said?"

Roup had to think about it. At last, his expression cleared and he laughed. He picked up his pace a little, forcing Arcove to break into a run to match him. In a voice that must have approximated his younger self, he said, "You and me until the world ends, Arcove!"

Arcove's laugh made him sound much younger.

"And then I think I said, 'Run away with me,'" continued Roup.

Arcove's smile was bittersweet. "You did." He glanced at Halvery. "You don't know how close you came to being king."

Roup slowed to a walk. "Not that close." To Arcove, he continued, "You had all kinds of plans for Leeshwood, for your den, for your future council, and your reign. And I... I was selfish. I didn't want to share you."

Arcove went quiet.

The wind whispered among the tall trees overhead. Halvery could almost see the ghosts of Roup and Arcove's younger selves, chasing each other along the ridge. *Was that the last time you were carefree?*

Roup spoke again, his voice so quiet that Halvery had to strain to hear. "It felt like Leeshwood was going to eat you up."

Arcove, just as quiet: "Did it?"

"Yes." Roup hesitated. "And no."

"Surely no one can hang onto their eight-year-old selves," said Halvery, "no matter what path their life takes." He paused to catch Roup's eyes. "Thank you...for sharing him with us."

Roup smiled, and Arcove's face lost its distant expression.

"I'm sure I would be dead long ago if you hadn't come back to rule," continued Halvery.

"Oh, I don't know if that's true—" began Arcove.

"Sir!" Halvery couldn't quite stifle a dismissive huff. "Please don't patronize me. I would have made a perfectly competent king by the standards of our day and probably ruled for six or eight years like most kings, but I would have made plenty of enemies, and one of them would have killed me the moment I made a mistake. I certainly wouldn't have set out to change the way alphas behave towards cubs or built an army or taken on the ferryshaft herds and the telshees. I didn't have that kind of vision. No one did. Except you."

He stopped, aware that, while his words were complimentary, his tone was not exactly deferential. Arcove didn't say anything, though, and Roup gave Halvery's shoulder a friendly head-butt.

Halvery thought of Coden and Arcove playing around the edges of that vast lake when they'd been younger than Moashi. There'd been six years between that journey and Turis Rock—enough time for an entire generation of cubs to grow up with Arcove's strict no-killing-cubs policy in full force. It had created more adult creasia than the island had ever seen, and for the first time they'd been able to stand up to the ferryshaft herds.

Those herds had panicked when Arcove started attacking them. They'd chosen Coden as their war-time leader, even though he was a rogue with no herd. They'd chosen him because he was cunning and had friends among the telshees. Many of the ferryshaft leaders didn't even like him. No one had seen it coming. Three friends chasing each other through the mountains six years earlier could not possibly have guessed what the future would hold. *If they had, they would surely have run away together.*

Halvery glanced at Roup and Arcove and thought again, *Thank you. I knew it cost you something to build this more peaceful world. I guess I'm still learning what a high price you paid.*

* * * *

This chapter includes an author's note at the end of the book.

10

Another Cave

By midnight, they'd reached the far end of the valley. Arcove led the way down, moving in long leaps over steep, broken ground. Clouds had rolled in to hide the moon, which made the creasia less likely to be spotted, but also brought the worrying problem of rain or snow. The high pass loomed above them—a jagged, gray wall of rock, plunging down to the eastern edge of the lake.

After a final long slide over loose shale, the three creasia came to rest in a little stand of trees at the bottom. Halvery understood why Arcove had chosen to run along the ridge in order to get here. He wondered how hard it was going to be to climb out of the valley and whether they could really get back to the clutters tonight. His stomach growled, reminding him that he had not eaten in most of two days.

"The canyons turn into tunnels near the water," said Roup quietly. "The best place to access them if you're trying to get into the valley is well above the lake, before they go underground. The canyons also open up at some points near the bottom, but most animals coming and going from the upper valley would skip that part."

"Are we entering the canyons tonight?" asked Halvery in surprise.

"Only for a short distance," said Roup. "The curbs left my message in a cave that the creasia were passing at that time. This was before Thistle's cats were entering the upper valley, but they were evaluating the caves in the lower canyons as birthing dens. I'm sure they concluded that those caves are too dangerous."

Halvery frowned. "Aren't the canyons likely to be guarded by Sedaron's ferryshaft?"

"Yes," said Arcove pointedly.

Roup flicked his tail. "If we can't reach the cave, I'll accept that. But Sedaron isn't stupid, and guarding the lower canyons would be stupid. There's a confluence higher up. Storm and the curbs told me that one can look down on that confluence from above, although you have to actually get into it if you want to reach the upper valley.

"If Sedaron is smart, he'll keep a watch there. He'll tell his sentries to howl if they see creasia passing below. Sentries at the top would be safe from floods and from creasia coming out of the valley. They could direct the ferryshaft at the bottom to intercept Thistle's cats. There's no reason for ferryshaft to guard the mouths of lower canyons. It would be inefficient as well as dangerous. Water can come crashing through with little warning."

"Speaking of dangerous…" Halvery glanced up just in time to catch a silent flash of lightning.

"The cave isn't very far into the canyon," muttered Roup. "Neither of you have to go…"

Halvery rolled his eyes. "As though we'd even consider letting you visit a cave where Dazzle has been leaving messages *alone,* Roup. Ghosts. I didn't hurt my shoulder just to watch you do the same foolish—"

"Quiet," hissed Arcove.

Halvery subsided. They were getting into the area where one would expect to find ferryshaft, and they certainly shouldn't be loudly quarreling. Moments later, Halvery noticed the first tuft of red fur clinging to a thorny shrub. Soon they were passing other signs of ferryshaft habitation—hoofprints and scent, decaying scat, grass and foliage nibbled down to the dirt, flattened leaves and underbrush in places where they'd slept.

They passed a dead ferryshaft, stripped down to bones by scavengers. It was impossible to say what had killed it. *The battle?* wondered Halvery. *Or just a casualty of this forbidding terrain? Perhaps even a natural death. Sedaron has some very ancient herd elders.*

Halvery thought uneasily of what might happen if even a single ferryshaft spotted them and howled an alarm.HHikhl *Well, I did say I wanted to come back with the two of you or not at all.*

Arcove knew their danger as well as anyone. He led the way in absolute silence through the darkest of the shadows between jagged rock outcroppings, around the remnants of snowdrifts, and through dense stands of trees. Halvery had to remind himself that Roup's coat didn't glow in the eyes of day animals the same way it did to other cats. To Halvery, Roup remained luminous even in the shadows. However, to a ferryshaft, he would vanish from sight against the dim patterns of snow, rocks, and trees.

Halvery finally caught the flash of the lake between the trunks. He glanced east. There he was able to make out the dark mouths of half-submerged caves, choked with ice. Those massive chunks looked like they'd washed down from the high peaks, rather than forming here in the lake. Even at this distance, he could see the gleam of open water running between the chaotic debris. *The curbs will never make it to those islands.*

At the same time, he noticed that the most easterly of the little islands was tantalizingly close to the mouths of the caves. It was relatively far from the shore, but not so far from the mounds of ice around those openings. *I hope Storm doesn't do anything stupid.*

"Where *are* the ferryshaft?" whispered Arcove. "I confess, I'm baffled. I was expecting to see them all over this end of the valley."

"They could have gone up to that spot above the confluence..." hazarded Roup. "Perhaps they hope to leap on any escaping creasia from above and fight them in the narrow canyon."

"That seems needlessly risky," muttered Arcove. "I don't remember much greenery up there for them to eat. I suppose things could have changed..."

They all stood still for a moment, thinking. Overhead, a night-bird called, and a curb yipped from across the lake. The air smelled of ice and evergreens.

Halvery caught the distant rumble of thunder. "That storm is headed in this direction," he said softly. "If we are going into a canyon, we need to do it soon and then get out."

Roup looked at Arcove.

His green eyes were unfocused, still thinking. At last, he turned east. "Alright. Perhaps the lower canyons will tell us something."

They certainly did. As the creasia approached the extreme eastern end of the valley, they encountered a dry wash. It was the easiest way to move up the rocky slope, although it was still slow going with soft sand, interspersed with water-polished boulders.

In the dry wash, they found dead ferryshaft. These were fresher than the body in the woods, but still decayed and picked over by birds and small animals. They were probably eight to ten days gone—casualties of the battle that Keesha had told them about.

It looked to Halvery as though the bodies had been washed out of the canyons by floods. They didn't look as though they'd drowned, though. Even in their decayed state, the marks of violent death were easy to read—teeth prints that had gone all the way to the bone, skulls crushed at the back of the head in characteristic creasia style. *They died in a fight,* thought Halvery, *and were later carried away by water.* He saw only ferryshaft bodies. Not a single dead creasia seemed to be present, nor any curbs. *This is odd, but at least we know that the ferryshaft numbers have been reduced.*

The dry wash formed a trench that didn't give much of a view of the valley, even as they climbed higher. The rocks on either side were beginning to close up, forming solid walls that would quickly become a narrow canyon.

When they seemed to have passed the last of the bodies, Halvery whispered, "I counted fifty-seven."

"That was my number as well," murmured Roup, "and this is just one of eight canyons that come down from the confluence. If there were a similar number of casualties in all of them..."

"I would not assume that," muttered Arcove, "but Sedaron has certainly suffered some losses." He hesitated. "I find it strange that Thistle was able to take such a toll without losses of his own."

No one had an answer to that.

"The curbs must not have fought with them," observed Roup.

"That's not surprising," said Arcove. "Curbs make good scouts. They make good allies for gathering information, and they're dangerous to a lone creasia, but they would be slaughtered in a battle. Especially lowland curbs."

Lowland curbs were smaller than highland curbs, and Halvery had to agree that an alliance with them would be wasted by taking them into a major fight. Still... *Not a single one?*

"I wonder if the currents carried bodies of different weights to different spots," he hazarded.

"Possibly," muttered Arcove. "Maybe the dead creasia are higher up in the canyon. Maybe the curbs are down in the lake."

An uncomfortable notion was beginning to take shape in Halvery's mind. "Arcove...you were concerned that we might arrive to find Thistle's cats all dead. But...what if it's the other way around? What if they managed some trick or trap and have, in fact, decimated and scattered Sedaron's herd?"

"Well, then, I suppose we can all go home," said Arcove doubtfully.

Halvery couldn't help thinking of Dazzle, coming to Leeshwood all by himself with the goal of destabilizing Arcove's reign. Against all odds, he'd nearly succeeded. *If anyone could beat a thousand ferryshaft with fewer than two hundred cats... What if Dazzle really is the one in charge up there?*

They were winding through tight canyon walls now, some ten lengths across, but growing narrower. Halvery couldn't help looking longingly at the top. He could still jump out, but soon that would no longer be possible. As the walls got higher, he felt more and more trapped. There was no cover in the slot—just pale sand and sheer rock on either side. Halvery kept looking up, expecting to see ferryshaft, curbs, or enemy cats staring down at them. "How much farther, Roup?" he whispered.

"We're almost there. It takes a sharp jog to the right and then the cave is about halfway up the left wall."

It felt like an eternity before they reached the turn. Arcove led the way around the corner, all of them uncomfortably aware of how easy it would be to run headlong into an enemy. Even ferryshaft hoofbeats would be muffled in the sand. But the dim canyon corridor was empty. The fresh breeze that blew along the slot carried only the scent of pines and water.

All eyes turned to their left. The cave wasn't difficult to spot, although Halvery was a bit disappointed that it had an upper overhang. It would not be possible to use it as a staging point to reach the top. Still, the cave would get them out of sight and off the bottom, which seemed appealing at the moment.

"Wait," whispered Arcove as Halvery gathered himself to jump.

Halvery swallowed his impatience as Arcove sailed soundlessly over the lip of the cave. He stood there scanning the interior for a long beat. Then he gave a jerk of his tail, indicating that Roup and Halvery should follow.

The cave was empty. It was about ten lengths deep and perhaps half of that across—a comfortable size for a small den, although Halvery would have considered this a terrible location. The floor was rock, dusted with wind-blown sand. Pawprints wouldn't last long here, and Halvery didn't see any. He couldn't smell other animals, either, although scent did not cling to this sort of stone. Both the floor and walls were ominously smooth, as though exposed to water on a regular basis.

Roup went straight to the back wall, where an animal had, indeed, scratched a message with a stone that left faint white marks on the red-brown rock. Arcove and Halvery glanced at each other. Halvery thought Arcove was bracing himself to have an argument with Dazzle by proxy. However, this did not transpire. The marks on the wall were too faded to read.

Roup grew increasingly distressed as he wandered back and forth along the rows of scratches. "He tried to write so much," he whispered.

Writing was labor-intensive. Good surfaces were often limited, and the characters had to be traced repeatedly to make them last. Animals usually considered their messages very carefully and used as few words as possible. Dazzle had tried to leave three long lines of characters beneath the even more faded remains of what must have been Roup's message left by Storm.

Almost none of it was intelligible now. They all tried. Even Arcove, who obviously did not want to hear from Dazzle, squinted at the wall for long moments. However, the only word they could read with certainty was "sorry."

"He's sorry for what?" growled Halvery. "What he did? What he's *planning* to do? Didn't Dazzle tell you he was sorry right before he tried to kill you, Roup?"

Arcove didn't say anything. He stepped back from the wall and watched Roup for a moment.

Roup's tail and ears were down. He nosed around some stones at the base of the wall. "This is part of his counting system," he muttered. "He was trying to tell me something with these, too."

"Something we can't trust," said Halvery. "Roup, I don't know how we could trust anything he says! If Dazzle has somehow out-witted Sedaron, it's him and not the ferryshaft, who is likely to kill us and take Leeshwood. What was it you told me he said at the end…Treace's cats have got to come back 'on top or not at all'?"

Arcove turned away from Dazzle's faded message. "We need to go."

Roup looked up, his face desperate. "Arcove, he *answered* me. He tried to write so much. He tried to tell me something about their numbers…"

Arcove's voice was implacable. "We can't read it, and it doesn't matter right now. Something very odd has happened here, Roup. We need to get back to the clutters. I am beginning to be sorry that I came down here tonight."

Roup returned his attention to the rocks at the base of the wall. Halvery realized, with a sinking feeling, that he was looking for a stone that would leave a mark. "Roup, no…"

"I have to try—"

Arcove was beside them in an instant, his dark ruff bristling. "No, you don't," he growled. "Leave it, Roup. That's an order."

Roup went still, jaw set, staring at the wall.

Halvery wanted to shout at him, to tell him how absurd and unreasonable he was being, but the idea that Arcove and Roup might fight again made him feel queasy. He racked his brain for something Roup might listen to. "Dazzle won't get any message you write, Roup. He isn't coming here anymore. He would have renewed those marks if he was."

"Maybe," said Roup flatly. "Or maybe he has just lost faith that I'll ever be here to see them."

"I don't think that's true—"

"Let's—go." Arcove's voice had an unfamiliar edge to it. Halvery noticed for the first time how the wind was swirling through the cave. It had been blowing in their faces as they walked, but it seemed to have gotten stronger.

Roup registered Arcove's tone all at once and turned away from the wall. His face lost its cold stubbornness. "Arcove?"

Arcove darted across the cave and over the edge, forcing Halvery and Roup to run to catch up with him. The clouds overhead seemed a little thicker, though the pale gray sand of the canyon floor still shone luminous.

Thunder growled, but it seemed far off. Not a drop of rain was falling. The wind had certainly gotten stronger, though, and it had a complex scent that Halvery couldn't identify. It made the fur rise along his spine.

Arcove hadn't slowed down. He was running hard. They were all running downhill, back the way they'd come. They hadn't gone far when there came a rushing noise from behind. Halvery instinctively looked to either side, searching for some place he could jump out of the canyon. However, they were still well above the point where the top of the slot would be reachable, and there were no ledges in the water-polished walls.

Halvery gathered himself to run as hard as he could. Then, to his astonishment, Arcove checked. He spun in a spray of sand and bellowed, "With me, both of you!"

Halvery's every instinct was screaming at him to run down the canyon, away from that building rush and grinding sound.

But his sense of duty was stronger. He would follow orders, even in the teeth of his instincts. Roup, of course, would have followed Arcove into fire.

All three of them turned and flashed back the way they'd come. They reached the jog in the canyon, still running on dry sand, and saw the wall of water bearing down on them. The first gush crested over Halvery's paws, splashing all the way to his flanks. Then he was leaping, hind paws slipping in new mud, but still clearing the cave's mouth.

Arcove and Roup scrambled up beside him, none of them as graceful as they'd been the first time. They all stood there gasping, safe for the moment, as the flood churned below.

11

Share

The water was carrying tree branches and chunks of ice. "I don't think it will reach the cave," panted Roup. "I don't think the floods get this high, except during the first thaw. Otherwise, the writing wouldn't just be faint; it would be scoured."

This sounded logical. Still, Halvery didn't breathe easily until the water leveled off below the cave's mouth. Finally, he was able to tear his eyes from the opening. He began grooming his wet legs. To Arcove, he said, "Sir, your instincts are, as always, exceptional. We couldn't have outrun that."

Arcove shot him a brief, unhappy smile. Halvery was sure he was not pleased to be trapped here with Dazzle's cryptic message. He was worried about the clutters. He was confused as to the whereabouts of the ferryshaft. *But it could be worse,* thought Halvery. *We could be drowning.*

Arcove stretched out on his stomach at the edge of the cave and watched the flood, which showed no signs of abating. Halvery did the same, wondering whether he might be able to nap, since they were at least safe for the moment. He didn't think he could sleep, though. His nerves were twanging with the giddy euphoria of a near-miss. He wished he could hunt—run off this shaky energy. He wished he could find anything at all to eat.

To Halvery's disgust, Roup returned to the wall of faded text. He hunted around until he located a rock he liked, but after he picked it up in his mouth, he just stood there. Halvery felt certain he was considering and discarding message after message.

Finally, Roup put the rock down again. He walked back and forth along the wall, squinting at the illegible characters. He stopped at last before the only clear word and looked at it with his head on one side.

Dazzle does not deserve your attention, Roup. He does not deserve your compassion. He certainly doesn't deserve the opportunity to make you this miserable. Against his better judgment, Halvery got up and came to stand beside Roup.

When Roup ignored him, Halvery said quietly, "He crippled multiple cats who fought with him. He probably would have killed me, or tried to, if you'd given him the chance. I'm sure he would have killed Moashi. He bit through your back leg and then stood there watching you suffer and bleed out. He did that in order to kill Arcove in the cruelest way possible. And he had the gall to say he was *sorry.*"

Roup screwed his eyes shut and dropped his head. He didn't argue. His ears were low and flat.

Halvery ground his teeth. "If there was ever a time I'd like to take your mind off your troubles…" Before he thought too hard about it, he got hold of Roup's scruff. When Roup didn't resist, Halvery tugged him sideways off his feet and then dragged him back to the mouth of the cave where he deposited him beside a startled Arcove.

Roup uncurled from his side and rolled onto his stomach, laughing uneasily and bristling a little. Halvery flopped down beside him and started grooming Roup's ears. After a moment, Arcove began working on his shoulders.

"There, see, you've got both of us," said Halvery playfully. "What on earth are you thinking about Dazzle for?"

Roup laughed harder and tucked his nose under one paw. But when he raised his head and spoke, he still sounded serious. "Arcove, you killed a few ferryshaft during the war in ways that I think you regret, because they hurt me."

Arcove said nothing. He used the back of his tongue to comb through the fur over Roup's shoulders.

"You punished Charder because I got hurt in his herd," continued Roup, "and I think you regret that, too."

Silence. Halvery nibbled into Roup's cheek. Roup canted his head and blinked, but he kept talking to Arcove. "And I think you are about to do something else that you will regret...because of me." Another pause. "I don't like being the reason you make mistakes, Arcove. I don't like being your weakness."

Arcove finally spoke. "Don't you?"

His voice was so deadpan that it took Halvery a moment to catch the edge of humor. When he did, he felt immensely relieved. *Thank you, Arcove.* "Roup, you are the only one still working here."

Roup made a chuffing noise, but then he continued, "Can't you see that I *have* to write something? I have to—"

"No!" exclaimed Halvery. "Roup, you don't even know what you'd be responding to! Dazzle's note probably says, 'I'm sorry to hear you're still walking.'" Roup drew a breath to respond, but Halvery talked over him, "We all just came within a hair's breadth of drowning. Take a break. Go to sleep. We might need that busy little brain later."

"'Go to sleep'?" echoed Roup, and Halvery was relieved to hear a note of playful sarcasm in his voice. "Is that really what you're trying to get me to do?"

Halvery nuzzled under his chin and was a little surprised when Roup tipped his head back. "I don't know," murmured Halvery. "Would you rather do something else?" He had the dizzy sense that he was walking on a narrow ledge above an uncertain abyss, but the feeling of having come so close to death was making him reckless.

He glanced up and saw that Arcove was sedately grooming Roup's head. He was, in fact, licking the back of Roup's neck in a way that was making Roup blink and shift his body. That was all the encouragement Halvery needed to drop his nose into the fine golden down of Roup's throat and trace his pulse all the way to his breastbone.

Roup let out an uneven breath. At the same time, Halvery's stomach growled. He lifted his head with a grimace.

Arcove muttered, "We should have stopped to hunt…"

Roup tilted his head to look at Arcove upside down and said, "I suppose we're all a little hungry…"

For some reason, that made Arcove laugh. He couldn't stop for a moment.

Roup shot Halvery a sheepish grin and said, "I'm sorry. That was a very old and very private joke."

Well, you're not thinking about Dazzle anymore, at least.

Roup stretched languorously, back and tail arching, and then relaxed onto his side. He settled down against Arcove, but he was looking at Halvery. "Please continue telling me how you'd like me to go to sleep."

It was Halvery's turn to laugh.

Roup tipped his chin up a little, but Halvery did not accept the invitation to resume grooming him. "What did you mean earlier… when you said you have something in common with Ilsa?"

Roup looked at him with round-eyed innocence. "We're both scheming politicians?"

"No—"

"We both think Moashi will make a good alpha one day?" Halvery rolled his eyes.

"We can both push you around like a mouse in a circle?" Halvery did not take this bait. He shifted so that he was facing Roup more directly and said, "You don't want to share a mate... You want to *be* shared; I don't know why I didn't see that sooner."

Roup looked at him quizzically. "I believe I already am."

Halvery was confused for a moment. Then he realized what Roup meant. *Oh...* For some reason, this way of looking at things had never occurred to him. The idea that he was sharing anything with Arcove was enormously appealing to Halvery. He felt sure that Roup knew it. Halvery had that uncomfortable sense of being flattered and manipulated at the same time.

He wanted to feel like he was in control of the situation again, so he said, "You shine in this light, Roup. I swear, if there was only one star in the sky, it would find its way to your coat."

Roup's faintly smug expression dissolved and he gave a helpless laugh. "Now I'm in trouble."

Halvery's gaze flicked up to Arcove. He'd rested his head across Roup's shoulders. Halvery dared to meet his eyes and saw that he didn't look angry or jealous. He was certainly paying close attention, and possibly still deciding what to think about this.

Halvery leaned close to Roup's nose and murmured, "You're the same color as the hunter's moon; you know that? Like the golden moon turned into a cat and walked down to earth." Roup had that helpless look on his face—like he didn't know what to say. His ears had dropped. In a moment of inspiration, Halvery added, "Arcove is the night sky, and you look so bright against his coat, Roup. You don't know how you shine."

That made them both stare at him. *What?* thought Halvery. *Has it really never occurred to either of you that Roup is the same color as the hunter's moon?* The moon had been golden on the night that Arcove won the ferryshaft wars, and cats had called it Arcove's luck ever since.

"He talks like this the entire time," whispered Roup to Arcove.

"I am beginning to see why you like going down to his den," said Arcove.

Halvery chuffed. To Roup, he said, "I don't know whether you've noticed, but I'm flirting with you."

"I had some notion that you were."

"Do you want me to stop? Because the next thing I'd like to do is get my tongue all over you, and I don't want to offend anyone."

Roup tilted his head around to look at Arcove again.

Arcove hesitated. He was so very difficult to interpret. For one moment, Halvery almost lost his nerve. Then Arcove said slowly, "Well, I confess I'm a little curious." He smiled and rubbed his cheek against Roup's. "Because you, my friend, are the pickiest cat in Leeshwood."

That made Roup roll his eyes. He started to say something, and Arcove started washing his face.

Halvery turned away from them. He cuddled up to Roup, facing the other direction, and licked his way down Roup's spine to the base of his tail. He proceeded to nibble into the muscles there until Roup was breathing deeply. Roup tried to pull his back legs under him, but Halvery put a paw across his hips to keep him on his side. He nuzzled under one hind leg and licked his way across Roup's lower belly. Roup tucked his head against Arcove's chest and made a mewing noise.

I could make you finish right now, thought Halvery. *But I want to watch your whiskers twitch.* He nuzzled under Roup's tail and licked him there until he was squirming.

At last, Halvery stood up, turned around, and got hold of Roup's scruff. Arcove looked a little surprised, but he didn't resist when Halvery dragged Roup away from him, around the floor in a circle, to wind up facing Arcove a couple of lengths away.

Roup curled up and submitted in a very satisfying manner when he was dragged. The moment Halvery let go of him, he turned over onto his belly and flattened out. His body formed a long, perfect curve, his tail an elegant arch.

Halvery walked around him once and paused to give him one more wet lick. Roup's tail twitched even further to the side. "Roup," he murmured, "you have the most flawless presentation imaginable. You really are the prettiest thing on four legs. I don't know how anyone could look at you like that and not lose their minds."

Roup made a little impatient kneading pattern with his front paws. "Well, you just seem to be talking."

"Aw, so impatient this evening. Does Arcove not put you on your back when you're pouting? And you've been avoiding *me* the whole journey. Feeling a little tense, Roup?"

Roup made an attempt at a growl that was almost comical, and Halvery settled down on top of him. Roup climaxed the moment Halvery slipped inside, chin against the ground, eyes screwed shut, whiskers and ears fluttering.

Halvery caught his breath and set his teeth, blinking with pleasure, but determined not to be done yet. "You feel so good," he crooned. "Too good not to...stay inside you for a while." He stayed perfectly still, letting Roup recover. "That was quick even for you," he teased. "If you fight with both of us, don't be surprised if you end up frustrated."

Roup opened one eye and gave him an exasperated, upside-down smile. "I knew if I talked to you, I'd...tell you about Thistle's bargain, and I...wasn't supposed to."

"And here I thought you were just bored of me."

Roup caught his breath. "I suppose I forgot how terribly sensitive you are and how easy it is to hurt your delicate feelings."

Halvery snorted a laugh. He started moving again, minutely. He knew he was getting the angle right when Roup's eyes fluttered shut. "Hunter's moon," murmured Halvery, "Arcove's luck. That's what you are. Brightest thing in the night sky."

"You are really...laying it on thick this evening," managed Roup.

"I love the way you forget how to talk when I tell you how beautiful you are," continued Halvery. "And all that nervous bristling... Ghosts, you are pretty when you fluff up."

Roup's breathing was starting to deepen again. Out of his peripheral vision, Halvery could see Arcove coming a little closer. He had the sense that Arcove was curious and not upset or embarrassed. He dearly hoped so. Halvery didn't quite have the nerve to look up and make sure. He focused on Roup, on getting him a little closer with every gentle thrust. Halvery leaned close to Roup's ears and purred, "You want us to share you, sweetheart? Want us to take turns on you? I will if you like it, Beautiful. You smell so good when you're happy."

He got hold of Roup's scruff, intending to pin his head down this time, because Roup liked that. But then Halvery accidentally raised his eyes.

Arcove was right in front of him, and he did not look entirely pleased.

For one moment, Halvery's stomach dropped. He wondered whether some part of Arcove's brain was insisting that Roup was being hurt. It was possible. In that case, Halvery had no doubt that Arcove's instincts were telling him to kill whoever was hurting his dearest friend.

Roup must have felt Arcove's breath across his whiskers, because he opened his eyes and Arcove's attention dropped immediately to his face. Roup was clearly having trouble focusing, but he managed a lopsided grin and whispered, "I told you he never shuts up."

Arcove immediately dropped down to his belly on the floor with Roup's head between his paws, watching his face.

"Feels good," Roup whispered. His eyes blinked shut. "Feels *so* good."

Arcove relaxed.

Halvery had another idea that he hoped wouldn't get him killed. He reached down and got hold of Roup's scruff again. But instead of pressing his head against the stone floor, he drew it back, presenting Roup's throat to Arcove.

Arcove, he will love this if you'll do it…

There was a moment's hesitation, and then Arcove was licking. Roup's breath gave a hitch. He whined. His whole body tensed, and Halvery had to pause for a moment to get control of himself.

Then he brought his weight down, forcing Roup's body into an even tighter arc. There was no way to tell Arcove what he wanted him to do, but Halvery growled and Arcove *got it*. He put his teeth completely around Roup's throat, and Roup responded with exactly as much enthusiasm as Halvery had expected.

He wailed between his clenched teeth. His whole body spasmed, and Halvery couldn't keep himself from finishing in a wash of shuddering pleasure.

He let go of Roup's nape, Arcove let go of his throat, and Roup sank bonelessly to the ground. Arcove was sitting up, and Halvery caught the flash of pink on his lower belly before he stretched out to put his head beside Roup's again.

Thank all the peaceful ghosts, thought Halvery. *You* are *actually enjoying this.*

Halvery eased off his partner, feeling proud of himself when Roup did not so much as flinch. Withdrawing painlessly was difficult, and some cats called it unnatural. Halvery just called it good manners, though not always achievable.

Arcove was washing Roup's face. Roup leaned into it with a dozy smile. Halvery flopped down beside them. He felt pleasantly relaxed, but also a little apprehensive, now that the haze of desire had passed. "Sir, I would feel very much better if you would say something..."

Arcove cocked an eye at him. Halvery was afraid he was going to say something like "This is an absurd time to call me sir" or "You're doing enough talking for everyone," but Arcove only said, "My turn?"

"I cannot spar with you right now," breathed Roup, but Arcove got him by the scruff and flipped him onto his back.

"No sparring," he murmured.

"Then what—? Oh..."

Arcove settled down half on top of him, facing the opposite direction, and started to lick. Roup shut his eyes and let his head fall back. He gave a long purr on a single breath.

Halvery wondered whether he was allowed to participate. He scooted forward hesitantly and stretched out on his belly with his head next to Roup's. After a moment, he started to groom Roup's face and throat. No one objected. Roup's half-unconscious purrs came and went. "You're so cute, Roup," whispered Halvery against his ear, "with all your flower-petal paws in the air."

Roup gave a breathless snicker. Halvery could tell that Arcove was doing more than one thing. Halvery couldn't see very well, and he didn't have the nerve to go stick his face between Roup's legs, but every time Roup's breathing started to deepen, Arcove would pause or change his rhythm.

He's doing the same thing to Roup that I do to myself, thought Halvery in surprise. This idea had never occurred to him. Halvery had always assumed that his role was to make his partner finish as many times as possible while delaying his own release. He accomplished this by changing what he was doing whenever he got too close to climax. Halvery had never felt deprived by his particular style of mating. He felt that it had its own peculiar pleasures and rewards, and yet he'd never considered doing it to someone else on purpose.

Well…did I really expect to watch Arcove put Roup on his back and not learn anything?

After a while, Arcove started purring. He began kneading Roup's stomach with his forepaws, still licking and then suckling.

Halvery felt suddenly awkward. *This* was the sort of behavior that he would have expected from a cat who started mating at three years old. It was why den mothers usually stopped that sort of thing on the rare occasions when cubs tried it. At that age, a cat's attachment to his mother could become confused with attachment to a mate. Cats who began mating too young sometimes engaged in odd behaviors later or displayed unusual bonding patterns.

But you were both motherless cubs, Halvery realized. *Ghosts, Arcove might not have been fully weaned when he was rejected by his den.*

Part of Halvery wanted to recoil from the oddity of the way Arcove was behaving. Another part of him whispered, *"He is letting you see something intensely private. Trust doesn't get any greater than this."*

Roup was whimpering and writhing. He kicked like a rabbit, and Arcove got right on top of him, pinning him down. Halvery scooted back a little, just watching them.

"You are...showing off," panted Roup.

Arcove paused to drawl, "I can't think what would inspire me to do that."

A moment later, Roup was past the point of forming sentences. "Arcove...please," he choked. "Please, please, please..."

Arcove was sucking and purring and kneading, but he kept pausing right before Roup reached the peak.

Halvery didn't feel awkward anymore. He watched with a sense of shared delight as Roup completely lost his mind, thrashing and begging, until at last Arcove spun around and took him by the throat. Roup curled his hips, and they became a solid mass of entwined black and gold. Halvery was sure they finished in the same instant.

Arcove sat up at last, breathing hard. Roup remained stretched beneath him. Halvery noticed that Arcove didn't withdraw immediately. *We've both learned that trick, I guess.*

Halvery inched forward to put his head beside Roup's again. "Are you done, Beautiful? Or have you got another round in you?"

Roup opened his eyes, and Halvery was pleased to see that floating, glassy look. "Anything you want," he murmured.

Oh, Arcove does know how to put you in a good place, doesn't he? "Anything I want?" purred Halvery. "Alright. Make a litter of cubs with Arcove and Shazel."

Roup's eyes focused a little and he shook with laughter. "You are relentless."

"You have no room to talk. Have you figured out what to write on the wall to Dazzle?"

Roup was practically slurring. "What wall? Who's Dazzle?"

"I'm so glad we could provide inspiration!" crooned Halvery. "Allow me to provide some more." He dragged Roup out from under Arcove, who made no attempt to stop him. "Have you ever pinned him on his side, Arcove? It's adorable. Let me show you how he kicks."

12

Tell Me

By the time they'd finished, the storm that had created the flood in the upper valley had moved into the canyons. Rain gushed from a dark sky streaked by lightning. The floodwaters had risen a little higher, the torrent fast and dangerous.

No one seemed very concerned about this. Halvery and Arcove were watching the rain with Roup on his back between them. Roup was purring, half asleep, his front paws fanning and closing in a contented kneading pattern that Halvery had once found juvenile and that he'd now decided was charming. *I guess you feel pretty safe, Beautiful. I guess you are.*

Arcove had both paws over Roup's stomach. He was still grooming him from time to time. Halvery put his own throat down across Roup's and felt that barely-audible, half-asleep purr resonate through his own face. The sensation made him feel peaceful and content.

At last, he raised his head and said, "Have the two of you really never noticed that he's the same color as the hunter's moon?"

Roup didn't even twitch. Arcove smiled. "I...never thought about it."

Halvery wanted to say, *"How could you possibly have not noticed that he's the color of a flower?"* But that sounded like criticism. "Well, he lies down in the prettiest way possible. I hope it doesn't sound to you like we're arguing. I just like to talk. He likes to talk back. He is so much fun to mate."

Arcove quirked another smile. He hesitated for a moment and then said, "I think *you're* bringing all the fun."

That caught Halvery off-guard.

Arcove put his head down across Roup's stomach and continued quietly, "This was never about fun."

Halvery was lost. *Well, it's not about making cubs. What else could it be about?*

Arcove's eyes strayed away from Halvery's face to the rainy night. "It's about comfort...trust...remembering who you are when it feels like you're being swallowed by your role...when you can't tell anymore where you end and Leeshwood begins and you need to remember your own name..."

Halvery stared at him. In his mind's eye, he saw the flash of confusion on Roup's face when Halvery had said, *"I don't do sad mating."*

Arcove spoke so softly that he was barely audible, "When you're a leader, you have to make decisions that cause problems for some animals, even as they solve problems for others. You know this, Halvery; you've been a den alpha nearly your entire life. You have to make compromises. It's difficult to make everyone happy. Often it feels like you make *no one* happy." Arcove hesitated. "But I could always make *him* happy...without being anyone other than myself." Another pause. "Maybe that's what you mean by fun."

No, it really isn't.

Halvery knew he needed to say something. But Arcove trying to explain himself was an alien creature and somehow frightening. *Why?* Halvery wondered. *I suppose I need you to be infallible and unafraid, with never a second guess. Every cat in Leeshwood wants that from you.*

He could almost hear Roup saying, *"Let him show a little fear, Halvery."*

Halvery leaned across Roup and caught Arcove's eyes. "Sir, I hope you know how tremendously grateful I am that you made the sacrifices you made. You are the only person who could have given us three decades of peace, and I am still learning how much it cost. You deserve any comfort, any pleasure you can create for yourself. You and Roup both."

Arcove gave him a sad smile. After a moment, he continued in that same quiet voice, "It often feels to me as though I *am* Leeshwood. I speak with Leeshwood's voice. Leeshwood's needs and desires are mine. Even my den, my mates, my cubs... These are things that a king *must* have, *must* love, *must* make...something Leeshwood wants and needs."

Halvery remembered Roup's words from earlier in the evening: *"It felt like Leeshwood was going to eat you up."*

"He is the *one* thing," said Arcove softly, "that is just for me."

Halvery did not know where to put his eyes.

Arcove straightened up a little and shook his ears. "I am making you uncomfortable."

Halvery chuffed. "You never explain yourself, Arcove."

"Is it tedious to listen to me try?"

Halvery forced himself to meet those sharp green eyes. "Of course not. I'm just...so afraid that I don't deserve this much trust."

Arcove's eyes strayed down to Roup's silky belly. "Roup trusts you. So I do."

Halvery laughed. "Oh, we both know it's not that simple. Roup trusts all kinds of people, including cats who tried to murder him in cold blood. He would try to have a peaceful negotiation with the Volontaro if he could find a way to talk to it."

Arcove started to say something and then laughed. Then they were both laughing.

"You hear that, Roup?" said Halvery. "Your judgment is suspect!"

Roup did not respond. His paws had stopped fanning. Halvery could no longer hear his purr, although he could still feel it very faintly.

"He hasn't been sleeping well," murmured Arcove.

"I guess we put him to sleep," said Halvery smugly.

Arcove smiled—less sad this time. "Roup doesn't *trust* Dazzle. He's just willing to give him the benefit of the doubt. Roup has always been very willing to show mercy, but he actually trusts very few people. You are one of them."

Halvery swallowed. "Well, I will try to deserve it."

"He's never lain down for anyone else apart from me. You know that, right?"

Halvery blinked. *Did I know that...?* He knew that Roup was devoted to Arcove and would never have gone behind his back or made him uncomfortable. But creasia were promiscuous by nature, particularly male creasia. Arcove had a den full of female mates, and if Roup preferred lying down, it should have been easy for him to find partners.

Halvery had vaguely supposed that Roup had some favorites among his clutter. Those cats loved him, and it would have been simple for him to say to a handsome clutter-mate, "I'd like to lie down for you, but we need to keep it quiet." It was common for male creasia to do this sort of thing, get bored of each other after a while, and part ways with no negative repercussions.

He's never...?

A thousand things Roup had said and done over the last two years flashed through Halvery's head. His occasional confusion, hesitation, and uncertainty. Halvery asking him over and over: "Have you ever done this? Have you tried it that way? How about this position?"

Roup, always answering, "No."

His relationship with Arcove was clearly about sameness, not variety. It was about reproducing familiar patterns to remind them both of who they'd been before they took on these roles that threatened to consume them. But that didn't mean Roup had never had other male partners.

"No one else?" echoed Halvery in a small voice.

Arcove watched his face.

"Ghosts, why *me?*"

Arcove finally laughed. "Because you're fun, obviously."

Halvery rolled his eyes. "You are also fun. I've never seen anyone do...what you were doing to him. He completely forgot how to talk!"

Arcove smiled.

"Roup loves you more than he loves to breathe," continued Halvery.

"I know," said Arcove softly.

They watched the rain in silence for a while. Roup was so deeply asleep that he'd completely stopped purring. At last, Arcove said, in that same soft voice, "The day I met him, I'd been driven from my den...after seeing my brother and sister killed..."

"How *did* you win that fight, Arcove?" whispered Halvery. "I've always wondered. You were two years old. He was an adult! An officer!"

Arcove screwed his eyes shut. He thought carefully, and then said, "I didn't actually see my father die. I was in the den with my siblings. Horrible noises started coming from outside. Everyone told us to stay where we were. We didn't understand what was happening. Then my mother started keening.

"The triumphant challenger came into our den. He killed a spring litter so fast we didn't even have time to react. Then he turned to us. My brother ran, but he didn't reach the den's mouth. My sister made it outside, and I followed them. The challenger caught her... Then he turned to me. I guess he expected me to run."

Halvery could easily imagine the ugly scene. It had played out with startling frequency before Arcove threatened death to any cat who killed a cub.

"So he made a mistake?" guessed Halvery.

"He charged and I went straight at him. He missed me with his front paws, because he expected me to be moving away."

Halvery couldn't help laughing at the audacity of it.

"I ended up under his chest," continued Arcove. "I jumped straight up, caught his throat, and bit down as hard as I could. I let go immediately. I knew I had to get out of his way. I climbed a tree and watched him die. It took a while."

Halvery winced. "Did you tear out his throat?"

"No. I wasn't strong enough. I crushed his windpipe."

"That's amazing, Arcove. At two years old… Amazing."

Arcove's eyes remained on his paws atop Roup's golden fur. "I thought for a long time…if I'd done it sooner…my brother and sister wouldn't have died. If I'd just run out to meet him…"

Halvery gaped. "Arcove!"

He shook himself. "I know. But I was a cub. Cubs have foolish ideas and nobody was around to tell me otherwise."

"I cannot believe the den drove you away. After displaying skills like that."

"They were afraid. All the officers were friends. My mother thought that one of the others might show up and slaughter the whole den." He went quiet.

Halvery's thoughts wandered far away, into that more violent world in which he'd grown up—a world that cats like Moashi couldn't even imagine. Cubs hadn't died *every* time a den got a new alpha. Even before Arcove, there had been males who would either raise their rival's cubs or, more often, allow the female to flee with her litter, raising them as best she could on her own. But it was considered a winner's right to do as he saw fit with the cubs of his deposed rival. Their mother would not come into season as long as she was nursing. She would be ready for breeding sooner if he killed the cubs.

Halvery's first den had consisted of only three females barely older than himself. He'd beaten their alpha, though he hadn't killed him. There'd been only one cub in the den at the time—a scrawny yearling, who looked at Halvery with enormous, terrified eyes.

He remembered looking down at the cub, smelling his challenger's scent, and feeling the instinctive urge to strike. At the same time, he remembered being that small. He remembered ferryshaft tearing apart his brother.

Halvery had walked away, stiff-legged, and ignored the cub for several days. Later, he realized that he should have made his intentions clear, because the mother ran away with her yearling shortly thereafter. She proceeded to rejoin the cub's father in a distant den. Halvery didn't pursue them. He felt guilty about the whole episode for years. *I should have told her that she and the cub were safe. They could have stayed or walked away in peace. They didn't need to run from me.*

Later, when he took Velta's den from an officer whom he actually killed, he'd raised three litters of his rival's offspring in spite of the fact that their father had been a bully who was barely missed. By that point, Arcove's prohibition against cub-killing was in full effect, and Halvery had had to enforce it. He'd fought and killed a number of den alphas for slaughtering their rivals' cubs. He'd found that, in general, cub-killers were troublemakers, and his territory was better off without them. The females, in particular, were quietly delighted to have them gone.

But there had been no adult to defend two-year-old Arcove. His reward for avenging his father and siblings was rejection by the den and banishment from their territory. He thought king's officers might be hunting him. And he'd apparently believed that he was somehow responsible for his siblings' demise.

"Surely Roup told you it wasn't your fault," said Halvery aloud.

Arcove hesitated. "I was drinking at a stream just before he showed up. It was daytime, and I was tired and disoriented. I was looking at the stream and thinking…that the water would be over my head in the middle…"

Halvery went still. He didn't know what to say.

"I don't believe I would have done it," continued Arcove in an oddly detached voice. "I've always been…stubborn. I was just having a bleak moment. But then Roup walked up and he looked even more lost than I was. He talked oddly. He was a strange color. After we fought, he seemed so grateful that I didn't keep attacking him. I only beat him to establish dominance, so that he would do what I said and not get us both killed. I had no intention of hurting him. I found out later that when ferryshaft cliques attacked him, they didn't stop kicking him, even after he rolled over. So he expected me to…" There was a note of bewildered rage in his voice.

How could they? thought Halvery. *How could anyone?*

"I suppose I've always had an instinct to…protect someone," continued Arcove. "When I met Roup, I'd failed my siblings. But then he walked up and gave me his trust. He told me he'd come straight from a ferryshaft herd, that his only real friend was a ferryshaft whom he considered his brother. He knew these things would be viewed with suspicion in Leeshwood. He knew I could kill him. And yet he trusted me. He held nothing back."

Halvery smiled. "So then you had someone to protect."

Arcove thought about it. "Yes."

"First Roup, and then our clutter, and then all Leeshwood."

Arcove smiled. A moment's silence, and then, "He was the brightest thing in my sky for a long time."

It's quite obvious that he still is.

Arcove shook himself. "You joined us…what, two years later? You were four? You and I both."

"Yes," said Halvery. "I heard about this amazing cub my age who'd killed an officer and I just had to go fight with him."

Arcove laughed. "Were you a rogue? That doesn't seem right. I can't remember why you weren't in a clutter."

Halvery shifted uncomfortably. "Oh…that's because I never told you."

Arcove cocked his head curiously. "You were an officer's cub. Lamar. I seem to remember that was a stable den with no turn-over for a long time. But you didn't come to us from his territory…"

Halvery looked at his paws. "It was a stable den. I was lucky."

Luckier than you and Roup, at least.

"I remember your only litter-mate was killed by ferryshaft…" continued Arcove slowly. "You were vocal about your hatred of them, which, unfortunately, had the effect of making Roup afraid to speak around you."

Halvery screwed his eyes shut. "Yes, I thought he just didn't like me." Before Arcove could speak, he added brightly, "I'm sure he *also* didn't like me."

"You fought well and you didn't seem inclined to kill cubs," said Arcove. "You were smart, willing to take risks, and you knew Leeshwood's politics better than I did, because you grew up in an officer's den. In any other situation, you would have been my beta. I know it seemed unfair to you that I gave that to Roup without even letting the two of you fight."

"Oh, Arcove," began Halvery, "we don't need to retread that—"

"Your skills and background being what they were," interrupted Arcove, "it suddenly seems odd to me that you were at loose ends with no clutter."

Halvery looked at his paws.

"You don't have to tell me," said Arcove at last. "I'm not… You can stop calling me 'sir' right now."

Halvery laughed. "It's not that bad. Just embarrassing. Around the time I turned four, one of my father's mates started flirting with me. She wasn't any blood relation. I should have just told her to stop, but I…didn't understand." *Why is that the worst part?* "I…I thought she was just being friendly. I thought we were playing a game. She was only a couple of years older than me. My father caught us one day and nearly killed me."

Halvery remembered the pain of the deep bite that had gone all the way through his scruff and had doubtless been intended to sever his spine. But more than the pain, he remembered his bewildered humiliation. His sense of hurt and betrayal had mingled with his embarrassment at having truly not understood his stepmother's foreplay or where it was leading.

He didn't look at Arcove as he continued. "My father didn't just drive me from his den. He drove me entirely out of his territory, which meant that all the clutters of my acquaintance were inaccessible to me. I was suddenly a rogue in a territory I'd never entered before. I fought my way into a clutter, but they didn't know me, and they quickly learned the story of why I'd been rejected from my father's den. They weren't friendly, and they didn't seem inclined to employ my...skills and background, as you put it. They seemed to think I had betrayed my father and would likely betray other leaders."

Halvery was surprised when Arcove started grooming his ears. He laughed and put his head down across Arcove's paws. "Do I sound dreadfully pitiful? It was a long time ago. I've got no business complaining about my cubhood. It was mostly peaceful, and others had it much worse."

"I think that if Roup were awake, he would say that you've always smelled too nice for your own good," rumbled Arcove.

Halvery laughed.

"I'm sorry." Arcove's voice was kind. "What happened to you was unfair. You are the most loyal officer any king could ever ask for."

Those words shouldn't have mattered. The unpleasant event had been so long ago. Halvery felt certain that he shouldn't *need* anyone to tell him that he hadn't deserved his father's rage or the distrust of his first clutter. But something inside him clung desperately to this bit of compassion all the same.

"I'm surprised you didn't hear about it," muttered Halvery.

Arcove yawned. "My first clutter was full of rogues with sordid pasts. None of us said much about where we came from. I had more important things to do than gossip." He hesitated. "I didn't want anyone to ask where Roup came from."

Halvery raised his head, feeling a bit more confident and very grateful. "I wish I'd found a way to talk to him back then. I wish... I wanted so badly to be your friend."

Arcove looked away. "I know you did." He shifted his massive paws against Roup's downy belly. "Do you still?"

How can you even ask that?

Arcove did not meet his eyes. "I know the way I behave with Roup is...odd, and not the sort of thing that...inspires respect..."

"Arcove!" Halvery dared to lean across Roup and rub his face against Arcove's cheek. "I respect you so much that I don't even know how to say it. There is *nothing* you could do that would make me think less of you. I am so flattered that you are sitting here talking to me and that you trust me with Roup and...and with your confidence. I have admired you since the day we met, and I cannot imagine a better leader."

Arcove was laughing now. "Alright." He pushed back gently. "Alright, Halvery."

Halvery settled down again. He laid his head on Roup's chest and watched the rain, which finally seemed to be slackening.

At last, Arcove said, hesitantly, "How are his paws like flowers?"

One of Roup's paws was lying pads-up not far from Halvery's nose. *How can anyone look at it and not see a ring of petals?* But Arcove sounded completely serious.

"He's so pretty, Arcove. I know you can't see it. You were too young when you met. Looking at his paws must be like looking at your own."

Arcove hesitated. "Yes." Very softly he added, "But I see it... when you say it."

Oh... Halvery felt a warm flush of happiness that seemed to radiate through his stomach and chest. "Well, then, I will tell you, Arcove. I will tell you how beautiful he is."

* * * *

This chapter includes an author's note at the end of the book.

13

Shale

Roup woke from a deep and pleasant dream. The details began to slip away even before he opened his eyes, but he remembered that Coden had been there. He hadn't died on Turis Rock after all. He'd fallen into an otherway and returned after many years. Roup told him about Storm's chases and antics. "He thought he saw you in the Ghost Wood," said Roup, "but that can't be right."

Coden, Roup, and Arcove were all running beside the sea on a summer day, and for some reason Halvery was with them. They were talking and telling jokes, and the world was so bright and so warm. Roup had a sense of deep unity and peace, a feeling that he was folded up in love.

He opened his eyes.

He was in a chilly cave on his back, but fairly warm, because Arcove and Halvery were lying against him on either side. They were sound asleep with their heads on top of him. Arcove had one paw across his stomach. *Well, I suppose I am folded up in love. It's a bit less comfortable in waking life.*

The rain had stopped and the sky had cleared a little. It glowed with the luminous quality of predawn. Roup couldn't hear any water in the canyon, although he didn't try to look. He experimented with moving, but there was no chance he was going anywhere without waking his companions. *Let them sleep.*

Roup himself felt well-rested and sharper than he'd felt since leaving Leeshwood. *Did I have a genuine fight with Arcove last night? Did I say...? Ghosts. I should never speak to anyone when I haven't been sleeping.*

But maybe with all his wits about him, he wouldn't have been drawn into the evening that followed, and that... *I couldn't regret that. Halvery, I hope you're not feeling left out anymore.*

Roup squirmed again. *Love is heavy.* But they were so warm and after a while, his eyes started to blink shut again.

A distant swishing noise. Roup came sliding back out of his dream. *Footfalls in sand?*

Something was coming up the canyon from the direction of the valley. Roup tipped his head all the way back and managed to get an upside down view of the narrow slot. As he'd expected, there was no more water in the bottom, just shallow pools and mud.

He instinctively wanted to flip over, to be less vulnerable to the approaching animal. *But if I wake Arcove and Halvery right now, we'll all be moving around when the creature comes into view. Halvery will start talking. We're less likely to be spotted if we remain still and quiet.* Roup steeled himself to remain as he was. However, his resolve nearly faltered when the animal came into view.

Flurry! Thistle's juvenile messenger was all-but running up the slot, dodging puddles and pausing occasionally to look over his shoulder. He did glance once at the cave's mouth as he came around the corner, but the cave must have looked like a mass of motionless shadows from below. Flurry ran on without a pause.

Roup forced himself to wait three full breaths before he heaved himself up, dislodging Arcove and Halvery in a muttering, bleary-eyed pile. "Wake up, wake up!" hissed Roup. "Flurry just ran by down there!"

"What?" Arcove blinked hard.

Halvery squinted into the canyon. "Are you sure?"

"Yes!" whispered Roup. "And he's barely gone, so keep your voices down. He came up from the valley, running and looking over his shoulder."

"I threatened him with death if he left the clutter," growled Arcove.

"Well, he seems willing to risk death," returned Roup.

Halvery jumped down into the canyon, sniffing. He looked up almost immediately and murmured, "Definitely Flurry's scent and tracks."

Roup and Arcove jumped down, sinking a little into the wet sand. "You were right last night, Halvery," muttered Roup. "This feels like a trap. I should have seen it earlier…"

"Yes, but why would Flurry run away from the clutters?" returned Halvery. "If he's meant to lead us into a trap, why risk losing our goodwill and the rapport he's built with Arcove?"

Roup didn't have an answer.

"There could have been a disaster," said Arcove. Roup could tell that he didn't want to say the words aloud, but he continued, "If the clutters were attacked and scattered… If Flurry escaped… of course he'd try to run home."

In that case, I wish I'd called to him, thought Roup.

Halvery swallowed. "If the ferryshaft herd was at the western end of the valley and we somehow didn't see them… If they figured out where the clutters were sleeping and attacked while they were still recovering from their journey…"

"No," said Roup with conviction. "Ferryshaft would have howled. They would have been signaling to each other. We would have heard it all the way down here. *Storm* would have howled, Arcove. He would have tried to let you know what was happening. I grew up with ferryshaft. Even when they are trying to be quiet, the instinct to signal is strong."

Arcove let out a long breath, his eyes darting back and forth as he considered Roup's words. He relaxed a fraction. "You're right."

Halvery spoke, his relief giving way to new suspicion, "Well, in that case, Flurry came here on business of his own—something so important that it was worth breaking his word to you, Arcove. And I confess, I have no idea what that could be. Even a trap doesn't quite make sense."

"He could have trailed us last night," said Roup. "Maybe he hoped to let Thistle's cats know that they could catch the three of us alone."

Halvery cocked his head. "An interesting idea…"

Arcove gave an ironic smile. "If that's the case, our near-miss has foiled them. Flurry could have only have tracked us to the base of the dry wash. After that, the flood would have obliterated our trail. He'll know that we're in these canyons somewhere, but he'll have no idea where."

"That would explain him running and looking over his shoulder," said Halvery.

They all stood still for a moment, thinking.

"What are we going to do, Arcove?" asked Halvery at last. "Follow him or go back to the clutters?"

Arcove looked torn, as well he might. It was a critical decision without enough information. At last, he said, "If there has been a disaster among the clutters, it has already happened. But I think Roup is right, and we would have heard howling. It could have happened during the storm, but..."

Roup winced. He hadn't thought of that.

"But in that case," continued Arcove, "Flurry would have had to travel all the way down the valley during that storm, which began late in the night. It's hard to imagine him making the journey that quickly and in bad weather. I think the more likely explanation is that Flurry slipped away from Hollygold's clutter early in the evening on some mission of his own. I think it's critical that we learn what that mission is. The flood gifted us with a bit of luck. Our trail has been obliterated. Neither Flurry nor Thistle's cats will know we are here, and Roup saw him run past, so we can follow him closely. We'll never get a better opportunity to learn what is going on."

"So we follow him," said Halvery.

"Yes." Arcove turned up the canyon.

Roup knew it was the best decision, based on the information available to them, and yet he was plagued by thoughts of Lyndi, either fighting for her life, or worried by their failure to return at dawn. She would be making hard decisions soon if they didn't come back. *Did I say good-bye properly? Is there any proper way to say good-bye to a friend of thirty odd-years, who has walked with you through triumph and sorrow?*

The canyons began to branch as they rose higher. It was truly a maze. Without Flurry's trail, they would have had no idea which way to go, but his recent scent and wet pawprints were easy to follow.

Roup noted several winding chasms that definitely ran away to the lake caves. He noticed tree limbs wedged high over their heads between the rock walls. *Maybe Flurry was only running for fear of floods. Maybe we should be running, too.*

Arcove kept up a swift lope, but not a headlong charge. He didn't want to come upon enemies unaware. They were all straining their ears for calls or voices. Few animals lived in the slots, and the world seemed unnaturally quiet. Tiny birds chirped in the underbrush at the top, and there was a constant, ominous creak of distant ice. Occasionally a loud popping sound issued from the lake, probably the debris that had washed down from the mountains, applying pressure to the ice near the caves.

They were going steeply uphill now. Flurry's trail did not always lead through the broad, obvious passages. He occasionally squeezed into the narrowest of openings, into spaces that looked too small for a creasia, but after several tight turns, the canyon would broaden out again.

Always, they followed the wet sand. This made sense if Flurry was headed for the upper valley. Water was the reason this pass existed, cutting its way from the higher lake to the lower one. Still, Roup couldn't help looking longingly into the canyons where the sand was dry. They were so obviously safer.

The creasia passed more and more such offshoots as they went higher. These were canyons that had been cut long ago, before the water changed course. Some of these inlets had inviting stands of trees around little pools. They looked like good places to hunt.

"Later," said Arcove when Halvery stopped to gaze into one such tributary.

Roup kept looking at spots where they might be able to get off the bottom. Plenty of the canyons had narrow ledges, where he suspected sheep and highland curbs might run, but not a full-grown creasia. "We could get to the top there," he said at last, eyeing a spot where a rockslide created steps. "We could follow Flurry from above."

"It would be safer, but more visible," said Arcove. "There's not much cover on top, as I'm sure you remember. If we want to creep up on him, we'd best stay in the slots."

"Flurry knows his way around," Halvery pointed out. "If he thinks it's safe, it probably is."

"It can become *unsafe* in the blink of an eye," muttered Roup.

They passed another dry, overgrown canyon, and this time, all of them stopped. There was a freshly killed sheep just visible among the distant rocks, lying at the mouth of a cave. It was half eaten, but inviting morsels remained. Roup's mouth watered. He heard Halvery's stomach growl.

"No," hissed Arcove. "Look at the ground. *Look* at it."

They all looked down and saw, in the wet sand leading into the canyon, tracks at least double the size of creasia pawprints. The tracks had very long claws. Roup could almost hear Cohal saying, *"Ice bear."*

"Sir, I think we could get the meat and run…" began Halvery, but Arcove had already moved on.

"Leave it," he said in his most implacable growl.

Halvery shut his eyes and turned away. Roup followed him, feeling hollow, but relieved.

The morning dawned cold and clear. The sun was just sending its first rays over the edge of the slots when Roup caught the sound of voices at last. Sound carried oddly in the echoing canyons, and it was difficult to say exactly how far ahead the speakers were standing. All three creasia froze.

Flurry: "I just need to speak to him for a moment."

A stranger, sounding annoyed: "I'm afraid that won't be possible; he's busy. Chief isn't going to be pleased about you turning up this way."

"I'm telling you, Arcove and his lieutenants are up here somewhere—"

"Our scouts haven't seen them, and there was a flood last night. They might be dead. More likely they went back to their army. We'll send someone out to look for them, but it would have been easier if you'd done what you were supposed to—"

"They're not fools!" snapped Flurry. "They'll have seen the ferryshaft bodies. I'm sure they were looking for the ferryshaft herd. They'll bring attention to—"

"*You* are the one bringing unwanted attention. Were you followed when leaving their army? You're behaving like a hunted animal."

"It's hardly an army," returned Flurry. "It's about sixty cats. I don't know whether I was followed. They have a couple of highland curbs and a ferryshaft—"

A gust of treacherous wind swept up the canyon from the lake, no doubt bringing Arcove, Roup, and Halvery's scents to the speakers. The voices ceased at once. Arcove gave up on subterfuge and bounded forward. The three of them whipped around the next tight turn, and there, on a ledge about halfway up the canyon wall, stood two surprised-looking creasia.

One was Flurry, who shot up the wall and disappeared over the top. The other cat turned to hiss something after him. He didn't run, though. He looked down at Arcove, Roup, and Halvery with an expression that Roup couldn't interpret. Curiosity, surprise, and excitement seemed to flicker over his face and then vanish into a bland smile.

He jumped down from the ledge. "Arcove Ela-creasia… Welcome to Thistle's Leeshwood. We are dreadfully honored that you've come, although…we were expecting a bit more of a warning, and…" His eyes strayed past the three cats to the jog in the canyon behind them. "I don't meant to sound ungrateful, but we were expecting a larger party."

Arcove did not respond at once. Silence had always been his weapon of choice when speaking to those he didn't trust.

They were only a few paces from the other cat, and Roup took the opportunity to study him. The fellow was a dark, brindled gray, the color of mountain stone. He had a muscular build, heavier than Flurry, and completely filled out. He was in his prime, eight years old at the youngest, and probably closer to fifteen or twenty. He could have fought beside Treace on Kuwee Island, although Roup thought it more likely that he'd been born shortly after the rebellion. His ears were notched from many a fight, and he seemed confident.

At last, Arcove said, "I have come at Thistle's dire request... because we are kin...because I do not like to see creasia anywhere suffer. But, as Thistle himself pointed out, there hasn't been much love lost between our two Leeshwoods. You are not inspiring me with trust. Furthermore, you know my name, but I don't know yours. I do not carry on conversations with mysteries."

The other cat gave a startled laugh. "Your name is a legend, sir, and mine means nothing. But if it matters, it's Shale. Now, if you will excuse me, I'd like to ask my leader how to proceed. Flurry was supposed to let us know when to expect you. He was supposed to bring your entire army. Instead, he has panicked for some silly reason and arrived early with you alone."

He hesitated, as though expecting Arcove to correct these misstatements about Flurry's behavior, to ask questions, or to offer an alternative explanation.

Arcove just waited.

At last, Shale said, "I don't know where your...payment for helping us...might be located at the moment."

Roup's eyes widened. *He's talking about Dazzle.*

"You can surely understand how this puts us in an awkward place," continued Shale. "If you run into the wrong cat, there could unnecessary conflict. We want you to feel welcome, sir, and to receive your due without injury to yourself or your officers. We definitely need your help and do not wish to offend you."

Arcove looked at him narrowly. At last, he said, "Where is the ferryshaft herd? Why were there so many dead ferryshaft at the foot of the canyons?"

Shale had probably been expecting questions about Flurry or Dazzle. This line of inquiry seemed to catch him off-guard. He started to speak and then hesitated. *He's concocting a lie,* thought Roup.

"As you probably guessed, there has been a battle," said Shale. "The ferryshaft came up into the canyons and fought with us. They were driven down on the southern side of the lake. They are licking their wounds over there beneath the trees."

Roup frowned. This was possible. It was easier to access the canyons from the northern side, but the herd *could* have ended up on the southern side, and there were enough trees over there to hide them.

"Did Sedaron not kill any of your cats in the battle?" asked Arcove. "We saw only ferryshaft bodies."

Another pause. "I'm pleased to tell you that Sedaron is dead, Arcove. He was killed in the fighting. One of his lieutenants, Macex, is leading. As to the battle, we certainly lost cats, but not in the lower canyons. The cats who were killed were washed into the lake."

He didn't volunteer numbers, and Arcove didn't ask. *You think he's telling you a pack of lies,* thought Roup, *and you're not interested in hearing any more of them.*

"Well," said Arcove slowly, his green eyes boring into Shale, "that is momentous news. Are you hoping we will wait here while you...consult?"

Shale gave a little snort of laughter that was not entirely respectful. "I was hoping that, yes, Arcove. You may wait at the top if you'd prefer." He inclined his head towards the ledge that created a stepping point to the top of the canyon.

Yes, thought Roup, who was feeling more and more hemmed in by the canyon's walls. *Let's get to the top.*

But Arcove surprised him by saying, "No, I believe we are fine right here. I take it we are near the confluence?"

Shale twitched his tail. Roup thought he was annoyed and trying not to show it. "Yes, sir, the confluence is just ahead. I can assure you that all debts will be settled before we go to sleep today."

He gave Arcove a meaningful smile and then bounded up the wall and out of the canyon.

14

Thistle

"He's awfully full of assurances for a sentry who hasn't even spoken to his superiors yet," muttered Halvery.

"I don't think he's a sentry," murmured Arcove. "I think he's an officer. If Dazzle has the kind of support Thistle implied, then only Thistle's inner circle would know about our agreement."

"*If* the whole thing isn't Dazzle's ruse," said Halvery.

Arcove grunted.

"Arcove, why can't we go to the top of the slot?" whispered Roup. "I don't like feeling trapped here."

"Nor do I, but it's easier for them to keep an eye on us up there in the open. Down here we can at least decide to leave unobserved if we so choose."

"I'm not sure about that," muttered Halvery. "They could have cats all around us by now. They could be waiting if we go back down the canyon."

"True," said Arcove, "but they invited us to go to the top, and I am disinclined to do exactly as they expect."

The sun was halfway up the sky, throwing light down the wall over the shelf. Roup watched it creep lower. He was glad that they'd all had a good nap last night. At least he didn't feel sleepy.

Finally, three new cats appeared, this time wending their way downhill from the direction of the confluence. The cat in the lead was of average size, with a coat the color of light brown sand and eyes like sunbaked earth. His winter coat was so dense and his ear tufts so long that it was impossible to tell whether his ears were notched, but his muzzle was certainly scarred from fights. He moved with a grace that reminded Roup of Dazzle. *Dangerous,* was the word that went through Roup's head.

Interestingly, the two behind him were both a little bigger. They looked like brothers and had pale gray fur like Moashi. They were obviously guards.

"Arcove," said their leader in a soft, conciliatory voice, "I'm Thistle." He continued quickly without waiting for a response, "I'm sorry that this meeting has occurred in such a haphazard manner. I am overwhelmed with relief that you responded to my plea for help. Thank you for coming.

"I beg your pardon for the behavior of my messenger. When Flurry learned that you'd left your clutters last night with only two officers, he panicked. You seemed intent upon coming up here and meeting with us unannounced. He thought you might run into Dazzle or his supporters. He followed you, found the ferryshaft bodies, and became even more frightened when he realized there'd been a major battle. He was afraid that I was dead and that Dazzle was leading. He did not know what you would do in that case, but it hardly matters, because I'm still here. Again, I apologize for the suspicious circumstances under which you arrived. Your presence and assistance are very much appreciated."

Thistle's explanation made more sense than Roup wanted to admit. Arcove sat down slowly, studying him.

Thistle gave a thin, sad smile and added, "If, in fact, you were hoping to find me dead and Dazzle in charge, you may still get that wish. He would like to challenge me. He doesn't quite have enough support, but it's closer every day. I can't be sure who would win, but I suspect that if I survived at all, I'd be limping for the rest of my life. I'm sure you can understand..." His eyes flitted to Roup.

You are well-informed, thought Roup, and couldn't help bristling, even though Thistle hadn't actually said anything to deserve it.

At the same time, Roup recalled, unwillingly, how Dazzle had injured Lusha. Roup had shifted Dazzle out of Halvery's clutter to keep Halvery from harm. Then he'd trained Moashi all summer, so that Moashi could just barely avoid injury. And here was one more cat who didn't want to fight with Dazzle. *I'd be a hypocrite to fault Thistle there.* Roup searched for some flaw in Thistle's presentation of events, but it fit with everything they knew.

Out of the corner of his eye, he could see Arcove relaxing ever so slightly. *You just want to kill Dazzle,* thought Roup bitterly, *but... maybe you should.*

"Is Sedaron actually dead?" asked Arcove.

"He is," said Thistle. "Killed by Dazzle, actually, so maybe it's just as well you didn't get here earlier." He laughed, and Arcove allowed a faint smile in return.

"As it happens," continued Thistle, "you've arrived just in time for a parley with Macex. Do you want to attend?"

That took them all by surprise. "What are you expecting him to offer?" asked Arcove.

Thistle sighed. "I'm expecting him to offer to leave us alone in exchange for favors. We gave a good account of ourselves in the battle, but we're still desperately outnumbered. I think they've got about six hundred ferryshaft who can still fight. We've got maybe a hundred and twenty creasia, and that includes pregnant females."

Arcove cocked his head. "Why would he let you surrender at all? He could annihilate you."

Thistle rocked his head. "Not without losing more of his herd. They were shaken by Sedaron's death, and Macex has different goals. He'd like..." Thistle made a face. "*Tame* creasia. Creasia who will do his bidding. He's ambitious, but unlike Sedaron, his ambition isn't to rule an island with no living cats."

Roup glanced at Arcove to see whether he was going to say anything about the herd's plans for attacking Leeshwood, but Arcove just watched Thistle. At last, he said, "My understanding was that Macex was willing to parley with cats, but not with me."

A toothy grin spread across Thistle's face. "Well, he may have no choice. Surprise?"

That made Halvery laugh.

"With you up here, the situation is altered," continued Thistle. "Flurry says you arrived with only sixty cats, but I assume they're the best fighters in Leeshwood."

Arcove did not confirm or deny this.

Thistle continued, "In any case, we don't actually have to tell the ferryshaft the size of your army. Just the sight of you and your officers will convince Macex and his ferryshaft that you've arrived to tip the balance in our favor. They think they're here to dictate the terms of our surrender, but instead, you can tell them that you'll generously let them live if they leave at once. I'd love to see the expressions on their faces."

Roup could tell that Halvery liked the sound of that. He particularly liked the idea of forcing a confrontation on Macex after he'd publicly disdained to parley with Arcove. Roup wasn't sure what to think. "What about Dazzle?" he asked quietly.

Thistle turned from Arcove. His eyes slid over Roup. "I'm impressed that you're still walking, friend. You got very lucky."

His tone was kind, and yet Roup thought, *I am not ready to call you 'friend,' and I don't like this overly familiar manner.*

Thistle continued, "Here is what I propose. Dazzle will be at the conference. I do apologize if this makes you uncomfortable. He is my beta, so this is unavoidable. You don't have to speak to him.

"Afterward, when we all leave, I suggest that you follow a little behind me and my officers. We'll make our way towards the high valley through a canyon with deep mud at the bottom. I will make certain that Dazzle gets pushed into this mud. It won't kill him, but it will slow him down. He'll likely need help getting out. We'll be sure to bite him 'accidentally' as we're dragging him up the bank. His claws will be caked with mud, and he may be…" Thistle gave a delicate laugh. "…limping. He's all yours after that. My officers are loyal, and they will not interfere. In fact, we'll probably just leave you to it. You may do whatever you like for as long as you like and meet us to share some hunting afterward in the upper valley."

I do not like you at all, thought Roup.

But Arcove only said, "His supporters?"

Thistle flicked his tail. "Did Roup tell you what happened after your officer Moashi beat Dazzle in a fight? The entire assembly turned on him, including his former friends. He is feared by other cats because of his skill. They follow him in the way cats follow cruel and cunning leaders, but the moment he is gone, everyone will claim they never liked him.

"You were extremely provoked by his behavior, as everyone knows. You have a justified right to vengeance. None of my cats will fault you for killing Dazzle, Arcove. No one will miss him or even mention his name once he's gone."

15

Confluence

Roup wanted time to discuss the situation with Arcove and Halvery. He wanted time to think. He wanted something to eat.

But they weren't going to get any of those things. According to Thistle, the conference was now. "The ferryshaft are already waiting. I had to choose between letting them wait and letting you wait. Of the two, I prefer letting Macex think I don't respect his time."

Roup glanced sidelong at Halvery over Arcove's back. *Are you swallowing all of this silky stuff?*

Halvery looked like he was amused by Thistle's jokes, but he caught Roup's eye and gave a little twitch of his lip. *Too smooth. Thank you.*

Thistle kept up an easy chatter as they walked and the canyon walls shot up around them. "Don't worry," he paused to say, "there's no rain in the upper valley right now. My sentries would pass the word quickly if there was. With sufficient warning, there is plenty of time to get out of the slot, and we know the fastest ways."

The corridor broadened as the walls grew higher, until it was some twenty lengths across, running steep and straight towards a distant point of dawn light. Roup noted, longingly, that sheep were moving high on the walls. He felt certain that no creasia could reach them.

The floor of the canyon lay in deep shadow. Roup supposed it must always be twilight here. The sand was cold underfoot, crackling with a film of ice. Roup realized, with a jolt, that parts of the canyon walls were composed entirely of ice. He glimpsed creatures frozen in the dark depths—fishes and things like enormous lizards, something with red fur.

Thistle caught him looking and smiled. "It's melting. A little more each summer. I wonder sometimes if anything is alive in there. It's amazing how some animals can sleep through the cold… just waiting for their moment."

Roup wanted to ask questions about the creatures in the ice, but he was too worried. They came over a rocky rise, full of water-polished boulders, and saw a nexus ahead. Some half dozen canyon waterways, large and small, converged here, amid a jumble of rock, driftwood, and gleaming chunks of ice.

The confluence.

As Thistle had said, a group of ferryshaft and creasia were waiting in a clear spot on the sand, looking tense and impatient. Roup counted nearly twenty ferryshaft, clearly ready to defend themselves. He was a little surprised they'd agreed to this location, although he supposed they must be itching for a closer look at the heart of the pass.

Thistle's party included five other cats in addition to himself and the two guards behind him. Shale was in the group. It took Roup a moment to spot Dazzle on the farthest edge of the circle. He was in dense winter pelage, but no winter coat could hide the claw tracks across the fine fur of his muzzle. The scar went all the way over his left eye, although he had apparently kept his vision.

Roup couldn't help thinking of the last time they'd seen each other. He'd been dizzy with blood-loss and pain. Dazzle and Halvery had crashed around the cave in a shrieking blur of claws. Roup could still see Dazzle stumbling backwards, blinded by blood, and Halvery lunging forward to finish him. Roup's voice had cracked out, "Stop!" and Dazzle had escaped with his life.

Roup had tried his best to have a follow-up conversation. He'd come so close, and yet he hadn't quite succeeded. *Arcove is right. I don't know enough to judge his character.*

Dazzle froze as the three of them took a seat more-or-less across from him in the circle. Roup supposed that Thistle had arranged this on purpose. He *had* said that they wouldn't have to speak to Dazzle. Their relative positions made it impossible for him to say anything to them that wasn't public.

Dazzle's eyes met Roup's.

Roup had been hoping for a shocked reaction of the sort that couldn't be faked—bristling or dilated pupils. Then he would know for certain that Dazzle had had no part in bringing them here.

Dazzle did freeze, staring at Roup. He was certainly surprised, but his reaction wasn't as definitive as Roup would have liked. Without taking his eyes off Roup, Dazzle muttered to the cat beside him. He clearly found his neighbor's reply unsatisfying. He stared some more.

Are you surprised I'm walking? wondered Roup acidly.

Thistle strolled into the middle of the circle and faced the ferryshaft who must be Macex. As Roup had expected, he was a big male in his prime, more brown than red, with the distinction of pale legs and tail tip. He did not look pleased, and Thistle's smirk couldn't have done anything to pacify him. Macex shot a glare at Arcove. "I didn't agree to this."

"Quite right," crooned Thistle. "We don't always get what we want, do we? The situation is altered. We have reinforcements who can surround you and slaughter every last ferryshaft in the valley. Fortunately, I am willing to offer terms."

Macex sputtered. He matched Thistle's condescending tone. "I see three cats. Three *old* cats from a generation that is dying. If you think I'll spook just because one of them is black, you don't know me as well as you suppose."

Arcove looked annoyed that he was being treated like a bargaining chip, rather than an ally and peer. "Thistle may be ready to offer you terms," he said ominously, "but I'm not."

"I'm not talking to you, old one," snapped Macex.

"Then perhaps you'd like to be at war with me," said Arcove. "Your herd is battered, wounded, and reduced. You've lost your leader. I'm sure some of your people are questioning your decisions. But by all means, pick an avoidable fight with me. If you reject the terms you're being offered today, the next ones will look a lot like my treaty terms of years past."

Macex looked like he was about to start shouting. The ferryshaft around him were muttering and shifting.

Thistle wasn't doing anything to conciliate his opponent. "*My* terms," he hissed, "are that you will vacate the lower valley *immediately.* However, you will leave three ferryshaft of my choice to live as our guests here. If you *ever* even slightly inconvenience me again, I will kill them in the most creative ways I can devise. And we both know I can get quite creative."

"You are a monster and a coward," rasped Macex.

"Maybe, but I'd be hard-pressed to keep up with you. I'll allow you to switch hostages from time to time. How's that? Quite generous, really. I should make you stay yourself. See what kind of leader you really are."

Arcove looked a little baffled by the speed with which the confrontation had escalated. Roup suspected he was annoyed that the hostage idea had not been presented to him before they arrived. It was an extreme measure and Roup doubted that Arcove would have agreed to support it.

Roup could feel Dazzle's eyes on him. The rest of Thistle's creasia were on their feet, offering muffled commentary regarding Thistle and Macex's standoff. But Dazzle just stared at Roup. Finally, he looked down and moved one of his front paws delicately through the sand. He looked up again, eyes intent.

Macex and Thistle had moved on to shouting at each other about various skirmishes during the spring siege, including the one in which Sedaron had been killed. "You broke your promise and nothing you say can be trusted!" shouted Macex.

"You tortured a messenger and have no right to my mercy or forbearance!" snarled Thistle.

Halvery nudged Roup, who couldn't bring himself to take his eyes off Dazzle. "No wonder they can't come to an agreement," Halvery muttered in Roup's ear. "It's like neither of them has ever heard of civil discourse. If this is the future, I don't like their odds."

Roup couldn't help but smile. "I'm sure Moashi would do better."

"I'm actually inclined to agree with you."

"Well, it's obvious you won't see reason," said Thistle at last. "I suppose Arcove will have to put you back under creasia law, and we can cull your herd every winter."

Macex sneered. "He'll be too busy trying to protect his precious cubs. We know how to kill creasia: when they're small and tasty." He turned, his ferryshaft closing up to watch his back. "We're done here."

"Very well," snarled Thistle.

Roup felt an unpleasant heave in the pit of his stomach. He knew what was supposed to happen next. *Too fast. This is happening too fast.*

The ferryshaft were already moving away towards a canyon behind them. Thistle and his cats turned in the opposite direction, vanishing quickly among the boulders. No one paused to look at Arcove, Roup, and Halvery. Everything was happening exactly as Thistle had predicted. *Everything except that farce of a parley.*

Roup half expected Dazzle to hesitate, to try to speak to him. But Dazzle got up along with the rest of Thistle's cats and trotted away without a backwards glance. There was a moment of silence, wherein Arcove, Halvery, and Roup looked at each other.

Then Roup got up and crossed the circle to the spot Dazzle had been sitting. *He couldn't have written anything intelligible... could he?*

Writing even a single character with a paw in a small space was nearly impossible. Dazzle hadn't tried. He'd made a line with a hook at the end. Roup stared at it.

It's not a word; it's a notation. Ghosts, Dazzle, you do put a lot of faith in my knowledge of cave writing. Such notations never appeared in the ferryshaft writing caves or even in the telshee Cave of Histories. One found such things in caves where an animal was trying to leave transitory information, perhaps guidance regarding which direction to go for water or food or safety. Such notations were often temporary and not renewed.

Storm would know what it means, but I don't.

Arcove and Halvery came up behind Roup.

Halvery sighed when he saw what Roup was looking at. "He just keeps playing with you, doesn't he?"

"Do you know what it means?" demanded Roup.

Halvery didn't answer. He turned to Arcove. "Let's go kill him, Arcove. I think Thistle is a terrible negotiator, and Macex is an arrogant rat's pizzle. But everything Thistle said about Dazzle aligns with what we know. Dazzle is just going to keep toying with Roup until you get rid of him. Then you can decide whether you need to get rid of Thistle, too, because I don't trust him, either."

Roup turned to Arcove desperately. "If you ever trusted my judgment, Arcove... If you ever thought I had any meaningful contribution to your reign or to your council..."

Arcove let out an exasperated breath. "Do you know what it means, Halvery?"

Halvery screwed his eyes shut. At last, he said heavily, "I believe it means 'This way.' I'm not *sure,* mind you. I overheard

Storm explaining these things to Costa once, but I wasn't paying much attention."

They all looked in the direction the hook was pointing. It was not the way the ferryshaft had gone, nor was it exactly the way Thistle's cats had left, although it was the same general direction.

Halvery peered through the boulders. "Dazzle is probably waiting with his followers to ambush and kill us."

Roup looked at Arcove, "You said you didn't want to do exactly as they expect."

"As who expects?" demanded Halvery. "Dazzle or Thistle?"

Arcove's eyes remained on Roup's. At last, he turned and stalked in the direction that the hook indicated. Roup let out a breath and followed. He expected Halvery to grumble, but he only sighed and matched Arcove's careful, soundless footfalls.

They hadn't gone far when they encountered another line drawn in the sand, directing them towards a fissure in the cliff wall ahead. Roup tried to go in first, but Halvery gave him a pointed look and nudged him aside. "My shoulder still twinges," he hissed.

"Well, then, let me go first and take my own consequences," snapped Roup.

Arcove gave them both a *look* that meant, "Be quiet" and jerked his head for them to get out of the way. Halvery moved aside and Arcove went first. After a moment's hesitation, Halvery smiled sweetly and jerked his head for Roup to go next.

Roup thought, *I have beaten both of you in fights.* But he took the sheltered middle spot as indicated. This tunnel appeared to be made entirely of ice. It ran straight and very steep, with bright daylight at the far end. This had the unfortunate effect of preventing their eyes from completely adjusting to the shadows. Reflected light gleamed all around them.

The tunnel opened out a little, so that they could walk abreast. Arcove was going slowly. He stopped all at once, a ridge of fur rising from his hackles to his hips. A shadow moved ahead, then became recognizably the silhouette of ears and whiskers. Dazzle's voice out of the gloom: "Roup?"

"I'm here," said Roup.

"So am I," snapped Halvery. "So is Arcove. What do you—?"

Dazzle spoke softly and rapidly, "Roup, you are unbelievable! You've got me, alright? You win." He caught his breath. "Don't go up there; they're going to kill you."

16

More Chaos

All three of them stared at Dazzle, who continued in a rush, "Thistle and Macex made an alliance earlier in the spring. They were just putting on a show for you back there. Macex let Sedaron and his closest followers get slaughtered in the battle. He told Thistle where we could ambush them and then pulled his own ferryshaft back. Thistle killed Sedaron for Macex, and Macex is supposed to kill Arcove for Thistle. Then they're going to take Leeshwood together.

"They expected you to show up with an army, Arcove. Macex has about six hundred ferryshaft left, and they are all waiting just beyond the confluence to pounce on your animals in the narrow pass. I can't believe you showed up alone; what were you thinking? I'm not even sure why they bothered putting on a show—"

Dazzle stopped, his eyes skipping between their faces. "I've missed something, haven't I? Why *did* they put on a show? They could have just killed you. But they... Ghosts. They offered you something to get you up here, didn't they? It was more than just begging." He laughed—a dark, brittle sound. "Me. They offered you me. Why else would you have come? Even Roup isn't that merciful."

Dazzle drew another quick, ragged breath. He looked away from Roup and focused on Arcove. "I'll keep that bargain. My life in exchange for my cats. Get them out of here. Take them back to Leeshwood. Your Leeshwood. Not Thistle's."

Roup cut his eyes at Arcove. *What do you think of his character now?*

But Arcove looked like he wasn't sure what to think. He was clearly being lied to by someone, possibly by everyone, and Arcove despised liars.

Halvery stalked forward and was suddenly nose to nose with Dazzle. "You always say the right thing, don't you, Dazzle?"

Dazzle dropped to his belly, his voice a hurry of nerves. "Say? Yes. Do? Not so much."

Halvery glared down at him. "We're in agreement there. You've *done* the wrong thing so often that I, for one, do not trust a word you've said. We're free to kill you? That's what you just told us. You'll roll over and die right now? No fight?"

Dazzle swallowed. "I would advise you to wait until we've gotten these creasia away from Thistle and out of the valley. They won't follow you otherwise."

Halvery's lip curled. "Ah, I knew there was a catch!"

"I am telling you the truth—"

"Enough," growled Arcove. "Dazzle, you came into my wood under false pretenses, as a spy, to undermine my rule. That alone ought to carry a death sentence. But then you attacked my beta in cold blood for the sole purpose of doing me a personal injury. You did this while he was offering you mercy."

"I know that," whispered Dazzle. "I tried to kill the best person I have ever met—"

Arcove spoke on, "If what you've just said is true, you were party to a plan to lure me and my officers into these mountains with a plea for help, playing on our mercy and goodwill, and then trade our lives to Macex for control of Leeshwood once we arrived. You seem to have been unaware of the price offered for my assistance... but you knew the rest."

Dazzle had stopped trying to interrupt.

Arcove continued, "You have utterly forfeited my mercy, Dazzle Ela-creasia. I put a great deal of store by promises. If we make this bargain, your life is mine when this is over, and if you cross me in any way, there will be consequences for these cats you'd like me to rescue. I'll leave them up here to deal with their own mess, for one thing. If they're at all like you, I can't imagine that I'd find them an asset to my Leeshwood."

Dazzle bowed his head and tucked his tail.

Roup hated everything about what was happening, but he thought, *Get out of here first; worry about the rest later.*

Halvery sniffed. "Sir, any liar can roll over and make promises he doesn't intend to keep. I'm still not convinced—"

"Peace, Halvery, I'm not going to follow him anywhere just yet," returned Arcove.

Dazzle looked up in alarm. "We need to get away from the confluence. Thistle and Macex—"

"Are planning to murder me; yes, you said." Arcove began walking up the tunnel towards the light at the far end. "You also said, 'Don't go up there,' so I assume that's where they went."

Dazzle stood up, glancing between the three of them. "Yes, but—" He had to trot to keep pace with Arcove.

"According to Thistle, *we* are supposed to kill *you* up there," said Roup gently.

"How?" asked Dazzle. He sounded genuinely curious.

"You were supposed to be pushed into the mud," said Roup.

"Oh. Yes, I suppose that would slow me down."

"Roup, stop talking to him," said Arcove. "Dazzle, in front."

Dazzle moved reluctantly to the front of the group. "It is possible to get up the sides of this canyon," he said. "We'll be visible on top, but...we can jump down into some of the lava tunnels and disappear. I just don't know how we'll get word to the others..."

Roup pushed up beside Arcove and muttered in his ear, "Do you *really* have to do this? Why can't we just run back the way we came?"

Arcove shot him an exasperated look. "Because either Thistle or Dazzle is lying to me—"

"Or both," put in Halvery from the other side of Arcove. "I would not discount the possibility of both, sir."

Arcove spoke with distaste. "Forcing a confrontation between them may reveal which of them is lying *less*. Also, I am increasingly disinclined to do exactly what either of these cats wants or expects. So, we'll go in there, but not the way Thistle would like. Then we'll see what happens. Also, if we do have to run for our lives, I would prefer to be on top of the slots. There's no place to get out for a long way behind us."

Roup had to agree with him about that. The daylight at the end of the tunnel loomed brighter. Roup realized that the time must be near midday. *None of us is thinking as clearly as we should be.*

They emerged, blinking, and found themselves at one end of a relatively short canyon with broad walls open to the sky. The floor of the canyon dropped off sharply into a trench of deep, wet clay. A narrow ledge hugged the canyon walls all around the clay pit, probably worn by generations of curbs and sheep long before Thistle's creasia came up here. The uneven walls offered many small footholds. Roup saw several places where he could probably reach the top.

Dazzle looked to their right, and Roup followed his gaze just a little further to the western end of the canyon. The same creasia who'd been at the parley were gathered around the spot where the canyon must wind down to the confluence. They were apparently waiting for Arcove and his officers. Roup realized that Dazzle must have slipped away while they were all watching the tunnel.

Dazzle glanced over his shoulder to make sure Arcove and company were following, then trotted boldly to the rear of the waiting creasia. "Lose something, Thistle?"

Thistle spun around. His eyes skipped over Dazzle, Arcove, Roup, and Halvery. He gave a cautious smile. "I didn't realize it would be so easy to get lost..."

Dazzle ignored this. His voice came out flat and bitter. "What were you going to tell the others? That Arcove treacherously murdered me? And then you had to kill him for it? After everything we've been through, the very least you could do is kill me yourself, Thiss. Surely we can agree that you owe me that much dignity. You used to think you could take me in a fight. Have you changed your mind about that? Lost your nerve, old friend?"

Thistle's eyes narrowed. Roup sensed a string of ideas rapidly considered and discarded. Thistle didn't say anything.

"Or are you afraid the assembly would revolt?" continued Dazzle speculatively. "Afraid they wouldn't forgive you for killing me? Well, that's possible. Blaming it on Arcove would be much easier. And you'd never have to find out whether I was humoring you every time we sparred—"

Thistle interrupted him at last, "Your paranoia is showing, Dazzle. I don't know what you're talking about." He walked forward and Dazzle backed away. His eyes flicked rapidly between Thistle and the other officers behind him. Roup thought Dazzle was speaking to them as much as to Thistle.

"It's my fault I didn't see it sooner," murmured Dazzle, "after you murdered Coldstep and Serot. After I saw how you roll over for a treacherous tyrant like Macex. You'd trade *me* for something like *that*? I have been on your side since Bitter Pool, since Kirsh's treachery, since the Great Thirst, since—"

"On—my—side..." grated Thistle, finally showing a trace of pique. "And yet you've got half the assembly thinking I am somehow leading them astray."

"I think you are."

Roup glanced at Dazzle's face. He'd seemed remarkably calm earlier in the tunnel—calm for a cat who'd made a split-second decision to undermine his leader, then learned that that same leader was planning to trade his life for an alliance, and then traded his own life to accomplish similar goals. *It's no wonder Arcove doesn't believe him. He's too smooth.*

255

But Roup didn't think Dazzle was actually as smooth as he looked and sounded. Dazzle was an accomplished spy, accustomed to hiding his reactions and processing information rapidly. Roup suspected that Dazzle was actually reeling with the revelation of Thistle's betrayal, reckless with his own life as a result, and in danger of making mistakes.

Thistle's eyes skipped between the edge of the drop-off and Dazzle's mincing paws. "You've always got to be a hero, don't you, Dazzle? Coldstep and Serot were dying—"

"They weren't!" hissed Dazzle.

"They were suffering and *dying*," said Thistle with an implacable chill in his voice, "and you were feeding them meat that should have gone to those who had a chance." Dazzle tried to answer, but Thistle talked over him. "You did this in order to build support against *me*. Because you don't care how many cats you hurt or kill as long as you win. While you're being a hero to dying animals and their shortsighted friends, *I* am making the hard decisions that will allow *any* of these cats to walk out of these mountains alive!"

"Do you believe your own lies?" shot Dazzle. "Sometimes I think you do."

He is definitely distraught, thought Roup, *and about to make a mistake.*

"Arcove, let's go," hissed Roup in Arcove's ear. "While Thistle is focused on Dazzle, let's run." *Dazzle will follow us. I think. I hope.*

But Thistle still hadn't said anything to corroborate Dazzle's version of events. It was clear that the two of them were involved in a power struggle, but everything else remained inscrutable. Arcove stayed where he was.

Thistle inched closer. "Clever, clever Dazzle, always three steps ahead of everyone else. You understand how to take control of the story, don't you? But the one thing you've never understood…is that I don't work with heroes."

And with that, Thistle lunged sideways and slammed into Arcove. Even Roup hadn't seen it coming. He'd expected Thistle to attack Dazzle and fling him into the mud as planned. Thistle hadn't even looked at Arcove.

Arcove tried to get his balance on the edge of the steep shelf, but then Thistle lashed at him with splayed claws. Arcove turned and jumped in order to avoid an uncontrolled fall. He landed on all fours without a stumble, but instantly sank hock-deep in the quivering mud.

Roup looked down, spotted a dry place near the edge, and jumped without a second thought. Snarls echoed off the canyon walls overhead. Roup hoped desperately that it wasn't Halvery trying to take on Thistle and all his officers.

"Halvery, help me!" he bellowed. "That's an order!"

Roup had managed to land without touching the sticky slime. Arcove had already sloshed halfway to the edge of the mud pit, but he was struggling. Every time he tried to pull a paw out, he sank a little deeper. The mud was up to his belly now.

Roup leaned towards him, bracing his back paws as much as possible. He couldn't reach. He wasn't even close. *I have to go in.*

"No!" snarled Arcove. "Roup, don't you dare."

Then Halvery was beside him. Roup didn't wait to discuss what he intended. He lunged out far enough to get hold of Arcove's scruff, front paws sinking into the mud, hind paws sliding. Next instant, Halvery had hold of Roup's scruff, and they were all pulling with whatever purchase they could manage. Arcove came free with a wet gulping sound and they landed panting on the edge of the mire. All of them were slick with gray mud to one degree or another. Thistle had been right. The mud clung heavily in fur and caked in paws.

Roup's eyes flashed to the edge of the pit and saw that Thistle and Dazzle were the ones making all the noise. They were fighting, or at least Dazzle was trying to. Thistle kept dancing away from him, and his officers were trying to intervene. They finally managed to get between the two cats. Dazzle tried to leap over them, but Shale smacked him right out of the air and into the pit. Dazzle twisted and managed to land, soft as feather, on the edge a little past Halvery.

"Well, this is interesting!" came a voice from the far end of the canyon. Roup recognized Macex. "I didn't think Arcove had the creativity to take this long killing Dazzle. What are you doing with them, Thistle?" Macex came into the view on the southern edge of the canyon, along with most of the ferryshaft he'd brought to the sham parley.

Dazzle made a leap for the northern edge of the pit—an idea that occurred to Arcove, Roup, and Halvery in the same moment. They were driven back by Thistle's cats, who ran to intercept them. Roup's paws were sliding and clumsy with mud. Arcove and Halvery were having the same problem.

Well, we've corroborated his story, Arcove, thought Roup. *Was it worth it?*

Thistle gave a hiss of exasperation, but when he spoke, his voice was full of lazy assurance, "Oh, I'm doing what we should have done to begin with: having a bit of fun."

"Doesn't look like fun to me," said Macex. "Looks like a mess. You should have killed Dazzle months ago and these three as soon as they showed up."

"And I told you we would have split the assembly," spat Thistle, "but at least we can still tell them that Arcove and his friends killed Dazzle after our peaceful and productive parley. And after such a shocking act of treachery, we could only respond by killing Leeshwood's old heroes." His eyes settled on Arcove and he murmured, "I would have given you that, Arcove. I would have let you have your revenge before dying. Instead, you have listened to this storytelling assassin, and now you're going to die alongside him."

Arcove sat back on his haunches. His legs and belly were gray with mud, but if he was regretting his decision to force a confrontation between Thistle and Dazzle, he hid it well. "I value the truth more than revenge. I believe you have finally given me that. So thank you."

Thistle laughed. The ferryshaft and creasia were all lining the edge of the pit above them now, their faces full of mingled malice and curiosity.

"Take a good look, my friends," said Macex. "You'll be able to tell your foals and grandfoals that you were the last to see Arcove Ela-creasia alive, along with his infamous lieutenants. You are seeing the passing of an era."

"Heroes of another generation," agreed Thistle. "Today, we kill a legend…in order to make our own."

Arcove cocked his head. "I'm waiting…"

"Oh, no one is going to fight you, Arcove," said Macex indulgently. "Not until tomorrow, at least. You'll be weak with thirst by then, and none of you look like you're eating well. Takes a lot of meat to feed a cat your size, doesn't it? You've been living soft in your woods, enjoying the results of your victories, but all things come to an end. Your end is going to be messy. You'll be as weak as a cub by the time we take you apart." He snorted a laugh. "But do posture and growl at us. It's interesting to imagine what you must have been like in your prime."

Arcove was not, in fact, growling, but Halvery was—a low, sustained rumble that made the mud vibrate.

Thistle scratched an ear. "You're assuming that it won't start raining in the upper valley before they start dropping of thirst. I find that unlikely. A flood will come and batter them lifeless in the confluence."

Roup noticed Halvery's shoulders bunching and hissed, "No!"

"One of them doesn't want to die like a rat," murmured Macex. "Perhaps you'd like to come out and fight us, Halvery, before you're too weak to stand? It's what *I* would do. But, then, I'm not old and timid…"

Arcove murmured, "Halvery, stay."

"Sir—"

"Trust me," said Arcove. He did not sound worried.

Halvery subsided.

Roup's eyes narrowed. *What have you seen that we haven't, Arcove?*

Roup glanced at Dazzle, who was pacing back and forth along the edge of the mud. He'd left plenty of space between himself and his cornered companions. Roup couldn't blame him. Halvery looked ready to fight just about anything at the moment.

Dazzle's restless movements kept drawing the eyes of their enemies. He shot a glance at Roup and then spoke to the creasia officer above him. "I found your cub, Sundance. When she was lost in the desert, and it was so hot that no one else would go out, when no one else would even try..."

The cat, Sundance, turned away, his expression suddenly strained.

"Flash!" shouted Dazzle. "I took your messages to Astari for twelve years!"

"And I paid for that!" snapped one of the cats. "You don't do favors for nothing, Dazzle."

Dazzle gave a hollow laugh. "Do you think summer meat is equivalent? Anyone can hunt in summer; *no one* else could do what I did. I accepted your gifts to soothe your pride—"

"Your condescension is noted."

Dazzle threw another desperate look at Roup before calling, "Shale, you'd be dead in a canyon if I hadn't gotten in front of that bear—"

"And I got between you and a lot of angry curbs," snapped Shale. "But the way I see it is, whoever kills you without paying you back wins. By all means, keep pointing out the debts we'll settle by finally getting rid of you."

Dazzle's movements were becoming quicker and more agitated. *He's going to make a break*, thought Roup. *He's drawing their attention and trying to let me know that we should run in the opposite direction.*

Roup glanced at Arcove to make sure he understood. Arcove was frowning. He spoke with implacable calm, "Dazzle, shut up and sit down."

That took everyone by surprise. Halvery laughed.

Roup had no idea what Arcove was planning, but he was certain of one thing: *Arcove wants to see whether Dazzle will actually follow orders. Did his promises to us mean anything?*

Dazzle looked at Arcove in bewildered frustration. He was clearly accustomed to being the smartest cat in the clutter and a law unto himself. Roup had no doubt he would have been a source of frustration to any leader, even one he liked and supported. Dazzle glanced at the edge of the pit again. *He's going to ignore Arcove. He's going to run...*

Dazzle sat down.

One of the ferryshaft snickered. "Well, you've got to give credit where it's due. The old tyrants know how to train their underlings quickly."

"Oh, look, Dazzle's afraid of something," crooned Shale. "Are you worried that Arcove might still enjoy killing you before he dies? Personally, I'd find it very satisfying if someone shut you up with a lung-full of mud."

Arcove spoke again, this time to Thistle, "So you intend to take Leeshwood...with some hundred cats. Dazzle must not have given you an accurate account of our numbers."

Thistle looked down at him coolly. "I have the support of the largest ferryshaft herd on the island, and you have foolishly brought all your officers and their best fighters up here to die with you. I agree that it would have been easier if you'd brought your full strength. I can't decide whether that was brilliant or stupid on your part. It's like you couldn't decide whether to fully commit. But I suppose soft living makes a leader hesitant."

"And I suppose hard living makes a leader faithless," said Arcove blandly. "You beg me for help and then try to kill me. Macex sends his own alpha to his death. I'm not sure how either of you intends to manage your affairs with the rest of the island. Your reputation will be in tatters. No one will parley with you. Every intelligent animal on Lidian will despise you."

Thistle's lip curled. He ignored Arcove's broader points in favor of something more petty: "Did you really think I would *beg* you, Arcove? You're letting your ego do your thinking these days."

Halvery spoke up, "Sounds to me like Macex will be ruling Leeshwood. He's got far more animals and will doubtless be doing the bulk of the fighting."

"A fine sentiment from cats who have been hiding behind telshees," sneered Thistle.

Halvery sniffed. "Telshees haven't fought alongside us in a single engagement apart from the rebellion, you snide little coward. Telshees have not helped us win battles or hold territory. They've offered counsel, but no one is in doubt as to who is king of Arcove's Leeshwood." Halvery waited a beat and then added, "But I think in your case, that would be Macex."

Thistle wasn't easily goaded, but Roup had a sense that he didn't like this angle in front of his officers. *He's going to say something cruel to regain control of the conversation. Don't respond. Don't let it get under your skin...*

"I'm sure the ferryshaft will want some payment for their assistance," said Thistle. His eyes slid half closed. "The cubs from all the officer's dens ought to do it."

"Do they taste better when their daddy was a war hero?" asked Macex with a laugh.

"I'm sure they must," chimed in one of his subordinates, "fatter, probably."

Halvery was growling again, his ears flat against his skull.

He's trying to make us lose our nerve, thought Roup, *lose our tempers, do something stupid... Don't react.* But he was thinking about Ilsa. He was thinking about that litter that probably wasn't his.

"We'll take your dens and kill your cubs and mate with your females," said Thistle sweetly, "and they'll lie down for us, because they won't have anyone left to protect them. Are you enjoying the truth, Arcove? Are you happy you made me say it to your face?

You've ruled for so long that losing you will leave Leeshwood crippled and in chaos."

Arcove laughed. It was so out of character that Halvery stopped growling in surprise. Arcove's laugh echoed around the canyon. "As it happens," he said, "chaos is a friend of mine."

Then Storm Ela-ferry leapt from the wall of the canyon and slammed into Thistle.

Thistle plunged over the edge of the pit with a startled yelp, and Arcove was on him in a heartbeat.

Roup had to give Thistle credit. He thought fast. Arcove's muddy claws couldn't find purchase on the first pounce. Thistle slipped away from him and jumped into the middle of the pit. He sank to his flanks, but Arcove didn't follow. "So you'd rather get filthy than fight with me," he bellowed. "There's certainly a metaphor in that!"

Halvery wasn't so willing to let mud stop him from taking a bite out of Thistle. He made a lunge into the center that caused everyone to snarl and shout. Three of Thistle's cats, including his two pale gray guards, leapt down to defend him. The ferryshaft were howling and shouting and running wildly around the canyon in the kind of chaos that only Storm seemed capable of producing.

Roup was suddenly fighting with two of Thistle's officers. In moments, they were all covered in mud. No one's claws were doing proper damage, and it felt like they were moving in slow motion. Halvery and Thistle were grappling near the center of the pit in an almost comically awkward manner. Arcove managed to wade out far enough to get hold of Halvery and drag him out of the fight without losing his footing. Thistle's officers were all in the mud now, striking at their opponents, but mostly trying to get to Thistle, who was trapped and sinking.

Roup helped Arcove pull Halvery completely free, and then they were all leaping out of the pit, slapping aside disorganized ferryshaft, to follow Storm in a messy ascent to the top of the canyon.

Highly Suspicious

Cohal and Moali were waiting at the top. Storm, Arcove, Roup, and Halvery followed the curbs over broken ground in the blinding sunlight. The top of the slots felt like a different world. At their backs rose the unscalable cliff, offering no passage to the upper valley without descending into a canyons. Before them, rocky ground sloped steeply towards the lower valley and the lake. The descent was broken by stands of scrubby trees, brush, and boulders. The rocky sections looked deceptively smooth from this angle. Upon closer inspection, Roup knew they would be riddled with slot canyons, some of which were too wide to jump.

"Have I brought chaos to yet another council, Arcove?" asked Storm cheerfully.

Arcove was struggling for breath, but managed a note of fond sarcasm, "Your consistency is a comfort in an inconsistent world, Storm."

"When did you spot him?" demanded Roup.

"Just after I fell into the mud," said Arcove. "I'm surprised you didn't."

"I was entirely focused on getting you out, so no."

"I needed Thistle to give me his full attention and get near the edge of the pit so that Storm could knock him within reach," continued Arcove. "I thought Dazzle was going to do something stupid; where is he?"

"I'm sure he has rejoined his supporters by now," said Halvery blandly. "They're probably hoping to slink away and attack Leesh-wood on their own while Thistle and Arcove fight it out."

"Dazzle was attacking ferryshaft last I saw," said Storm. "I think he killed one, maybe two. It'll take a few moments for them to pull themselves together and for Thistle and his creasia to get out of the mud—"

A howl from somewhere farther up the slope cut him short. At the same time, Dazzle came flashing around the boulders and brush from downhill. He'd somehow gotten ahead of them and waited, panting, until they reached him. "We've got to get off the top," he breathed. "Ferryshaft are keeping watch at the highest point against the cliff. They can see us and signal to the others. Come on." He turned, and Roup saw a dark crevasse in the ground behind him—the top of a narrow slot.

"Absolutely not!" spat Halvery. "We are not following you anywhere!" He turned to Arcove. "Sir, please—!"

"We don't have time for this!" exclaimed Roup. He could tell from the ferryshaft barks and howls that Dazzle was right. They *were* signaling directions.

"Storm?" growled Arcove. "An opinion?"

Storm came forward and stuck his head into the crevasse. "It's a lava tunnel. The curbs and I didn't spend much time in these, because they're so dangerous during floods."

Maoli spoke, "I know these tunnels. We could get down to the lake without being seen. They are death traps during floods and easy to get lost in, but if we don't stay down there for long, the risk might be worth it."

"Then you lead," said Arcove.

Dazzle didn't comment.

The drop from the opening to the tunnel floor was only a couple of lengths. The black rock was smooth and it gleamed like ice in the light from above. Nevertheless, darkness swallowed them quickly as they walked. The tunnel turned and dropped and twisted and branched, with no opening to the sky for long stretches. Even creasia eyes could not penetrate the gloom. Roup tried not to think about being caught here during a flood. At least their coats were drying quickly, the mud flaking and crumbling with every step.

"Storm, a word," said Arcove.

Storm dropped back to walk between Arcove and Roup.

"Have the clutters been attacked?" asked Arcove quietly.

"Not as far as I know," said Storm.

"Then why are you and the curbs out here?"

"We came after Flurry. Everyone woke up last night and you were gone, and then Hollygold's clutter realized that Flurry was missing, too. Lyndi didn't think you'd want your cats tracking him down the valley and possibly giving away our location to the ferryshaft herd. But she also didn't think you'd want her to let him get away. So I offered to track him and at least try to see where he went. We lost him during the flash flood, but then we spotted you from the top of the slots and I thought we'd better stay close. Something wasn't right. There were ferryshaft bodies and evidence of ferryshaft patrolling the area around the slots, but no sign of the rest of the herd."

"Macex and Thistle have conspired to kill Sedaron and Arcove," said Roup.

"I overheard that part," said Storm. "Why is Dazzle with you? Is he on our side now?"

Halvery made a rumbling noise from beyond Arcove. Roup drew a breath to try to explain, but Arcove spoke first, "For the moment."

Up ahead, Maoli and Dazzle had begun a discussion about which way to go. They all stopped walking and waited in total darkness. Roup gathered that they were standing in an intersection. "The left fork will get us down to the lake faster," insisted Dazzle.

"I don't think so," returned Maoli. "We never went that way when I lived here."

"And how long ago was that?"

Silence.

"The tunnels change," said Dazzle. "Some of the ice has melted. It was probably a dead end when you lived here."

"All I can say is that I have no knowledge of the tunnels in that direction," she said stubbornly.

"And we did not use lava tunnels at all when I lived here," put in Cohal, "because of the extraordinary risk. Arcove, we have probably lost our pursuers and should consider going back to a point where we can jump out of these tunnels. We should return to the slot canyons, which are a little safer and with which Maoli and I have more familiarity."

"Just a little further," pleaded Dazzle. "The left fork will bring us out more than halfway to the bottom, on the edge of Wave Canyon."

Maoli's voice sounded cautiously hopeful, "Wave?"

"That's what I call it. The one with the swirl in the rock; it looks like a cresting wave?"

Maoli considered. "I know the canyon. It *is* in that direction."

"We will try the left fork," said Arcove. "Dazzle, come here." His voice held an edge of warning. "I wouldn't want to lose our guide in the dark."

They started down the unknown tunnel. Roup could tell that Halvery had come up on the other side of Dazzle. "Don't think I haven't noticed," he growled, "that you're the only cat who managed to walk out of that canyon *not* muddy."

"Do you take that as a personal offense?" asked Dazzle dryly.

"I take it as highly suspicious."

Roup noted, with relief, that the tunnel was brightening. He could see the silhouettes of Maoli, Cohal, and Storm leading the way. They turned a corner, and diffuse daylight spilled around them. It was still muted by several turns, but getting brighter. It gleamed on walls composed entirely of ice, with icy puddles underfoot.

Maoli crouched suddenly, and Cohal flinched back. "Something's coming," he hissed.

Roup caught the soft swish and splash of paws over wet stone. Then a creasia rounded the curve ahead and ran straight into them. It was Flurry.

18

Charisma

Dazzle was the first to react. He trotted forward from between Arcove and Halvery. "Well, this is interesting."

The instant Flurry saw Dazzle, he seemed to have eyes for no one else. Cohal and Maoli began growling as Flurry passed them, but he went down on his belly in front of Dazzle without giving them a second glance. His ears drooped, and his tail curled nervously around his haunches, threatening to tuck underneath him. "Dazzle…" He was out of breath and had to struggle to get words out. "Shale s-said you were up on the…up on the ice cliffs…"

Dazzle's voice came in a dangerous croon, "Oh, you should know better than to believe everything Shale says."

Flurry's anxious gaze skipped to Arcove and then back to Dazzle.

"There's really no reason to keep pretending," said Dazzle blandly. "Did you just come back to check whether I was dead?"

Flurry gave a full-body shudder and burst out, "They said it was your idea! That…that there was no other way to take Leeshwood, that you would lure Arcove here because he would want to kill you and…and…"

Dazzle's voice was as cold as winter ice, "And you didn't think to double-check that with me?"

Flurry spoke in a miserable whimper, "They said I had to leave right away, that Macex's ferryshaft couldn't take me out of the mountains otherwise, and—"

"Your capacity for self-deception is extraordinary," said Dazzle. He paced slowly around Flurry, who remained crouched against the icy floor. "What did they offer you?"

Flurry screwed his eyes shut. "Ash," he whispered. "They said that if we took Leeshwood, there would be enough mates for everyone and they wouldn't stop us from being together…or kill the cub when it's born…I…I…wanted to believe them." His voice broke. "Dazzle, I'm sorry; I wanted to think it was true. I wanted it to be true so badly, but I knew… I knew…" He petered into silence.

Roup glanced sidelong at Arcove. He was watching closely, but he did not look like he intended to interfere.

Dazzle stopped in front of Flurry. "You knew," he said with deadly finality.

A heartbeat's terrible silence and then Dazzle continued in a detached voice, "Well, Flur, your sense of self-preservation is about as good as your ability to detect deception. You've tried to lead Arcove into a trap. You've tried to lead me into a trap. And now that you're out here talking to me, I can't imagine that Thistle will have any use for you. You've managed to offend just about everyone—"

"I don't care!" wailed Flurry, reminding Roup of exactly how young he was. "I don't care about everyone else. I'm sorry, Daz! I'm so sorry. You're the only officer who ever cared whether I lived or died, and if you're done with me, I don't want to keep going. We both know who would win if we fought, so let's just skip that part." He put his chin against the ground and shut his eyes.

Dazzle screwed up his face in some combination of extreme emotions. When he spoke, however, his voice betrayed nothing, "Stop embarrassing yourself. Of course I have a use for you. Get up; I need you to take a message to Eclipse. Abyss, too, if you can find her."

Flurry opened his eyes and stared at Dazzle as though he didn't quite believe it. "You…you want me to…"

"Yes, there really isn't time for wallowing. You won't be able to get up to the dens now. Thistle's cats would kill you. But Eclipse can do it. She needs to tell Shimmer: I want every cat she trusts—every cat who's mine—to meet me in the lake caves. Tell Shimmer…" Dazzle thought for a moment, half smiled, "tell her that we're going somewhere green."

Flurry shot a look at Cohal and Maoli. "If Eclipse finds out you've brought highland curbs up here, it'll be a non-starter—"

Dazzle gave a dismissive flick of his tail. "For anyone else, maybe."

"What if she's already heard about them, Daz? Because she might—"

Dazzle looked impatient. "Tell her this will clear all debts. Tell her *I'll* owe *her.* Tell her I said please. Tell her whatever you like and get Shimmer down to the lake." Dazzle paused and then added, "Tell her she can hurt me. I'm sure you'll find that rolls off your tongue easily enough."

Flurry crumpled.

Dazzle turned away, and Roup saw the flash of pain in his eyes before he managed to bury it. Flurry took a step towards the daylight, ears and tail low. Dazzle drew a deep breath, as though forcing himself forward through sharp rocks, and said, "The only reason Thistle sent you to Leeshwood was to get you out of the way. Because he knew you were mine."

Flurry's ears perked up and he spun around. "Yes. I was. I am. I still am. Dazzle—"

"Then prove it," snapped Dazzle. "Go."

Flurry went, paws flying over the stone.

Dazzle seemed to deflate as he stared after him. Finally, he said, without turning. "Arcove..." When Arcove did not speak, he added, "Please."

"You're going to have to get more specific," said Arcove dryly.

Dazzle turned around. He looked unspeakably weary. "Please take him back to Leeshwood. Please don't kill him."

Halvery gave a snort. "He tried to lead us to our deaths, so that's asking a lot. And you seem to be out of things to trade."

Dazzle kept his eyes on Arcove. "He did it for Ash, a five-year-old female who loves him. He's a four-year-old cub."

"He came to Leeshwood to offer me your life..." said Arcove slowly.

Dazzle just looked at him.

Arcove looked almost as weary as Dazzle. "I will withhold judgment until I get a better look at your cats and their situation. I distinctly heard Flurry say that he does not care about my opinion of him. He'll have to do better than that if he wants to live in my wood."

"He might also try not changing sides for two days running," said Halvery. "I realize that might be a challenge for your lot."

Roup wished, again, that he could slow everything down. "We all need sleep," he said quietly, "and some of us haven't eaten for three days."

Halvery shot him an aggrieved look. Roup was certain that he thought they shouldn't reveal weaknesses in front of Dazzle, but Roup continued, "This is not the time to plan the future or ask for favors, Dazzle. It's the time to find somewhere safe to rest."

Dazzle became instantly brisk. "Understood. And it's time to get out of the lava tunnels, because I hear ferryshaft howls. That sounds like the signal they give for water in the slots."

Storm spoke up, "They're certainly signaling danger. Those short yips, followed by a long howl means trouble is coming."

"And they're not signaling for our benefit," said Dazzle, "which makes me think we've got trackers behind us in the tunnels." He took off at a lope, and they all followed. The tunnel took two more sharp jogs and then opened into a very steep straight-away towards a point of bright light at the bottom.

"The floor is ice!" called Dazzle. "Don't try to run down; you'll break a leg. You've got to jump from rock to rock."

Roup saw what he meant—boulders with more purchase jutted out of the ice at random intervals. Dazzle leapt to one, then another further down, displaying that perfect grace and conservation of movement that Roup remembered from Moashi's fight. Storm followed him with a similar level of dexterity. The curbs took a little more time choosing their jumps. Arcove, Halvery, and Roup came last. Roup found that he needed to think hard about every series of movements. *I am so tired. Focus. Don't make a mistake.*

They emerged near the bottom of a canyon only four or five lengths across, but open to the sky. The walls were rock, with a swirling pattern that did, indeed, resemble a cresting wave. The floor was wet sand with a trickle of water at the bottom.

"Alright, here is what we are going to do," said Dazzle. "At this point, there's enough cover on top of the slots to hide us from watchers near the cliff. I want to get up there, because we can reach the lake caves faster. But I want whoever is tracking us to think we stayed in the canyons, so—"

"Ghosts, you are quick to take command, aren't you?" exclaimed Halvery. "What makes you think you can start giving orders?"

"I thought you were tired and hungry and in unfamiliar territory," snapped Dazzle, "but if you have a plan, by all means, execute it, Halvery. We've got just a few moments to get out of sight before whoever is tracking us shows up, probably just ahead of a flash flood."

"Enough," growled Arcove. "Halvery, let me deal with him. Dazzle, what is your plan?"

"We'll walk downstream to that boulder. You see it?"

The boulder split the stream further along the canyon. It was impossible to miss.

"There are a few footholds. You can get to the top of the boulder, and then I think all of you should be able to jump out of the canyon. Someone might have to carry the curbs."

"We are highland curbs," said Cohal disdainfully. "We can run up these walls. We'll be out of here faster than any of you."

Dazzle gave a wry smile. "In that case, maybe you would like to help me leave a false trail. I'm going down the canyon a little ways in the wet sand and then I'll come back without touching the bottom. You want to join me?"

"I think I just heard you tell Flurry to send a message to lowland curbs," said Cohal, "so no."

Dazzle flicked his tail. "Just as well. Let's go." He hopped down onto the canyon floor and they all followed, leaving a rather obvious trail in the wet sand.

"How are you going to come back up the canyon?" asked Storm.

"You'll see."

Roup thought Halvery might demand details, but even Halvery seemed tired of arguing at this point, and they all reached the boulder in silence. The way up was not obvious, and the lichen-encrusted rock didn't show their footprints. The jump from the top of the boulder to the lip of the canyon was manageable for a creasia, though all of them struggled for a moment on the edge. Roup noticed that Halvery was favoring his right foreleg.

The curbs declined to jump to the top. Instead, they jumped to some barely visible shelves along the canyon wall and then made their way gradually upwards. Storm watched where they went and then followed.

As Dazzle had said, there was cover at the top—jagged rock hillocks and stands of scrub. They all crouched on the edge, breathless from the scramble, and looked back down. Beyond the boulder, the stream spread out over stretches of loose stone, interspersed with sand. Dazzle walked along the bottom, making sure to leave footprints in every available patch of mud. He went further and further, until he was almost out of sight.

"He's going to run off," muttered Halvery.

"I don't think so," said Roup.

"If he does, I'll deal with him later," muttered Arcove.

Dazzle stopped and turned in the hazy distance. He stood perfectly still for a moment, staring hard at a canyon wall. Then he jumped. He hit the wall about a third of the way up, pushed off immediately, and hit the opposite wall a little higher. He bounced back and forth, higher and higher, until he managed to reach the top of the canyon. As far as Roup could tell, there was not a single real ledge at any of the points where Dazzle touched. It was an astonishing display of strength, skill, and dexterity.

Storm was not too proud to say so. "*That* was elegant," he told Dazzle as he came gliding low along the edge of the canyon.

Dazzle shot Storm a grin that seemed genuine. "High praise coming from you. If that worked, we might be able to hide and rest for a while." He led them away from the slot, hugging a ridge of broken ground, and staying under the scrubby trees whenever possible.

The time was well past noon. Roup's legs felt clumsy and too heavy, as though he were still moving through mud. He couldn't help noticing how sunken Arcove's sides looked in the bright light of day—how the glossy shine of his coat delineated his hips and lower ribs. Roup knew he wasn't looking any better himself. His skin felt too loose. *We have to find something to eat soon. But first we have to sleep.*

Storm trotted up beside Dazzle. "Were those really lowland curbs that you told Flurry to contact?"

"Yes. Eclipse is the alpha of the dominant pack in the upper valley. Abyss is the lower valley. They're sisters, but they don't always get along."

A pause. "Are they your friends?" asked Storm cautiously.

Dazzle gave a grimace that was difficult to interpret. "I would not presume to call them that, no." After a moment, he added, "They won't attack your curbs. I'm sure I can get at least that much out of them. Hopefully a good deal more."

Storm looked doubtful. "Were they here when lowland curbs first overran the upper valley?"

"I doubt it," said Dazzle. "I don't think they're old enough for that."

Storm hesitated again and finally said, "How long did it take you to learn that trick in the canyon?"

Dazzle's voice registered that flash of genuine warmth again. "Most of a summer. I kept losing my nerve and falling. You can do that at the beginning, but if you panic near the top, the fall is deadly. I'd sabotage myself before I got too high. I stopped trying for a while. Then a flood caught me in a canyon, and it was do or drown. After that, it was easy. Once you know you can do such a thing, you never forget." He flashed a conspiratorial grin at Storm. "Maybe you understand."

Storm looked like he was trying not to like Dazzle and failing. "Maybe I do."

Dazzle looked at him sidelong. "I talked to every cat I could find who chased you."

Storm laughed in surprise. "Why?"

Dazzle tossed a look over his shoulder at Arcove, Roup, and Halvery. "Because you outwitted *them.*"

Roup knew Halvery was tired, because he didn't manage to growl out loud, although Roup saw him bristle.

"You and I were born the same year," continued Dazzle to Storm.

Before he could say anything else, Halvery pushed up between them. He turned to glare at Storm. "Let's not forget, *friend,* that you spent all summer training Moashi to avoid getting maimed and probably killed by this fellow. Do you like Moashi? Maybe don't get too cozy with his would-be killer."

Storm looked instantly guilty, but Dazzle made a noise of startled pleasure. He poked his head around Halvery to continue talking to Storm. "*You* were involved in that? Oh… The way he jumped in the air… That's not how creasia fight, but most alphas aren't that small." He gave Halvery an incredulous look. "I didn't think you'd care if I killed Moashi; I thought you *wanted* him dead. But, then, you didn't orchestrate any of that, did you?" He turned to look over his shoulder. "Ghosts, Roup, I'm flattered that you thought I mattered enough to…" His expression changed. "You're limping."

Halvery finally found the energy for a growl.

Roup hadn't been aware of limping, but he certainly felt the ache in his left hind leg. Before he could formulate a reply, Dazzle said, "Right up here. There's a place to rest where we can get a view of the lake and maybe the caves. And I think I can find us something to eat."

The spot Dazzle chose did, indeed, offer a view of the eastern end of the lake. They were more than halfway down. The afternoon was bright and chilly. No ferryshaft cries had broken the silence for some time, nor had any of the canyons they passed contained water. "Sometimes it rains in the upper valley and then stops and we don't get a flood," said Dazzle. "Sometimes ice blocks the slots and the water comes crashing through a day later. It's not perfectly predictable."

"It sounds the opposite of perfect," agreed Storm. He looked around at Arcove and the others. "I am a day animal, and I slept some last night. I will keep watch if that is acceptable."

"Just as long as it's not Dazzle," muttered Halvery.

"I was going to find you something to eat," said Dazzle. "Do you trust me enough for that?"

Arcove spoke. Roup could tell that he was foggy with exhaustion and trying not to show it. "What are you planning to hunt, Dazzle?"

"Mud turtles. There are usually some in the next canyon over. It's not far. I won't be gone long, but I'll stay here if you tell me to."

Arcove lay down. "Go."

Dazzle *wasn't* gone long, but Roup was already asleep when a soft-shelled turtle landed under his nose, smelling of blood and rich fat. Someone had already chewed its head off. "They bite," Dazzle tried to explain.

"Thank you." Roup's mouth was running with saliva. He consumed the turtle in crunchy mouthfuls, the warm blood dripping down his chin. It was the most delicious thing he had ever tasted. Not until he was chewing his way through the last of the bloody shell did he pause to look around guiltily to make sure everyone else was eating. They were. Or they had. Dazzle must have brought back half a dozen turtles before waking any of them.

The other creasia had consumed theirs with the same ravenous speed as Roup. Halvery was already asleep again a few paces away. He hadn't even bothered to clean the blood from his whiskers. Arcove hadn't performed the customary post-meal grooming, either. He was drifting off at Roup's side. Roup turned to put his head across Arcove's back.

He saw that Storm had positioned himself in a ray of sunshine close to the edge of the drop-off, where he could watch the lake and get a view up the slope without exposing himself. He was taking more time with his turtle, enjoying the chewy bits. Cohal and Maoli were nowhere in sight. Roup assumed they'd gone to keep watch nearby.

Dazzle had curled up a little way apart from everyone else, in the deep shadows beneath a thorny bush. Roup saw that he was not asleep. He was blinking, but still looking out over the lake.

"Thank you," whispered Roup.

Dazzle looked around at him. That spark of charisma he'd displayed with Storm had vanished, and his eyes looked dark and hollow. "I'm sorry." He spoke almost too quietly to hear.

"I'll stop limping once I've had some sleep," said Roup.

Dazzle's ears fell. He did not meet Roup's eyes. "I'm amazed you're walking at all."

"It pays to be friends with a telshee king."

Roup half expected some curious question in response to this, but Dazzle just looked away.

"Dazzle." Roup waited until he raised his eyes again. "*I* didn't come here to kill you."

Dazzle stared at him for a moment. Then he gave a mirthless laugh. "Of course you didn't."

"I'd really like to talk to you," continued Roup, "about the message you left and your counting system, but..." His eyes were already sliding shut.

Dazzle's voice seemed to come from far away. "Sleep, Roup... you unbelievable creature. I'm sure we'll have a chance to talk before Arcove kills me."

"He won't," muttered Roup.

"Well, the smartest thing would be to let me drown in my own mess. But if you were my den-mate...I'd kill me."

"You didn't kill Flurry." Roup wasn't sure he was making sense. Arcove's breathing had gone deep and even under his chin.

Dazzle's voice sounded soft and distant. "Is that all it takes to get mercy in Leeshwood? Show it to someone else? Ah, but I needed Flurry to do something for me. Surely you can see that."

"You didn't need to beg for his life." Roup wasn't sure he said it out loud. He felt warm and his stomach was full of turtle, and even the possibility of finally having a conversation with Dazzle couldn't stop him from floating down into dreamless sleep.

19

Costa

Halvery woke to evening light and a sense of returning sharpness. Yesterday felt like a dream or a nightmare, but now that he was thinking more clearly... *Where is Dazzle?*

Halvery bolted upright. He could hardly believe he'd gone to sleep with that spy so near. *Thistle called him a storytelling assassin. I guess Thistle knows him pretty well.*

At the same time, he was uncomfortably aware that he was rested and fed as a direct result of Dazzle's actions. *What's your game, assassin?*

Halvery felt no relief when he spotted Dazzle talking to Storm on the edge of the drop-off. *Dazzle was trying to charm Storm earlier. Seemed like it was working.* Cohal and Maoli were sitting beside them, which seemed a bit odd after the revelation of Dazzle's connections to lowland curbs. They were all looking at something below.

"—can't be a ferryshaft," Dazzle was saying. "None of Macex's ferryshaft would be out there."

"It doesn't look like a curb to me." Storm sounded apprehensive.

"I do think it's a curb, Storm," said Cohal, "although I agree that it's in an odd color. It's yipping like a curb."

"It's too small for a ferryshaft," said Dazzle.

Halvery stood up and joined them. He poked his head over Storm's shoulder. "What are we looking at?"

Storm glanced at him guiltily. "I'm sorry we woke you. It's just... There's an animal down there on the ice, and it...it looks like..."

Halvery followed his gaze to the lake below them. The sun had already dipped behind the mountains. True dark was still a ways off, but even the hazy evening light was making it difficult for day animals to see details at a distance. To Halvery's eyes, however, the world had become much clearer.

He saw the animal that Storm was talking about immediately. It was about halfway between the northern shore of the lake and the easternmost island. It was not alone. Some distance to the west, a pack of what looked like lowland curbs were in pursuit. They were surely running by sight out there on the ice, but the hunted animal had a wide lead and seemed to be taking its time. It was moving slowly south, further onto the lake, occasionally calling. The noise did sound like a curb's yip, although they were too far away to hear it clearly.

"Ghosts!" exclaimed Halvery. "She's trying to reach the island. And she's already well past the thin edges... I think she'll succeed."

"She?" demanded Storm, his anxiety giving way to naked alarm.

Halvery laughed. "Don't you recognize your own foal, Storm? That's Costa."

"What?!"

"She's been following us since the beginning. Did you and the curbs really miss her trail?"

Storm was on his feet now, bristling all over. "You...you knew this? And didn't tell me?"

Halvery's ears flattened. "I didn't think it was any of my business. She's a young adult. I also figured you knew. Some scout you are—"

"She's a three-year-old *foal*, Halvery!" Storm was fairly vibrating with anger.

His furious voice had woken Arcove and Roup, who came blinking to the edge of the drop-off. "What are we arguing about now?" asked Roup.

"Costa is about to do Storm's job for him, and he's ready to challenge me to single combat over it," said Halvery sourly.

"I thought you cared about her!" spat Storm. "I thought that after teaching her to fight—"

Halvery was becoming truly irritated. "Do you think I coddle my own cubs, Storm? What part of 'she's practically grown' do you not understand? Besides, what good would it have done to tell her to go away? I didn't have any luck telling *you* what to do at that age."

"Nor will you at this age!" flashed Storm.

Halvery's voice rose in a crack of anger, "She wants nothing more in life than to live up to your legend, you obstinate, ungrateful sheep turd!"

Dazzle muttered, "Keep your voices down, please. I'm sure our pursuers this afternoon were ferryshaft, and they're mediocre trackers. But now that it's evening, Thistle will have sent creasia after us, and they are better."

Arcove looked between them and then back down at the lake. "Costa followed us, and that is her down there on the ice?"

"Yes," grated Storm. "Halvery knew and didn't tell me."

Halvery let out an exasperated breath. "I found *one* footprint when we were coming up the lower slopes, Storm. One! In mud. I couldn't be sure who it was."

"She's trying to reach the islands to find highland curbs," murmured Roup, his gaze now focused on the scene below. "She's lighter than any of us, so she's got a better chance. It looks to me like she's testing the ice. That's why she's going so slowly." He paused, his gaze shifting to the pack of lowland curbs closing in. "She may have to give up and run for cover if she doesn't find her way soon."

"She must see them," said Halvery. "She must have been dealing with lowland curbs since we started into the mountains. She'll get out of there if she can't figure out how to reach the island."

"She sees the curbs," agreed Arcove, "but does she see the creasia?"

Storm was on his feet again, voice tight. "Where?"

"In the boulders near the shore," murmured Arcove, his eyes narrow. "Look carefully. I think I see at least a dozen."

They all looked. Halvery had to stare for a long moment before he noticed them, but once he caught the outlines, he was sure. There were creasia waiting on the shore near the entrances to the canyons.

"Well, that's not good," muttered Dazzle. "Those will be our trackers. Instead of trying to find us in the slots, they've gone straight to the lake caves to ambush us. So either Flurry was caught and made to talk, or..." he swallowed. "Or Shimmer..."

"Or one of them betrayed you and changed sides," said Halvery with easy malice. "That seems to come as naturally as breathing to your sort."

Dazzle didn't get angry. He gave a mirthless laugh. "Or that."

"Or they simply figured we'd be coming out of the canyons on our way back to the clutters," said Roup. "That's not an unreasonable guess, even without a tip-off."

Storm was pacing back and forth now. "Those boulders leading into the canyons are the most obvious cover. That's where she's going to head when she runs from the curbs!"

No one said anything. Halvery felt an unpleasant drop in the pit of his stomach. *But she's smart. Smart like Storm. Like Coden. Clever. She got all the way out here alone. Surely she'll be alright...* "Those cats aren't here for her," he said aloud. "Would they even attack her?" He glanced unwillingly at Dazzle, who gave a noncommittal flick of his tail.

"If she runs straight into them...and they know she's not with Macex...they probably *would* attack her. They would at least want to catch her and find out who she is and why she's here."

"And they'll kill her then, if not before," finished Storm in a hollow voice. He didn't even sound angry anymore. He sounded stricken.

Halvery rolled his eyes. "She's not dead yet. Have a little faith in what you taught her."

Below them on the ice, Costa had given up trying to reach the island. The curbs had started to yip as they closed in, and the small red and gray ferryshaft made straight for the shore...straight for the boulders and canyons...straight for the waiting cats.

"Why isn't she testing the ice?" burst out Storm. He was pacing again. "Why is she just running like that?"

"It's thicker towards the caves," said Dazzle, obviously as caught up in the drama as everyone else. "She probably doesn't need to worry there."

The creasia had seen her, their attention likely drawn by the yipping curbs. They were moving around more, making them easier to spot from above, but probably still hidden from the view of anyone on the lake. These cats were an ambush party sent to deal with Arcove, Halvery, Roup, and Dazzle. They would be skilled fighters. And one three-year-old foal was about to encounter them all alone.

Come on, Costa, thought Halvery. *See them...smell them... You could still run towards the lake caves.* But the ice in that direction was littered with debris washed down from the mountains. It probably looked like treacherous footing and more daunting than the canyons.

Storm gave a whine of distress.

Halvery's chest felt tight. As Costa approached the shore, it became harder and harder to breathe. He heard Roup whisper, "Storm, don't look."

The first creasia pounced. He didn't wait for Costa to get quite into the boulders, but lunged out onto the ice.

Costa checked and stumbled.

Halvery knew, then, that she hadn't seen the cats. He could read the surprise in her body language—body language he'd learned without thinking about it on all those summer evenings when they'd sparred. He could almost hear her baby laugh as she bounced back up after he'd knocked her down. She'd been knocked flat by creasia paws more times than either of them could count. But not with claws. Never with claws.

"*You're my favorite.*"

Halvery almost shut his eyes along with Storm. *I never told her my brother's name...*

Costa changed directions. She doubled like a rabbit under a hawk. The creasia landed *right* beside her, but not on top.

He lashed at her.

And missed.

And pounced.

And missed again.

Halvery was on his feet now, shouting, "Good cub! Perfect dodge! Run, Costa! Run!"

Roup was shouting right beside him, "Go, Costa! Come on, foal! You can do this! Run!"

Costa was a dancing blur on the distant ice, a zig-zag line between cats. They were all after her now, but their numbers were actually hindering them. They were colliding with each other.

When she entered the boulders, they converged. For one sickening moment, Costa seemed to disappear under several twisting shadows. Then she was ahead of them—a streak of red and gray fleeing into the canyons, running for all she was worth.

20

Familiar Tactic

Halvery was over the edge of the ridge, bounding down the steep slope before he thought about what he was doing. "That's enough near-misses; I'm going to help her." He listened for Arcove's voice calling him back, but didn't hear it.

Instead, Storm caught up a moment later. "You can't fight all those cats," he spat. "She's my foal; let me do this my way."

"How's that?" asked Halvery breathlessly. He slid down a nearly vertical section and almost plunged into a canyon. It was too wide to jump. He ran along the edge, going downhill, but maddeningly in the wrong direction.

Storm threw back his head and howled. The sound rang off the cliffs. "Well, if Thistle's cats didn't know where we were before..." muttered Halvery. But a moment later, the call was answered—a thin, distant cry. Costa knew her father's voice.

Halvery glanced back and saw that the rest of their party wasn't far behind. They were all slithering and jumping down the steep rockface. The curbs were trying to catch up to Storm, who'd gone down into the canyon. Halvery didn't dare follow. He couldn't run on canyon walls and wasn't sure he could get back up. He did, however, arrive at a point where he could jump the gap and follow along from above.

Storm and Costa kept signaling to each other as their paths converged. Halvery wondered what Storm planned to do once he found her, since Thistle's creasia had to be right on her tail. *They must feel like they've had a stroke of luck,* thought Halvery, *since we are coming to them, making a lot of racket.*

Below Halvery, Storm veered into a new canyon. It was one of the dry ones. Something about it looked familiar. Halvery caught the scent of carrion. "Storm!" he hissed from above. "Storm, don't go in there. It's a—"

"Yes, I know! I'm surprised you don't recognize this tactic, Halvery. I don't need your input right now. Just meet us down at the lake caves."

His shouted retort got the attention of the canyon's resident, who lumbered out of the cave at the far end. Halvery had never seen a land predator larger than a creasia. Until recently, he hadn't known that such a beast existed. The ice bear was gray and white, shaggy, and as big as a boulder. As he watched, it reared on its hind legs, which put it at half the height of the canyon.

Halvery took a quick step away from the edge. Dazzle came sliding down the slope at his back and nearly ran into him, Arcove and Roup just behind.

"What—?" Roup panted.

"Storm has decided to antagonize a bear!" exclaimed Halvery.

As though to confirm this statement, a howl floated out of the canyon, along with curb yips.

The bear did not roar. Its snuffling was almost more ominous. It clearly did not regard Storm and company as a serious threat, but merely an item of curiosity. When Halvery looked down again, Storm and the curbs were fleeing out of the bear's tributary with the creature ambling briskly after them.

"What is he doing?" demanded Arcove. "What are *you* doing? I do not like being left out of deliberations, Halvery. It would be easy to get separated in these canyons, easy for Thistle's cats to pick us off one by one."

Halvery hung his head, forcing himself not to turn and follow Storm and the bear at once. "I believe he intends to lead it into Costa's pursuers, sir. He did something like that when I chased him."

Arcove frowned. "How are Storm and Cohal and Maoli going to avoid getting killed by the bear? How is Costa?"

"I…I don't know, sir."

They all started running again. The evening light was perfect for creasia eyes, and most of the canyons here were narrow enough to jump across. They soon caught up with the bear. They were on the lower slopes now and so close to the lake they could no longer see it. Halvery caught the yip of a curb, the sound echoing off the canyon walls. He'd lost sight of Storm and his companions, but the bear was easy to follow. It ambled along, stopping occasionally to scent the air.

It was starting to slow down, perhaps losing interest, when the snarls of cats floated from the slot ahead. Next instant, Storm, Costa, and the curbs came tearing up the canyon, and ran headlong into the bear.

Halvery thought at first that Storm had made a terrible error in judgment, but then he remembered his own clutter running into Eyal's pack, some fifteen years ago. Storm had run through the pack just ahead of the clutter. The curbs had been too startled to attack him, but the encounter had put them in a frame of mind to fight. Then Halvery's clutter had slammed into them, primed for combat and hot with running.

The bear was certainly startled by the sight of its quarry running towards it. One enormous paw slapped at Storm, who was in the lead, but then a curb nipped at the bear's opposite flank. Costa darted between its legs, quick as a fox, and then all four of them were behind it, running hard.

The bear snarled, finally enraged. Then, in true Storm-induced chaos, the clutter of creasia rounded the corner and ran straight into the bear.

Halvery would have laughed if he'd had breath. There was a cacophony of shrieking feline voices, snarls, hisses, and screams. Unfortunately, there was no time to stay and watch. Storm and his companions had turned up a new branch of the canyon below. Arcove loped along the edge above them. "Storm!"

"I see you!" He was breathless and clearly didn't want to slow down.

"Where are you going?" asked Arcove, struggling to keep pace among the underbrush and small trees at the top of the slot.

"This way leads to…to the lake," panted Storm. "We'll…get there from below. You…come along the top. We'll meet you—"

"Storm!" It was Dazzle. "Floods converge in this canyon. The slot goes underground at the end. It's a bad place to travel, even for a short distance." He hesitated and added, "I hear something that sounds like water."

"He's right, Storm," panted Maoli. "This canyon is about to turn into a tunnel, and I do hear water."

Storm finally stopped running. "Alright, let's find a way up."

"Costa!" called Halvery.

She raised her head, too winded to speak, but grinning.

"His name was Charsel. Chars."

He thought for a moment that she wouldn't remember what he was talking about. Then her eyes crinkled and she managed, "But I'm…like you."

He laughed. "Well, you're like someone. That's enough near-misses to put you ahead of your daddy at the same age, I'm sure."

He thought this might get some friendly sarcasm out of Storm, but Storm wasn't ready for jokes. He'd turned his attention to helping the curbs find a way up the wall of the canyon. Dazzle and Maoli were right: water was coming. The stream at the bottom was rising, and there was an ominous rushing noise from further up the cliffs.

The curbs—so quick to scamper up the walls of most canyons—were having difficulty with this one. Frequent floods had polished the walls smooth. The slot was narrow enough that Halvery could have jumped across, and he was sure that Dazzle could have gotten out by performing his back-and-forth trick. But neither Storm nor the curbs could jump that far. Costa certainly couldn't.

The stream was rising fast now. It wasn't exactly a wall of water, but it would soon sweep them off their feet if they didn't find a way out. "Go back a ways!" shouted Dazzle. "The walls are rougher; I've seen sheep back there." So the curbs and ferryshaft ran back the way they'd come, sticking to the edges of the canyon, where the water hadn't yet reached.

Finally, the curbs identified a wall they could work with. It wasn't great footing. Cohal fell while leading the way—something Halvery had never seen in all their journey through the mountains. He landed in the middle of the rising stream and went under. Storm jumped down and waded in to drag him out.

Maoli paused halfway up the wall. "Cohal, are you alright?"

"Yes," he gasped. "Costa, Storm, go!"

Costa was following Maoli, her hooves light and careful on the narrow shelves of rock. The floor of the canyon was completely underwater now. Storm pushed Cohal up the canyon wall ahead of him. "You go first. Don't argue with me. You just fell."

There was no time for arguing, but it was obviously impossible to go fast. The footing must have been slippery. Costa staggered once. Then Moali made a leap and reached the top. She turned to guide Costa.

At that moment, the rushing noise grew to a grinding roar. A wave crashed into the canyon. Costa made a bound and reached the top. Cohal jumped forward and got high enough to escape the water.

Storm didn't. The wave swept him off the canyon wall and sent him spinning into the roiling center of the current.

Halvery started running. He saw Roup and Arcove out of his peripheral vision, struggling to keep pace with the current over the uneven ground. Amazingly, Storm hadn't gone under. He was swimming, trying to reach a wall of the canyon, as the flood carried him with terrible speed down the slot.

He managed to swim to the far edge and get a little purchase on an outcropping of rock. Arcove jumped the gap, but before he could reach Storm to help him, a bit of debris caught the ferryshaft, drove him briefly underwater, and then back into the middle of the flood. His swimming was less coordinated now, closer to flailing.

Halvery could imagine how cold the water must be, full of snowmelt. Just like the Igby River that spring fifteen years ago, when they'd both gone swimming…

"I'm surprised you don't recognize this tactic, Halvery."

He caught sight of something up ahead—a scrubby tree that overhung the slot, and a gnarled branch that looked more dead than alive. Halvery put on a burst of speed that he felt, not just in his shoulder, but in his hips. *I am getting too old for this.* He launched himself at the branch, hitting it with all his weight and momentum.

Crack!

Halvery had an instant to ponder his life choices and character flaws, particularly impulsive risk-taking. Then he struck the water.

* * * *

This chapter includes an author's note at the end of the book.

21

A Good Friend

The icy water shocked the breath from Halvery's lungs, but he didn't lose his grip on the branch. As he'd hoped, it wedged in the narrow slot. Halvery craned his head to look over his shoulder and found the breath to shout, "Storm!"

A pale face bobbed into view, driven by the current. Halvery got a glimpse of Storm's surprised and desperate eyes before he washed into the branch and managed to get his front hooves over it. *Thank all the friendly ghosts.*

Arcove and Roup were on either side of them now, trying to figure out how to help. The flood waters were still well below the top of the canyon, but the walls were rougher at this height, less polished, with more ledges. Halvery thought that he and Storm could climb out, possibly even jump out, if the branch would bear their weight. Halvery worked his way towards one edge, Storm the other. Arcove looked like he was thinking of climbing down. He could almost reach Storm.

Snap!

The branch buckled. Fortunately, Storm was not thrown free, but he was having trouble hanging on without claws. Halvery hoped that the branch would wedge again. The slot was so narrow, the sides tantalizingly near...

Too near, in fact. The top was closing up over their heads. Halvery raised his eyes with a sense of despair. The canyon was about to become a tunnel. They were headed into the dark. They were going to drown. They were going to be tumbled like river rocks.

Halvery glanced at Storm, his gray eyes dilated to pools of blackness. "The branch might keep us safe if we stay in the middle!" shouted Halvery as he scrambled back towards the center. *It might keep us from being battered against the tunnel, but you'll never hang on without claws.*

The evening sky was only a sliver now, rapidly narrowing. Storm's eyes followed it like vanishing hope.

Halvery had an idea. "Don't panic, Storm." Before the last of the light winked out, he inched over and got hold of Storm above the shoulders. Ferryshaft didn't have a scruff, a fact that Halvery suddenly found extremely inconvenient. However, ferryshaft did have plenty of neck, a thick pelt, and fairly loose skin. Halvery got a good grip.

He assumed that if this was unwelcome, Storm would say, "Let go of me."

He didn't, although the flood was so loud in the echoing tunnel that Halvery might have missed it. The water grew suddenly choppy. One end of the branch struck with a bone-jarring crunch.

Storm slid completely free. Water churned around them so fiercely that it was hard to breathe. Halvery almost lost his grip on both Storm and the branch. *This isn't good enough.* He dragged Storm back to relative safety and then got a front leg around him, so that Storm was wedged between Halvery's chest and the branch.

Halvery gave up trying to hold him by the looser skin above his shoulders and just got a grip on the back of his head.

Don't panic, thought Halvery. *If you struggle, you'll push us both off.*

Storm did not panic. Or perhaps he was in such a state of panic that he couldn't move. The ends of the branch bashed against the tunnel walls again and again. Halvery felt the crush of stone at his back and knew that, if the angle had been just a little different, the impact would have broken his spine.

Don't panic, he thought and wasn't sure whether he was saying it to Storm or to himself. *Don't panic, don't panic.*

They went over a waterfall.

Halvery would certainly have panicked if he'd seen it coming. Instead, he was simply falling without warning. Then he was underwater, then straining to breathe in some mixture of water and air. His claws remained locked in the slippery wood, Storm's skull between his teeth. He pushed his head desperately upwards amid flying foam and thought, *His nose is higher than mine. If I can breathe, he can breathe.*

A scrap of evening sky flashed past overhead. And then again, along with the reflected glint of ice.

Quite suddenly, the ordeal was over. The water slowed, and they were gliding through crystalline caves with a view of the lake coming and going through a honeycomb of ice and rock. The branch bumped against something, and Halvery felt shifting pebbles under his back paws.

Storm spoke at last, his voice rough as though he'd been shouting. Or possibly screaming. "Halvery, please let go of me."

Halvery let go. He tried to stand. They both tried, shaking violently. They staggered and weaved their way up the shallow bank to a mostly dry stretch of stone above the water. It was miserably cold, but Halvery didn't think they were going to die. They would be uncomfortable until they dried out, but if they were lucky, they might avoid frostbite.

Storm began pacing almost immediately as his coordination returned. "I cannot believe you did that," he whispered. "Ghosts, Halvery... You could have just watched me drown!"

Halvery was less inclined to pace. He felt sore all over. He wondered whether he really had been seriously injured and hadn't yet felt it. He sank to the ground and curled up, shivering.

Storm stopped in front of him, eyes searching his face. "You have the most phenomenal bite-control of any animal I have ever met! How did you not crush my skull when we hit the wall? Or when we went over the waterfall?"

"Only amateurs crush someone's skull when they don't intend to," muttered Halvery.

Storm gave a laugh that was half-hysterical. "That is untrue, and you know it!" He was still staring into Halvery's face with an earnestly searching expression.

"You didn't seriously think I would let you—" began Halvery.

"I know *Roup* wouldn't," said Storm. "I know *Arcove* wouldn't. But *you...*" He caught his breath and said again, "I cannot believe you just did that. And after I was just shouting a lot of cruel nonsense at you."

"Oh, it wasn't exactly nonsense—"

"I know you care about Costa. You were so patient when you were teaching her two years ago. I know you're just treating her the way you'd treat your own cubs. I know I'm being overprotective, and maybe I don't deserve to know what she's doing..."

Halvery was accustomed to dealing with quick-witted Storm who always had a sharp retort and a playful insult. He was accustomed to grandstanding, get-the-job-done, always-one-step-ahead Storm. Storm babbling explanations and apologies was an alien creature, and Halvery wanted him to stop, so he leaned forward and said, "Could I get you to lie down here? I am cold, and I don't think I can stand yet."

He expected Storm to lie down beside him, but instead, he wrapped himself around Halvery's chest and the front half of his body. Halvery held his head up awkwardly for a moment, but then

Storm rested his head over Halvery's shoulders and Halvery put his head down in Storm's fur. The warmth was welcome. "I could *not* have watched you drown," he muttered.

"Why?" asked Storm. "I've humiliated you on I-don't-know-how-many occasions, told that story about dumping you in the river more times than I can easily remember. I'm the reason the curbs hate you—"

Halvery rolled his eyes. "Oh, and how you love to rub it in—"

"From now on, every time I tell that story about the river, I'm going to follow it with this one," said Storm. "The time you jumped into a flood to save my life. You almost died, Halvery."

"We both almost died." *And we may still.* They were shivering. Being wet in this weather was quite dangerous. Halvery wondered whether he should force himself to his feet, try to get warm by moving. But he could tell he wasn't steady. He was in no shape to fight. *Thistle might have other cats waiting in these caves. Better to lie still until Arcove and Roup find us.*

It's really not that cold, he told himself. *We weren't in the water for long.*

"I never asked what happened to you after that chase when we fell in the river," whispered Storm. "I was a quarter of the way to the lake by the time I managed to swim to shore, and then it took me the rest of the day to dry out and stop shaking. You didn't come after me, so I figured your clutter must have been busy getting you out."

"The branch hit me on the head," muttered Halvery. "My beta swam in and held my nose above the water until I came to my senses, but we were swept downstream. Took a while for the clutter to find us. I was in no shape to keep chasing you." *I never told that part in council. It was too humiliating. I thought Roup would enjoy it too much.*

A long silence. Finally, against his better judgment, Halvery said, "Were you truly Costa's size...when we were hunting you?"

Storm snorted a laugh. "I was a runt. I was smaller."

When Halvery didn't respond, Storm raised his head and craned around to look him in the face. "Oh..." Some of his usual cheekiness returned. "Oh, regret doesn't look good on you, Halvery."

Halvery refused to meet his gaze. "I know. I am becoming soft in my old age."

Storm started washing his face.

Halvery gave a sputter, but then he just shut his eyes. "Don't tell anyone I let you do that."

"You are such a good friend," whispered Storm. "I am sorry I haven't been. I haven't been a good friend to anyone lately; is that any consolation? Tollee says I came up here looking for death. I guess she was right. I guess I almost found it."

"What happened," asked Halvery quietly, "with the foal you lost?"

Storm shifted back around to put his head across Halvery's shoulders. Halvery thought for a moment that he wouldn't answer. Then he said, in a very low voice, "He was following me. We were in the foothills of the Great Mountain on the seaward side—an unfamiliar place—and I was picking my way along a sheep trail. Paeden missed a step."

When he did not continue, Halvery said, "That could happen to anyone—"

"No, it could not," said Storm in a voice so tight it cracked. *"Anyone* doesn't take their yearling onto unfamiliar sheep trails."

Halvery said nothing.

After a moment, Storm continued, "My first two foals were afraid of the things ferryshaft are supposed to be afraid of. They did what I told them to do. I took them all over the island. Afterward, one of them settled down in Sauny's herd and one in Charder's, which is now my mother's. They took mates. They're happy. But Paeden... He was restless. And he wasn't afraid. Not ever. He was following me from his first spring. Teek was like that, and Teek turned out alright, so I thought... I guess I thought we were invincible—me and mine. And because we were in an unfamiliar place, where ferryshaft do not usually go for *good* reasons, my yearling foal made a mistake…and died for it."

Storm stopped talking.

Halvery couldn't think of anything to say. At last, he ventured, "Does your mate blame you?"

Storm gave a miserable snort. "She never said so. She didn't say much of anything for a while. We split up for the rest of the summer. I stayed in Leeshwood or ran with the curbs, and she went to live with Charder's herd. But then fall came…the mating season. I showed up and she was happy to see me. We didn't do anything to make a foal that year, though. We ferryshaft avoided making a foal on purpose; can you imagine?"

Halvery smothered a laugh in Storm's fur.

"Next year, though, we made Costa."

"So Tollee doesn't blame you?" persisted Halvery.

"Tollee saw her parents killed in front of her when she was just a baby, Halvery. And then creasia killed her first mate when we foals tried to start that rebellion all by ourselves. Sometimes I think she just expects everyone she loves to die in front of her, and she's pleasantly surprised when some of us don't."

So the only person blaming you for this is yourself. "You know that creasia cubs frequently do not survive…"

Storm tucked his head against Halvery's side with a miserable whine. "Halvery, if you tell me that I am being weak and silly because I can't handle the death of one foal—"

"Don't speak for me, please. I was going to say that I lose a cub or two nearly every year, often while I am training them to hunt or swim or fight. It is *never* easy. There is no number of dead cubs that makes it easy."

Storm shifted so that he could look Halvery in the face again. His eyes were large and dark, and there was pain in the angle of his ears.

Halvery looked at his own paws and continued, "A few years ago, one of my favorites…the most promising tracker I have ever trained…she got kicked in the head by a buck on her first real hunt.

She misjudged her timing. Anyone could have made that mistake, especially on their first try, but she happened to catch a hoof to the head. She thrashed around for a moment, and then just…died. I was the one teaching her."

He'd thought he could tell this story dispassionately, but the bite of that moment caught him like a different kind of blow. *She trusted me.*

Storm was still looking at him. "How do you stand it?" he whispered.

Halvery growled because he didn't want to whimper. "What's the alternative? *Don't* train them? Send them out into their adult lives *not* knowing how to hunt or swim or climb or fight? Everyone needs a bit of luck when they're doing something dangerous for the first time. You just hope that your cub gets that luck, that second chance, but sometimes they don't. That's what I was trying to tell Costa when she was lamenting her inability to live up to your legend."

Storm gave a mournful chuckle. "When was this?"

"On the way here. That first night, when she wanted me to hunt her. She stayed ahead of me as well as you ever did, right up until the end. Then she got tired and careless. She knew I wasn't going to kill her if I won, so I did. Afterward, she wanted to know why she wasn't as good as you, and I told her: you succeeded because you had to, because you had no other choice except to die." He thought, unwillingly, of Dazzle unable to learn his canyon jumping trick until a flood threatened.

"You have to have some near-misses," continued Halvery. "You need to get lucky a few times when the stakes are real. She hasn't had those high stakes or those near-misses." He smiled. "Until now."

Storm was silent a moment. "I should have let her come with us," he said at last. "Then she wouldn't have been down there on the ice alone."

"Or maybe she needed to do this alone and now she has valuable experience that will keep her alive in the future," said Halvery.

"I think she would have escaped even if we hadn't gone to help her." He hesitated. "You trained her well."

Storm laughed. "*You* did. Don't think for a moment that I didn't recognize the way she reacted to that cat coming at her."

"Looked like your moves to me," said Halvery placidly. "I did wonder…" He fidgeted. "But I suppose it worked out."

"You wondered what?"

"Oh, when I was hunting her by the lake. After I caught her…I thought I should scare her a little…and I just…I couldn't make myself do it."

Storm was suddenly washing his face again.

"That's not kindness," snapped Halvery. "I wondered for a moment if she was going to die this evening because I didn't have the stomach to make her afraid. Paeden wasn't afraid enough; you just said so."

Storm became instantly serious. After a moment, he said, "I thought I'd made peace with his death. But when Costa got to that age, I started dreaming about him. And not just him. My friend Tracer, who died during the foals' rebellion. Callaris from our old clique, Mylo, Ishy, Ally… Nearly all the friends I grew up with are dead."

"Because of creasia?" asked Halvery unwillingly.

"Oh, I'd be a fool to credit you with all that. We were a bunch of orphans—exactly the sort of ferryshaft the elders were willing to sacrifice to the cull. We were starving in winter and fighting with each other year-round. Kelsy is the one who killed Ally. Most of my clique would have died of something before reaching adulthood. But Tracer was doing what I encouraged him to do—fighting with cats—and I do feel that was mostly my fault."

Halvery made a grumbling noise. "This sounds like Roup's style of nonsense. A cat killed him. How is that your—?"

"Tell that to my nightmares, Halvery!" Storm shut his eyes and ground his teeth. "Anyway…when Costa started insisting on coming to the mountains, disobeying me, inviting herself to creasia conferences…the dreams got worse. I've spent more time training

Costa than any of my other foals, but I can hardly bear to hear her call me father. The last person who did that wound up dead at the bottom of a cliff."

Halvery said nothing. His own cubs usually called him "sir," but ferryshaft had a less hierarchical social structure. He *had* noticed Costa's unusual tendency to refer to her father by his given name, although he hadn't attached much significance to it.

Storm's ears were flat. He stared at a patch of sky, now velvet black and gleaming with stars. "Maybe I shouldn't have any more foals. Maybe I shouldn't even have a mate." He gave a mirthless laugh. "Maybe I *don't* have a mate. I wouldn't let Tollee come with me up here. We were still arguing about it when I left. I'm only good at taking care of myself."

Before Halvery could formulate a response to this, Storm continued, "*Of course* you were doing Costa a kindness by not making her afraid of you. She adores you and Roup and Lyndi. She's spent more time around creasia than ferryshaft; it would be a shame if she were afraid of you. Whose name did you tell her when we were climbing out of the canyon?"

Halvery hesitated. "My brother's. Littermate."

Storm frowned. "Have I met him?"

"He died when we were yearlings. He and I went hunting away from our den, and a couple of ferryshaft caught us. He didn't make it up the tree in time. Not for lack of skill; just random chance. I told Costa that she might be like me or she could be like him, and she can't know which until she has those near-misses."

Silence. "Your littermate was killed by ferryshaft when you were a year old…"

Halvery made a face. "Ghosts and little fishes. I didn't want Costa's pity, and I don't want yours. I am trying to make a point—"

"Did they eat him?"

"Of course they ate him."

"In front of you?"

"I'm beginning to think you're enjoying the mental image—"

"Halvery!" Storm's outburst came so close to his ear that he flinched.

Halvery continued stubbornly, "I told Costa that if she wants to live up to your legend, that's what it will take, and she might get lucky like I did. Or she might not. She might be like my brother. He was just as special."

"Oh, Halvery…"

"And so was Paeden. He had an instant of bad luck at a critical moment. Like my brother, like my daughter… You can't shield your offspring from that. They've just got to take their chances like everyone else, but it *hurts* when they don't make it. You wouldn't be any kind of a parent if it didn't hurt worse than anything."

Storm went quiet. Halvery listened for sounds of approaching animals—either friends or foes. He heard a creak almost like footfalls from the direction of the lake, but that would be an odd direction for approach. It was probably just the ice settling.

At last, Storm said, "Did you take your brother to the Ghost Wood?"

Halvery snorted. "I was a year old. And there was nothing left."

"Ferryshaft write names sometimes for dead friends. Or we used to. Ferryshaft who lived before the war would write a line or two about a friend's life. We did it for Charder, but it's not a common tradition anymore."

"Did you do it for Paeden?"

"No. It seemed ridiculous to do that for a yearling. His life hadn't even started."

"Maybe you should. Maybe you should write all of their names—the friends you grew up with."

A pause. "Why didn't you tell Costa your brother's name until now?"

Halvery shifted uncomfortably. "No ferryshaft knows that name. Or they didn't."

"Would you be offended if I wrote his name in our caves?"

A long pause. "I don't know. I'll think about it." Halvery was starting to feel a little steadier. His fur had gone crunchy with ice. He stood up, backed away from Storm, and shook himself. Frozen droplets showered the cave floor. His paws were tingling. He paced up and down to warm them. Then he began to groom himself, stopping to pick shards of ice from between his toes.

Storm shook himself as well and trotted around the cave. His winter undercoat was very dense. Halvery didn't think he'd been wet to the skin even after their dunking. "You say Costa wants to live up to my legend... Halvery, *I* can't even live up to my legend! I did the most important thing I will ever do when I was three years old. *Nothing* I will ever manage for the rest of my life can equal that."

Halvery harrumphed. "I take exception to the notion that dropping me in a river was the most important thing you'll ever do—"

Storm barked a laugh. "I meant—"

"You got the ferryshaft out of a muddle they'd gotten themselves into by being relentless bullies. Yes, I know not everyone agrees about that, but I'm right and they're wrong."

Storm laughed again.

Halvery continued, "You always seem to be in the middle of whatever trouble is happening on Lidian. Who's to say that what we're doing right now isn't just as important as what you did when you were three?"

Storm sighed. "I do go looking for trouble, don't I? I am incapable of settling down to a peaceful life. Kelsy said it: a legend, not a leader. I've tried to live in a herd, but I get so restless. I think I would walk off a cliff if I had to go through the same round of social niceties and seasonal routines endlessly year after tedious year..."

Halvery tried to swallow a laugh. "As far as I can tell, you live in a clutter."

"Oh, don't even start. Maybe Kelsy was right about that, too. I saved the ferryshaft, but I can't live with them. Do you know what was happening right before you chased me fifteen years ago? The herd had rejected me. My clique had disbanded. No one wanted to talk to me or sleep near me. I felt like I was winning with the creasia and losing with my own herd. It wasn't bravado that caused me to run such risks when I led your clutter into Eyal's pack. It wasn't fearlessness that caused me to jump onto that branch and send us both into the river. It was despair. Because right then, I didn't care whether I lived or died. And I'd never wish that on Costa. I hope no one I love *ever* feels as lost and alone as I felt that day."

Halvery stopped beside Storm. After a moment's consideration, he started grooming Storm's ears.

Storm's tail waved. "You are such a good friend."

Halvery sighed heavily. "Thanks to Roup's machinations."

"Oh, no. It was *your* idea to bring me to Moashi's training."

"Can we forget that you know that?"

Storm laughed. The spark of mischief had returned to his eyes. "You and Roup got *really* close that summer we trained Moashi."

"We did. It's going to break his heart when I can't forgive Dazzle for nearly killing him."

Storm cocked his head. "I'm confused. Is Dazzle on our side now or not?"

"Well, if you're confused then that makes two of us. Here's what I know: Thistle offered Arcove and Roup Dazzle's life in exchange for assistance. That's the part of Flurry's message that no one else received."

Storm's eyes widened. "Oh..."

"But," continued Halvery, "Flurry believed that he was leading us into a trap. Thistle told him that the whole thing was Dazzle's idea. Dazzle and Thistle were supposed to trade our lives to Macex once we arrived. Macex was supposed to help them take Leeshwood after they helped him kill Sedaron."

Storm cocked his head. "Treachery seems to be everyone's favorite pastime up here. I take it that Dazzle was not, in fact, the initiator of this scheme? That's why he behaved as though Flurry had betrayed him?"

"Supposedly. Dazzle would have us believe that he never knew his life was on offer. He came to warn us about Thistle's treachery and that's when he realized he was part of the bargain. But Dazzle told Arcove he would keep that bargain—his life in exchange for his cats returning to Leeshwood."

A long silence while Storm tried to make sense of this. "You don't believe him?"

"I..." Halvery could almost see Roup's anxious face, *wanting* peace, *wanting* forgiveness for everyone, but... "No! I don't. I think Dazzle is still playing some game with us. I don't think he has any intention of dying. And even if he did...even if he's got enough loyalty to his own cats to make that bargain...in that case, I think we should take him at his word and kill him. I don't see how we can ever trust him again or bring him back to Leeshwood. Storm, he stood there and watched Roup bleeding out...in order to make Arcove grieve himself to death. I just can't..."

Storm butted his head against Halvery's shoulder in a creasia-like gesture of comfort and goodwill.

Halvery tried to laugh, but it came out hollow. "I'm not as good as Roup."

"You are *so* good."

"I'm not that generous, not that kind, not that trusting—"

"You may be right about Dazzle," said Storm quietly. "He's very likable, though. It's hard not to like him."

Halvery snorted. "When he's flattering you with every other word." He hesitated and added grudgingly, "When he can do the same kind of clever tricks you can."

"The way he moves looks like he's floating."

"Yes, and meanwhile Roup spent all winter learning to walk again."

Storm winced.

"I'm not saying don't admire his skill," continued Halvery. "Just don't assume you're talking to a friend."

"Understood." Storm's head whipped suddenly towards the lake. "Did you hear something?"

"I keep thinking I hear someone walking out there," said Halvery. "But surely Arcove wouldn't approach from over the ice, and I can't imagine why Thistle's cats would come that way. It's one thing for curbs and a ferryshaft foal to risk it and quite another for a full grown creasia to walk around out there."

Storm reared up on his hind legs to see better. "Could be that pack of lowland curbs."

"I suppose, but why would they skulk?"

"Could be Cohal and Maoli."

"Again, the skulking."

Storm sank back down. "I hope our group finds us soon. Roup will be losing his mind."

Halvery laughed. "Oh, he'll be sad, but—"

"Are you joking? He'll be frantic." Storm hesitated and then added in a lighter tone, "You know he does not want to raise that litter of Ilsa's all by himself."

"Well, you're right there. But Arcove would just take her into his den, so it would work out. And, ghosts, wouldn't that satisfy Ilsa's ambitions! She might be happier."

"Utter nonsense," replied Storm. "She would be heartbroken if you didn't come back. And it would be a desperate shame if you didn't get to see those cubs. *I* want to see them, and I didn't spend all fall trying to bring them into existence."

Halvery couldn't help preening a little. "You don't know the half of it. And, yes, I do want to see them. Roup acts like he doesn't care, but—"

Storm snorted. "Oh, he cares. If you're ever tempted to wonder whether Roup cares about something, the answer is always yes."

Halvery burst out laughing. "His temperament is entirely wrong for a creasia."

"And yet you have made an enormous effort to get more of his blood into Leeshwood."

"Yes, well, that coat—"

Halvery froze all at once. An animal stood in one of the openings to the lake, silhouetted against the star-studded sky. Storm saw it, too, and went rigid. The creature was too small for a cat. The shape of the head was wrong. Medium-sized, shaggy. A curb…?

The animal vanished, and Storm dashed after it. "We're friends! Friends of highland curbs! Don't run! Please!"

He and Halvery splashed through one of the cave's meandering streams, through an opening in the honeycomb of rock, and out onto the edge of an icefield broken by all manner of frozen debris. There would be no tracking the animal over this ice.

To Halvery's relief, the curb stopped a little distance away. A long silence. Then it spoke: "An animal was on the lake calling to us. She howled like a highland curb."

Storm's face broke into a grin. "Yes! Yes, that was my daughter, Costa. We came into the mountains with two highland curbs, Cohal and Maoli. They're from a pack on the northern plains. We've been looking for you."

————

* * * *

This chapter includes an author's note at the end of the book.

22

Curbs

The curb's name was Tsueri. Storm and Halvery had been talking to him for only a few moments when there was a patter of hooves, and Costa came tearing out of the caves. "You're alive! You're both alive! Halvery, you are the very best cat who ever lived. Storm—"

Storm came forward to embrace her with his neck and she tucked her face under his chin. She spoke in a babble, her voice an octave too high, "I thought I'd killed you. I thought you got killed rescuing me. Because I did something dangerous, and I meant to risk my life, but I never meant to risk yours, Storm. Please don't make me live with that. Please..."

Storm gave a tired laugh. "Now you know how *I* feel."

Costa pulled back to stare at him round-eyed. "I'm sorry. I'm so sorry; please don't die."

Halvery spoke up. "He's quite difficult to kill."

Cohal and Maoli came flying out of the caves at that moment, followed by Arcove, Roup, and Dazzle. Halvery got a look at Roup's face—ears low, eyes huge and dark. *Maybe Storm was right.*

"Halvery..." Arcove's voice was rough with relief. "You scared us." He turned to Storm. "*You* also scared us. I am frankly shocked that you're both alive."

"Well, he's nearly impossible to kill—" began Halvery at the same time that Storm said,

"Halvery pinned me to the branch and held my head above the water. I have no idea how he did it without crushing my skull. The branch slammed against the walls I-don't-know-how-many times."

Halvery sighed. *Next thing I know you'll be telling them I let you wash my face afterwards.*

But Storm was busy being greeted by the curbs.

Roup hadn't said a word. He came right up to Halvery and sniffed over him—not in greeting, but like a cat searching for injury. "Roup, I'm fine."

Roup walked all the way around him, nudging him gently this way and that. "Roup, I'm fine. Alright, a little bruised. Don't poke me."

He stopped in front of Halvery and tucked his head under his chin. He was shaking—a faint tremor that was probably invisible to everyone else. Halvery felt suddenly guilty, although he could not have said for what. He spoke again, this time right against Roup's ear, "Roup, I—am—fine."

Roup let out a single, ragged purr.

Halvery started grooming his head and neck.

"We saw a waterfall…" began Arcove.

"Oh, Storm and I noticed it," said Halvery brightly. "It did not escape our attention."

"I have no idea how you didn't crush my skull," repeated Storm.

"Yes, well, I have no idea how you didn't panic and shove us both off the branch."

"Frozen terror."

The curbs were crowding around Storm. "We thought we'd lost you, friend," said Maoli.

Cohal's ears and tail were low. Storm bent to sniff noses with him. "Are you hurt?"

"No," said Cohal in a near-whisper. Halvery suspected he was feeling some responsibility for the whole episode, since his fall from the ledge had precipitated it.

Roup spoke at last, his voice almost steady, "We couldn't get down here right away. The tunnels were all flooded, and the lake ice seemed precarious. Dazzle thought it might take even longer to find you if we went through the more accessible caves, so we just waited for the water levels to fall."

Halvery glanced around for Dazzle and saw him standing a little apart from everyone else. *So, you didn't take advantage of our separation. You still need us together. Why?*

Costa went suddenly rigid. She'd noticed the strange curb, standing in the shadow of a slab of ice. Cohal and Maoli followed her gaze and started. Halvery gave them a smug smile and said, "We met someone at the end of our little adventure. Tsueri says that his pack lives on the islands, but that a ferryshaft was howling to them like a highland curb, so he came to investigate. He recognized your names, so I assume you know each other."

There was a heartbeat's pause, and then Cohal, Maoli, and Tsueri converged in a tail-waving mass, exclaiming and talking at once. Apparently Tsueri had been a cub when Cohal left the valley and a young adult when Maoli left. They talked, yipped, whined, laughed, and then ran around each other in circles. "We have established a den on each little island," Tsueri told them. "We rarely go to the mainland; it is too dangerous. We didn't think there were any other highland curbs left..."

"How many are you?" asked Maoli.

"I am not sure," said Tsueri. "More than fifty, less than a hundred."

Maoli's tail waved. "This means there are twice as many of us in the world as we thought."

"You have such dens on the northern plains?" asked Tsueri in wonder.

"We have such dens," said Cohal. "We need to speak to your queen. These ferryshaft are friends to highland curbs—very dear friends. The adult's name is Storm, and his daughter is Costa. May they come with us? Will the ice bear their weight?"

"They may and it will," said Tsueri, "so long as they follow me closely."

Costa danced around the curbs. "Did you hear me? Did you hear me howl like a curb?"

"We heard you," said Tsueri. "No one has howled like this from the mainland in a very long time."

Storm glanced at the creasia. "Will you wait here?"

"Yes, in the caves on the southern edge," said Dazzle. "It should be easy for you to get there from over the ice, although it's more complicated over land." He glanced at Arcove. "At least... that's where my cats will expect to find us."

"I assume it's also where Thistle's creasia will expect to ambush us," said Halvery.

"Not necessarily," said Dazzle. "If he thinks you're heading back to your clutters, there would be no reason to go to the lake caves." He paused and then added unwillingly. "Unless he has intercepted my message."

"Sir," murmured Halvery to Arcove, "I do not like the idea of waiting in unfamiliar territory under the direction of this dubious ally. I propose we head back to the clutters and return with our full strength or a better plan. Presumably, Dazzle's cats will still be here."

"They will have difficulty waiting here for very long," said Dazzle. "They will likely be pursued. There will be pregnant females who are near their time for birth."

Arcove spoke at last. "Are there any spring cubs already born, Dazzle?"

"Not unless they've arrived in the last day. Our birthing season has been starting later than yours, probably because the weather warms up later."

Arcove thought for a long moment. At last, he turned to Storm and said, "We will wait here tonight. If Dazzle's cats do not arrive by early dawn, we will head to the clutters. If you cannot find us, don't linger. Meet us on the far side of the valley." He hesitated. "If there is a battle, I trust you'll hear it."

"I hope it doesn't come to that," muttered Dazzle. "Macex outnumbers you severely."

Halvery did not like the fact that Dazzle knew this. He didn't like the idea of waiting in a vulnerable position of Dazzle's choosing.

Tsueri spoke up, "Consider leaving at midnight instead of dawn, Arcove. There is bad weather coming. We know the signs."

Halvery didn't know the signs, but he could tell the temperature was dropping.

"Dazzle, how likely are your cats to reach us by midnight?" asked Arcove.

Dazzle considered. At last, he said, "It depends on too many factors, Arcove. I just can't say."

"How convenient for you," said Halvery.

Dazzle's calm was more irritating than an impatient response, "Halvery, I've had plenty of opportunities to lead you into an ambush if that's what I wanted."

"Yes, you must want something else."

"I must."

"Costa and I will try to return by midnight," said Storm. "If we can't find you, we'll head west."

Flurry

Roup knew he wasn't following along as well as he should be. *Focus.* But he'd been hollowed out with sorrow, and relief hadn't caught up yet. The sick feeling of loss was still sloshing around in his stomach.

"Wait," Arcove had said in his ear when Halvery and Storm disappeared. He didn't say anything else, but Roup knew what he meant.

Wait to feel things. Do what has to be done and save the rest for later. Don't run ahead of me. I need you here. Wait.

And Roup had tried. While Costa panicked and the curbs tried to calm her and Dazzle looked for a way past the flood, Roup had held those feelings in check. But when he'd gotten a look at that shadowy waterfall—the height of it, the narrow, unforgiving walls—then Roup had not been able to wait any longer. Grief had seeped through him like ice water, blurring the world with pain.

But Arcove had been right. He should have waited. Because here was Halvery, joking with Storm, making suspicious remarks about Dazzle, and being snide with the curbs. And he was fine.

Storm was fine, too. Not dead at an age just a few years older than Coden had been. Not a broken body floating in a pool. Not missing, never to be found or properly mourned. He stopped to give Roup a lick on the ear before taking off with the curbs. "Are you alright?" he whispered.

"I'm…" Roup almost choked. "I'm fine."

Roup knew he should be paying attention to the way that Dazzle took them through the caves to his rendezvous point. It was only prudent, even if Dazzle wasn't leading them into a trap. But Roup couldn't concentrate. He watched Halvery out of the corners of his eyes, alert for some sign that he was more injured than he seemed, bleeding internally, perhaps. But he really did appear to be well, apart from noticeably favoring his right shoulder whenever they had to climb.

When they finally reached the cave where Dazzle wanted them to rendezvous, Roup was feeling less like vomiting. The moon had risen, gleaming off the lake ice just visible through the lattice of rock to the west. Access from the canyons was limited to a narrow tunnel, cut by water in the distant past, but rarely flooded now according to Dazzle.

The four creasia had barely begun to sniff around the cave when there came a soft rustle from the tunnel. Halvery dropped into a defensive crouch, lips peeling back in a snarl. Arcove bristled, his legs going stiff, and even Dazzle's tail fluffed up as he backed away.

Then Flurry trotted out of the shadows, his voice cracking with relief, "You made it."

Dazzle's fur smoothed at once. "We made it, but an ambush party was waiting at the bottom of the canyons. Do they know we're coming here?"

"I don't think so. I was chased, and they may have seen me talking to the curbs."

"Which curbs?"

"I found both packs."

Dazzle sat down, his tension easing. "Good." He hesitated and then added, in a gentler voice, "That's good, Flur."

The hint of kindness seemed to prompt Flurry to ask, in a whisper, "Is Serot really dead?"

"Yes."

"Coldstep?"

"Also, yes."

Flurry rattled off a dozen other names, growing more distressed with each pronouncement of, "Dead, dead, dead..."

Dazzle only said three were, "Still alive."

"Why was it mostly your friends who got killed in that battle?"

Dazzle snorted. "Why do you think?" He hesitated and then added, "If you'd been here, you'd probably be dead, too."

"This was the battle in which Sedaron was killed?" asked Arcove.

"Yes," said Dazzle. "He and a group of his best fighters thought they were sneaking into the valley through a little-used canyon. Meanwhile Macex attacked the main confluence with a larger force to provide a diversion. Except, of course, Macex had told us where to expect Sedaron's ferryshaft, and we trapped them in the slot."

Flurry shivered. "Are we talking about Sliver Canyon?"

"You got it in one," muttered Dazzle.

"That's a terrible place for a fight...even with surprise on your side."

Dazzle said nothing.

"And Thistle sent you in there...with Serot and Blacktip and Coldstep and all your old clutter..."

"We were a logical choice; I can't fault him for that. And it's not like there wasn't hard fighting in the confluence. Plenty of Macex's ferryshaft didn't know about the bargain he'd made. Most of them never will. Thistle and Shale were both bitten and kicked pretty badly, and Flash is still limping a little. But the fighting in Sliver Canyon... It was like nothing you've ever seen."

Flurry gave a bitter laugh. "I bet Thistle said, 'Make it rain blood, Dazzle.'"

"He did." Dazzle sighed. "And I did."

Flurry stared into the middle distance, apparently lost in a mental image of the battle. "It's so narrow in there that even outnumbering them wouldn't help much. You'd be fighting them one or two at a time and then the bodies would pile up."

Dazzle turned away, as though he were tired of this conversation. "We should rest while we can." He went a little further into the cave to a dry, sandy spot where they had a view of the tunnel, but plenty of space to react to anything coming through.

Dazzle stretched out on his stomach. Flurry promptly lay down beside him, facing the other direction, and put his head over Dazzle's back. Dazzle grunted, but he didn't say anything.

Halvery lay down a few paces from Dazzle with the obvious intent of keeping an eye on him. After a moment's consideration, Roup lay down between Halvery and Dazzle, much to Halvery's obvious annoyance. He expected Arcove to lie down on the other side, so that Roup would have to talk to Dazzle over Arcove's back. Instead, Arcove lay down on the other side of Halvery. Not just next to him, but right up against him.

Roup couldn't help but smile. *Maybe you didn't wait to feel things after all.*

Halvery looked surprised to be in the middle. Roup scooted over and leaned against him, so that Halvery could not possibly miss the fact that they'd curled up around him.

Roup could feel the way Halvery's posture softened. After a moment, he said to Dazzle, in an almost civil voice, "Who really killed Sedaron?"

Dazzle kept his eyes on the tunnels. "Who do you think?"

"Well," muttered Halvery, "you're good for something."

After a moment, Dazzle murmured, almost too low to hear, "They were retreating. They almost made it. They were using their own dead as a barricade; it was difficult to get to them. And Sedaron was in the middle. The canyon was too high to jump down on them from above, but..."

Flurry laughed. "But you walk on air."

"Up, up, up," said Dazzle, his eyes flicking back and forth as though tracking his passage up the sides of the slot, "down, down, down. Right on top of him. Still a nasty fight. Sarot followed me. He got hurt keeping them off me. Coldstep was injured, too, but they both survived the battle, and they *were* getting better. I was feeding them. Not from clutter kills, either. I was hunting for them myself. Then, two days ago, Thistle killed them."

Raw hurt and anger slipped into his voice for a moment, instantly smoothed over by his usual dispassionate way of speaking. "He said they asked him to do it, that they were dying and consuming food that should go to others. He claimed they asked him because they couldn't bear to ask me. Everyone was out of the dens at the time. There were no witnesses apart from Shale and Sundance."

"Oh, Daz..." whispered Flurry.

"I should have seen it coming," snapped Dazzle. "I *really* should have. I think Coldstep fought for her life. They'd already dragged away her body by the time anyone arrived. They probably killed Serot first. He died in his sleep, at least."

"I can't believe Thistle is doing this to you!" exclaimed Flurry. "To *you*. What is he thinking? He can't win without *you!*"

Dazzle shut his eyes. "Well, he has obviously decided that he can't win *with* me."

"Why?"

Dazzle didn't answer. Instead, he said, "Flur, I'm trying to get these very important people not to kill you, and you're not making it easy."

"Oh..." Flurry got to his feet and came around in front of Arcove.

Arcove raised his head and sat up.

Flurry crouched. Roup couldn't see Arcove's face from this angle, but he doubted that his expression was making Flurry's task any easier. "I...I don't know what to say, sir."

"Well, that makes two of us," said Arcove dryly. "Perhaps in the Southern Mountains, it is customary to change sides with the changing moon, but in my Leeshwood, we rarely give our trust more than once."

Flurry looked at his paws. "In Thistle's Leeshwood, they tell a lot of stories about you, Arcove—how you killed the ferryshaft for generations because they made you angry. How you killed Treace because he was clever and wanted to change things and had good ideas. You were bigger and meaner, so you won. And Dazzle...he's clever, too, and I thought... I imagined it was like that." His eyes flicked up to Arcove's face and he added defiantly, "Dazzle is the best commanding officer anyone could ever have, and he saved my life when no one else would have bothered. I thought you wanted to hurt him. So I didn't feel guilty for leading you into a trap."

Arcove said nothing.

Flurry took a deep breath and continued, "But your cats seem happy. I can tell you take care of each other. Even the ferryshaft and telshees like you. And you didn't have to be kind to me, but you were. And I…I started feeling not-quite-right about bringing you up here. And I was afraid I was about to get Dazzle killed, too, because I didn't really think this was his idea. I felt worse and worse the whole way. I kept telling myself that, as soon as we got near the valley, I'd go find Dazzle. I'd make sure this was really his plan and…and maybe ask him to reconsider it."

His gaze skated to Roup briefly and then back to Arcove. "I know Dazzle must have saved your life in the confluence. That's why you changed your mind about killing him."

The way he said it made Roup prick up his ears. Flurry wasn't sure. He was guessing. Arcove's face and posture betrayed nothing.

On the far side of them, Dazzle gave a heavy sigh. "I know you can grovel better than that, Flurry."

Flurry looked earnestly at Arcove and continued, "Sir, there is no point in me fighting with you, any more than me fighting with Dazzle. If you want my life, you'll take it. If not…I'll do whatever you ask to redeem myself. I'll hunt for you or take messages or do something dangerous. I can see how you wouldn't trust me, but if Dazzle is on your side, then so am I, and I'll prove it any way you like."

Roup looked hard at Arcove. *You are not going to kill a four-year-old in cold blood.*

But Arcove *really* didn't like being lied to. "Even favors require trust," he growled. "At the moment, I wouldn't trust you to tell me the direction of the wind, Flurry. But my beta doesn't want me to kill you, and for the moment I'm going to humor him. I'll let your hero over there explain why that's ironic."

Arcove lay back down, and Flurry slunk back to Dazzle.

Roup let out his breath. *That's as good as you're going to get right now, Flurry. Leave him alone until we've managed to bring everyone home alive.*

Flurry spoke to Dazzle, almost too low for Roup to hear. "I feel like there's something you're not telling me."

Dazzle didn't take his eyes off the tunnels. "That's always true."

"Alright, but—"

"Each and every time we speak, you may assume that there are dozens of things I am not telling you, Flurry."

Flurry flicked his tail. "I meant—"

Dazzle was making a joke out of it. "Hundreds of things. Thousands."

"Very funny."

"The things I have not told you could fill the lower lake—"

"What did you trade for this?"

"Nosy four-year-old cubs."

"Daz..."

"Shut up and go to sleep, Flurry."

"Please—"

"You just called me your commanding officer, which is a dubious claim at best, but if I am, then shut up and sleep. I may need you for something later."

Flurry subsided. Roup had no doubt that he was exhausted in the way that only growing juveniles could be. He put his head over Dazzle's back and drifted off almost as soon as he stopped moving.

Roup wanted to talk, but he wondered if he ought to let Dazzle sleep. Dazzle hadn't offered to keep watch, although perhaps that was just because he knew he would be refused. Roup suspected he was as tired as the rest of them, although he was in his prime and handling it better.

"I'll watch," murmured Roup.

Halvery made a grumbling noise. "I'm not leaving you alone with him."

"How does this qualify as alone?"

"You managed to get yourself into trouble via written message last time."

Roup couldn't decide whether to laugh or be irritated. Arcove wasn't volunteering an opinion, but Roup saw his ears rotate to listen.

Dazzle spoke in a tired voice. "Ask, Roup. You unbelievable creature. Ask me anything."

24

Losing

"Why did you cripple the cats you fought with?"

Dazzle raised his head to stare at Roup. "*Surely* you don't want to listen to me make excuses. *I* don't want to listen to me make excuses. Let me tell you something that might actually be useful. The counting system I was using—"

"I do want to hear about that, yes. I'd also like to know what you wrote after Storm and the curbs left my message in the canyon."

Dazzle gave an impatient flick of his tail. "What I wrote isn't important now. Here's something that might actually matter: there were strange animals in the upper valley once. Humans, maybe, or something like them. They created…dens, I guess you'd say. Unnatural caves that have been filled with ice for hundreds of years, perhaps thousands. But the ice is melting now, and amazing things are coming to the surface. It's dangerous to get up to those caves, but worth it. I found a place full of things I can't even describe. These creatures wrote—more than us and better—on animal skins, but preserved somehow."

"Did you figure out how to read their writing?" asked Roup in wonder.

"Some of it. Not the words, but the numbers. They made symbols for numbers. I don't think they're phonetic. Each symbol just means one, two, three and so on. You only have to memorize ten of them, though. After that, you can write any number in existence. It's very clever."

Roup's level of interest must have been apparent, because Halvery laid his head down across Roup's back and proceeded to glare at Dazzle over top of him. "My shoulder hurts," he murmured.

Dazzle ignored him. "They were doing all kinds of things with numbers, these creatures. More than just counting. I used what I saw to figure out things like how many ice oxen we'd need to kill to feed all our cats…and how many we'd need if we had so many cubs in the spring and so many next spring. It gets complicated, those numbers."

"It does," agreed Roup. "You were predicting your needs a year or more in advance…accurately?"

"Yes. These ancient creatures had an object that was helpful: smooth little rocks on strings, and you slid them back and forth to make multiples and divisions, so that you didn't have to keep it all in your head. The device was small and fragile, and I didn't try to carry it out of the mountains, but you can do the same thing with stones of different sizes. The smallest represent ones, the bigger stones are tens, and the biggest represent hundreds. You can go higher, but I usually don't need to."

"Fascinating," murmured Roup. "That's how you were keeping track of your counts in that cave in the Garu Vell."

Dazzle's teeth flashed in a genuine smile. "Most of the cats I tried to teach were looking right at the device, listening to me, and I *still* couldn't make them understand. You looked at what I was doing without any explanation and just…figured it out."

Roup laughed. "I didn't, though. I just knew you were counting and using stones to represent some number of cats. I thought for a while that the biggest might represent dens."

"Well, that almost works," said Dazzle. "Since ten cats to a den is pretty common. But the counting device has a few more tricks to offer. It's easier to understand once you see how the symbols work. I've taught a few of the females whom I hope will end up in Leeshwood; they can show you. Also, it would be worth sending someone up to the ice caves in summer. There are other things up there that I can't begin to explain."

Dazzle paused and his eyes drifted towards the lake with a worried expression. The temperature was definitely dropping. The moon had disappeared into a bank of clouds.

"What did you write in the canyon?" asked Roup. "We couldn't read any of it. Except one word."

"Oh, I was trying to tell you about Macex and Thistle," said Dazzle. "I wasn't sure I'd be alive by the time you got here. That was before the battle with Sedaron. I was playing coy with my language because I didn't know who else might wander by. Most cats here can't read, or not very well, but some of the ferryshaft can. I also tried to explain my counting system. I know I said too much."

"The only thing left was 'sorry.'"

Dazzle snorted. "Appropriate. If I say nothing else to you, Roup."

"Dazzle..." Roup waited until Dazzle turned to look at him. "The way you fight..."

Dazzle made a face. "Roup, surely it doesn't matter." When Roup said nothing, he said, "Alright. You want to know why? Fast is my only real advantage. I was always underweight—coming and going from the mountains, long journeys, never enough to eat. If I grapple with a cat who severely outweighs me, I usually lose." His eyes crinkled in bitter amusement. "As Halvery conclusively demonstrated."

Roup suspected that Halvery had been having difficulty keeping his mouth shut from the beginning, and now he lost his battle with his self-control. "I hope you know," he hissed over Roup's back, "that there is only *one* reason you are still alive, and he nearly bled to death while you were running back to Thistle."

"I am aware," said Dazzle quietly.

"It took telshees to save him and all winter for him to learn to walk again!"

"Halvery, enough," murmured Roup. At the same time, he thought, *If you suppose that Dazzle cares about that, then you're starting to believe him.*

"I trust you'll make sure I know how he felt when the time comes," said Dazzle. He gave a sudden, worried glance at Flurry, but the juvenile was sound asleep. "Don't tell that one what happened to me. Don't tell any of them."

Out of the corner of his eye, Roup saw Arcove give a twitch that he couldn't interpret. He was certainly listening. "I would like to know why you behaved the way you behaved," said Roup patiently. "Halvery, please let him talk."

Dazzle sighed. "I'm fast, but if an opponent closes, I'm usually in trouble. So I should use my speed to kill them in the first rush, right? But that's not what Thistle told me to do. He told me I needed to cripple them and leave them alive if I wanted cats to remember me when I was away. He said, 'Creasia fear weakness more than they fear death. You have to make them afraid.'

"I didn't believe him at first. I was young; I thought I knew better. Things were chaotic in Treace's territory for the first few years after the rebellion, especially in the far eastern corner around his old den. It took Stefan years to get control of the entire area. There were ugly fights all the time—rogues attacking dens, ambushing females, sometimes killing them, killing cubs... No one wanted Stefan's attention, let alone Arcove's. So we just...took it. Other clutters seemed to think we were getting what we deserved. Some cats even came into our territory to fight with us for fun... because none of the officers would know or do anything about it."

Roup might have said that interference from Arcove's officers had not been welcome among Treace's old dens during that period of time, but he held his tongue. Dazzle had been a six-year-old spy taking messages into the most lawless part of the wood, and he had doubtless seen some ugly things.

"I was challenged several times my first summer," continued Dazzle. "I killed two cats, and I beat one whom I didn't kill. I thought that, by winning those fights, I'd made my friends in Leeshwood safer. I returned next year to find that the cat I *hadn't* killed had killed my cousin and taken over my old den. So I challenged him again, beat him, and this time, I left him limping. I had to do it a few more times, but word got around. Turns out, if you kill an ambitious male creasia, his friends still want to fight with you. But if you cripple him, they get scared. An injured cat is a constant reminder of what might happen. After that, they left my old den alone."

There was a pause. Roup started to say something and Dazzle spoke first, "And you can say it's a nasty way to fight, and you'd be correct, but it works. I've always been the cat who did the jobs others were too squeamish to do. Two years ago in that cave, I wasn't going to leave you crippled, Roup. I was going to kill you. Because I saw a clear opportunity to destabilize Leeshwood and give my cats a chance to survive. Sedaron killed all our cubs that spring. All of them. We couldn't stay in the mountains, and Leeshwood turns murderous at even the rumor that a cat fought on the wrong side on Kuwee Island. I thought somebody had to be the villain, and I've always—" He stopped abruptly. "But I detest excuses, and I can't imagine that mine are interesting to you."

"I like to know why animals behave as they do," said Roup mildly. "Thank you for telling me."

Dazzle screwed his eyes shut as though waging some inner war. Finally he said, with more emotion than he'd previously displayed, "I don't like losing, Roup. You beat me, and I don't like losing. How's that for honesty?"

Halvery harrumphed.

"You moved me around like a cub playing with a grasshopper and I didn't see it. Not until Moashi had my chin against the ground. *Then* I knew someone had gotten the better of me. Cats like me are most dangerous when we're losing." Half under his breath, he muttered, "Thistle is about to learn that the hard way."

"I realized later that I should have tried to talk to you when your back wasn't against a wall," said Roup quietly.

Dazzle gave a mirthless laugh. "I'm not sure that would have worked any better. I couldn't understand why you didn't let Halvery kill me."

"Me neither!" burst out Halvery.

"I thought," continued Dazzle, "that maybe you just weren't thinking clearly on account of all the bleeding. It wasn't until you sent that message last summer that I realized the truth. I hadn't just tried to kill a kind, clever cat; I'd tried to kill someone extraordinary. *Then* I knew that you meant what you said. *Then* I believed you."

Roup had to stifle the impulse to turn and give Arcove a nip on the ear. Halvery, too. *See! I was right to send that message. The conversation I started, the price I paid, was not for nothing.*

Dazzle didn't look like he shared Roup's optimism. He spoke with his head on his paws. "I believed you...too late. You did manage to drive a wedge between me and Thistle. After you sent that message...I told him we needed to parley with you, that we might be able to return to Leeshwood without bloodshed. He was not receptive at first.

"Then he let me think I was changing his mind...or that I *might* change his mind before you arrived. He asked me not to argue with him publicly because it would split the assembly. And because even I can be too trusting, I went along with it. He *didn't* change his mind, of course, and I said I would abide by his decision. But when you showed up—not just Arcove, but *you*—I couldn't do it. And I know it must seem as though we all betray each other as often as the moon turns up here, but *I* have never changed sides. Until now."

Halvery gave a snort and Dazzle added, "I realize that's a distinction of no interest to you."

He stopped talking. Outside, the wind was picking up, moaning in the rocks and caves. Roup thought he saw a peppering of snow. At last, he said, "What is Thistle to you?"

Dazzle hesitated. "He raised me. More-or-less. He's a couple years older. He taught me to fight, saved my life a few times, hunted for me when I was hurt, protected my mates when I was gone until Pace started doing that. He…"

Roup could hear the struggle again in Dazzle's voice, reaching through the familiar story of his own life to grasp the painful truth at its center. "Thistle always had a mean streak. He held onto power through some serious challenges. He's not big enough to manage that with fights alone. Thistle knows how to make an example of someone. He knows how to make cats afraid of him. And I helped him do it. I've seen him turn on friends who threatened his authority. I just…never thought he'd turn on me."

A long pause. When Dazzle spoke again, his voice was brisk, the bleak bitterness replaced by dark humor. "Are you tired of listening to me yet, Roup? I really cannot justify my behavior. I don't like losing. Nobody does. You beat me and then put your life between my teeth. For such a clever cat, you can be very stupid."

Halvery laughed in spite of himself.

"It was the only way to show that you could trust me," said Roup.

Dazzle turned and looked at him searchingly. "It doesn't seem like you hold a grudge. I still find that nearly impossible to believe—"

"He doesn't—" interrupted Halvery.

"That sounds like personal experience, Halvery." Dazzle clamped his mouth shut around the flash of sarcasm.

Roup felt Halvery bristle. He continued in a growl, "He doesn't, but I do. And Arcove does. For a cat who claims to be losing, you seem to be maintaining remarkably tight control over this situation. You tell a good story."

Dazzle had regained his composure. "Old habits," he said with an easy smile. "I think I hear something in the tunnel. I hope it's my cats."

* * * *

This chapter includes an author's note at the end of the book.

25

Shimmer

"Don't tell them what happened to me. You can never tell them."
It was what Arcove had said to Keesha during Treace's rebellion, when he'd thought that he could barter his life—or perhaps his reputation—for the lives of his followers. He'd been particularly concerned that if Roup learned exactly how Arcove had died, he would refuse to cooperate with Keesha and get himself killed.

"When future generations are born, you can tell them I was responsible for the war. Blame me for the raids, make Coden their hero. Let them hate me or forget me."
Arcove remembered saying those words and meaning them. More, he remembered the absolute certainty that there was no way out, that he was going to die a painful and terrifying death that he didn't remotely understand. He'd felt certain that if he thought very hard about this, he would panic and flail and pull everyone he loved down with him. His focus had narrowed to the next breath, the next step, maintaining his nerve for the next moment…right up until he had waded into a shallow lake to die…and Keesha had changed his song…changed his mind…forgiven the unforgivable… and given Arcove back his life.

It should not have been possible. There was too much bad blood between them. *I didn't just* try *to kill his friends. I did kill some of them.*

More than that, Keesha had offered genuine wisdom and, slowly, over the fourteen years since the rebellion, trust. A few days before Arcove's company had reached the high pass, Arcove and Roup had spotted an ely-ary. Roup had laughed and said, "You know he's down there in the lake, tearing his fur out because he's worried about you."

Arcove had harrumphed. "Tearing his fur out because something important is happening that he cannot control."

"Can't he do both?" asked Roup sweetly. "*I do both.*"

"*Don't tell that one what happened to me,*" Dazzle had whispered over Flurry's sleeping head. "*Don't tell any of them.*"

Dazzle was on his feet now, ears pricked. Arcove watched him suspiciously as they all got up. *I told Roup he was giving Dazzle unwarranted second chances because of a superficial personal resemblance. Now I suppose I'm trying to do the same thing. Halvery thinks he's still playing games with us. Halvery may be right.*

The first cat through the tunnel was the same brindled tan as Dazzle, and there was something similar in the way she carried herself. Like most female creasia, her head was a little smaller than a male's, without much of a ruff around her shoulders, but the resemblance between her and Dazzle was hard to miss. She checked when she saw him. "You're alive."

"It would have been rude of me to call you out here if I wasn't."

She let out a hiss of exasperation and relief. "Thistle is saying that Arcove killed you."

Dazzle rolled his eyes. "Thistle is stating his wishes as though they were facts."

Behind her, a stream of other creasia filed into the cave, bristling with nerves and glancing in every direction. The group seemed to be composed almost entirely of females. Arcove couldn't help noticing that many of them were smaller than Leeshwood's females, even though they appeared to be adults. *That's what happens when they start having cubs at four or even younger.* None of them were noticeably pregnant, although most had swollen teats, indicating that they were, in fact, soon to deliver. Under the stress they'd been experiencing, Arcove doubted they were carrying more than one cub each.

Flurry gave a little cry and shot across the cave to greet a dark gray female, who met him with trilling enthusiasm. The whole group was murmuring and whispering.

Dazzle nodded at the cat who'd greeted him. "Arcove, this is Shimmer. She's in charge of this group, not me."

Shimmer's green eyes shifted to Arcove, and they studied each other.

"Your sister?" Arcove guessed.

Dazzle hesitated and Shimmer answered for him, "Littermate."

"She hasn't been in Leeshwood since we were cubs," said Dazzle quickly.

Shimmer's eyes darted between Dazzle and Arcove, then over Roup and Halvery. "They know everything," said Dazzle quietly.

Her gaze returned to her brother in wonder. "And you're still alive?"

"You keep asking that like I might say no."

Shimmer came forward and crouched down in front of Arcove, who took a step back in confusion. Females did not usually engage in the same submissive displays as males, but Shimmer was tucking her tail and turning her head as though she thought he might strike at her. "Sir, thank you for not killing my brother. I know he hasn't always made the best decisions."

"I'm standing right here," said Dazzle blandly.

Shimmer ignored him. "Whatever promises he made, we'll keep. Please tell me what he has traded to create this opportunity for us in spite of...everything that has transpired."

Before Arcove could decide how to respond, Roup said, "Is no kindness ever freely given in the Southern Mountains?"

Shimmer's eyes focused on him. "No," she said frankly, and then seemed to really *see* him. Her posture became, if anything, even more submissive. "Sir, are you...?"

"This is Roup," said Dazzle easily, "the nicest person I've ever tried to kill. That other one is Halvery; he gave me this scar. I really did earn it. Now, I'm guessing you don't have much time before you're missed. Also, the weather is deteriorating. We need to get out of here. How many did you manage to bring?"

Shimmer's eyes narrowed. Roup thought she knew her brother too well to be easily deterred.

Arcove spoke, "You have not harmed me, Shimmer Ela-creasia, and there is no need for appeasement. Be at ease. I would like to know the answer to Dazzle's question. How many?"

His gentle tone seemed to surprise her. She stood up straight and her ears came up. She glanced at Dazzle and gave a smug smile that made the family resemblance unmistakable. "All of them."

Dazzle's answering grin showed his teeth. "You astonish me."

"No, I don't. You knew this would happen. Seventy-eight cats—all the females and all the males under four, plus Pace, Rain, and Blacktip."

Dazzle's smile became a grimace—a look of disappointment, instantly buried.

Shimmer sighed. "I know some of the other males would have come, Daz, but I couldn't be sure which ones. I couldn't risk asking them. They feel like they've got a lot to lose. They don't think they'll be treated kindly by Leeshwood, and they're afraid of Thistle. They're even more afraid of Arcove." Her curious gaze shifted once more to Leeshwood's king. "Sir, if you don't mind my saying so, you are not at all what I expected."

Dazzle made a show of mock surprise, "You thought he'd be even bigger? He's a creasia; not a bear!"

Shimmer rolled her eyes. To Dazzle, she said, "I would have expected you dead in a puddle of blood. And I would have expected an army."

Halvery spoke, an edge of sarcasm in his voice, "This adventure began as a reconnaissance mission, which has gone horribly awry. Please allow me to clarify your situation, Shimmer: you took *all* of Thistle's females?"

Dazzle's mouth twitched in a smirk. "I told you Thistle is going to find out that I'm dangerous when I'm losing."

Shimmer gave them all a longsuffering look. "We took ourselves. Because we don't want to watch our babies die again. We've all had enough of that."

Another new creasia pushed his way out of the cluster around the tunnel and approached. He was dark brown, almost black, and a little bigger than Dazzle, with a pale belly, cheeks, and facial markings. "Dazzle, if someone told me that you died five years ago and you've been a ghost on four legs ever since, I'd believe them. It would explain how you keep walking out of impossible odds."

Dazzle butted his head against the other cat's shoulder. "Pace! Well, it's good to know my den-mate can be trusted to take my side, at least. Although you all seem to think I'm dead, which is worrying."

"Of course I'm on your side, but…" He shot Arcove an incredulous look and then, in a barely audible murmur to Dazzle, "Stop joking for a moment, and tell me how you did this."

Three females joined them abruptly, along with a couple of scrawny cubs. The cubs were about the size of Leeshwood's two-year-olds, although Arcove suspected they were closer to three. The group swarmed around Dazzle, exclaiming and nuzzling. One of the cubs leaned up to lick his muzzle.

Dazzle looked suddenly worried. Arcove thought he'd already been rather careless, considering what he'd tried to do in Leeshwood. *Some cats would expect me to kill his family in reprisal.*

Dazzle whipped out of the group and said, "This is Pace. These are his mates and cubs; they are kind enough to let me sleep in their den when I am home."

Arcove considered asking whether Dazzle thought he had the intelligence of a pigeon. *They're your mates and den-mate. The cubs are either yours, or you're not sure whose they are. Probably the latter.*

But if there was one part of Arcove's legend that even Treace's old followers could not twist or vilify, it was the fact that he did not kill cubs. Every intelligent species on Lidian knew that. *And if Dazzle has spent half his life in Leeshwood, he knows that I don't punish dens for an alpha's misbehavior. I certainly don't punish females and cubs because a male did something cruel or stupid.*

Shimmer had been joined by several other females who'd gotten up their nerve to approach. They stood around her, asking whispered questions and receiving equally soft answers.

Dazzle padded up beside Arcove. "Sir, I would like to rejoin your clutters as soon as possible. These females will be aggressively pursued once they are missed, and they have probably already been missed."

Arcove opened his mouth to respond and Halvery spoke in his other ear, "Arcove, a word."

Arcove glanced at him. Halvery was looking pointedly at Dazzle. "For your ears only, sir."

Dazzle had the grace to back away. Arcove moved further into the cave, although he kept the group in sight. Roup appeared to be already in the process of making friends with Dazzle's mates and cubs. *Of course he is.*

Halvery spoke in a murmur, "Arcove, you keep me on the council to balance Roup."

Arcove couldn't help but laugh. "You think that's the only reason?"

"I'm just saying, sir: I know he won't agree with this, and maybe he's right, but just hear me."

"I'm listening."

"Thistle and Macex put on a convincing show of antagonism during their parley. I thought they were terrible negotiators, but I didn't think they were colluding. They fooled us. Dazzle's little spat with Thistle could be the same sort of thing. It could all have been an act."

"Yes, I had thought of that," said Arcove, "but why?"

"I've been asking myself that all the way from the confluence," said Halvery, "and I finally see a reason. Thistle and his cats were surprised and disappointed that you didn't turn up with an army. They had a plan with Macex for dealing with your army, so that Leeshwood would be left unprotected. They didn't expect you to turn up alone. At this point, they know that you didn't bring your full strength, but that you *did* bring all your officers and their carefully-selected clutters."

Arcove could see where Halvery's theory was leading. "It would be easier to take Leeshwood if all of those cats were dead."

"Exactly," continued Halvery. "Of course, we all tried to leave our territories in good shape in case we didn't return, but, let's be honest: we didn't expect to *all* die. We thought one or two officers might not come back. If all of us died up here, Leeshwood would suffer a leadership crisis. Thistle knows that. He wants to kill the whole group. He knows where *you* are, but he doesn't know where we left the clutters. It's a huge valley..."

Arcove let out a long breath. "You think he is hoping we will lead him to them."

Halvery's ears flicked. "I grant it's a bit of a stretch. But consider what happens if Thistle *doesn't* make an effort to find them. If Lyndi got wind that we three were dead, and that Macex and Thistle had united against Leeshwood... Lyndi's not a fool, Arcove. She wouldn't attack all those ferryshaft with a few dozen cats, not even to avenge Roup!

"She'd run home and raise an army to crush them. And I think she'd succeed. She and Carmine and the others *are* capable. The future doesn't absolutely need you and me and Roup, but I do think Leeshwood's future would be precarious without the younger generation of officers."

A moment's silence. Arcove watched Roup chatting away to Pace. Dazzle was talking to Shimmer and the cats around her. More were gathering, lying down in concentric circles to listen.

"So Dazzle pretends to switch sides," said Arcove slowly, "allows Roup to see what Roup wants to see. Then he stays with us until we lead him back to the clutters, whereupon he alerts Thistle in some way? How do these females figure into such a scheme? They're near their time for birth. Surely they wouldn't agree to travel."

"I can't imagine they'd be in on the ruse," said Halvery, "but that doesn't mean a ruse isn't what's happening. If Thistle lets his females give birth up here, he's stuck in the mountains, helping to guard them and hunt for them, until the cubs can travel. These cats seem to have lost nearly all their cubs for the last two years, which means they're all pregnant at the same time—"

"Which means he's got a large number of vulnerable infants on the way," muttered Arcove. "Yes, I see your point. He needs to move fast if he wants the females to give birth in Leeshwood or at least on the plain. Otherwise, he's tied up here for a year or more. And maybe the females wouldn't agree to knowingly take this risk for his war, but—"

"But they'll follow Dazzle," said Halvery darkly, "because he's the sweet one—at least to these cats—and Thistle is the other one. But Roup and I play that game all the time, Arcove. Everyone may think we don't get along, but we're very much on the same side in the end."

Arcove's eyes tracked Roup through the group of creasia. More and more of them were lying down to listen to whatever Shimmer and Dazzle were saying. Roup crouched to talk to one of Dazzle's cubs, a little female with pale belly and paws. She looked like she was telling him a story. Aloud, Arcove said, "I'm not completely convinced, Halvery."

"Neither am I," said Halvery quickly. "And even if things are as they seem, I'm not sure I can forgive Dazzle, which I know is what Roup wants."

"One thing at a time," murmured Arcove. "You are proposing we avoid taking Dazzle and his cats straight back to the clutters. How?"

Halvery flicked his short tail. "I don't see why they can't start for Leeshwood on their own. Dazzle knows these mountains better than we do. Let him take them the best way he knows how, and we'll meet them by the lake. Thistle and Macex will have to choose between going after them or going after us. That ought to complicate things to our advantage.

"Frankly, it will complicate things to Dazzle's advantage as well, if he's telling the truth. With the best will in the world, I don't see how we could protect this group, Arcove. Not from an attack by six hundred ferryshaft and forty or fifty male creasia, all of them skilled fighters of Dazzle's caliber. We don't have that kind of army."

At that moment, heads began swiveling towards the lake-facing side of the cave. Arcove caught the flash of moving bodies coming towards them through the honeycomb walls and washed up debris. A few of the gathered creasia looked like they might retreat back up the tunnel from which they'd come, but it was only Storm, Costa, and the highland curbs—half a dozen of them now—returning over the ice.

The group milled around in surprise for a moment, and then Storm approached Arcove with an uncertain smile. "You've increased."

"We have."

"Are they all female?"

"Most of them."

"All Thistle's females," put in Halvery.

"Well, he's going to love us even more, isn't he?" said Storm. "Listen, you need to leave soon if you don't want to be trapped here. It's snowing hard out there, and the temperature is dropping. The curbs think the storm will be severe."

Halvery frowned. "In that case, I think Dazzle's cats might want to shelter right here until it passes. Especially if some of them might give birth. It's not a great location, but I doubt anywhere nearby will be better."

Arcove considered. "But you think that you and I and Roup should leave?"

"I do, sir, but I respect that this is not my call, and I will support your decision, whatever that may be."

Storm was looking at them with his head on one side.

Arcove spoke briskly. "Halvery, please acquaint Storm with what has happened in his absence and...tell him your theory." Arcove turned, leaving Halvery to explain things to Storm and company, while he delivered his unpleasant verdict to Dazzle and Shimmer.

26

No Promises

The group around Shimmer was looking quiet and more set-tled now, most of them lying down, those on the edges straining to hear. Arcove heard Shimmer say, "And they'll probably split us up, but I don't think they'll split dens, and I'm sure they won't take cubs from—"

"Is it really green all the time?" interrupted one young female longingly. "Even in winter?"

"All the time," said Dazzle.

"And there are things to eat? Everywhere?" marveled one four-year-old.

"No one starves."

"Never?" She didn't sound like she believed him.

"Never, Naveya. If you die in Arcove's Leeshwood, it won't be because you starved."

Roup fell into step beside Arcove as he approached Dazzle and Shimmer. He was watching Arcove's face.

Arcove sighed. *I am about to disappoint practically everyone. That is, so often, what it means to be king.*

Dazzle and Shimmer looked around as he drew nearer. "I'd like a word with you two," he said quietly.

One of the older females got up immediately and began speak-ing in a calm voice to the group. "I was there as a young cat," she said. "Deer are less dangerous than ice oxen, but you must not kill does. It's spring there now, full spring with no ice."

"It's warm there right now?" whispered someone.

"Yes, right now."

Their voices grew fainter as Arcove led the way to the far side of the cave. He wished Roup would say something, but Roup knew how to employ silence to his advantage just as well as Arcove did. Dazzle and Shimmer weren't saying anything, either.

When they were well away from the group, Arcove turned. "It's snowing heavily, and there's about to be a storm. Surely you don't propose taking females who are near their time into a blizzard."

Dazzle and Shimmer glanced at each other. Then Shimmer spoke quietly, "I feel that if we do not put some distance between ourselves and Thistle, there will be no point in our escape, sir. I do not think a snowstorm will stop him from tracking us to this cave. It's too obvious of a rendezvous point. I *do* think that it might stop him from tracking where we go next, and we should take advantage of this at once."

Arcove looked hard at her. "If your cats go into labor while traveling through a storm, they could die. Their cubs will certainly die."

Shimmer looked at him steadily. "We make hard decisions in the mountains every day, Arcove. If we are caught, there will be reprisals. Both for us and for our cubs. If you think that being female protects a cat from the consequences of treachery in Thistle's Leeshwood, you're wrong. If you think we're not risking everything right now for a brighter future, you're wrong."

Arcove watched her. It was impossible to imagine that she did not believe what she was saying. Dazzle, however, remained silent and inscrutable. *If he's determined to follow us to the clutters, he's being quite smart by letting Shimmer do the pushing. But I would expect nothing less of a cat who tricked Roup.*

Aloud, he said, "It has been suggested that we should part ways with a promise to rendezvous by the lake."

Dazzle gave a minute twitch that Arcove interpreted as emotion quickly concealed, though what emotion he couldn't say. Shimmer's mouth opened, but she couldn't seem to think of a reply. Arcove refused to look at Roup. After a moment, he continued, "We do not have the kind of army that could protect you from hundreds of attackers, Shimmer. We can, however, provide those attackers with another tempting target."

He paused, waiting for someone to argue with him or to become angry. Shimmer's gaze dropped. She had the expression of an animal absorbing a setback and trying to rearrange her strategy without giving in to despair.

"We have reinforcements by the lake," said Arcove. "We can protect you if you can get yourselves there. It is my impression that Dazzle knows these mountains better than me or anyone in my party and would make an excellent guide."

Dazzle gave a fleeting smile. "Certainly true."

Arcove focused his gaze on Shimmer. "You and your cats are welcome in my Leeshwood, Shimmer. You have my goodwill if you can get yourselves there."

She raised her head at this and put on a bold smile. "That means a great deal, sir. I know it's more than we have any right to expect." She took a deep breath. "We'd better get going. Dazzle, do you need to consult with anyone about where we should aim to shelter during this storm?"

Dazzle frowned. "Possibly. Flurry was outside the valley most recently—"

"Then go talk to him."

Dazzle fidgeted. "Shimmer—"

"You just said I'm in charge, Daz. Prove it."

A law unto yourself, thought Arcove, watching him. *You don't like taking orders from anyone.* Dazzle clearly didn't want to leave Shimmer alone talking to Arcove, but she glared at him a moment, and at last he got up and moved grudgingly away.

Arcove sighed. He felt certain that Shimmer was about to initiate another awkward conversation regarding Dazzle's likely future. He didn't want to lie to her. But he didn't want to tell her the truth, either.

Shimmer surprised him by muttering, "Arcove, I'm going to tell you something that Dazzle would argue about if he was standing here: Thistle was always going to kill him."

This was not what Arcove had expected. He cocked his head and waited. When he didn't try to interrupt, Shimmer continued,

"If Dazzle had won Leeshwood for him two years ago, Thistle would have kept him until the fighting was over and then quietly pushed him off a cliff. Dazzle has always been a little too...*dazzling* for his own good. He's too popular, and Thistle won't tolerate it. He knows that if he and Dazzle parted ways, he'd lose at least half his cats. He's known it for years, and he's tried to mitigate it by asking Dazzle to stay for longer and longer in Leeshwood, but it hasn't worked. The only reason Dazzle is still alive is that he can do things other cats can't, and Thistle still needs him."

"Why can't Dazzle see that Thistle considers him a threat?" asked Roup quietly.

"Because they are friends!" Shimmer's voice cracked with emotion that seemed genuine. "They used to share a den. Long time ago. They used to have each other's backs. We all went through some rough years right after the rebellion. The meanest rogues in Leeshwood followed Treace or joined us here after the battle. The fight for control was brutal. You have no idea..."

She broke off, swallowed. "We were all friends once and on the same side. I understand how hard it is to accept that someone you trusted would turn on you. I didn't think Dazzle was going to see it in time. I thought Thistle was going to kill him when he came crawling home the autumn before last. But I guess Thistle still thought he needed Daz. I guess he's regretting that now."

Her eyes focused on Roup. "Whatever you said to my brother when he tried to kill you...it changed his mind. Dazzle doesn't say 'I made a mistake' very often. I've never seen him argue with Thistle like that."

Roup spoke again, his voice very quiet, "Who is your mate, Shimmer?"

She hesitated. "His name was Serot."

"Ah."

Shimmer screwed her eyes shut as though burying that line of thought somewhere deep inside. She looked at Arcove squarely and said, "My brother is not incapable of loyalty, sir. He was *very* loyal for a long, *long* time, and it's gotten him betrayed by a cat he loved and trusted. I know he's behaving as though he doesn't feel it, but I assure you, he does. He is risking everything to get us out of here, and I'm certain he bargained with his life."

Well, I guess I don't need to explain that, thought Arcove wearily.

Her eyes searched his face. "If there is anything you would take instead, Arcove?"

It was tempting. Desperately tempting, with Roup standing there, to say that he would, at least, not do anything cruel. *But I don't make promises I'm not certain I can keep.* "You need to organize your cats, Shimmer." He tried to keep his voice neutral and as kind as possible. "You need to decide how you're getting out of here. Dazzle is all yours for the moment."

She gave a mirthless snort of laughter. "You're good at this, Arcove."

He couldn't help but smile. *So are you.*

She swallowed. "No promises, then, but please think about what I said. He's very useful."

"I have no doubt."

At that moment, there was a commotion around the tunnel. Creasia scattered in alarm. Arcove expected to see Thistle's cats pouring out. Instead, he saw lowland curbs—dozens of them, quickly organizing themselves into a defensive ring several animals deep. They were a little smaller than the highland curbs, and their dense pelts were sleeker. *Ferryshaft allies?*

Arcove doubted that even multiple packs of curbs would be a match for this many creasia. *But they could hold the tunnel for a while.* It was the only safe exit. *This could get ugly...*

Then two of the curbs pushed their way to the front. They were both unusually dark in color, black in places, with white streaks and brindling. One had a completely black face and the other had a striking two-toned face, half black and half white.

Dazzle threaded his way through the uncertain creasia towards the curbs, smiling. "Eclipse and Abyss... I was beginning to think you wouldn't show up. What did Flurry promise you anyway? You must *really* want a piece of me. But, then, everyone does lately."

27

Eclipse and Abyss

The two lead curbs left their pack and came to meet Dazzle without showing much concern for the creasia around them. "Dazzle Light-foot," murmured the one with the two-toned face, who must be Eclipse. "You're not walking on air tonight."

"Indeed, I seem to have gotten mud on my paws," he said blandly. "What do you want?"

"Dazzle Sheep-thief," growled Abyss. "When you cannot bargain, you steal."

"I'm sure I don't know what you mean. Come, little sisters, I am in a hurry. What do you want from me? I'm afraid I'm rather low on kills that can be traded, and I would have some difficulty enforcing your territory borders, but if you have a bargain in mind—"

Abyss cut him short with a nasty laugh. "Sisters he calls us!"

"Oh, *big brother*," crooned Eclipse, "I suspect that you are running short of more than kills. You have absolutely nothing left to offer us but your life, and maybe not even that."

"He has a cub," whispered Abyss, "two cubs, in fact. The curbs from the plains say that creasia cubs are tasty, but I've never eaten one."

Arcove could not help glancing at the spot where he'd last seen Dazzle's mates and cubs. Pace had gotten in front of them. At Arcove's side, Roup had started to bristle.

If Dazzle was shocked or frightened, he didn't show it. "You are mistaken. I have no cubs. If you attack anyone else here, you'll be slaughtered. There are nearly a hundred of us. I'm the only one who made a deal with you. Don't be greedy, little sisters."

Eclipse stopped to scratch an ear. "You call us greedy, but you're the one who takes more than he gives, and it's about to catch up with you. You seem to be shedding friends like a winter coat, big brother. Thistle doesn't love you anymore, and you've offended Arcove. Now half the ferryshaft on the island want to kill you. Dazzle-oh-so-charming-always-says-the-right-thing, what are you saying now?"

Dazzle said nothing and the curbs laughed.

"Thistle's creasia are moments behind us," continued Eclipse, "and they've got hundreds of ferryshaft with them."

"And packs of the curbs from the plain," said Abyss with distaste, "more sheep thieves."

Arcove thought, again, that these curbs could easily defend the narrow tunnel, even from a hundred creasia. They could certainly hold it long enough for Thistle and Macex to arrive. *We may already be trapped.*

"Arcove," whispered a voice at his shoulder. He turned to see Storm, looking earnest and worried. "I think you and Roup and Halvery could leave over the ice if the highland curbs will guide you. Shall I ask? They are grateful that you brought Cohal and Maoli to meet them. I think they would do you this favor."

Across the cave, Dazzle was speaking to Eclipse and Abyss as if they hadn't just threatened to kill him and eat his babies. "It was kind of you to bring me this warning. I really do not see how I can pay you for it."

Eclipse cocked her head. "You will simply have to owe us a favor, Dazzle Light-foot Sheep-thief."

Dazzle quirked a smile. "A future favor, Eclipse? How optimistic are you that I'll be around for you to collect?"

"You've given your word," sniffed Eclipse, "so you'd better."

Arcove realized, then, that he'd misunderstood the entire tone of the exchange. *They like him. They just have a funny way of showing it. Perhaps they need to maintain appearances in front of their packs.*

Dazzle looked almost touched. He opened his mouth to say something, and Abyss interrupted, "My sister may be content with future favors, but I'll tell you what I want: no more creasia in my valley. Get out of here, Dazzle Sheep-thief, and take all these cub-carriers with you. And when Thistle catches up with you, kill him."

They turned away, and Dazzle shut his eyes as though letting out his breath. Shimmer came darting up to speak to him in a low voice. Her creasia gathered around them, murmuring and pacing, eager to be off, now that they knew their pursuers were closing in.

The wind was keening in the honeycomb caves, the driving snow completely obliterating the view across the ice. It moaned plaintively in the tunnel as the curbs moved aside to let Shimmer's creasia pass. A gust sent a burst of white flakes whirling across the cave floor. One gangly four-year-old in the mouth of the tunnel hung back as the wind flattened her fur.

Shimmer said something to Dazzle and then pushed her way forward to lead the group. She spoke with determined calm, "This is the best possible weather to lose pursuers. Come on, friends; if it was easy for us, it would be easy for them. This is better. Stay close to your den-mates. Count each other as often as possible. If you get separated, try to reach Chelby Lake; that's all that matters now."

Arcove couldn't help thinking that this was the last he would ever see of most of these cats. He could feel Roup's eyes on him. Halvery had come up beside Storm, looking unhappy. He started to say something and stopped.

Arcove had a mental image of these pregnant females struggling through blinding snow, freezing to death in ones and twos, perhaps giving birth under hideous circumstances, getting picked off by pursuers who would kill some of them and punish the rest in ways that didn't bear thinking about. *They ran to me. They asked to be my cats. They asked for my protection.*

"Wait." He spoke in a voice that carried across the cave and cut through other conversations. Shimmer raised her head and Dazzle looked up from talking to Flurry and Pace. Arcove turned to Storm. "You said the ice would hold creasia."

Storm swallowed. "I think so."

"Explain."

"I..." Storm's eyes strayed to the deep shadows in the direction of the lake. Arcove realized that the highland curbs must have retreated there when Eclipse and Abyss showed up. Storm didn't want to speak for them or give them away.

We don't have time for this. "Eclipse and Abyss," rumbled Arcove, "how badly would you like my misplaced creasia removed from your mountains? Do you want it badly enough to behave civilly to your cousins?"

The pack leaders had melted back into the shifting knot of their companions. Arcove wasn't even sure they were going to acknowledge him for a moment. Then the sisters detached themselves from the group and approached. "*Your* misplaced creasia?" asked Eclipse.

"Mine," said Arcove.

He could almost feel Roup smiling at him. *Don't be so smug; I'm sure it's bad for your health.*

Abyss sat down slowly.

"We do not have time for formalities," said Arcove. "You know who I am. Let's skip the part where you call me old and feeble."

That got a laugh from Abyss. "Neither of those words come to mind, Arcove Always-wins-his-fights, Breathing-legend."

Arcove ignored the flattery. "I would like your guarantee that you will not harm my allies if I promise to get these creasia safely away. I will do my best to see that Thistle and his companions do not remain in these mountains to trouble you. Do we have an agreement?"

"Your allies..." murmured Abyss. "Do you ally with ghosts, Creasia King?"

Arcove was confused.

"There are some ghosts who haunt the islands in my lake," said Abyss in a dismissive tone.

"Ghosts…" echoed Arcove. *An interesting way to avoid admitting that you did not entirely win your war.* "Yes, the ghosts are my allies. I would not see them…" He searched for a word, "Disturbed."

Dazzle and Shimmer had joined the group, looking confused. "Have you changed your mind about coming with us, sir?" asked Shimmer.

"No," said Arcove, "I have changed my mind about *you* coming with *me.*" He raised his voice. "Cohal and Moali and whoever else is hiding over there, please come out! You have my protection and a promise of truce. I am calling you all to council. Right here, right now; I do not think we have much time."

The group emerged together—Cohal and Maoli in front, followed by Tsueri and two others that Arcove hadn't met. In spite of their talk of ghosts, the lowland curbs stiffened and their hackles went up. Their packs began to growl behind them. Eclipse turned and barked, and the others subsided, but their ears remained pricked like animals who scented blood.

The highland curbs were just as on-guard, bristling to their tail-tips.

Before any more unpleasantness could ensue, Arcove turned to Tsueri and said, "We are about to be set upon by Thistle's cats and a great many ferryshaft. Storm believes the ice would hold us. If we leave that way, there will be no trail, and I do not think our enemies would expect it. Even if they do realize where we've gone, they might be afraid to follow. Storm says you can tell us where to walk."

The local highland curbs began whispering among each other at once. Cohal looked uncertain. "To the shore, Arcove?"

Arcove thought about it. "No. To the island."

That got all of their attention. "If it's possible," he continued. "If we could move from island to island, right down the center of the lake, and then go ashore near the western end, we would reach the spot where we left the clutters well ahead of Thistle. Even if we have to move slowly, even if he figures out where we went, he'll never be able to follow us over the ice without a guide. He'd have to go all the way around the north shore and its many inlets."

"Oh..." breathed Storm. "Oh, that's good, Arcove. That's what I would do."

Arcove smiled, but his eyes were on Tsueri. "Is this possible, friend?"

The curb raised his head from the consultation he was having with his companions. "We think so, Arcove, but...I want to be honest with you: it is risky."

"Ghosts walk on ice where others dare not tread," said Eclipse with a baleful look at Tsueri. "Be careful where you follow ghosts, Creasia King."

"We'll need a cat to go in front and test the weakest places," admitted Cohal. "I'm sorry, Arcove. Ice that will hold us may not hold you, and this will require someone to risk—"

"Sounds like a job for me," interrupted Dazzle. "I like this plan."

A ferryshaft howl cut him short, ringing off the rocks above them, disturbingly close.

"Time to go," said Arcove.

Eclipse and Abyss were whispering to each other. At last, Eclipse said, grudgingly, "There is unstable ice and loose rock above the tunnel. It's even more precarious now with a layer of new snow. We could probably cause a rock slide."

Dazzle cocked his head. "Seal us in?"

"It would slow them down," said Eclipse, as though the words hurt her.

"Oh, Eclipse, you're going soft," crooned Dazzle.

"You owe me a favor," she hissed. "Don't forget it!"

Another ferryshaft howled. The two curbs made for the exit at a lope, and their packs followed. "Good-bye, Sheep-thief!" shot Abyss over her shoulder.

"Good-bye, little sisters!" called Dazzle with evident mockery. And then, under his breath, in a completely different voice, "Good-bye, friends."

28

On the Ice

Halvery couldn't help a thundering sense of relief when he heard Arcove's plan. He'd been feeling increasingly guilty at the notion of sending pregnant females off on their own in a blizzard, but he couldn't see a way around it that didn't jeopardize all of Leeshwood.

If they could pass right down the center of the lake, though… *Even if Dazzle intends to betray our position to our enemies, I don't see how he'll do it from out on the ice in this storm.*

True, Dazzle had volunteered to go first, which made Halvery wonder whether he hoped to slip away. Snow was swirling down out of a black sky without even a fitful moon or patch of starlight. Visibility would be terrible.

"There are weak places in the ice," Tsueri told them. "And I do not know whether all the strong places will actually hold a creasia. We will test as we go and you must make sure your cats do not stray from the path we mark."

"We can do this," Arcove told him. "Creasia are very good at walking in each other's steps."

Shimmer and her closest confidants moved among their companions, explaining the plan. "You must follow the cat in front of you perfectly. We are going to walk where Dazzle walks. You've never seen him fall, have you?"

They were afraid. Halvery could see it in their eyes. He could smell it. But they would listen to Shimmer, and they would follow Dazzle.

The first part of the journey was somewhat sheltered and included landmarks and windbreaks. They threaded their way between towering blocks of ice that had washed down out of the mountains, along with jagged boulders and twisted trees, half buried in the frozen lake. Even creasia eyes had difficulty penetrating the dark, whirling snow, and they quickly lost sight of all but their nearest traveling companions.

Behind them, ferryshaft were howling in unison—a sound of mixed aggression and frustration. Halvery felt certain that they meant to intimidate their quarry, but they were also signaling to each other, trying to avoid getting lost in the storm. They sounded like thousands of animals. *They always sound like that,* Halvery reminded himself, *when they howl together.* He couldn't help remembering the war and hard fights when Arcove's cats had been heavily outnumbered, when no one had yet proven that creasia could cooperate in groups large enough to beat a herd of ferryshaft.

At last, between the ferryshaft's wails, came a clear creasia rally cry. *Thistle has definitely reached the tunnel.* He would be confused by the buried entrance. He wouldn't be sure whether it had been filled in on the way out as a decoy, or whether the females had decided to hunker down in the cave, perhaps sacrificing one of their number to seal them in. There were other possibilities as well. The snow could have covered a trail departing from the cave, or Shimmer's creasia could have risked the ice to reach the shore without using the tunnel.

Thistle would need to split his party to investigate and eliminate each possibility. Some contingent of cats and ferryshaft would begin digging out the tunnel into the cave, while others would spread out over the surrounding area. And all the while, Shimmer's creasia would continue to spool quietly in a long line onto the ice, leaving no scent trail.

No scent, thought Halvery, *but there will be footprints because of the snow. Will they all get covered up or blown away before Thistle breaches the cave? Probably not.* Halvery didn't think he needed to voice this aloud. They could all see how the snow was creating prints, as well as the way those prints were preserved in the more sheltered areas between half-submerged boulders and blocks of ice.

Arcove had chosen to travel near the front, just behind the curbs, Storm, and Dazzle. He'd told Roup and Halvery to stay with him, for which Halvery was grateful. Roup looked like he was thinking about wandering down the line to encourage stragglers, and yet Halvery noticed that he was limping again.

Halvery himself was feeling the strain of staying awake for most of a night and a day, coupled with his spontaneous dip in a flood to rescue Storm. Bruises and strained muscles were making themselves felt with every step. *This is going to be a long night.*

They definitely could not stop to rest anywhere on the ice. Standing still for even a moment made Halvery feel as though he were risking frostbite. The chill wind cut through fur to skin, and they were all soon wearing a dusting of snow.

The curbs led the way, occasionally calling Dazzle forward to test various places on the ice. "Bears make holes to fish," explained Tsueri, "and then those holes freeze and disappear. They leave a weak place where you wouldn't expect one. Also, warm currents flow into the lake from hot springs in the mountains and cut rivers beneath the ice. You can't see them, but you can smell the warm water if you know exactly what you're scenting for. Sometimes you can even hear the gurgle if you listen very carefully. But it's easy to make a mistake. We curbs have been out here for years, learning the ways of the ice, but even we break through sometimes. The warm water changes course, tunnels to a new place, and catches us unawares."

Halvery suspected that Arcove was staying near Dazzle to keep an eye on him. It would be easy to disappear into the snowy darkness. *Maybe Dazzle "knows the ways of the ice," too,* thought

Halvery darkly. If Dazzle reunited with Thistle and told him where they were headed, the race would be closer than anyone liked.

Halvery imagined Thistle's cats lying in wait for them to come ashore at the western end of the lake, then quietly trailing them back to the clutters. They would fall upon the group with devastating numbers, and none of them would ever go home. He couldn't help thinking of Ilsa, her cubs that might already be born, and Macex's lazy sneer, *"Do they taste better when their daddy was a war hero?"*

They reached the first island without mishap. It loomed out of the whirling snow—a dark mass of towering fir trees and a forbidding, rocky beach. A shadowy throng of curbs met them, whispering to Tsueri. Costa was with them. She had apparently run ahead. She pattered up to Halvery and bumped her head against his shoulder in a feline gesture that made him laugh. "Ferryshaft don't do that."

"Maybe I'm not a ferryshaft. I lived in Carmine's den all summer."

"Costa Ela-curb, perhaps? That's what you're acting like lately."

"No, I'm Costa Ela-creasia."

"The way you dodged those cats on the ice looked like Storm Ela-ferry."

She preened. "You could see that from the cliff?"

"I saw the whole thing."

Creasia were coming ashore, some of them taking the opportunity to flop down on earth that wasn't frozen, panting clouds of steam into the chilly air. Halvery noticed that they almost never lay down alone. They were accustomed to sharing warmth, and they cuddled up in twos or threes or fours, wrapped around each other and their juvenile cubs.

Arcove and Roup were talking to the curbs. Halvery doubted that they would linger here for any longer than it took to regroup. Shimmer's cats had picked up their pace, now that the trail to the island had been firmly established. The second half of the party came ashore at a loping run. Shimmer herself arrived, along with a few females that Halvery had begun to think of as her officers. They were counting heads. Halvery was impressed by their organization.

He considered joining Arcove and Roup, but they were talking to Dazzle now. *I've given my opinion about that, and I suppose I don't need to keep driving it home.*

Storm approached him, frowning at Costa. Halvery suspected that she had run ahead without asking for advice or permission. He thought Storm was about to ask Halvery to keep an eye on her. *Let's not start this again...*

Instead, Storm said, "Costa, would you mind looking out for Halvery this evening? I'm afraid he got banged up saving my life. He's elderly and tired and he hasn't been eating enough. I'd really appreciate it if you'd watch over him."

Halvery gave an outraged sputter.

Costa laughed aloud, but then she looked at Storm's too-bright smile and said, "You just don't want me running off on my own again."

"Oh, it's quite clear that you can handle yourself on your own, but I'm worried about this old fellow." He walked right up to Halvery and tucked his head under his chin.

Halvery didn't know what to do. He somehow could not bring himself to growl.

Costa giggled. "I know what you're doing, Storm."

"Yes, and neither of us appreciates it," snapped Halvery.

Storm turned away. "Thank you for taking care of him, Costa."

"We can spar *right now*, Storm!" Halvery called after him. "You can decide how weak I am after I smack you out of the air again!"

Storm ignored him.

Costa said, "I was chased so many times coming here through the mountains. And I remembered what you told me, Halvery. When I was tired and hungry, I remembered how I got careless at the end of that hunt beside the lake. It saved my life. Because I didn't take shortcuts when it mattered. Do you want to hear about it?"

He couldn't help but smile. "Yes."

So she told him about her near-misses as the last of Shimmer's creasia came ashore.

Arcove didn't let them rest for long. "I want to reach the western edge of the lake by dawn," he told the group. "Unfortunately, our footprints will have alerted Thistle to our initial course away from the cave. However, I do not think enough of a trail will remain for him to follow without a guide, and he will not be able to see us from the shore in this weather. Consequently, he can only guess at our destination. I suspect he will send groups of cats and ferryshaft around the lake in both directions. Even if we are so unfortunate as to meet one of those groups, it won't be his full strength. Still, I would prefer to reunite with my clutters without encountering enemies at all, and I think we have a good chance of that if we press on quickly. The sooner we reach the end of the valley, the sooner we can get off the ice."

So they crossed the island and kept going.

Costa told Halvery the details of her most harrowing escape in the mountains. Halvery pointed out her errors and offered suggestions for improvement. In spite of his snarls at Storm, he was finding her company a welcome distraction. The ice was so cold. The wind was relentless. His stomach felt like it was trying to digest itself. His right shoulder throbbed.

The first time Dazzle went through the ice, Halvery didn't see it, but he heard the unmistakable crack. He looked up in time to see Dazzle in mid-leap, a splash behind him. *Light-foot, indeed. Maybe he really was the best animal for this job.*

Dazzle jumped clear of the rotten ice, but Halvery heard the curbs say, "You need to clean your paws, friend. Right away. Your toes will freeze."

"I know that," said Dazzle.

They crossed another island around midnight and another soon after. Curbs came and went. Shimmer and her officers moved up and down the line of cats, counting, always counting. The last time, Halvery saw that she was carrying a cub—probably close to three years old, but scrawny enough to be mistaken for two. He thought he should offer to carry the cub himself, but he wasn't sure he could manage it. He wasn't sure she would trust him.

Costa kept talking. He could hear the exhaustion in her voice. *She's a day animal, even if she's been keeping a creasia schedule.* He tried to keep answering, to keep thinking of questions. *Stay awake. Don't lose sight of the animal ahead of you.* The group was becoming more strung out. They moved with heads low, eyes focused on the prints of the cat in front of them. There were no landmarks now, nothing protruding from the ice. The night was as black as a deep cave.

The second time Dazzle went through the ice, he wasn't so quick. Halvery actually saw it happen. Dazzle must have felt the ice give way, because he jumped sideways, drawing Halvery's attention. He landed on something unstable, and his back legs disappeared to the hocks before he managed to push off and achieve firm footing.

He paused to groom himself vigorously as the curbs turned to look for a way around the weak place. No one said anything this time. There was nothing to say. Dazzle was risking frostbite, and everyone knew it. *Storm and I got wet earlier,* thought Halvery, *and we're fine.* But that was before the temperature dropped.

A little further on, it happened again.

And again.

And again…

Halvery opened his eyes to the sensation of Costa biting his ear. He turned to snap at her.

"You're off the trail," she hissed.

Halvery realized he'd fallen asleep while in motion. He turned to see the line of creasia filing past. They were only paces away, and yet if he'd gone just a little further, they would have been invisible. He managed, "Where are Roup and Arcove?" Every cat looked the same now—grayish white with snow.

"Up ahead. We just fell a little behind," whispered Costa. Worry leaked through her voice like cold water. "Are you alright?"

"Yes."

She stayed right against him after that. Halvery was annoyed and exhausted and angry—at whom he couldn't have said. Costa stumbled once, and he grabbed her too hard. She yelped.

"Sorry," he muttered. "I thought…" *I thought you were going through the ice. But that's silly. Dazzle has already gone through it everywhere anyone is likely to do that.*

Dazzle was limping now whenever Halvery got a glimpse of him. Halvery thought of cats he'd seen die of frostbite. It didn't happen very often in Leeshwood, but sometimes, during a bad winter, when cats got lost while hunting. Frostbitten paws and tails tended to fester. They turned black and smelly and then rotted away. The unfortunate victim would develop a raging fever as their limbs turned to pus and blood. Left to themselves, they died slowly over many days or even a month. It was an excruciating death that was usually cut short by the merciful intervention of family or friends. Nobody in their right mind would choose to die of frostbite.

Halvery sensed that dawn was not far off when they reached another island. He had no idea where they were in relation to the wider valley. The world had shrunk to the dim shapes of the cats around him, the constant low murmur of curbs discussing the way forward, and Dazzle's tired voice answering questions about the ice ahead.

They had not crossed an island in quite some time. This one had almost no shore, but rose out of the lake in a steep embankment, almost a cliff. The curbs bounded nimbly up like sheep. Storm followed them. The creasia jumped. It was a long jump, but achievable for any adult cat. Nevertheless, most struggled a little on the lip, too exhausted for grace.

Halvery jumped with the first wave of creasia coming off the ice. He stopped to make sure that Costa managed to scramble up behind him. Arcove, Roup, and Storm were in consultation with the curbs again. Halvery joined them.

Storm stopped to give Costa a lick on the nose, and Halvery caught his whispered, "Thank you."

He thought, with a grimace, that Costa might loudly tell everyone that Halvery had fallen asleep on his feet, but she only said, "He picked me up when I fell."

Shimmer met them a moment later, her gait unsteady. "Arcove, they need to rest."

"I know," he said quietly.

"Two of them miscarried out there on the ice."

Arcove grimaced. "We're at the western end of the lake, Shimmer. There's only a little more ice between us and the shore. I am concerned that we might meet enemies there, and we're in no shape to fight. So we'll rest here and go ashore in the daytime. Perhaps our pursuers will be asleep then like sensible creatures. In the meantime, the curbs think they might be able to spare a few sheep for us."

Shimmer gave a tired smile. "Thank you, Arcove. Food would be very welcome." Her eyes shifted to the curbs. "This is a debt we can never repay…"

Maoli returned her smile. "Someday, a highland curb might need to shelter in your den, Shimmer Ela-creasia. Perhaps you will remember this kindness then."

"I will remember," said Shimmer. "We will all remember."

Arcove turned to Halvery. "Roup is going to help with the food. I am going to have a look at the western shore. I would like you to go back to the eastern edge of the island and monitor the stragglers coming off the ice. They're worn out, and they might need help getting up the embankment. Also, there's a bit of a view from that cliff and you could call to any you see getting lost."

"Yes, sir." Halvery stopped beside Roup as Arcove turned away. "Where is he?"

Roup glanced at him, ears low with exhaustion. Halvery thought he was going to ask who Halvery meant, but then he just said, "He turned straight around when we reached the island. He went back along the line to make sure the stragglers didn't lose their way."

Halvery stared at Roup. "You're joking."

"Please tell me you're not going to say he ran back to Thistle," continued Roup.

"No," muttered Halvery, "I was not…going to say that."

Costa had disappeared among the curbs, but she rejoined Halvery a little later on the bluff. She was carrying the leg of a sheep, which he accepted with ravenous hunger. He devoured the leg in great crunching bites. It was all gone in a moment.

Costa watched in admiration. "You eat bones like they're twigs."

"Yes, well, you eat twigs like they're bones," said Halvery, cleaning his whiskers. "I can't eat twigs at all."

Costa giggled. "Roup said I was to feed you that *before* you had to talk to Dazzle."

Halvery grumbled under his breath. "Ghosts and little fishes! I am not going to *eat* him."

"If you were going to eat anybody, you'd eat me," said Costa mildly.

Halvery matched her playful tone. "Exactly."

Costa settled down beside him to watch as creasia continued to trickle into view. The slowest had fallen far behind the main group. A few of them were carrying three-year-old cubs in their mouths. Halvery came forward to help them up the embankment. He had to grab more than one by the scruff to drag her the rest of the way. His shoulder twinged.

Shimmer came by to ask about her brother. "Not here yet," said Halvery curtly.

"We're only missing four," she said, squinting into the driving snow. She looked like she was thinking about jumping down and going to look for them.

"They've been arriving steadily," said Halvery. He hesitated. "The last one said that she saw Dazzle only moments ago."

Shimmer relaxed a little. She looked like she could barely hold her ears up at this point.

"Go sleep," said Halvery.

She didn't argue with him.

Another cat arrived, then another. Costa fell asleep, curled in the snow with her tail over her nose. Finally the last exhausted four-year-old appeared, weaving. Dazzle was limping behind him. The youngster had to try twice to get up the embankment. Halvery could see why the journey had been too much for him; he was skin and bones. Halvery helped the juvenile over the edge, where he promptly lay down as though he never intended to rise again. "I believe there might be some sheep carcass left," Halvery murmured in his ear.

The youngster found a bit of energy at this news. He dragged himself to his feet and stumbled off towards the sounds and smells of his companions.

Halvery looked back down the embankment. Dazzle was still sitting there. He was crusted with snow, and his lower body had the telling spiky pattern of wet fur frozen into ice. Halvery doubted that Dazzle could feel any of his paws at this point. He'd been moving with uncharacteristic clumsiness.

Dazzle tensed for the jump, eyes on the ledge. He bobbed his head a couple of times, gauging the distance and then...stopped. He looked down as though he needed to regroup.

Halvery remembered watching this cat make an impossibly graceful ascent of a canyon. Now he looked like he wasn't sure he could clear a modest bluff. His wandering gaze strayed to Halvery.

Whatever he saw caused Dazzle to settle back onto his haunches. Something like relief flitted across his face, mixed with disappointment and resignation. He gave a mirthless smile. His voice came in a rough whisper, "I'm not g-going up there...am I?"

Halvery was confused. "Of course you are! Why do you think I'm still sitting out here in the wind? Get up here so that I can go to sleep!" Halvery didn't move forward to help, though. He wasn't quite sure he could bring himself to pull Dazzle over the edge.

Dazzle was shivering violently, but he seemed to be past the point of noticing. "Did *I* hurt your sh-shoulder?"

The question caught Halvery off guard. He answered automatically, "No, I did...when I jumped out of that cave with Roup."

"You c-carried him out of the cave?"

"Jumped out. Dragged him all the way back to Arcove's den. Keesha did the rest." Halvery stopped talking.

Dazzle's eyes were pools of blackness with a bright sheen that did not bode well. Halvery wondered whether he was going to fall over dead right here. *What an awkward conversation that would be with Shimmer.* "Dazzle, stop wasting time."

"I had no idea you and Roup were so c-close," whispered Dazzle.

We weren't, thought Halvery, *until you.* But he wasn't about to give Dazzle the satisfaction of saying it aloud.

"I d-didn't think you'd c-care if I killed Moashi," continued Dazzle. "I c-can't believe you jumped into a flood to save Storm...or his foal. You've done such a good j-job with your legend...making everybody think you're all claws. That's some extraordinary p-politicking, Halvery. Imp-pressive."

Halvery wanted to say, *"It's not politicking. I'm an unfriendly, uncreative, old-fashioned den alpha, and the only reason I became friends with any of those animals is Roup...and training Moashi to fight you."*

Dazzle was still talking. "So you must unders-stand...if these cats know you and Arcove k-killed me..."

Halvery didn't like where this was going. "I am not about to kill you—"

"Now, later, it doesn't m-matter when. Some of these cats will fight. I don't want them to. I want them to have a f-future in L-Leeshwood." Dazzle turned and stared back over the ice.

Halvery realized, with a jolt, that he was thinking about walking back out there. "Dazzle," he growled, "get—up—here. That is an order."

Dazzle turned back around and said, with desperate earnestness, "Halvery, just let me go through the ice. It would be so much better for everyone." He tried to smile again. "If it would make you f-feel better to come down here and have a s-swipe at me first..."

Halvery snarled at him. "You are not mine to kill. You are not yours to kill. You are *Arcove's!* Now, for the last time, get up here."

Dazzle didn't look like he was listening. He'd turned back to the ice again. *Is there anything I can actually do to stop him? I'm certainly not going to follow him out there; we'll both go through.*

At that moment, Pace and Flurry burst through the trees and came loping to the edge of the bluff. They started to speak to Halvery, then caught sight of Dazzle. "Daz!" exclaimed Pace. "Everyone is asking about you. Why are you just standing there? We've got to get the ice out of your paws *right now!* Come on!"

Dazzle hesitated. He shut his eyes, and said wearily, "I just need a rest before making that j-jump."

"You've never needed a rest before a jump in your life," snapped Pace. "Now!"

Dazzle had to try three times before he managed to get high enough for them to grab him. Halvery did not try to help. He watched Pace and Flurry tug Dazzle gracelessly over the edge and then nudge him to his feet. "We have to get your paws warm," Flurry was muttering. "Daz, I'm so sorry, but we're going to make you run."

Halvery watched them disappear into the trees. *Can they save his paws?* He supposed that if any creasia on Lidian knew how to prevent frostbite, it would be these creasia. *And I'm sure they also know exactly what it's like to die that way.*

Costa was sound asleep. Halvery felt utterly drained. He considered curling up around her and just drifting off right there. Instead, he nosed her to her feet and guided her back into the trees. He found where Storm was sleeping and left Costa curled beside her father.

Then he went in search of Arcove.

29

I Told You So

The curbs had made their dens in rocky ground near the center of the island. Their tunnels were too small for creasia, but the area was heavily wooded and sheltered from the wind. Shimmer's cats had settled down there, sleeping in furry piles.

Halvery wasn't surprised to learn that Arcove and Roup weren't with them. The place they'd chosen was on the western end of the island, against a little hillock in the lee of the wind. They were facing in opposite directions, heads over each other's backs, exactly the way they always slept far from home.

Halvery stopped a few paces away, unsure of whether he should wake them. But then Roup raised his head, and Arcove looked up immediately. They hadn't been asleep. In fact, Halvery had the sense they'd been waiting for him. He closed the last few paces and stretched out beside Roup, facing the same direction. He was unpleasantly aware of every joint and muscle in his body.

His companions both looked at him, waiting.

Halvery sighed. "Dazzle made it off the ice."

"Do you think he's going to live?" whispered Roup.

Halvery screwed his eyes shut. "I don't know." He hesitated. "His own cats seem to think they can save his paws. They ought to know something about frostbite up here."

Roup let out a breath.

Arcove looked over Roup's back at Halvery. "Do you still think Dazzle is likely to betray us?"

Halvery looked away. "No one would do that for a trick."

Roup leaned over and gave him a lick on the muzzle.

Halvery gritted his teeth and raised his eyes to Arcove again. "He...um...seems fairly determined to go through the ice."

Roup went still.

Halvery continued wearily, "He'd rather be remembered as a hero than take the risk that his followers might try to avenge his death."

Arcove dropped his head onto Roup's back with a grunt. He looked completely exhausted, as though he didn't quite trust himself to make one more decision.

"He's not going to do it with them fussing over him," said Halvery. "But…if you'd like him to walk off the ice alive tomorrow…I think you'd better talk to him before we leave." Half to himself, Halvery muttered, "Maybe he just knows he's going to die of frostbite. Maybe he just doesn't want to go out that way—"

Roup rubbed his face against Halvery's jaw. "Your eyes aren't focusing together. You'll think better after you sleep."

Halvery didn't argue. He curled up against Roup, the warmth and familiar scent equally comforting. He could feel Arcove shifting on the other side. His rumble vibrated through Roup's body. "Your advice, councilor?"

Halvery tried to rally the conflicting tumble of his thoughts. "Dazzle only follows orders when it suits him. He's prone to keeping secrets. He *does* like to be a hero, and coupled with the other two things…" Halvery broke off. "But Thistle's characterization of him as a bully who wouldn't be missed was an utter fabrication. These cats love him. I do think you'll have permanent problems with this group if you kill him and they know it. But you'll also have problems with them if he lives and decides to change sides again. Or if he just doesn't follow orders one day. As long as he's alive, he'll be a source of division." *And there's the little matter of how I can't stop seeing Roup in a puddle of blood every time I look at him.*

"So you still think I should kill him?" asked Arcove.

"I…" Halvery tucked his head against Roup's shoulder. "It's not my call, sir." He was annoyed that his own voice sounded plaintive.

Arcove relented. "Thank you for speaking your mind, councilor. I know it has been a long two nights."

"Has it only been two nights?" muttered Roup.

Halvery gave a miserable laugh. "It feels like two years." He continued to Arcove, "I'm glad we didn't leave these cats behind, sir. Thank you for not listening to me when I'm wrong."

Roup raised his head again and started licking Halvery's face and ears.

Halvery shut his eyes with a bitter smile. "That is the sweetest version of 'I told you so.'"

Roup kept grooming. Halvery was already losing his grip on consciousness. "I'm not trying to be cruel," he muttered.

"I know," whispered Roup.

"I am not the villain here."

"I never said you were."

"He nearly killed you."

"Go to sleep, Halvery."

30

Bright Side

Arcove woke around noon to a dim world, still cocooned in falling snow. The air felt warmer, the smell of spring reasserting itself. *All this snow will turn into slush very shortly.* The woods were completely quiet, save for the sigh of the wind through the trees and the occasional thump of snow sliding off a branch.

Arcove rose without waking Roup or Halvery and padded deeper into the trees, around the drifts, until he reached the spot near the curb dens where Shimmer's creasia were sleeping. Arcove could not detect clear separations between dens. They seemed to be almost a solid mass of animals, curled around and on top of each other, and so soundly asleep that most of them had accumulated a layer of snow.

He'd almost despaired of identifying Dazzle without waking anyone, when a nose pushed up from the center of the pile. Dazzle shook snow off his head, blinked at Arcove, and then began to extricate himself.

Arcove was impressed to see that he looked both warm and dry. *I suppose they do know how to deal with icy paws up here.* Dazzle's companions stirred and muttered as he waded through them, but he continued to live up to the nickname the lowland curbs had given him, mincing over them so lightly that they never fully woke. Dazzle jumped over the last few cats and staggered as he hit the ground. He was obviously sore, but he got his legs sorted and came to meet Arcove without a limp.

Arcove gave a jerk of his head towards the western side of the island and started away. Dazzle caught up and walked beside him. The moment they were out of earshot of the group, he began talking quickly, "I need to tell you a few things about these cats, Arcove. I should have told you last night; I wasn't thinking clearly. They're sick to death of watching their cubs die, it's true, but most of them still love their mates. Most of those mates didn't get a chance to make a choice between you and Thistle. Shimmer didn't dare ask, because even one betrayal would have been the end of the whole escape.

"Many of the adult males will try to rejoin their mates and cubs in Leeshwood. They'll probably trickle in with their tails between their legs over the next year or so. Please let them. It's what these females are hoping for. If you kill their mates, they'll be hurt. They might run away again and create another hostile colony. But they won't cause trouble if they're allowed to resume their lives with some dignity. They'll be your cats if you show them a little mercy."

They'd reached the western shore of the island. Dazzle paused to catch his breath, but before Arcove could say anything, he raced on, "I know what you're thinking. You're thinking that there have to be consequences for cats who lied to you and tried to lure you to

your death. But even most of the males didn't know what Thistle
had planned for you. Some of them fought with Treace on Kuwee,
it's true, but they've paid for that. Paid and paid and paid, Arcove.
It's been fourteen years.

"Roup said it was possible for us to come home…without being
attacked for sport and malice, without becoming rogues, without
half of us dead within a year…and I didn't believe him. That was a
mistake. I didn't believe him two years ago, but I do now. I know
you're willing to do this for the females, but I'm asking you to do
it for the males, because then you will have the unreserved loyalty
of the entire group."

Arcove finally managed to get in a sentence, "Do you believe
that all these cats are capable of being good citizens of my wood,
Dazzle?"

Dazzle hesitated. "I don't think *all* of them will try to join
you."

"Thistle's officers?"

Dazzle screwed up his face. "Flash misses his old den. He was
heavily involved in the rebellion, but I don't think there's anything
he wouldn't do to rejoin Astari if he thought there was a chance."

"And the rest?" continued Arcove.

Dazzle looked away. "If Shale or Sundance turns up, watch
them. I'm not saying don't give them a second chance. Just…keep
an eye on them."

Arcove looked at him narrowly. "Shale seemed to particularly
dislike you." *He invited me to 'shut you up with a lungful of mud.'*

They were walking along the western shore of the island.
Arcove had hoped for a clear view of the mainland beach. The
gray light was perfect for creasia eyes, but the fine, driving snow
still hampered visibility. The far shore was a hazy, indistinct mass
of dark trees and pale drifts.

Dazzle was moving too fast. Arcove slowed, forcing Dazzle to
slow with him. "Shale was Thistle's second in command whenever
I wasn't around," said Dazzle. "I've been gone even more in the last
few years, and he got used to that."

"Every time you showed up, he got demoted," said Arcove with a trace of wry humor. "That will cause resentment in most animals." *And that one obviously has a taste for cruelty.*

"He's not my biggest admirer," said Dazzle. He laughed mirthlessly and added, "Surely that's not a strike against him from your perspective. Just know that Shale is very invested in Thistle's notion that the only way we can safely return to Leeshwood is on top. If he changes his mind about that, he might make a good citizen. I don't know."

Arcove looked at him sidelong. "And Thistle?"

Dazzle looked away. His hurry of words seemed to fail him and he didn't answer for a moment. They passed the western-most tip of the island and started around the backside. It was the most isolated area, far from earshot of the others.

"If Thistle rolls over for you and asks to come home, I wish you'd let him," said Dazzle at last. "He has two mates who love him." Half under his breath, he muttered, "And he has two who have never forgiven him for killing Restri."

Before Arcove could decide how to reply to this, Dazzle said, "Please don't kill Flurry."

Arcove rolled his eyes. "I am not going to kill your foolish protégé unless he exercises further errors in judgment."

"He's not my protégé."

"Dazzle, do you think I am stupid?"

"Flurry is just a cub whose father lost a fight! His mother asked me to find him a new den, so I did. I checked on him now and then. I suppose I was the only one checking. It's hard for male cubs out here."

Arcove found that he really did not want to hear the details of this, but he forced his way onward. "Explain."

Dazzle looked at him as though he were asking for an explanation of the obvious. "Resources are limited. Mates are limited. For an adult male creasia, male cubs represent future rivals, future competition. They *might* represent future allies, but most males in their prime don't want to risk it."

So they've been living the old way, thought Arcove. It was the world he'd grown up in. A world he'd set out to erase. "How did Thistle expect to win a war while killing most of his male cubs?"

Dazzle snorted. "He didn't! He wasn't even thinking about taking Leeshwood until Sedaron started attacking us. And don't make Thistle the villain as regards the cub situation, Arcove. It's creasia instinct to kill cubs that aren't your own. Thistle actually encouraged them *not* to kill female cubs, even when they took over a den. He just...didn't say anything about the males."

Arcove listened with distaste.

Dazzle seemed to sense this and hurried on. "Until Sedaron started attacking us a couple of years ago, Thistle didn't have any notion of leaving the foothills. He wasn't interested in growing our numbers, because the land couldn't support more creasia. Too many mouths would mean famine for all of us. There's no bitterleaf out here, Arcove. We couldn't stop the cubs from being born, and killing some of them kept us all from starving."

Arcove had the sense that Dazzle was repeating an oft-rehearsed line of reasoning. "And yet you went out of your way to find a home for a cub whose father had lost his den to a challenger?" *A cub whose father was dead and whose mother had rejected him...*

No, Arcove told himself sternly. *That is not what he said. Stop creating parallels where none exist.*

"I..." Dazzle seemed to be searching for words. "I come and go from Leeshwood, where things are different. I...have a different perspective." He gave a bitter flash of teeth and added, "Shale would tell you that I was cultivating a future ally—making life harder for everyone by creating another mouth to feed, in order to have another cat who owed me something."

Before Arcove could formulate a response to this, Dazzle continued, "I know what you're thinking: these cats are accustomed to living in a manner of which you disapprove. But, Arcove, they will come around to your way of doing things *so* quickly. Most of them *are* capable of being good citizens.

"I know that allowing them to return would require an enormous amount of forbearance, trust, and compassion. That's not your reputation. Cats who fought with Treace say that you never forget a slight, that you hold a grudge forever, that you are merciless to those who've wronged you." Dazzle's voice dropped to a near-whisper. "But that can't be true. You love Roup, and he is *made* of compassion. Arcove's Bright Side—that's what they call him. So I know you have one."

Arcove almost laughed. *Roup...always telling my secrets.* They were strolling along the shore that faced the open lake now, looking out over a vast expanse of ice, fading into snow and fog in the distance.

Dazzle's breathing had developed a catch—a betrayal of mounting anxiety. Arcove watched him out of the corner of one eye. *He's the same age as Storm. Two years older than Carmine.*

When Arcove finally stopped walking, Dazzle blurted, "Please just let me go through the ice tomorrow, Arcove. Some of these cats are already suspicious about how I bargained for this. They'll be much better citizens of Leeshwood if they see what happened to me...if they know you didn't kill me."

Arcove had a distinct memory of standing on the edge of a different lake. Keesha's exasperated voice: *"Will you stop trying to control everything? Even after you're dead, you think you can control what's said? What's believed? Trust that I am not a fool."*

He wished Keesha's words would stop going through his head. He wished his own sentiments would stop coming out of Dazzle's mouth.

Arcove started to speak and Dazzle interrupted him again, "I should tell you some things about the mountains between here and the plain. There are several good places to hide if some of the females need to give birth and there are places to hunt for game—"

"Do you always talk this much?" demanded Arcove.

Dazzle flinched. "Only when I'm terrified." He shut his eyes. There was a fine tremor in his paws.

Arcove sighed. "Are *you* capable of being a good citizen of my wood, Dazzle?"

Dazzle opened his eyes. He'd been afraid before, but now he looked truly off-balance. Panicky, even. He swallowed and his voice came out in a whisper, "Please don't toy with me, Arcove."

Arcove thought he finally understood. *You've accepted your own death. That's why you've been so calm. What you fear most is disappointment. To be disappointed, you'd need to first have hope.*

Dazzle's eyes skittered around the ice and shore, as though searching for something. "I know what you're thinking. You're thinking that it would be more convenient if I led you through the mountains myself, and drowning in the lake is probably not what you had in mind for me—"

Arcove brought his head down until they were nose to nose. "Dazzle."

Dazzle's pupils were huge, his breathing quick and uneven.

"You have no idea what I'm thinking," growled Arcove. "Stop putting words in my mouth."

Dazzle's ears dropped and he crouched down a little. He gave a ragged laugh. "I'm sorry, Arcove. I did say that I'm not very good at losing."

Arcove could almost hear himself say, *"I'm not very good at begging."* He made a rumbling noise of frustration. "Halvery says you only follow orders when it suits you."

Dazzle gave a laugh that was all nerves. "I'm sure he'd be willing to cure me of that for you permanently."

"Good citizens follow orders. Don't go through the ice. That is an order."

Dazzle's ears drooped. He wrapped his tail around his body, almost under his haunches. "Yes, sir."

Arcove watched him. *You really do think I'm playing with you. You think I'm giving you hope so that I can jerk it away, like a cub with a mouse.* Arcove wasn't sure what else to say, though. "We're going to cross to the mainland in the afternoon. Go back to your cats. See if you can get a little more sleep before then."

Dazzle inclined his head without raising his eyes. As he turned to go, Arcove thought of another angle, "Dazzle…"

He waited until Dazzle looked up.

"You *tried* to kill my…bright side. But you didn't."

Dazzle swallowed. Arcove could see the battle between the calm of despair and the fragile, chaotic flame of hope. He thought, *What would Roup say?* He knew immediately. "Trust me."

Dazzle shut his eyes, opened them again. "I'll try, Arcove."

"Good. Now go get some more sleep. I have a feeling that the last bit of ice may be a challenge."

31

So Close

Later that afternoon, Halvery sat on the western shore, along with Arcove, Roup, Storm, Shimmer, Dazzle, and Tsueri. All of them were squinting into the gray haze at the blurry outline of the mainland.

"I wish I'd gotten everyone up at noon," muttered Arcove. "This is worse."

The wind had dropped, which was a relief, but the temperature had begun to rise, so that the snow was wet and mixed with rain. The changing temperature had brought a rolling mist across the frozen lake and along the shore.

"At least they won't see us coming off the ice," observed Storm, "not unless we're so unlucky as to walk straight into them."

Arcove frowned. "That may, in fact, happen, because this is the logical spot to leave the lake." He glanced at Tsueri as though to confirm.

"It is," agreed the curb. "This is the closest island to the western shore. There are enough stepping stones to cross the weakest ice."

"But does Thistle know that?" persisted Storm. He was looking at Dazzle.

"*I* didn't know it," said Dazzle, "so I doubt *he* does."

"We'll hope you're right," said Arcove. "Shimmer, get your cats ready to move. I'd like to be at the top of the valley before dusk. Hopefully our enemies had an exhausting night and are still fast asleep."

Halvery hoped he was right. *But even if we have to fight our way through, I'm glad we stopped to rest.* He felt sharp again. He was still sore and hungry, but he didn't feel weak.

Shimmer's creasia were already up and moving around. No one appeared to have died while they slept—a remarkable outcome, given the amount of pressure being placed upon underfed, severely stressed animals. Apparently a number of highland curbs from the islands were planning to accompany Cohal and Maoli back to the plain. The rest of the curbs seemed anxious for the creasia to be gone. They kept a small number of sheep on the island, and they seemed concerned that the hungry cats might decimate their carefully controlled food supply.

They're not wrong if we stay here much longer, thought Halvery. *We need to bring down a few ice oxen before starting for Chelby Lake. Half these cats will die if we push them through the mountains while fasting.* He couldn't help thinking, *One of them might be me.*

Soon they were following Dazzle and the curbs onto the ice again. An ominous creaking began underfoot as they approached the shore, and this time, the curbs did not look for a way around it. "The ice will be rotten from here on," they said, "but there are boulders and ridges of rock underneath. If we stay overtop them, we probably won't go through."

The curbs had memorized the locations of these rocks during times when the lake melted. The rocks were hard to see under ice, although Halvery could detect their shadows at certain angles.

The curbs still needed to test whether the ice would hold a creasia, so they kept sending Dazzle ahead. Halvery was impressed that he seemed mostly recovered from last night. *Maybe you're not going to die of frostbite after all.* Dazzle didn't look like he was trying to go through the ice, either. He appeared cautious.

"I talked to him," said Arcove quietly.

Halvery cocked his head. "Anything I need to know about?"

"Not yet."

Roup was still favoring his left hind leg this morning—a worrying development, since his limp usually disappeared after he'd slept. "It's the cold," he muttered. "It'll get better after I move around...after we're off the ice."

Halvery wasn't so sure. He suspected that what Roup needed most was a few days of unbroken rest and something to eat. *The sooner we get out of this valley, the sooner he's likely to get those things.*

Visibility remained terrible. The shore was startlingly close by the time it finally materialized out of the mist. The land fell towards the water in a series of rocky hills, currently hock-deep in wet snow. Stands of pine dotted the slopes, casting dark shadows amid the sliding fog. *So many places to hide,* thought Halvery uneasily.

Above the fog, Halvery glimpsed the edge of the valley. Over that ridge lay the little clearing and waterfall where they'd left the clutters. Friends, reinforcements, perhaps even food, waited just out of sight. Halvery had to repress the urge to run for it. *We could be there in no time.*

Instead, Arcove brought the head of the column to a halt. They all stood still in the drifting fog, listening and sniffing. There was not a breath of wind. The mixed snow and rain pattered straight down around them. Halvery strained his ears, but all he could hear was the drip of thawing snow, and creak of settling ice. His nose brought him scents of spring earth and pine. He saw no footprints, although the melting crust made the ground more difficult to read than he would have liked.

Costa pressed against his side and shoulder. "I wish there was wind," she whispered.

"Good thought," he murmured. He tipped his head at Arcove. "You see that even creasia kings don't rush in blindly. Not even when the goal is so close. *Especially* when the goal is so close."

Arcove didn't look completely satisfied, but he murmured, "Well, we're not going to learn anything else standing here. Shimmer, please pass the word for your cats to proceed as quietly as possible."

They reached dry land without mishap. Arcove led the way up the slope to the first stand of trees. "We regroup here. I don't want us proceeding up the valley this strung out."

Shimmer's creasia were coming ashore quickly now that they had a clear path and a destination. The first quarter had reached the trees when Flurry came dashing into the group in great distress, "Ash broke through the ice and now she's trapped on an unstable slab. She...she says a cub is trying to be born."

He'd addressed himself to Shimmer and Dazzle, but Arcove answered. "How far back?"

"Near the beginning," said Flurry miserably. "She was pacing because of the pain, and she got off the path."

Arcove turned to Shimmer and Dazzle. "You stay with your cats. If there's trouble, try to get them to Chelby Lake."

Halvery was surprised. He'd expected Arcove to send Dazzle back to deal with the stranded cat. Possibly Shimmer. However, Leeshwood's creasia were the biggest in the group, and if a cat needed to be pulled to safety or even dragged all the way from the island, they were the most likely to be successful.

Halvery was relieved when Arcove said, "Roup, Halvery, with me."

At least he's not splitting us up. Arcove had hardly let Roup out of his sight since they started into the mountains.

Flurry pleaded to come with them. Apparently, there was some chance that the cub about to be born was his. Arcove did not argue. The four of them moved quickly back along the line of creasia.

Flurry had not been exaggerating about the distance. They were nearly back to the island by the time they encountered the dark gray female called Ash. She was about five lengths off the trail, lying on her belly with her eyes closed. As they came nearer, Halvery saw that she was resting on a shelf of ice surrounded by cracks. A newly-visible stretch of open water separated the shelf from the trail, lapping greedily at the crumbling edges.

A cluster of other females were gathered there, trying to help Ash, but also impeding the progress of those trying to leave the island. Some cats were hanging back, unwilling to risk leaving the trail to skirt the distressed group. Others were boldly going around or over them, increasing the risk of another break.

"The ice creaks every time she moves," said one female as Arcove's party joined them, "and the piece she's sitting on starts to tip."

Ash wasn't saying anything. Her body tensed and her back legs slid as a contraction wracked her bony frame. Halvery saw that the ice around her back paws was stained with blood. As the spasm intensified, she set her teeth and screwed her eyes shut as though determined not to cry out. She had obviously gotten the message that silence was imperative. She began to purr on every breath—a ragged sound of pain and distress.

Arcove turned to her friends. "I will allow one of you to stay here, but the rest need to keep going. You are blocking the trail and endangering others. I will handle this. I will not leave her here, but you must continue to the mainland. That is an order."

They looked at him and then at each other. *Well, this is interesting,* thought Halvery. *Let's see whether any of you can follow orders.*

Then the foremost turned to her companions and said, "I'm her sister; I'm staying. You all go on."

They went unhappily, looking back. The line began to move again.

Arcove turned to the stranded cat. "Ash," he said softly.

Her eyes opened, huge and dilated. She panted clouds of steam into the frosty air.

"How close is the cub?" asked Arcove.

"Don't know," she said through gritted teeth. "First time."

Halvery wanted to jump across the gap and just pick her up, but he knew he couldn't manage it.

Arcove looked at the sister.

"She was having pains yesterday on the ice," said the other cat miserably. "I think the cub will come soon."

Arcove's eyes narrowed in concentration. He turned to Ash again. "It will be harder to pull you out of the water with a cub. Harder to swim, too, if you land in the lake. Newborn cubs don't survive in ice water. I think you'd better jump now."

She stared at him hopelessly. Her voice sounded as small as a cub's. "I can't."

Beside them, Flurry gave a wordless whimper of distress.

Arcove's voice was gentle, but adamant. "You can. We'll pull you up. You'll get a little wet, but the temperature is rising. Have your cub on safe ground. Come on, Ash. One jump. You've come all this way to raise this baby somewhere green."

She looked at him and the panic cleared from her eyes.

Halvery felt a wave of pride in his king. *The thing about Arcove is that he's always so certain. He tells you that you can do something you didn't think you could do. And you believe him.*

Ash gritted her teeth, rose on wobbly legs, and jumped. The shelf gave way beneath her, stealing some of her momentum. She landed mostly in the water, but her front claws locked onto the edge of solid ice. Arcove caught her by the scruff and dragged her onto the trail. Flurry and her sister crowded around her, whispering encouragement, licking her face, cleaning the water from her fur. Blood was pooling rapidly under her tail. She gave another agonized straining motion, and the cub slid onto the ice.

Halvery saw with relief that it was already moving in its sack. Ash's sister tore it free and then scooted the placenta around for Ash to devour. They both began licking the cub vigorously, placing it atop their paws, so that it was not lying on ice. Flurry stared, wide-eyed, for a moment, then joined in.

Roup had taken on the task of keeping the line moving around them. "She's alright," he told the cats who kept stopping to stare. "The cub is fine. You need to keep going. Don't get off the trail."

Halvery looked back at the island and saw that the clump along the shore had disappeared. The last of Shimmer's creasia were filing past them. Arcove had noticed the same thing. "We need to go," he murmured. "Flurry, carry the cub. Ash, can you walk?"

Flurry came right up to Arcove, tail and ears low and whispered, "Thank you, sir. Thank you, thank you…"

Halvery thought Arcove might give him a brief lecture about the value of loyalty, but instead, he just gave him a lick on the head. Flurry looked at him with naked gratitude and something like reverence. Halvery leaned over and said in Flurry's ear, "You can tell him how you would die for him later; right now, pick up your cub and let's go."

Flurry picked up the cub, pausing for a moment to figure out how. *You've never carried one before,* thought Halvery. *Of course you haven't. You're barely more than a cub yourself.*

Ash staggered to her feet. "I can carry it."

"You can barely walk," said Arcove. "Let Flurry do something. Ghosts know you already did the hard part."

That made them all laugh.

"Let's get you to the mainland, and then you can clean up the cub. Hopefully you'll have something for it to eat."

Halvery grimaced. *She might not.* Under these circumstances, milk didn't always come. In that case, the cub would die…unless another female had milk. Which seemed entirely possible now that Halvery thought about it. *How on earth are we going to get these cats out of the mountains if they all start having cubs?*

He took a deep breath. He could almost hear Arcove say, *"One thing at a time."*

At that moment, a terrible racket erupted from the shore—the wail of fighting cats and the fierce howls of ferryshaft.

32

Blood in the Snow

Arcove whirled to Ash and said, "I would suggest that you go back to the island until the fighting is over, but that is not an order, and I will not tell you what to do in this situation with a newborn." Then he was running, Halvery and Roup behind him.

Visibility remained dreadfully poor. Halvery could barely see the shore and he couldn't make sense of what was happening. Animals were definitely fighting. The line of creasia laboring across the lake wavered and then broke into a flat-out run.

Halvery was sure they were all doing the same terrible calculations in their heads. They were running towards a fight that might involve impossible odds, but if they went back to the island, they could be trapped there with little to eat. Shimmer and Dazzle were on the mainland, and these were their most trusted leaders. So they ran towards the awful noises and the moving bodies in the swirling fog. The line of females was well ahead of Arcove's party, and they soon disappeared into the confusion on shore.

The trail over the ice was, at least, mercifully easy to follow, marked as it was by so many footprints. Arcove and his officers tore along its sometimes zig-zag course, slipping occasionally on the turns. They were three quarters of the way across when Arcove spun, and Halvery saw that Roup was falling behind. He was limping badly now.

"Roup, take your time," panted Arcove. "Better yet, stay out here; I don't want you involved in this."

"Arcove—" gasped Roup, his voice thick with emotion, but Arcove cut him off.

"I cannot win fights when you're in the middle of it limping like that!" he thundered. "Stay out of it; that's an order! Halvery, with me." Then he was *really* running, and Halvery had to concentrate on the trail.

By the time they reached the mainland, the noises had stopped. Halvery found the silence almost more ominous. No enemies were visible in the drifting fog, but there was blood on the snow, a multitude of footprints, and a single dead creasia sprawled in the shallows.

Halvery felt a pang when he saw him—the emaciated juvenile straggler from last night. *He tried so hard...*

Halvery's thoughts were turning in a dark direction. *Maybe Dazzle brought our attackers. They certainly found us quickly. And we left him alone on the shore for quite a while. Plenty of time to slip away and find his friends, especially if they were already in the area.*

The trail of blood and trampled snow was easy to follow, and it seemed to be leading back to the stand of trees where they'd left the main group. Arcove flashed over the snow, Halvery right behind him. *Roup never could have kept up. Because of what Dazzle did to him.* Halvery ground his teeth. *I'll kill him myself if Arcove doesn't want to do it.*

They whipped out of the fog into the trees, and a cat leapt at them. Arcove and Shimmer recognized each other just in time to avoid blows. "We were attacked," panted Shimmer.

"I heard," breathed Arcove. "What's happening now?"

"I don't know!" Her eyes were bright with battle nerves. "They came at us from all sides. Scattered us. I couldn't tell how many. I think they killed someone."

"A juvenile by the water," said Arcove. "You rallied here?"

"Yes, and then they disappeared into the fog."

"We need to move," said Arcove. "That was probably a scouting party, and they drew back to gather reinforcements."

"Where's Dazzle?" demanded Halvery.

"I don't know," said Shimmer in great agitation. "He got separated from us in the rush."

"Of course he did," muttered Halvery.

"Storm!" called Arcove.

No answer.

"I think the ferryshaft and curbs ran when we were attacked," said Shimmer.

Halvery felt ill. He wished they hadn't left Roup on the ice. He wanted to start calling loudly, but that might make the situation worse. He looked at Arcove.

Arcove's face held that deadly calm that Halvery remembered from battles—putting everything aside except the current problem. "We make for the top of the valley," he said at last. "We left some cats on the ice, who've probably gone back to the island. We will return for them when we have reinforcements, but right now, we need to get away from the spot that our enemies expect to find us."

"Oh, it's too late for that, Arcove."

The voice came from the sliding fog, but it was immediately echoed by yowls and howls all around them. The group of creasia pulled closer together under the trees, forming a circle with the smallest and weakest in the center. The rest stood shoulder to shoulder, bristling, their eyes darting in every direction. The late afternoon light had the unfortunate tendency to reflect off the fog and snow, making it impossible to see more than a few lengths beyond the edge of the trees.

Arcove backed into the circle beside Shimmer. Halvery squeezed in against his opposite shoulder.

"This is not their full strength," said Arcove quietly. "Otherwise, they would have already attacked. They mean to hold us at bay here until reinforcements arrive. We cannot let that happen. When I give the signal, I want you to all break for the ridge at the western end of the valley. There's a basin and a waterfall up there. That's where we regroup. Hopefully it's where we'll find my clutters. Shimmer, you need to talk to either Lyndi or Carmine. Tell them..." He thought for a moment and smiled. "Tell them you're on my bright side; they'll know what that means."

"I hear you..." crooned the voice out of the fog, "whispering some plan to each other about running away." Halvery thought it was Shale. It didn't sound like Thistle. "You can try," the voice continued, "but it won't work. We vastly outnumber you, and frankly, we could outfight you even if we didn't. A bunch of pregnant females, likely to give birth at any moment, a few half-grown cubs, and some elderly males. Quite an army you've got there, Arcove."

Arcove raised his head with an intent expression. Halvery thought he was trying to catch sight of Shale so that he could attack him. That would doubtless be the signal to break.

And I'll attack with you, thought Halvery. *Maybe we'll kill whoever is leading this group, but...* It seemed likely that their enemies would throw everything they had at Arcove and Halvery, abandoning all other targets in order to kill them. *We can put our backs to each other.*

But it wouldn't be enough. Not with the kind of numbers likely present or soon to arrive.

"Shimmer," came the voice again, "I know this was your idea. You're mad with grief over Serot, and you blame us. You've allowed yourself to be misled. You probably expect to die, but I'll give you this one chance. Lie down. All of you, and we'll take you back, along with those cubs you're carrying. Otherwise, I don't see how your babies can hope to survive."

"Never," spat Shimmer. "But come fight me one-on-one like a real alpha, and we'll consider it."

Shapes began materializing out of the fog. Halvery had hoped that Shale would come forward in front, but he was too wily for that. More than a dozen creasia were suddenly visible, providing no clear target. Halvery recognized several from the confluence, including Thistle's pale-colored guards. They were flanking Shale, who was wisely hanging back.

"*Real* alphas don't engage in challenge fights with females," sneered Shale. "And real females don't lead their den-mates to their deaths with empty promises."

Shimmer was glaring at him, ears flat. Her shoulders were bunching, and Halvery realized that she was serious about this fight. "You're just afraid I'd do to you what Dazzle should have done years ago," she breathed.

Shale matched her tone. "You are a lying, arrogant traitor—you and your brother, both. I am going to lame you and leave you to freeze on the ice one limb at a time!"

The group was closing around the stand of trees. Halvery couldn't tell how many there were. *Dozens? Hundreds?* They were all going to attack at once; that was obvious. *And they will kill Arcove and me first. I'm sorry, Roup. I hope you get to see that litter of Ilsa's. I hope they make you want to live.*

One of the pale guards had come right up to Shale, as though to whisper some message in his ear. Shale inclined his head to listen.

Then he jerked back. He whipped his head around and stared stupidly at the other cat. Halvery realized that there were, in fact, three pale guards. Shale blurted, "Who are you?"

Halvery noticed suddenly that the cat who'd whispered was a little smaller than the others. His enormous ears flicked up, and he gave Shale a cheeky grin. "The future." Then he went straight for his throat.

33

Dazzle

Roup felt like he was four years old again, watching Arcove take on cubs who wanted to steal their meat or their tiny sleeping cave, or who simply wanted to kill a future rival. They would ignore Roup in favor of Arcove, driving them apart so that they could attack him together. Arcove would let it happen. *"Go hide; I don't want you in the middle of this." "Leave me alone; I'll handle it.*" *"Stay out of it, Roup."* Roup had been left feeling furious and helpless, tagging along behind.

The fact that, this time, Arcove actually had a point was scant comfort. Roup's left hind leg had begun to cramp during the long, cold night of finding their way over the ice. By morning, it was stiff and sore, sending darts of pain all the way to his hip whenever he fully extended it. Walking helped, but running was intolerable. He yearned, hopelessly, for the warmth of Smoky Branch and a full meal.

Roup knew he was nothing but a liability in a fight right now. He knew.

And yet it took every bit of his self-control to watch Arcove and Halvery race away and not try to follow them. *You said you would take me with you when you go.*

They're not going to die, he told himself.

He could almost hear Arcove say, *"Wait for me."*

I guess I don't have a choice.

They were soon lost to sight amid the lazily rolling fog. Glimpses of the shore came and went. Roup was still walking slowly towards it. *I can't stay on the ice,* he told himself. *It's too cold. My leg will keep cramping.*

He glanced back towards the island, visible only as a silhouette in the mist. He was pretty sure that Ash had taken her newborn cub there, together with Flurry and her sister. *I should join them, wait for someone to come get us.*

But he kept hobbling towards the mainland. *Arcove said to take my time. He didn't say, "Go back to the island."*

Sounds from the shore had stopped. Roup couldn't see any movement. He gritted his teeth as a spasm brought him to a standstill. His hind leg curled against his body. He whimpered and then lay down, panting with the pain. *I have to get off the ice.* But right now, he couldn't move. Roup turned instinctively to lick the painful leg, although he knew this would not help. He began to massage the muscle with his teeth, and that did help a little.

Long moments slipped by while he waited for the cramp to pass. Noises broke out again—not right on shore, but very close. Roup's heart sank as he heard the howls of ferryshaft and the yowls of cats. *How big is the group that found us?* He strained his eyes, but the late afternoon light was glowing off the fog, making it impossible to distinguish details on shore.

Suddenly a pair of fighting animals shot into view, whipping around each other, snarling. Roup blinked. They were both ferryshaft. Neither of them was Storm or Costa. *Are Macex's ferryshaft fighting with each other?* That didn't make sense. *Who else is out here?*

* * * *

Halvery did not think. He simply acted, charging into the midst of Shale's entourage to keep them off Moashi, who was flipping over and over with Shale in a screaming, snarling mass. Halvery deflected one attempted intervention, caught the cat behind the head and crunched through his skull.

Next thing he knew, he was fighting back-to-back with his acting beta. Cats from his own clutter and Moashi's swarmed around them. Arcove and Shimmer had backed up against each other, and the females under the trees were striking out at any enemies who came too close. Carmine flashed out of the fog beside Arcove, backed up beside him and began speaking quickly. The noise was too great for Halvery to catch their words. He glimpsed Lyndi, Stefan, and Hollygold, all of them racing through the fog after attackers.

"It's good to see you, sir!" panted his beta.

"Likewise!" returned Halvery.

"You had us worried for a day or so."

"Unfortunately, I'm about to worry you some more," said Halvery. "Thistle is allied with Macex, who has around six hundred ferryshaft who can still fight. We think they've split up to search for us, but we need to get out of the valley before their full strength arrives."

"Oh, I wouldn't worry about that too much," said his beta with a laugh.

Halvery wanted to turn and look at him. "Why not?"

"Because Kelsy showed up with half his herd."

"You're joking!"

"No. I guess he took a vote. He didn't make them come, but a lot of them came anyway. We spotted your attackers gathering from the ridge. Lyndi decided to ambush their ambush."

Halvery felt a giddy laugh bubble up from somewhere deep inside. He heard a howl in the near-distance. He couldn't be sure it was Storm, but it sounded like him. He glanced towards the lake. *Are you seeing any of this, Roup? I hope so.*

Halvery scanned the racing bodies in the fog. *Where are you hiding, Dazzle? Come on out. I'd like to hear what you have to say. And then I'd like to take the rest of your face off.*

* * * *

The fog had closed in again. Roup couldn't see the battle at all, but he could hear it. He was almost certain he'd seen Hollygold rush by before the mainland disappeared. *Lyndi... Ghosts, I hope you're alright.*

The cramp had passed, and he limped forward slowly, not so intent upon reaching the fight now as simply getting close enough to see it. However, as the sun slipped behind the mountain peaks, casting the valley into premature dusk, the fog grew thicker. Roup could hardly see three lengths in front of him when he heard the soft swish and creak of someone running over the ice from the shore, following the well-marked trail.

Roup almost called out, but some premonition stopped his tongue. The other animal was certainly a cat—no clip-clop of hooves. They were moving fast and quietly.

Roup considered getting off the trail. He would only need to go a few lengths to become invisible in the fog. But the ice was so obviously rotten, and the image of Ash atop the unstable shelf was too fresh in his mind. *I couldn't make the jump she made. I couldn't swim very well, either. My leg would cramp the moment I hit that cold water.*

The other cat was upon him before he could consider other alternatives—sliding like a ghost out of the fog—a cat the color of desert sand with eyes like sunbaked earth. He stopped when he saw Roup, and they looked at each other.

"Thistle."

"Roup."

Thistle's smile was almost welcoming—an expression of relief, mixed with dark pleasure. "I figured he would have left you on the island." He glanced down at Roup's left hind leg, the toes of which were barely touching the ice. "Or maybe you just couldn't keep up?" He laughed gently. "Cats who've had a run-in with Dazzle tend to have some trouble keeping up."

Roup resisted the instinct to back away. He couldn't win a race right now. He had a terrible notion that the only way out of his predicament was to win a fight, which seemed equally unlikely. He didn't think talking to this cat would do much good, but he needed to do something. "It's not too late to walk out of this alive, Thistle."

Thistle cocked his head. His smile reached his eyes. "Oh, I know that. In fact, I think I'm about to win a battle against stunning odds! Your party has been reinforced and I'm sure they're congratulating each other. But they've forgotten that it's possible to win a battle and lose the war…just by losing track of one little detail."

He struck like lightning. He was as fast as Dazzle, but he couldn't run around Roup without risking the unstable ice. Roup shifted his weight onto his good back leg and jumped. He managed to propel himself over Thistle, effectively switching places with him.

Now his enemy was no longer between Roup and the shore, but that didn't do much good when Roup couldn't outrun him. He whirled, not an instant too soon, because Thistle was already closing again. He went for the side of Roup's neck, latched on, and Roup flipped him.

They were both suddenly off the trail, the ice groaning and shifting underneath. They were both on their feet again in an instant, bodies low, paws spread to distribute their weight, backing instinctively away from each other.

"Come on, Roup," purred Thistle, "tell me a story. Dazzle seemed to think you were very convincing. Let's hear what you have to offer me."

"Your life," said Roup flatly.

Thistle laughed. "I think I'll take yours instead." He struck again and this time, Thistle's teeth closed around Roup's throat.

Forty years of sparring with Arcove took over, and Roup folded up and twisted under Thistle, hind legs lashing. It was the only move that might have worked, but still poor odds. Roup felt the slide of his own loose skin from the long days of small meals. It gave him just enough space to twist loose of the crushing jaws. Nevertheless, Thistle had him on his back now in a cross-pin, and the next bite would doubtless find purchase.

Snap!

Freezing water seeped through the fur of Roup's back, ice shifting beneath him.

Thistle was suddenly gone, leaping away to avoid breaking through. Roup rolled to his belly, gasping, heart trying to beat its way out of his chest. The ice was cracking and shifting, but it hadn't actually opened. His left hind leg curled under him, and he snarled in pain. Thistle was only a couple of lengths away, trotting daintily back and forth, putting a foot out, only to draw it back when the ice creaked. He was going to find a way forward any moment.

Roup tried to stand. His legs were shaking. He drew in his breath and let out a long, clear caterwaul—the loudest and most carrying cry for help he could manage. *Please hear that, Arcove. Halvery, Lyndi, anybody...*

Thistle didn't look concerned. "Oh, I do hope he comes running. It'll save me trying to get his attention."

Roup called again.

Thistle cocked his head. "You know what would be even better than me killing you? If Arcove had to do it himself... Perhaps I'll just gut you and leave you on the ice." He surged forward, and Roup skittered backwards, hopelessly slow.

Something sailed over Roup's head and slammed into Thistle. The two creasia flipped over in a spray of cold water, blood, and flying fur. Roup thought it was Halvery. Then the two separated, ice creaking ominously, and it was Dazzle.

Thistle seemed to recognize him in the same moment. "Daz," he spat with a mixture of disgust and relief. "Well, I suppose this is your victory as much as mine. You want to hear me say it? You were right. All is forgiven. Now let's finish this."

Dazzle was shifting his weight from foot to foot, bristling all over. Thistle had raked him from shoulders to hips. They were both leaving bloody prints on the ice. "No, I wasn't right." Dazzle's words came in a breathless hiss. "I nearly destroyed our only way home— the only way back to a *good life*. That's what you want, isn't it?"

Thistle stared at him. "Dazzle, did I rattle your brain just now?"

Roup took the opportunity to back carefully away from them towards the trail. Thistle shot him a contemptuous look over Dazzle's shoulder.

Dazzle was completely focused on Thistle. "I'm serious. We can go home without more bloodshed. We might even be able to stay together. Arcove will let us, but not if we kill the voice of compassion on his council. Stop fighting. Call off our cats. They'll listen to you."

Thistle's gaze shifted back to his would-be beta. "He said that to you?"

"Yes, he—"

"And you believed him?"

"Thistle—"

"Roup, I take it back; you truly are a master dissembler. You and Arcove both. What nonsense!"

"It's not a trick!" exclaimed Dazzle.

"Of course it's a trick!"

Roup spoke at last, "It's not."

Thistle's eyes shifted to him with a look of fury. "You expect me to believe that after fourteen years of leaving us out here to burn and freeze and starve, you've generously decided to give us a place in your kingdom?"

Roup watched him. "I understand that trust is difficult. It's always difficult when things have gone wrong. But we came out here to help you."

Thistle's lip curled. "That's not even clever, Roup. And yet you have somehow scrambled the thinking of my previously savvy, suspicious beta. That's some remarkable politicking."

"It's not politicking," said Dazzle. "It's genuine friendship and trust."

Thistle leaned forward. "I'll tell you a secret, Daz. I don't care. I don't care whether we could return to Leeshwood with our tails between our legs and rule some miserable den in the most undesirable scrap of territory, while every cat who sees us says, 'There goes Arcove's mercy.' I don't want that *good life*. I want to *win*." He made a feint at Dazzle, the ice crackling around them. It was very clear that it would not hold two cats in the same place.

Dazzle backed towards the trail.

"Here's the thing, Daz," continued Thistle. "You might be able to win a fight with me. Maybe. But not while protecting your lame *friend* over there. You'll lose that."

"I know," said Dazzle, his voice oddly thick. "I know that, Thiss."

Thistle's gaze focused on Roup, and he charged forward, forcing Dazzle to move or risk disaster. Dazzle shot into the air.

He shot up...but not away.

Thistle was just short of the trail, a couple of lengths from Roup, when Dazzle landed right on top of him. The ice folded without even a pop, and they vanished.

Roup let out his breath. His eyes skipped back and forth over the yawning hole. A rush of bubbles broke the surface. Then fewer and fewer, and, at last, none at all.

Roup inched closer to the edge. "Come on, Dazzle," he whispered. "You landed on top..."

He heard fighting on shore again, the sounds carrying clearly over the ice. He stared at the dark water until his eyes burned. *Could I hold my breath that long in such cold water? While fighting? Could anyone?* Roup didn't think so.

He had an overwhelming sense of loss, disproportionate to how long he'd known Dazzle. *I suppose I did feel a bit of kinship with you. I wish we could have talked longer. I am so sorry I couldn't bring you home, Dazzle. I tried.*

A head broke the surface. Thistle and Dazzle were a similar color, but only one of them had a claw-mark scar right across his face. Dazzle made a weak, uncoordinated scrabble at the edge of the ice. He would have slipped under again if Roup hadn't grabbed him by the scruff.

Dazzle grunted. He was soaked through and weak—almost deadweight between Roup's teeth. Roup heaved and the ice crumbled around his forepaws. He backed away hastily, nearly letting go of Dazzle. He tried again, but he dared not apply pressure to the ice with his front legs, and his back legs weren't cooperating. The left one spasmed with his efforts, making him whine between his teeth. One front paw broke through, and Roup nearly slipped into the water.

"Roup, stop." Dazzle choked out words against his neck. "You'll fall in, too."

"Help me," growled Roup around a mouthful of Dazzle's scruff.

Dazzle was trying. Roup could feel him trying, but he was worn out and too cold, and the edge of the ice kept giving way.

"Let me t-try on my own," panted Dazzle. He actually attempted to twist out of Roup's grasp. "You can't pull me out, Roup. You can't pull me out, and it's my own f-fault."

You'll sink in a heartbeat if I let go of you, thought Roup, but he kept sliding towards the edge. *If I don't let go of him, I may really end up in the lake.*

A splash and swish of footfalls. Suddenly Halvery was beside him. He got hold of Dazzle near the shoulders, and then he and Roup were pulling together. Dazzle slid out of the water and lay on the trail, breathing in short, shallow gasps.

Roup was shaking and struggling for breath. "He s-saved me from—"

"I saw," interrupted Halvery, his voice coming harsh between pants. "I got a v-view through the fog. Couldn't…couldn't get to you fast enough."

Roup stared hopelessly at Dazzle's wet body, already adhering to the ice. He leaned down and lay his nose against one cold ear. "Dazzle, can you walk?"

Dazzle made a clumsy attempt to sit up. He didn't even manage to get all four feet under him.

Halvery huffed, "Of course he can't walk. Just give me a moment." He caught his breath, then said, almost gently, "Dazzle, curl up if you can. It'll make this easier." Then he got a good grip behind his head and started for the shore.

Dragging an animal over ice wasn't so hard. Roup thought Halvery could have managed it at a run, but he made sure that Roup could keep up. The fighting seemed to have moved away from the area right around the shoreline, and they reached the first stand of trees without mishap. A number of Shimmer's cats stood guard there, surrounding the smallest members of their party.

Halvery dragged Dazzle into their midst as exclamations ran through the group. "If you want him to live," rasped Halvery, "do something."

He turned to Roup, "I cannot force you to stay here, Roup, but for the love of everything you hold precious…"

"I'll stay," said Roup humbly.

Halvery gave him a lick on the nose. Then he disappeared back into the fog and the fighting.

This chapter inclues an author's note at the end of the book.

34

Good Job

Sometime after midnight, Halvery led his exhausted clutter up the ridge towards the clearing around the bowl of the waterfall where they'd started this adventure. The hard fighting was finished, although there were still little skirmishes and standoffs all over the valley.

Halvery paused to look back from the top of the ridge and saw only a sea of fog. Water continued to pour from the dark sky, although it was all rain now with no snow or even sleet. Howls and yowls floated up from below, occasionally breaking into the cacophony of a furious struggle. But Halvery was done. It was all he could do not to stumble in front of his clutter as he made the climb up the ridge.

A sentry met them at the top, a cat from Hollygold's clutter. "There are two ice oxen, killed recently, sir, off that way."

"Go eat," Halvery told his weary subordinates. He didn't follow them. Even food could wait on sleep. "Where are Arcove and Roup?" he asked the sentry.

"Roup is under some bushes on the north side of the basin, sir, near the spot where the stream exits. Arcove has been back and forth over the ridge all evening, but I believe he has gone to rest there now as well."

"Thank you."

Halvery found them deep under cover, dry among the leaves. Lyndi was curled up on the other side of Roup. Halvery collapsed beside her and began to drift off at once. He woke up enough to register her licking his face. "Thank you for watching their backs," she whispered.

"Not sure they needed me," he muttered.

Lyndi snorted. "That's not what Roup said."

Halvery wanted to ask what exactly Roup had said, but he was too sleepy to listen.

Sometime near dawn, he woke to see that the rain had stopped, and the world was very quiet. Arcove had gone out, but Roup and Lyndi were still fast asleep. Halvery considered going in search of food, but he still felt sleepy, and Roup's warm body was molded to his. Lyndi's head was resting on his flank. His eyes were sliding shut again when he noticed the shadow of someone skulking in front of the bushes.

Halvery blinked. "Who's there?"

No answer. The shadow didn't move.

Halvery extricated himself from his companions and emerged to find Moashi sitting hunched in the pre-dawn light. He was facing the clearing, apparently too lost in thought to hear Halvery come out. "Ears?"

Moashi turned, and Halvery saw that his right ear had been ripped. Blood had streamed down the side of Moashi's face and across his velvet nose, bright against his pale gray fur.

Halvery sighed. "It'll heal. It'll just leave a notch."

When Moashi said nothing, Halvery came over and started to clean the ear. Moashi flinched away from him. "You want it to heal evenly, don't you?" snapped Halvery. "Stop moping. I've had so many of these. It'll make you look like you know what you're doing. This is a silly thing to be upset about."

Moashi finally spoke in a strangled whisper. "Tetry..."

"Your beta? What about him?"

"He...he...had a bitten spine. He was dragging his back legs, crying and begging and I had to...I had to..."

Halvery stopped licking. He stepped back to look into Moashi's wild eyes. *Oh… Oh, Moashi.*

Moashi's gaze dropped. "I don't know whether I did it right. I don't know whether I said the right thing. I don't know why I ever wanted to be an officer. I shouldn't have brought him up here. None of us were ready. I can't face them again… I can't—"

"Stop that," interrupted Halvery with every bit of authority that nearly forty years of leadership had given him. "Did you tell him that you'll miss him?"

Moashi choked out, "Yes."

"Did you make it quick?"

Moashi screwed his eyes shut. He rocked back and forth. "Yes."

"Then you did it right. No one could have done it better."

Moashi was purring. He was making a keening noise in the back of his throat. Halvery stepped forward and folded his neck around Moashi's head. "That is the hardest thing an alpha ever has to do," he whispered.

Moashi buried his face against Halvery's chest.

Halvery shut his eyes. "You are a good cub. You did a good job. I am *so* proud of you."

Moashi's breathing gave a hitch. "I know you're not my m-mother," he choked out.

Halvery snorted. "Maybe right now I am."

Moashi kept his head tucked for a long moment, and Halvery didn't try to push him away. He didn't even try to wash the blood from his face.

At last, Moashi's distress purr subsided and he pulled back, looking embarrassed.

"Do you even know that your ear is ripped?" asked Halvery.

Moashi stared at his paws. "I do, yes. I suppose you won't call me Ears anymore."

"Oh, I will."

That got the hint of a smile. Moashi drew a shuddering breath. "I should go back to my clutter. They're so upset, and I…I couldn't fall apart in front of them." He still wasn't raising his eyes. "Thank you, sir, for…listening to me."

"Moashi." Halvery waited until he looked up. "The first time I had to do something like that, I went off by myself and vomited. Then I had to go talk to Arcove about it before I could face my clutter. There is no way to put down one of your own that *feels* right. You wouldn't be a good officer if it felt right."

Moashi looked at him with some mixture of gratitude, misery, and desperation. "Thank you, sir."

"Did you kill Shale? I didn't see how that ended. Was it your idea to sneak up on him like that?"

"Shale?" Moashi's eyes wandered around the basin. Halvery supposed that the beginning of the battle must feel, to him, like a long time ago. "Was he the leader of those cats attacking you? Yes, I killed him. But only because I took him by surprise. They were all so busy surrounding you that they weren't watching their backs. I thought that if I just walked in like a messenger, I could get close to him. Scent conditions were so poor that I didn't think they'd smell me. Sometimes, if you just act like you belong somewhere, animals think that you do." Half under his breath, he muttered, "Like pretending to be an alpha."

"That was foolhardy," said Halvery. "You weren't watching your own back."

Moashi didn't look like he intended to defend himself.

Halvery relented. "It's the sort of thing Storm would do. I suppose it worked out. If you're pretending to be an alpha, you're certainly fooling everyone. Including me."

Another watery smile.

"Tell me about the fight. What happened after you killed Shale?"

Halvery kept him talking until the sun rose. By the time Moashi left, he was looking calmer. Halvery crawled back into the thicket to find Roup and Lyndi awake and watching. Roup rubbed his face against Halvery's nose. "Good job," he whispered. "I am so proud of you."

"Don't mock me," muttered Halvery. "The cub just did something incredibly difficult."

"So did you, I think," whispered Lyndi.

"Again with the mockery," grumbled Halvery.

"Moashi grew up with his cousins," said Roup, "Tetry particularly. They were like siblings."

Halvery winced. "Is his mother even alive?"

"No. She was elderly and died when he was three. He was a singleton."

Halvery sighed and put his chin on his paws.

Roup rested his head across Halvery's shoulders. "You're such a good mamma cat."

Halvery considered a retort and then just shut his eyes.

35

Kinship

When Halvery woke again, it was midmorning and Roup and Lyndi were gone. He wasn't surprised to find Costa cuddled up against his neck, but he was a little surprised to find Storm on the other side. There was a chunk of meat on the ground near Halvery's nose, sticky with blood. "Everyone said you came in too tired to eat," whispered Storm, "and the carcasses were starting to get picked over."

Halvery grunted. He dragged the meat between his paws and started chewing. It was certainly the best thing he'd ever tasted in his life. Costa stirred in her sleep, but didn't wake.

"She was chasing after the fighting all night," muttered Storm.

"Seems like she took care of herself," said Halvery between bites.

Storm smiled.

Halvery was still eating when another ferryshaft pushed her way beneath the bushes. To his surprise, Halvery recognized Tollee.

"So Storm still has a mate? He seemed to think he might not."

Tollee rolled her eyes. "Yes, he still has a mate." She shot Storm a baleful look, "A mate who cannot be ordered to stay out of the mountains, because we are not a creasia clutter, and I am not his subordinate."

Storm fidgeted. "I said I was sorry, didn't I?"

Tollee turned back to Halvery. "I am told that I have you to thank for the continued survival of my family. So thank you."

Halvery snorted. "Costa would have been fine without me." He grinned. "Storm, however, certainly would have drowned."

Tollee glanced at Storm and then back at Halvery. "Oh, really?"

Storm rolled his eyes. "Why do I get the idea you're going to be telling this story at every opportunity?"

"Only as many times as you've told that tiresome tale about the river," said Halvery.

By the time he'd finished, Costa had woken and was adding her own details. "Did Storm tell you how we were chased by a bear just before the flood?"

"No," said Tollee dryly, "I don't believe he did."

"*Briefly* chased," interjected Storm.

"Because Storm teased it," continued Costa, "on account of all the creasia who were after me."

Tollee put her head on her hooves. "Were there a pack of hostile curbs before that? An avalanche, perhaps? Fire?"

"Yes, actually. Well, just the curbs."

"Of course there were."

After they'd finished the story, she said, "Jaden was looking for you earlier, Costa."

She jumped up. "He came with Kelsy's herd?"

"He did."

"I wish you wouldn't encourage that," said Storm when she was gone.

"Why not?" said Tollee mildly. "He's an easygoing fellow with a bright future. They're good friends."

Storm harrumphed. "He's Kelsy's foal."

"And Valla's," replied Tollee. She hesitated. "Kelsy was looking for you earlier. Did he find you?"

Storm put his head on his hooves. "No."

"You should go talk to him."

"And say what? 'Thank you for doing the right thing, Kelsy? Congratulations; you're a hero for grudgingly doing what you should have done to begin with'?"

Tollee gave him a longsuffering look. Halvery thought she must be a very patient creature. "You know, 'the right thing' isn't always obvious. It's not the same from every angle."

Storm said nothing.

"He didn't ask his herd whether they wanted to come save creasia, Storm. He asked them whether they wanted to come save *you*."

Storm finally looked uncomfortable.

"Kelsy told them that *he* was coming up here whether any of them came with him or not," continued Tollee.

Storm screwed up his face. "I'll go talk to him."

"His father is dead and he's not allowed to be sad about it," continued Tollee.

"I said I'd go."

"The most powerful herd leader on the island desperately wants to be on good terms with you, and you make him dance around like a yearling seeking an elder's favor."

Halvery couldn't help himself. "Isn't that what Storm does to everyone?"

Storm smirked.

"I wonder how long Kelsy will tolerate it," persisted Tollee. "He doesn't have to, you know, especially with Sedaron's herd in pieces. Also, his foal and our daughter like each other, and I wish you wouldn't antagonize him for no good reason."

"I said I'd talk to him." Before Tollee could say anything else, Storm continued, "Are Sauny and Valla up here, too? I didn't see them."

"No, they stayed by the lake with their smaller group of ferryshaft and a few telshees in case they needed to cover your retreat. I think staying behind nearly killed Sauny, though."

Storm laughed. "I'll bet."

Halvery drifted off again with their voices murmuring around him. When he woke, only Storm was dozing beside him. The day was overcast, but still well above freezing. Rain drummed on the leaves.

Halvery yawned and stretched. Storm shifted and put his head over Halvery's back. It was oddly companionable and somehow felt no different than sleeping with a clutter-mate. After a moment, Halvery muttered, "How does it work—writing the names of the dead. How does it...help?"

"Oh..." Storm sounded like he really had been asleep.

How bizarre is it that a whole family of ferryshaft feels safe to visit and sleep around me?

Storm cleared his throat. "Well, you have to renew it now and then or the writing will fade. We usually do it once a year. We retrace the name and anything we wrote about them. If they had other living loved ones, those animals might trace the name, too. The name gets renewed, year after year, until no one feels the need to do it anymore. Or until all of their family and friends have joined them in Groth."

Halvery thought about that. "And this...helps?"

"I think so," said Storm. "We think about them when we retrace their name, and sometimes we talk about them to others. We tell their stories. We have a designated time to do that...so that we don't do it *all* the time." He hesitated. "Keesha would tell you that we write the name *outside* our heads, so that we won't keep writing it *inside* forever."

Halvery said nothing. Storm shifted in order to look him in the face. "You've been writing your brother's name inside your head for forty years."

For some reason, Halvery couldn't bear to meet his gaze. He shut his eyes and pretended to sleep and thought about the telshee letters that would spell Charsel.

Shortly after that, Storm went away to find Kelsy. Arcove, Roup, and Lyndi returned to their sleeping place a little later. "Halvery, have you even been out to eat?" asked Roup in some concern.

"Storm brought me something," he muttered.

"I doubt he brought you enough. Go eat. The clutters and Shimmer's creasia have killed several more oxen. The walk to the one downstream is pleasant."

"I'll go with you if you like," said Arcove.

That made Halvery embarrassed and he heaved himself to his feet. "I'm just being lazy, sir."

Arcove gave him a look that said, *"Don't give me that nonsense."* Aloud, he said, "How is your shoulder?"

"Not too bad, all things considered."

"I am extremely grateful that you were close enough to respond to Roup's call for help."

Arcove's expression was almost fragile, and Halvery wasn't sure he could bear it, so he said lightly, "Dazzle is the one who should be grateful." He shot a sidelong look at Roup. "How is he?"

"Still alive...but awfully sick."

Halvery sighed. *He's not going to escape frostbite after all. I might not have done him any favors by dragging him out of the water.*

Halvery was feeling the gnawing bite of hunger in earnest now, so he started downstream towards the carcass Roup had mentioned. The way was easy to find, given the many animals who'd come and gone from it recently. Halvery took his time walking through the damp, pine-scented dusk. The rain continued to patter on and off among the leaves. The air smelled of spring shoots.

He encountered a few cats returning along the trail, some of them from Arcove's party and some from Shimmer's. He asked their news if he knew their names and learned that Hollygold and Stefan had each lost a cat. Moashi had lost half his clutter. *Well, Arcove did say they'd come back better fighters or not at all.* Carmine hadn't lost any. Neither had Halvery, although his clutter had been in the thick of the fighting and badly mauled. One member had severe injuries that might yet prove fatal. *Considering our odds and the situation we walked into, we did very well,* thought Halvery.

Shimmer's party had lost some animals, although nobody seemed to know exactly how many. More cubs had been born, about half of them dead or premature. Ash and Flurry's infant, however, seemed to be thriving.

No one had any clear idea of the state of their enemies, except that there were numerous dead bodies scattered over the valley. Halvery heard variously that Macex was dead, that he'd escaped, that Kelsy had killed him in single combat, and that he had killed Kelsy. "That's not true," he said when he heard the last. "Kelsy was talking to Storm when I left the clearing."

Halvery didn't encounter any ferryshaft. As far as he could tell, they had left the big game for the creasia to eat, since they could live on greenery or smaller prey. For this, Halvery was grateful.

By the time he reached the ox, it was full dark. He was relieved to see plenty of good meat still on the carcass, and he swiftly made a place for himself among the animals worrying at it. Creasia were instinctively possessive of food, particularly when they were dining among cats who were not from their den or clutter. Halvery put his head down in the bloody abdomen, ripping off chunks from the interior, and snarling at anyone who came near him. When at last he looked up, he found that he was alone, save for a single curb, feeding at the far end.

Halvery backed away from the kill, feeling better than he had in days. He began a thorough grooming of his person, starting with the ox blood on his face, paws, and shoulders, and then moving on to the scratches and bites of battle and the blood of enemies, still stiff in his fur.

When he looked up again, the curb had come around the carcass, and he saw that it was Cohal. He spoke the moment Halvery raised his head. "I did not get an opportunity to thank you for pulling Storm out of the flood." The words came out flat and fast, as though the curb had been steeling himself to say them.

Halvery snorted. "Well, don't strain yourself."

Cohal continued as though he'd swallowed something bitter, "It was my fault that he fell."

Oh, this is interesting. Halvery's first instinct was to rub it in a little, but he was feeling fed and rested, and everything that had happened in the last two days was still fluttering around inside him like birds trying to find a place to land. He said, "Have I redeemed myself, then?"

Cohal's eyes flicked to his face as though to gauge whether he was serious. When Halvery just looked at him, he turned away, shoulders hunched with discomfort. He started worrying at the ox carcass again. "Why would an alpha creasia care what a nearly-extinct minor predator thinks of him?" he muttered.

"Well, when you put it like that, it does seem pretty silly."

Cohal didn't laugh. He didn't look up from the rib he'd tugged loose, although he wasn't trying to eat.

Halvery stretched out on his stomach. "I am sorry that I and my clutter killed your packmates fifteen years ago. I'm sorry that we never officially acknowledged Eyal's sacrifice. You are right that if he hadn't helped free the ferryshaft, we all would probably have died on Kuwee Island."

Cohal turned to stare at him. At last, he said, "Do you know how members of the long patrol were chosen, Halvery?"

Halvery was surprised. "You mean, the highland curbs who came down to the plain?"

"Yes."

"No, I don't suppose I know that."

"Troublemakers," said Cohal. "Curbs who couldn't get along with anyone, who tried to mate out of turn, who didn't follow orders, who made mistakes that might have warranted death. We were so few that good fighters could not be sacrificed…even when they deserved it. So our queen sent such animals away to fight on distant plains and die far from home."

Halvery went perfectly still.

Cohal still wasn't looking at him. "I killed a packmate. Because I lost my temper. So my queen sent me away. And I deserved it."

For the first time, Halvery actually felt sorry for him. He also felt an odd stirring of what he suspected Roup would call "kinship."

"Eyal, though," continued Cohal. "He wasn't exiled for misbehavior. He would have been chosen for breeding rights. But he knew that we curbs were in trouble if we didn't establish a population outside the mountains. He knew the ice was melting, that we wouldn't be able to hold off our enemies forever. So he chose exile. He left a promising future and all his friends to come down to the plains with a pack of misfits who'd made terrible mistakes. He knew what I'd done, but he made me his beta, and he…trusted me. He treated every one of us as though we were precious. In the hierarchy of the valley, we were nothing, but he kept telling us we mattered, and we believed him."

Cohal stopped talking.

Halvery wondered what it must have been like—to be exiled as the most expendable members of the population, and then to discover that they were all that remained.

"*I* should have died that night," said Cohal softly, "not him." He drew a deep breath. "This was never your fault, Halvery Elacreasia. You are just conveniently loud and…combative."

Halvery laughed. "I've got a temper that gets me into trouble."

Cohal kept his eyes on his paws.

"I don't know whether you know this, but Eyal died in my territory."

"I do know this," said Cohal without looking up.

"We never moved the bodies," said Halvery. "There were several curbs. As far as I know, a few bones are still there. We could take them to the Ghost Wood. I don't know whether that's mean-

ingful to you, but if you want creasia to acknowledge his sacrifice…
that's how we would do it."

Cohal cocked his head. "I would like that."

"Also," continued Halvery, "Storm thinks we should write the names of those we've lost in order to honor them. I don't like the idea of writing creasia names in the ferryshaft caves, so I'm thinking about creating some spot for this in my territory. There's a cliff wall on one of the little islands offshore of my den…" He was feeling his way along as he said it, testing the idea.

Cohal's ears came up and something flickered in his eyes. Halvery continued with more confidence, "You could write Eyal's name there if you like."

Cohal's tail waved once. He hesitated and then came forward, ears and tail low. "I also apologize, Halvery Ela-creasia. I have been ungenerous and unreasonable, which is not at all what Eyal would have wanted."

"Oh, don't apologize to me," said Halvery cheerfully. "You'll never forgive yourself." He got to his feet. "Come on; I'll walk you back to your pack. What are you doing out here by yourself anyway? We didn't bring you all the way through the mountains so that you could get picked off by lowland curbs while coming and going from an ice ox."

Cohal gave a miserable snort. "It will surely not surprise you to learn that I had a fight with Moali."

"What about? The color of the sky?"

"You are insufferable."

"I'm practically famous for it."

"I want to stay up here. I want to join the curbs on the islands. She doesn't think I should."

"Well…" Halvery considered. "At least come down long enough to write Eyal's name and help us take him to the Ghost Wood."

Cohal smiled. "I will do this, Halvery."

So Proud of You

Five days later, Roup woke in the early evening. He rose without a wobble, stretched beside Halvery and Lyndi, who were still fast asleep, and padded towards the murmur of Arcove's voice beyond the trees.

The sky had been completely clear today, the sun bright outside their nest in the sleepy noon. Ferryshaft had been coming and going at that time, chattering to each other before heading down out of the mountains. They'd departed now, taking some dozen highland curbs with them, and leaving the creasia and a few injured ferryshaft, who planned to make the descent more slowly.

Arcove was standing in the clearing amid the glow of early dusk, talking to an enormous eagle. Roup still felt a jolt whenever he saw one up close. This animal might have almost carried off an adult creasia in its talons. It was listening while Arcove spoke of his plans to bring his cats down in stages, owing to the injured among them, and the newborn cubs. He said that their enemies had been scattered and their numbers greatly reduced. He did not think there was danger of further hostilities at the moment. He finished with, "So you can tell Keesha that we'll be at the lake in ten or fifteen days, a month at most, and we're alright."

The bird cocked its head at him and made a low trilling noise. Arcove sighed. "Tell him that *I* am alright."

Roup could have sworn that the ely-ary laughed. Then it spread its wings, and Arcove stepped back as it leapt into the sky.

Roup padded up beside him and rubbed his face against Arcove's shoulder.

Arcove grumbled under his breath. "You can stop laughing at me."

"I wasn't."

"It's the third one in as many days; they are making everyone nervous."

"And now you have given it the necessary information," said Roup with a twinkle.

"I suppose I should be glad that Keesha doesn't feel the need to check on me every time I leave my den in Leeshwood. To have those things following one around? It would play on anyone's nerves."

Roup leaned against him. "The only thing worse than having Keesha for a friend is having him for an enemy."

Arcove started to say something. Then he just laughed. He turned and rubbed his face against Roup's nose. "How's the leg?"

"Fine. Well, it's stiff, but it's always stiff when I wake up. Are we still having a council meeting at sunset?"

Arcove had told everyone last night that he intended to discuss the disposition of the creasia from the Southern Mountains this evening. He'd allowed no discussion of the topic earlier while the two groups were still counting their losses and getting to know one another. However, if they were to start down out of the mountains, they needed a functioning chain of command. New additions to Leeshwood needed to know whose clutter they were in and who their commanding officers were. In the unlikely event that they were attacked, they needed to know where to look for leadership.

All of the officers had met Shimmer at this point, along with many of her cats. They'd even met a few of the males who'd come slinking in with their tails between their legs. Arcove's officers were not without sympathy for these creasia, but they also knew that there would be altercations between the existing residents of Leeshwood and newcomers with such a charged history. Integrating these cats would be a great deal of work, especially since they wanted to stay together. Roup expected a heated discussion in council. And that didn't even touch on the biggest point of contention: Dazzle.

He'd come and gone from Leeshwood as a spy for years. He'd injured some of his rivals, leaving them with smoldering grudges. He'd been publicly denounced as a traitor, and then tried to kill the most beloved officer in Leeshwood. Dazzle was certain to be a focal point for violence, discontent, and division, even if he did not wish it.

Of course, Roup's opinion in this matter was well-known, and everyone had heard about events on the ice. Dazzle had paid a high price to come to Roup's defense. He'd been sheltering with his den-mates since the battle, mostly delirious by all accounts. He had blackened toes and patches of frostbitten skin sloughing off.

Dazzle had sustained terrible injuries saving Roup's life, but most of the officers seemed to regard this as no more than justice. It did not alter the fact that he would be a difficult addition to any clutter. Roup wasn't looking forward to the debate. He wasn't looking forward to the way the others were going to look at him, or the concessions he might have to make to find a place for Dazzle anywhere in Leeshwood.

Arcove had kept his own opinion on the matter opaque. No one knew what he wanted for Dazzle, not even Roup. He hadn't killed him, though, and he'd been checking on him.

"We've got a little while before sunset," he said cheerfully. "Let's see if we can get rid of that limp."

So they walked up the ridge and then along the edge of the valley, through pines where they'd played tag with Halvery a few days past and also thirty-six years ago with Coden. Evening light was making the rim of the sky glow golden, fading into clear blue overhead. The valley gleamed below with a combination of spring green, blue ice, and black rock. Roup could see all the way to the tumble of the slots in the clear evening air, the sweep of the valley drawing the eyes upward to the higher crags beyond. *It's difficult country,* he thought, *but so beautiful.*

Soon his muscles warmed up and his limp vanished. Arcove didn't want to talk about the council meeting. He certainly didn't want to talk about Dazzle. Instead, he talked about new plans he'd been making with Kelsy. "I'd like all the ferryshaft to come visit us at least once a year, even if there is not a Volontaro. I would like some sort of friendly interaction between Leeshwood and the big herds, so that they do not think of us as abstractions, but as individuals. As friends. I wish I could think of some group project or even a friendly competition."

"Lyndi and I have an idea," said Roup.

"What's that?"

"Common way trails all around the island."

Arcove considered. "An interesting notion." They talked about this as they jogged back to the clearing. The daylight was fading, and the council would be gathering beside the waterfall.

"Did you invite Shimmer?" asked Roup at last.

Arcove glanced at him sidelong. "No. I don't want the officers to mince words in order to spare anyone's feelings. I want them to speak their minds."

Roup quirked a smile. "You don't want them to spare her feelings…or you already know where she's going?"

Arcove's ears flattened in a rare show of discomfort. He stretched out on his stomach above the waterfall, watching Stefan and Hollygold chatting beside the basin.

When he did not continue, Roup said, "Have you asked her yet?"

Arcove looked at him guiltily. "No. I thought I should ask you first."

Roup was surprised. "Why?"

"You're my den-mate."

"Oh…" Roup hadn't gotten used to that yet. "So I am." A warm sense of belonging flooded his chest and he started to purr. He stretched out against Arcove. "In that case, I advise you to ask Nadine."

"Of course. But I'm certain she'll say yes after she meets Shimmer. She'd be an asset to any den. If I'm going to take these cats into Leeshwood at all, it's imperative that I avoid another rebellion. I need to integrate them, so that they do not seem like outsiders. Taking one of them into my den would go a long way towards showing my acceptance and respect."

"Yes, of course," said Roup with a hint of sarcasm. "Good politicking."

Arcove ignored his tone. "Also, there's the cub. It was born yesterday. It's male. If I raise this cub, who is not my own, it will set an example to these cats of the behavior I expect from them. The last thing I want is a return to the old ways." Arcove hesitated. "I raised my rival's cubs when I took my den, but that was decades ago. No one has seen me raise another male's cub in a long time. Maybe I need to set that example again."

Roup smiled. *I am so proud of you.* But when he spoke, his voice was full of mischief. "All very sound reasoning. Wise, kingly, self-sacrificing."

Arcove's tail lashed. "You can stop with the condescension."

"You could just say that you like her."

Arcove looked uncertain again.

Roup hated making him look like that, so he said, "I would be an utter hypocrite to tell you not to mate with anyone you like. You have, after all, put up with my odd tastes."

Arcove laughed and the uncertainty vanished. "You should ask Halvery to go hunting with us sometime."

"Perhaps we will get trapped in a cave during a flood."

"Perhaps." Arcove shifted his paws. "Shimmer might say no."

"I doubt that," said Roup.

"In any case," continued Arcove, "she will be occupied for two or three years, raising that cub. She won't be ready to breed until he's weaned. If, in that time, she decides she doesn't want a litter of mine, she can go somewhere else. Meanwhile, she'll be perfectly positioned to advocate for her cats during their critical adjustment."

"You are so good," whispered Roup against his ear.

Arcove chuffed.

"Raising Serot's cub will also put Dazzle at your feet," continued Roup. "They were close."

"I believe Dazzle is already at my feet," said Arcove dryly. He rose and shook himself. "Also, I'd like him to attend this council meeting."

Roup's eyes widened in surprise. "You're not serious."

"Perfectly serious."

"I'm not sure he can walk."

Arcove had an odd glint in his eyes. "Well, we'll just see."

Roup followed him, wondering, down off the ridge and a little way into the forest, along a tiny spring stream, fed by snowmelt. At last, they reached a sandy rock grotto. It was the time of evening when creasia went out to hunt. Dazzle's den-mates were all away, save for one of the scrawny three-year-olds, who was curled up against him near the water.

Dazzle looked a mess, with patches of missing fur and the telling blisters of frostbite scattered over his body. His ears and toes were practically hairless, the lower half of his tail likewise.

"Dazzle," rumbled Arcove.

Dazzle raised his head. He stared at them in confusion with eyes that were fever-bright. Then he saw Roup and struggled to his feet.

Roup wanted to tell him to lie back down, but he suspected that Arcove would say otherwise.

The cub fell over as Dazzle stirred. She sat up and blinked at them.

"You're coming to a council meeting," said Arcove. "I don't expect you'll need to say much. You'll be back sometime tonight."

The cub looked fearful and Roup crouched down to say gently, "We'll bring him back, Aila."

Dazzle swallowed. His voice came out rough with illness. "A council meeting with whom?"

"Just my officers," said Arcove, as though that were a triviality.

Dazzle seemed to fold in on himself. Roup could only imagine how vulnerable he must feel—barely able to stand, burning with fever, certainly not thinking clearly, and facing cats whom he'd tricked and threatened, who had every reason to want him dead or worse.

"Arcove..." began Roup.

Arcove ignored him. "They've probably already gathered. Let's not keep them waiting."

Dazzle came forward, head low, ears flat, tail almost brushing the ground. Arcove and Roup walked on either side of him to keep him from weaving. Roup looked at Arcove over Dazzle's shoulders and Arcove murmured, "Trust me."

The council had, indeed, already gathered beside the waterfall. They were retelling the highlights of the battle and speculating about when they might arrive home, when Arcove walked into their midst. He nudged Dazzle into the middle of the circle, then sat down with Roup on the edge. "Discuss."

A moment of startled silence.

Dazzle kept his eyes on his paws. He was breathing quickly. Finally, he crouched down and wrapped his pitiful tail around his haunches.

Roup thought he understood what Arcove was doing. Most of the officers hadn't gotten more than a glimpse of Dazzle since Leeshwood. The image they had in their heads was of a wily, confident, dangerous spy, taunting them and threatening their authority. The cat they saw in front of them inspired none of these feelings.

Roup looked sidelong at Arcove. *And you took me walking this evening to get rid of my limp...so that no one would see me and think, "Dazzle needs to be punished for that."*

Halvery was looking almost concerned. He shot Roup an incredulous glance, as though to say, "He's in no shape to be here; what are you doing?"

Trust me, thought Roup.

Stefan was the first to collect himself. He looked at Arcove across the circle, deliberately averting his eyes from Dazzle. "I'll take some of Thistle's cats, sir. Most of them came from my territory originally. They came from Treace's old dens, and they still have family and friends there. They're my cats in a sense. So I'll take the females and some of the males. But not all of them, and definitely not *him!* Surely you can see why. If a new rebellion is likely to foment anywhere in Leeshwood, it's in my territory, among those dens. These cats have support in that region and a long history of grievances. Dazzle had followers. They'll come back to him. If he tells them to do one thing, and I tell them to do something else, it will cause a rift." He finished with an earnest tone, tinged with defiance.

Arcove inclined his head, acknowledging Stefan and showing no inclination to argue with him. His eyes wandered around the circle. Hollygold cleared his throat and said lazily, "Can we just wait and see whether he's going to live before having this argument?"

That got a laugh out of Stefan and Halvery, and a grim smile from Carmine. Dazzle hunched up a little and pulled himself into a ball. Roup felt so sorry for him. *Arcove is doing you a favor, Dazzle. I know it doesn't feel like it. These jokes show that the officers are seeing you as less of a serious threat.*

"I think there will be a lot of fights if you put any of these cats in my clutter, Arcove," said Halvery. "I'm not refusing, but...a lot of fights. As for *him,*" he inclined his head at Dazzle, "he crippled one of my officers, who had many friends. I think putting Dazzle in my clutter would be a death sentence."

"Which is what he deserves," muttered Stefan.

Hollygold sighed. "I'll take some of Thistle's creasia, Arcove, but not the ones who were alive during the rebellion. There was bad blood between Ariand's clutter and Treace's. Those cats killed Ariand in a horrible manner. His command has never forgotten it. I don't care how sorry the perpetrators are, how they've suffered, or even whether they were personally involved in Ariand's death. If they fought on the wrong side in the rebellion, they can't come to my territory, because my cats would kill them." He glanced at Dazzle. "I'm definitely not taking him."

Carmine spoke up, "I'll take them, sir, but..." He hesitated.

"That's a bad idea," said Lyndi quietly. "Your leadership is too new, Carmine. You're off to a splendid start, but Roup's clutter has always been small. These cats would nearly double it. Diluting your loyal followers with that many unknown elements would be unwise this early in your leadership." She hesitated. "Of course, the ultimate decision is yours, and I will support you."

Carmine smiled at her. "Sir, I would never disdain your advice. I'm certain you are right."

"It sounds like we might be able to successfully split them among our territories on a case-by-case basis," said Stefan. "I know they want to stay together, Arcove, but that may not be possible. Not unless you order it, in which case, I'm sure the unlucky winner will do his best. Maybe Hollygold is right, and we should wait and see whether Dazzle lives before we worry about where he might go. Perhaps you could find something for him to do outside of Leeshwood. He seems prone to wandering."

A murmur of assent ran around the circle. Dazzle looked like he wanted to fold up and disappear.

"I'll take all of them." It was Moashi. He'd been listening to the debate with his head down. He'd been quiet and withdrawn ever since losing his beta and other friends in the battle, but now he lifted his chin and looked squarely at Stefan. "I'll take all of them," he repeated, "and Dazzle is technically my officer, so I believe I ought to be consulted before he's assigned elsewhere." His eyes roamed defiantly around the group.

They stared back at him in various postures of surprise.

Even Dazzle lifted his head and turned to look at Moashi.

Moashi returned his stare. "Dazzle, come here."

He came, bristling with nerves, slinking and unsteady. His gaze dropped to Moashi's paws.

Moashi said, "I owe you an apology."

That made them all pause again.

Dazzle was sufficiently shocked to raise his eyes to Moashi's face.

Moashi drew a deep breath and continued, "You were one of my cats, but I never treated you like one. From the moment you entered my territory, I started plotting to kill you. I didn't try to talk to you. I didn't give you the benefit of the doubt. You crippled Lusha. You made Stefan and Halvery nervous. Roup was playing the kind of games with you that only Roup can play. So I was afraid of you. I didn't treat you like one of my cats. I treated you like an enemy from the moment I saw you."

Dazzle cleared his throat. His voice came out soft and rough. "Moashi...I stirred up your clutter against you. I made them doubt your authority and fitness to lead. Then I tried to kill you in a fight. You don't owe me a thing."

Moashi flicked his tail. "You challenged me. We fought. I won. That should have been the end of it. But I encouraged cats to lie about you—to say you fought beside Treace on Kuwee Island when you didn't—so that a mob would murder you. Arcove has made it clear that he thinks this behavior was shameful, and he is right. You were mine, and I had an obligation to you that I did not fulfill, and I am sorry."

Dazzle looked overwhelmed. He actually wobbled as though he might fall over, and crouched to get his balance. In an uncertain voice, he muttered, "Forgive me, I feel that I may be having a fever dream, and none of this is real."

Moashi smiled. "It's real." His eyes rose above Dazzle's head. "Furthermore, I need to apologize to Roup and to this whole council, because much of what happened two years ago was my fault. Roup wanted Dazzle to know that he *couldn't* beat us, but that he *could* trust us. I undermined the second half of that message. I don't think Dazzle would have tried to kill Roup if he hadn't been running for his life from a mob of murderous liars. He didn't believe we could be trusted to show mercy to him or to his cats, and it's easy to see why."

Dazzle laid his chin on the ground at Moashi's feet. All around the circle, officers were watching in complete stillness. The gush of the waterfall sounded loud in the silence.

Moashi continued, "We all tell a story about the things that happen to us. This version of events is not the story Roup has chosen to tell, and that's kind of him. He has allowed you all to disparage his judgment, when, in fact, he probably would have succeeded if not for me. He has diverted blame away from me, because he thinks I'm young, that I deserve second chances, and that I'll make a good alpha one day. I hope he's right. But the story I have told is also true. Dazzle is still one of my officers. In fact, at this point, he may be my beta." Moashi swallowed. "Halvery and Roup say that I need a sharper one."

Halvery gave a snort that sounded suspiciously like laughter. There was a faint ease of tension in the group.

Moashi flashed him a relieved smile. "Sharp enough for you, sir?"

"So sharp you'll cut yourself," said Halvery dryly.

Roup shot a searching look at Arcove, who was keeping his eyes on Moashi. *You knew some of this would happen...but not all of it.* He thought Arcove actually looked impressed.

"Anyway," continued Moashi, "my clutter is elderly. I could use more cats in their prime, more breeding females, more young males who know how to fight. So I'll take Thistle's creasia, or Shimmer's cats, or whatever we're calling them."

"I think we're calling them yours," said Roup with a smile.

Moashi grinned at him. His eyes shifted to Arcove. "Permission to take him back to his sleeping place, sir?"

Arcove inclined his head.

Moashi turned back to Dazzle. "Come on, I'll walk with you." Half under his breath, he muttered, "I cannot *believe* they made you come to council like this."

"I really may not live," whispered Dazzle.

"Don't say that. And don't fall over. No, turn around; you're going the wrong way."

"Sorry. I feel as though my head is not attached to my body."

A hint of levity: "You're walking like it, too."

"You know, I used your move...when I dropped Thistle through the ice. Went straight up and landed on top of him."

"That's Storm's move."

Dazzle gave a ragged laugh. "Of course it is."

Their voices faded as they moved away, Dazzle weaving, Moashi gently turning him when he started in the wrong direction. The entire council watched them go in stunned silence.

Roup felt a warm glow of satisfaction. *Good cub,* he thought. *I am so proud of you.*

37

Cubs

Halvery sat in the mouth of his den on a day in early summer, chatting with Stefan, and watching his cats spar with some of their visitors. They were waiting for Roup, Lyndi, and Wisteria to arrive. The latter had asked to speak to Halvery and Stefan together "on den council business." Halvery wasn't sure what that meant. He hoped it wasn't going to involve an argument that might ruin Roup's visit.

Halvery and Roup hadn't seen each other in most of a month because Halvery had led the vanguard of Arcove's party out of the mountains. It had seemed prudent that some of the officers return to Leeshwood sooner rather than later, so Halvery had taken a select company down in advance of the slower group that included injured cats and females with newborn cubs. Roup and Arcove had traveled in the rear, reaching Leeshwood a full twelve days behind Halvery.

He'd sent a message to Roup the moment he heard they'd arrived: "Come to my den." It was all he would allow the messenger to say. He had no doubt that Roup was awash in nervous curiosity.

It was midnight by the time his guests appeared. Halvery was only slightly surprised to see that Caraca had come with them. She was carrying a fluffy oory kitten, which Halvery chose to ignore. Caraca always seemed to have an oory about her.

The night was beautiful and clear with a full moon. Halvery called, "Ilsa, they're here!" before trotting up to Roup and rubbing his nose against the side of his face.

Roup laughed nervously. "I suppose this means the cubs are born? And you're not too disappointed? I wish you'd stop being so mysterious."

"I wish Ilsa would," complained Caraca. "They were born fourteen days ago, but she won't let anyone see them."

"She let *me* see them," said Halvery sweetly. "Velta, too. And I'm told Wisteria came by."

"I *would* have let you see them, Caraca, if you'd come in person," said Ilsa, emerging from the shadows of the den. She looked lean and rangy, the way nursing females always looked. "I just swore everyone to secrecy, because I didn't want rumors flying before Roup arrived." She caught sight of Wisteria and beamed. "Wist! Do you want to help me carry them? Halvery, you too. Roup, sit. Caraca, you sit as well. Lyndi, do as you like."

Lyndi laughed.

Roup lay down on his belly, looking baffled. Halvery, Wisteria, and Ilsa trotted into the den, back to Ilsa's nest to retrieve the cubs. Their high-pitched mews filled the air as Halvery picked one up by the scruff. He carried it outside, laid the cub between Roup's front paws, and sat back.

Roup stared down at it. The cub was fuzzy and bobble-headed, just starting to open its eyes. It was also honey-gold—the color of a flower, of the hunter's moon, of Roup. Its tiny pink paw pads flailed as it tried to stand and toppled over.

Caraca trilled in delight. She stretched out beside Roup and put her nose between his paws to examine the cub from all angles. At last, she turned to look at Lyndi with an expression of glee. "We did it!"

"I beg your pardon," said Halvery in mock indignation.

"Technically, I believe Ilsa and Roup did it," said Lyndi sagely.

"I was heavily involved," objected Halvery.

"You never would have managed it without me," said Caraca coolly.

Roup said nothing. Halvery didn't think he'd ever seen him so dumbstruck.

Ilsa had been watching from the shadows. Now she emerged with a second golden cub and laid it between Roup's paws. She gave him a lick on the nose. "Twins. Both male. I told you we'd make amazing cubs."

Roup's eyes got even bigger. He stared up at her, back down at the cubs.

Ilsa looked almost sorry for him. "What did you expect? Say something, Roup; you're starting to make me nervous."

Roup cleared his throat. "Thank you," he whispered, "for… putting up with my constant whining."

Ilsa burst out laughing. "You really didn't."

"Only for the last half of their conception," said Halvery critically.

"Just the last quarter, surely," said Ilsa.

They both laughed, and Roup's ears dropped a fraction. Ilsa leaned down and rubbed her face against his. "You are ever and always charming, sir."

"No sirs, please." He couldn't seem to drag his eyes from the cubs.

"There's one more," said Halvery, "and she is definitely mine."

Wisteria brought out the last cub. She had Halvery's brindled, earth-brown coat. She was just beginning to show traces of darker color on her paws, tail, and face, which would darken into points as she grew older.

All the adults sat in silence for a few moments, admiring the cubs, who looked plump and healthy. Stefan had come forward cautiously, as though unsure of whether to invite himself into this domestic scene. Other creasia who'd been sparing were craning their necks, but they were too polite to intrude.

"There was one more," said Ilsa quietly, "but something was wrong with it. Don't ask me whose it was; I couldn't tell."

"Tithe to the Ghost Wood," said Halvery somberly. "That's good luck. Means we've paid our dues and the rest will live."

"That's nonsense, Halvery," said Caraca.

Halvery flicked his short tail. "It's what the old den mothers say."

"Because it makes a good story, because they want to make you feel better. I think we've all got some dangerous traits hidden inside of us, and sometimes they come together poorly."

"Well, obviously," said Halvery. "Roup and I have dangerous traits that have come together poorly on more than one occasion."

"That's not what I—" began Caraca and then she just laughed. She turned to locate the oory kitten, who was playing with her tail. "Halvery, this is one of the results of Munchy and Brindlefluff's pairing."

"Oh!" Halvery came over to examine the scrap of downy fluff, so absurdly tiny for a cat. "Will it have the long hair?"

"I think so, but I'm not sure yet. It definitely has the green eyes."

"Which means you were right about the eye color, but you're not sure about the fur."

"Correct. Anyway, it's a female, and I already have the maximum number of females who will tolerate each other around my den, so..."

Halvery backed away. "Oh, no..."

"You want to see whether it's going to have the long fur, don't you?"

"Caraca..."

She adopted a stubborn expression. "Every one of Roup's cubs has been raised with oory kittens, Halvery. Every single one." She dropped the kitten between Roup's paws, where it immediately cuddled up with the cubs.

"That doesn't mean it was good for them!" exploded Halvery.

"Are you saying that my mother was poorly raised?" interjected Wisteria.

Halvery turned to Ilsa, who said immediately, "I don't mind."

He made a face.

Caraca looked at him in exasperation. "You *liked* learning about coat color, Halvery. I've never seen someone else so interested in it. She'll have other unique traits in her blood, too. I think there's orange in there somewhere. Are you just so proud of your ill-tempered reputation that you can't lower yourself to be seen with a kitten?"

"No!" shot Halvery. "I just think someone will kill it." He hesitated and added with less certainty, "And then you will hate me."

"Oh." Caraca got up and came to stand by him. She actually rubbed her head against his shoulder. She was not usually so demonstrative. "No, of course not. Things happen sometimes; I know that. But I've found that kittens get along well with cubs."

Halvery made a grumbling sound. "Fine. Alright."

They all contemplated the odd tableau of the kitten settling down with the cubs between Roup's paws. Roup was still looking at them as though the rest of the world had ceased to exist.

"I wish my mother could have come," said Caraca quietly.

"Is she…still with us?" asked Halvery.

"Oh, yes. She just couldn't manage the journey."

"The cubs should be robust enough to handle a trip to Arcove's den by late summer," said Halvery. "Do you think…?"

"I think she'll be waiting," said Caraca with a twinkle.

"The one with Halvery's coloring…" began Ilsa. "She'll look a lot like Nadine when she's grown. I thought I might…might name her in honor of your mother, Caraca…if she wouldn't be offended."

"I think she'll be flattered," said Caraca happily.

"It's bad luck to name them this young," muttered Halvery.

"Luck has nothing to do with it," said Caraca. She gave him a sly smile and said, "Besides, I thought you already paid your tithe to the Ghost Wood."

Halvery rolled his eyes.

Wisteria cleared her throat. "Stefan, I'm sorry to make you feel like an outsider here. Thank you for coming."

Stefan smiled. "No need to apologize. I am honored to have gotten a look at these cubs, who are sure to be the talk of the forest."

Wisteria's smile showed her teeth. "Don't thank us yet. Ilsa and I solved your den dispute while you were away."

Stefan looked up sharply.

So did Halvery. "They were fighting *again?*"

"Shortly after you departed, yes."

Stefan gave a low hiss of frustration and Halvery growled. "Why haven't I been told? I've been back for twelve days; why hasn't anyone mentioned it?"

"Because we solved it," said Wisteria patiently. "The dens involved *asked* for my council's opinion. Stefan's alpha den mother came to our meeting. I asked Velta if she wanted to attend herself, or whether she would rather send a representative from Halvery's den. Ilsa volunteered."

Halvery had a mental image of his young, heavily pregnant mate walking into the middle of an ugly den dispute. "You took her over there just before she gave birth?!"

Wisteria started to answer, but Ilsa got there first, "Do not talk about me as though I am not standing right here, Halvery! I was not about to give birth. This is my territory as much as yours. I have every right to go help with a den dispute."

Halvery sputtered.

Stefan had his ears back. He looked like he was mentally rehearsing every objection he'd ever had regarding den councils and preparing his speech to Arcove.

"Would you like to hear what we learned?" said Wisteria with exaggerated patience.

"Yes," said Stefan sourly. "Please tell us what you've done so that we can figure out how to undo it."

"I'm assuming you split that thicket yet again?" asked Halvery. "We've split it along every imaginable line. You've probably just moved the boundary back to where it was before."

"No," said Ilsa primly. "We did not. We've given the thicket to Stefan's cats for the time being."

"What?" Halvery was confused.

"Here's what we concluded after talking to them," said Wisteria. "They don't want the thicket. They don't want a fair boundary line. They *want* to *fight*."

A long beat, and then Halvery burst out laughing. "Well, that's obvious, but—"

"No, no, listen to what I am saying," said Wisteria. "You can't give either den what they want by negotiating peace, because they don't want peace. They like scrapping!"

Even Stefan looked vaguely amused. "So, in your infinite wisdom, you gave them permission to scrap?"

"In a limited fashion, yes. We had a tournament. Stefan's den won."

Halvery bristled. "They *what?*"

"They won," said Wisteria, "although yours put up stiff resistance."

"Stiff resistance?" said Halvery with contempt.

Stefan suddenly looked like he was in a better mood. "Who was in this tournament?"

Wisteria rattled off a list of names, occasionally corrected by Ilsa. "You should have seen the final match, Stefan. I believe it involved one of your grandcubs. It was very exciting. Nobody was hurt. I told them they would forfeit if they seriously injured anyone."

Halvery looked balefully at Stefan, who was now smirking. "Don't worry, Halvery," he said sweetly, "it sounds like your den tried very hard."

"I am going down there tomorrow night and give them a few lessons," grumbled Halvery.

"Well, they'll get a chance to use those," said Wisteria, "because the deal we made with them is this: we'll hold another tournament every spring, awarding the thicket to the winner for one year. If they fight with each other out of turn, we've threatened to create a new common way trail through that area. Then the thicket will belong to no one."

Lyndi cackled with laughter. "That is brilliant, Wisteria. Ilsa, you're going to be such a good mother."

"So you can both go coach them if you feel your pride is at stake," continued Wisteria to Halvery and Stefan. "Or you can leave them to their own devices, because, frankly, they've taken up enough of your time and attention. But either way, they get to scrap and no one gets hurt. I can tell you that all the witnesses were highly entertained."

A moment of silence. Stefan and Halvery looked at each other sidelong. At last, Stefan said, "Well…" But then he didn't seem to know how to continue.

"If you are displeased with what we've done, feel free to go divide the thicket again," said Wisteria. "We are guests in your territory and in no way intend to countermand your authority. We've given our solution, and if it doesn't suit—"

"I believe," said Stefan slowly, "that there may be a place for den council consultation in the settlement of some disputes…"

"You're only saying that because yours won!" snapped Halvery.

Stefan gave him a guileless smile. "If you want to redraw the boundary line…"

"No, no, we'll just see what happens next spring."

One of the cubs had begun sucking on Roup's toe pad. Ilsa sighed. "They are hungry constantly." She lay down on her side in front of Roup, and the cubs tottered towards her, mewing joyfully.

Roup seemed to come out of his daze. He stood up and then bent to wash Ilsa's face.

Caraca and Lyndi came forward to have a closer look at the cubs.

Stefan said, "I would like to hear the details of this tournament."

Wisteria was an excellent judge of fights. She was a skilled combatant herself, Carmine's mate, and she watched her grandfather, Arcove, spar frequently. She launched into a detailed technical break-down of the matches, while Stefan listened with fascination.

Halvery sidled up to Roup, "Go for a run with me?" he whispered.

Roup looked around at him, still with that big-eyed, lost expression. "Alright."

38

At Your Feet

They loped along the edge of the lake. The night was peaceful, the hour very quiet with the full moon laying a bright trail across the water. Halvery considered pointing out the island a little off-shore where he planned to create a writing wall. But he felt that he needed to get Roup talking instead, so he said, "How's Dazzle?"

Roup shook himself. His eyes came back into focus. "Better. He's lost two toes and part of his tail."

Halvery chuffed. "However will he live without a tail?"

Roup smiled faintly. "It's not as short as yours, but it's notice-able. His ears are pretty chewed up, but the fur is starting to grow back, and his fever is gone."

"If the fever is gone, he's going to live," pronounced Halvery. "Does he have a limp?"

Roup rocked his head. "His gait is uneven because of the toes."

"Losing his tail will alter his balance," said Halvery seriously. "You don't realize how much you use it until it's gone."

"I'm sure," said Roup. "But he's already starting to compen-sate. Give him a year. I think he'll be walking on air again."

"Well..." muttered Halvery, "he deserves a limp, but...I sup-pose it would be a shame. And he'd be less useful to Moashi."

Roup smiled. "Moashi could not ask for a more devoted beta." He laughed. "Or a sharper one."

"Good. Moashi is skilled for a cat of his size, but he's always going to be at a disadvantage in fights against bigger opponents. And he's got that unfortunate tendency to second guess himself. If cats know they'd have to face Dazzle before or afterward, they'll be less likely to challenge Moashi at all."

"Agreed," said Roup. "I do think there are likely to be some fights. I heard that Lusha is not happy to learn that Dazzle is his new commanding officer, and other cats in the clutter are declaring that they won't share space with Thistle's creasia, particularly if more of the males show up. You'll have a few of Moashi's cats applying to join your dens and clutters, I expect."

Halvery flicked his tail. "Well, they're welcome. But they're making a mistake." He butted his head against Roup's shoulder. "That situation will sort itself out, Roup. Moashi can handle it. Dazzle is hard to kill."

"I know."

"Is Shimmer going to stay in Arcove's den, or did she decide to go to Moashi's territory with her cats?"

"I believe she intends to stay with Arcove, although we only just arrived, and she's still getting to know Nadine and the others. Shimmer is smart, friendly, and has a good head for leadership. She and Arcove like each other. She'll speak her mind to him, and that's rare these days. I predict she'll end up his alpha den mother after Nadine is gone."

Halvery rolled his eyes. "And you'll get lots of opportunities to talk to Dazzle because he'll be back and forth to visit his sister."

Roup smiled. "Don't forget his friend's cub. He was fairly staggered when he realized that Arcove intends to raise Serot's son in his own den. I think, at first, Dazzle thought Arcove meant to keep the cub as a hostage to his good behavior. Shimmer, too. But then Arcove carried the little thing most of the way back. He and Shimmer talked and talked. And Dazzle changed his mind."

"Did we ever learn what happened to Macex?"

Roup's nose wrinkled. "Multiple accounts say that he took off across the ice when he saw that Kelsy had shown up. Odds are, he's at the bottom of the lake, but he disappeared into the fog, and we can't confirm that. Our best estimates put the remains of Sedaron's army at about four hundred animals, most of them scattered. Kelsy thinks they'll join other herds or form small ones. He doesn't believe they'll try to band together under a single leader and continue Sedaron or Macex's goals."

Halvery shook his ears. "And in the meantime, Kelsy's herd has absorbed most of Sedaron's females and juveniles, along with any survivors who care to join them. Kelsy came out of this in better shape than anyone."

"Storm would agree with you," said Roup dryly. "But I find it hard to believe that Kelsy delayed his assistance in order to improve his position. He really did ask for volunteers. He didn't order any of those ferryshaft to help us."

"And Thistle's creasia?" asked Halvery.

"We think about a third of them are dead," said Roup, "mostly adult males, but also a few females and juveniles. Most of Thistle's officers are accounted for, but one of them, Sundance, is still missing. Dazzle seems to think he is particularly dangerous, so we're keeping an eye out."

They trotted along in silence for a while. Halvery kept glancing at Roup out of the corners of his eyes to see whether he was limping. He wasn't.

They finally arrived at a broad estuary where a stream met the lake. It was Halvery's favorite spot to take his cubs fishing. He leapt from rock to rock across the shallow, fast-moving water, Roup following, and picked a place where the fish were swimming lazily, sleeping in the moonlight.

Roup was a superb fisher. He grabbed one in the blink of an eye and carried it thrashing to the bank. Halvery jumped down into the middle of the school for the sheer joy of it and dashed after them through the shallow water, leaping and spinning like a cub, listening to Roup's laughter. At last, he snapped up a fish and marched to shore, head held high.

As they began to eat, he said, "Was Keesha waiting in the lake? I didn't see him, but I didn't stop to look."

Roup snorted around a mouthful of fish. "Oh, he was waiting. He had to sniff Arcove over and make sure he wasn't mortally wounded."

"You're joking."

"I am, but barely. He sent eagles to check on us almost every day. He lost track of us during the snowstorm, and I think it just about killed him."

Halvery laughed. "Did Arcove tell him to mind his own business?"

Roup smiled. "How do you scold a worried telshee? No. Arcove just told him about our adventure."

"Well, he did save your life without asking for anything," said Halvery. He took a deep breath and steeled himself. "I was thinking... Whenever Nadine is ready to go...if it's not as easy as she'd like...Arcove should ask Keesha to sing her to sleep."

Roup stopped eating. He turned to look at Halvery.

"What good is having a telshee king for a friend if you can't ask for something like that?" persisted Halvery.

"That's a wonderful idea," murmured Roup.

Halvery relaxed. "Well, I do have a good one now and then."

"You have so many good ones." Roup was looking at him with such earnestness that Halvery become uncomfortable and looked away.

"I'm afraid she's going to ask *me* to do it," he muttered. "I know she doesn't want to ask Arcove. He should ask Keesha; it would be painless, probably even pleasant."

"It's a wonderful idea," repeated Roup.

"When she wants to go, of course. I'm not suggesting any time soon."

"Last winter was very hard on her," said Roup. "I don't know whether she wants to do that again."

"She might do it for the chance to talk to your cubs," said Halvery with a grin.

Roup left the remains of his fish and came to sit beside Halvery. "I *am* sorry that I whined so much about that. You did something very kind for me, something unprecedented, and I complained the entire time."

Halvery laughed and leaned against him.

"I can't believe they actually *look* like me," whispered Roup. "It shouldn't matter..."

"Oh, Roup, it's alright to be a little shallow now and then. *I* am almost all the time!"

"You are not remotely shallow." He started to groom Halvery's ears.

Halvery stood up. "Don't start that when I've got fish blood all over me."

"Start what?" asked Roup innocently.

Halvery was feeling confident, so he said, "I wish Arcove had come with you."

Roup's mouth curled. "He did consider it. But he thought you might...prefer things as they are."

Halvery thought about that. "Well...I do like things as they are. But, if there's ever any doubt..." He put his face against Roup's cheek and murmured, "I *love* sharing you with him."

Roup smirked down at this paws. "I told him that. He did say you should come hunting with us sometime."

"Oh, good."

"We might even look for food."

Halvery shook with laughter. But then he turned and splashed into the stream, heading back the way they'd come. "I'm sorry, Roup, but I'm not going to be able to relax out here when I've got such young cubs at home. I don't like going very far away when they're so small."

Roup trotted after him. "Understood."

"I always imagine challengers...fire...hostile ferryshaft... I know it's silly."

Roup caught up and walked beside him. "It's not silly."

"I'll put you on your back somewhere closer to the den."

"You don't have to put me on my back at all."

"Believe me, I want to."

The moon had set, and the stars were very bright. The air smelled of water and the beginnings of verdant summer. "Do you know what you want to name your cubs?" asked Halvery.

Roup laughed. "I had not given it a single thought." He hesitated. "I always let Caraca name my others."

"Well, I'm sure Ilsa will be happy to provide names if you like," said Halvery, "and it really is bad luck to name them so young."

Roup smiled. "Tell me what you're thinking, Halvery."

"Well...my brother...my only littermate..."

"The one who was killed by ferryshaft," said Roup quietly. "Yes, I remember."

"His name was Charsel. We called him Chars." *And I have considered giving that name to so many cubs, but somehow it never felt right.*

"I like that name," murmured Roup.

"And I thought maybe...Coden...for the other one."

Roup stopped walking. He turned to look at Halvery, eyes wide and dark.

"If that isn't a pleasant association—"

"You didn't even like him!" interrupted Roup. And then, more quietly, "He bit off your tail."

Halvery fidgeted. "He was your brother."

Roup looked away.

"Chars and Coden—your brother and mine."

Roup paced back and forth for a moment. Finally he stopped and tucked his head under Halvery's chin. "You are so much better than I ever gave you credit for."

Halvery laughed. "Oh, don't say anything you'll regret."

"I mean it. I have gotten so much more attached to you than I ever expected."

Halvery surprised himself with a brief purr. "You like those names then?"

"I do."

"Not that we're naming them yet. We're just *talking* about naming them."

Roup snickered. "Caraca would give you a lecture about ignorant delusions."

"Happily, Caraca is not here."

"You've truly made friends with her, you know. I can't believe it."

"No, it's like you said. I'm a fellow-investigator…or possibly an experiment."

"No, you are a friend. She has maybe three of them."

"I really hope nobody kills that oory kitten," muttered Halvery.

"I am certain she would not hold it against you."

"I am certain that you are wrong."

They were approaching the den now from the backside. Halvery chose to climb the ridge above it. He thought he heard a sparing match in progress. He dearly hoped it wasn't a real fight. *I'm sorry, Roup. I know you prefer privacy, but I just can't relax out of earshot when I've got young cubs in the den. Your cubs.*

They climbed through the sighing pines with the lake sparkling on their right until at last they were able to look down on the den. To Halvery's relief, there was no real fight occurring. In fact, it looked like all this talk of tournaments had led to an actual one between the cats Stefan had brought and members of Halvery's clutter. Wisteria, Ilsa, and Stefan seemed to be offering pointers and enthusiastic commentary. Caraca and Lyndi were chatting with Velta and Samathi.

Halvery stretched out on his belly to watch. He felt a jolt of anxiety that his cats might not give a good account of themselves and embarrass his clutter yet again. "I am really going to have to evaluate the skills of my border dens," he muttered.

Roup stretched out beside him. Halvery realized, suddenly, that this was where they'd sat that first night, almost two years ago now, watching his cubs spar.

"Are you flirting with me?"

"I might be. Do you want me to be?"

Without taking his eyes off the fight, Halvery said, "You were worried when we started this that cats would disrespect you if they knew you lay down for me."

Roup shifted beside him.

"Are you still worried about that?"

Roup laughed uneasily. "Well, we've got cubs in the same litter now, so…"

"Exactly! Now cats will look at us and say, 'Roup and Halvery are extraordinarily good friends. They even shared a mate. Of course they lie down for each other now and then. Nothing unusual about that.'"

Roup glanced at him sidelong.

"They'll never say, 'Roup lies down for argumentative council members in order to get things done,'" continued Halvery.

Roup choked on a laugh.

"Because those two situations aren't even slightly similar."

"They'll say that you're special," said Roup softly, his tongue tracing the contour of Halvery's ear and along his jaw. "Because you are."

Halvery could almost hear Arcove murmur, *"He's never lain down for anyone else apart from me. You know that, right?"*

Roup nuzzled under his chin. "Did I just hear you say that we lie down for *each other?*"

Halvery squirmed. "Well…general principle."

Roup's tongue ran in long strokes from Halvery's chin to his breastbone.

"I don't think I'd actually like lying down, Roup. I…I think I'd panic."

Roup made a noncommittal noise against his throat. "That one time on the cliff...after you pinned me on my side...you turned over onto your back."

Halvery smiled. "You remember that?"

"I remember everything."

"You put your throat over mine."

"I did."

"That's not lying down, Roup."

"No, but it's what lying down *feels* like."

Halvery didn't think he would agree, although he had to admit he had no point of reference. He swallowed. "Do you...want me to try?" Anxiety washed through him.

Roup seemed to sense it and rubbed against his chin. "Can you imagine me enjoying anything that made you afraid?"

"No," admitted Halvery. He swallowed. "What do you want me to do?"

"Turn over," murmured Roup and then he laughed. "But come away from the edge of the bluff first, so that you don't make a spectacle of yourself."

Halvery shook with laughter. "You want to drag me?"

"I'm not sure I could."

Halvery got up and followed Roup away from the edge of the bluff. Roup was walking backwards and sideways, back arched in a playful posture. He lashed his tail and made a feint. Halvery accepted the invitation to chase.

Roup tore away from him, flinging up clods of earth and pine needles. They sprinted pell-mell to the pinnacle, where they'd had that awful fight the night before Moashi's challenge. Roup circled it, as though making a conscious attempt to create better memories here. He dodged Halvery's pounce, and then charged joyfully back down, into the shadows of the sweetly scented pines. He whirled suddenly, and they grappled in a clawless mockery of combat. Roup flipped them and came up on top. He caught Halvery's throat in the gentlest of grips, and pressed him back against the earth.

In spite of the barely-there pressure, Halvery had a momentary flashback of Roup pinning him in his den—humiliation, absolute helplessness, and then a sensation like drowning. *Please don't choke me.*

Roup was suddenly licking his muzzle. Halvery realized, to his embarrassment, that he was trembling. He opened his eyes to see Roup's worried face a nose-breadth from his own. "I shouldn't have suggested this. Come on, get up; I'm sorry."

Halvery felt like an idiot. "Well, I am curious," he managed. "I do usually like t-trying things."

Roup's expression of pity was almost too much to bear on top of everything else. "You're panicking," he whispered.

Halvery shut his eyes. "I feel like you have me on my back nearly all the time." He swallowed. "I know that doesn't make any sense."

Roup gave a sad chuckle. "Well…it sort of does."

"Roup, I can't do what you do. I will lose my mind, and not in a good way."

"Oh, ghosts, Halvery, I wasn't going to suggest that. But if you lie here a moment longer, you can tell me whether you like my idea, and if you don't, we'll stop." He leaned close to Halvery's ear and murmured. "And then I promise I will put my tail over so nicely, and you can keep me on my stomach for as long as you want."

Halvery gave a shaky laugh.

Roup stepped squarely over him. Halvery looked up, feeling acutely vulnerable. He had an intense, instinctive urge to turn over, to guard his softest parts, to protect himself.

Roup started licking his stomach. He licked and nibbled his way down, pausing over nipples to suck and nuzzle. It felt shockingly personal in a way that mounting another cat never had. Halvery's breathing deepened. He could feel his body relaxing. A sense of warmth spread through his innards. By the time Roup got to his lower belly, he was beginning to whine. The first lick over his erection made his toes curl.

"Ghosts, Roup," he whispered.

Roup paused to say slyly, "You want to turn over?" His tongue lapped under Halvery's tail, then back up over his lower nipples.

Halvery surprised himself with a spontaneous kick. He growled, "Only if I get to mount you immediately."

"That might be fun sometime, but no."

Halvery didn't think this could feel any better, and then Roup started sucking. He started kneading Halvery's belly with his paws, purring.

Halvery bit off a caterwaul. Climax hit him in a rush that blurred the world—pleasure mingling with that heightened sense of exposure, of intimacy. He lay still for a moment, gasping.

Roup slid back up his body and lay down belly to belly with him, licking his face, still purring. "*That* is lying down," whispered Roup.

Halvery put all four paws around him and tucked his head under Roup's chin.

Roup laughed.

They lay like that for a while, lazily grooming each other. At last, Roup said, "Lyndi and I have been toying with an interesting idea. Arcove wants some project that ferryshaft and creasia could cooperate on, and we've been thinking: common way trails all over the island."

Halvery frowned. "All over...?"

"Yes. We would need to patrol them, of course. To keep them safe and keep an eye on things everywhere. And if they were a joint project, ferryshaft wouldn't feel as though we were increasing our own range at their expense."

Halvery screwed his eyes shut. He shifted a little, and Roup got up and lay back down beside him. Halvery rolled over. "Patrol them... So, these trails would be part of our territory?"

"No," said Roup firmly. "'Common way' means everyone."

"But...we'd be defending them?"

"Yes."

"You just said they're not our territory."

"Correct."

Halvery had that sense of bewilderment that frequently plagued him when talking to Roup. His instincts rebelled at the notion of defending territory that somehow belonged to everyone and no one. He could feel anger trying to rise up and crowd out confusion and uncertainty. Roup shot him a worried look, as though Halvery might start shouting.

Instead, he tucked his head against Roup's shoulder and said plaintively, "Roup, I don't understand."

Roup leaned against him and licked his head. "I know. But you're listening?"

"I'm listening," groaned Halvery. "I don't think I'm smart enough for this."

"You are."

Halvery opened his eyes. "Wait a moment… I just realized you're *working*."

Roup blinked. "Well…I was just thinking about it—"

Halvery stood up. "Oh, no. Not while you're flirting with me, you're not." Roup laughed as Halvery grabbed him by the scruff and dragged him deeper under the trees.

"At least let me finish the thought—"

"No. I was promised you on your belly."

Roup smothered a laugh. Then Halvery got his tongue under Roup's tail, and he was no longer laughing. He let out a long breath, stretched out on his stomach, and arched his back. *Getting on top of me certainly put you in the mood.* Roup was making little impatient noises and pushing his hips up.

Halvery stopped licking and slid along Roup's body, letting his weight and heat settle down over his partner.

Roup whined. He pressed his hips up into Halvery's stomach with an eagerness that Halvery found extremely compelling. Halvery didn't press himself inside, though. "It's my turn to try something."

"You try something every time!" objected Roup.

Halvery continued in a cheerful murmur, "But you can go ahead and explain these new trails to me if you like. I won't stop you."

Roup choked on a laugh. He broke off in confusion as Halvery tipped them both onto their sides. He waited to see whether Roup was going to struggle. When he didn't, Halvery curled his hips and finally slid in under Roup's tail.

Roup squirmed in some combination of discomfort and confusion. "What are you doing?"

"Trying something," repeated Halvery. He raised the upper half of his body, careful to keep his hindquarters exactly as they were, and curled over. It was much the same posture he would have adopted to clean his own nethers. It was quite easy to lick Roup's erection, making him gasp and twitch.

Unfortunately, it was impossible to thrust in this position. Still, Halvery stayed inside and kept licking while Roup quietly lost his mind.

"You know," said Halvery between licks, "while I do love listening to you caterwaul, listening to you try to swallow it is even better. Shhh, Roup, there's a whole tournament down there."

Roup gave a desperate groan and climaxed in a toe-curling spasm. It was almost enough to push Halvery over the edge even without thrusting. He remained still and let the trembling subside. "Am I giving you something to think about, Roup?"

"I am not thinking about anything right now."

"Even better."

Roup caught his breath. "Why *are* we doing it like this? I mean, I'm not complaining, but…"

"Oh, I just wanted to see whether you like getting licked with me inside you."

Roup flailed awkwardly with his front legs. "Well, yes, but…it doesn't seem like the most enjoyable position for you."

"No, this was just a test. I thought Arcove might like to do the licking next time."

"Oh." Roup somehow contrived to look more embarrassed than he already was in this odd position.

Halvery uncurled and rolled them back onto their stomachs. By some astonishing turn of good luck, he managed to do so without breaking contact. He murmured against Roup's ear. "I thought he might like to lick you and knead your belly with me inside you. Does that sound like fun?"

Roup laughed, shaky with nerves. "Have you been lying awake days…dreaming up things for the *three* of us?"

"How could I possibly not!" exclaimed Halvery. He heaved a sigh. "I realize that the two of you are above such nonsense." He started to move—a gentle rocking, searching for the perfect angle.

"Oh, don't be so sure," panted Roup. "He's been…trying things lately."

Halvery was delighted. He brought his weight down and casually pushed one of Roup's back legs out from under him. "I do hope they were things that made you forget how to talk."

"Did you tell him something about my paws?" demanded Roup.

"I might have told him to try licking them."

"Well, he did."

"I hope the results were interesting."

"Let's just say we did not catch any deer that night."

Halvery lost his rhythm and buried his nose against Roup's nape, laughing.

"We've done things the same way for forty-odd years!" exclaimed Roup.

"Time for something new."

"You are certainly something new." He broke off in a gasp, whiskers and ears fluttering.

"You're so cute, Roup," murmured Halvery. "You're so beautiful."

Roup tilted his head all the way up to look at Halvery, nose to nose and upside down. "I love you," he whispered.

Halvery couldn't think of a single joke. Or even a proper compliment. "My heart at your feet, Roup."

Sometime later, after Roup had forgotten how to talk and then remembered again, after Halvery had lost himself in the pleasure of his partner's body, after they'd both watched his five-year-old daughter put one of Stefan's officers on his back, Roup said, "Can I talk to you about the new trails next time? Or will that upset you?"

Halvery sighed. "How can I even be sure you'll visit if you can't tell me something I'll hate?"

"Well, you've got my cubs for one."

"I suppose there is that."

"I'd like to sleep here today."

"Oh, good. I'd like to sleep in a pile with you and Ilsa and our shared litter. That would make me very happy."

Roup smiled so hard his eyes crinkled. "I'll be back before a month."

"Maybe bring Arcove?"

"Maybe."

Halvery gave him lick on the nose. "Come back anytime, Roup. I look forward to hearing the next thing that I'll hate."

Final Note

Dear Reader,

Thank you for coming along on this journey. I wasn't planning to return to this universe after finishing *Hunters Unlucky*. Now, over the last three books, I've added a number of words equivalent to the original novel!

As of this writing, I have drafted yet another Hunters Universe novel that continues the themes of *Bright Side*. It's called *Legacy*, and I'm not ready to publish it yet. I have quite a few other ideas for this world, ranging in length from short stories to novels. I don't know when those will be available, but you can get updates on my website (abigailhilton.com).

Yours,
Abigail Hilton
September, 2022

Chapter Notes

Part I, Chapter 3
One interesting thing I am finding about this story: the Coming of Age stuff from the original is still here. Moashi, Costa, Ilsa, Carmine, Teek, and Wisteria are youngsters and/or young adults who are learning and doing things for the first time, trying to figure out how to leave a mark on their world. But they're in the background. We're not in their heads, and a lot of their struggles are happening off-screen.

Adult-Abbie wants to put the adult characters in the foreground. And I don't mean *young* adult characters. I mean the ones who've been around for a while, the ones who've had some tragedies and some triumphs, and lived long enough to say, "We won. Now what?"

In the original *Hunters* novel, there were certainly adult dynamics, sexual and otherwise, going on between adult characters. But they were mostly in the background. The kids and their struggles were in sharpest focus. In the stuff I want to write now, that is reversed.

Part I, Chapter 4
I have been dying to write this conversation between Halvery and Lyndi since this book got started. It was one of those conversations I heard clearly in my head while brainstorming the novel. I may be giving Lyndi too much insight. I'm letting her say a lot of things that I know about these characters, but I never thought I'd get the chance to spell out.

A little context regarding the ages: a three-year-old creasia is the equivalent of a 13 or 14 year-old-human. A four-year-old would be about 14 or 15. A five-year-old would be 16 or 17. A six-year-old is 18-20 (this is when they reach true physical maturity).

There are several places in here where Lyndi tries to explain concepts for which she has no words. For instance, she doesn't have the phrase "midlife crisis." She's trying to tell Halvery: "Your midlife crisis was Ilsa. Roup's midlife crisis was *you*."

She also doesn't have words for things like "boundaries." She's trying to say that Arcove and Roup need some boundaries with each other. They sort of raised each other *while* fucking each other, and that is not a good combination or a recipe for any boundaries. However, they do, in fact, have some boundaries with each other. They have the ability to say "no" and to disagree. Lyndi is trying to tell Halvery that that's a good thing, and everyone should want them to maintain that amount of distance and perspective.

As an author, it's frustrating not to have the short-hand human vocabulary for these concepts. On the other hand, writing these characters and their world forces me to ask myself "What is a midlife crisis, actually? What *are* boundaries anyway?" Sometimes that's an interesting exercise.

The detail about postmenopausal creasia still occasionally mating is something I wish I had found a way to say earlier in the story, possibly back in *Distraction,* but there just didn't seem to be a good place for it. This means that Moashi does have some sexual experience with females, even though all of his mates are past breeding age. It makes his conversation with Halvery at the beginning of this book more meaningful, because he's not speaking from a place of total ignorance or exclusively homosexual experience.

The part at the end with Storm, Tollee, Myla, and Costa is funny to me, and it just keeps developing on the page. Storm had a role in this book when I first brainstormed it, but I wasn't planning anything for Costa. Her appearance at the creasia council was a surprise. I didn't know Tollee would get to talk, or that I'd have Myla show up, but here they are!

Part I, Chapter 6
We've hit a point in the story where I had to make decisions about how to cover a lot of ground fast. The book could easily sprawl and turn into a 250K brick...or three books.

One thing I'm doing to prevent that is sticking to Halvery's point-of-view as much as possible. We're not seeing Roup's plotting, thinking, and maneuvering during this period. We're not getting Storm's point-of-view, which would add entire subplots. We're not seeing Arcove's back and forth with his various officers, the telshees, other advisors, etc. We're not getting point-of-views from the kids, seeing their goals and maturing.

We just get Halvery's view…which is a lot simpler.

Part I, Chapter 8

Obviously, the part with Costa is pretty darn cute and the irony is pretty darn thick. Here we've got Arcove, Roup, and Halvery babysitting Storm's foal, whom he has willingly left with them as the safest option.

The different ways they deal with her illustrate their personalities. Halvery physically restrains her and is quick with the threats of violence. But he's kind of a softy underneath. She knows him too well, and this is not terribly effective.

Roup plays word games with her. He would eventually get what he wants, but at the cost of revealing more about himself than he'd like.

Arcove is a little of both. He'll dialogue with her, but unlike Roup, he never tips his hand. He's got no qualms about threatening her, but he uses words to dissect down through the layers of her reaction until he identifies the threat that actually means something to her. *Then* he applies force. Ironically, the thing that scares her the most is the loss of his goodwill. Once he realizes this, it softens his response to her behavior.

Part II, Chapter 1

Things are about to get twisty, guys. Wheels within spinning wheels.

My short stories often have the characters solving two interlocking problems. While *Bright Side* is a hefty novel, it's episodic, and the structure is more like a short story. So in this case, Halvery's attempt to reproduce Roup's coat color is one (lighthearted) problem, while Roup's struggle to save the creasia in the Southern Mountains is the other (much more serious) problem.

Since this is a novel, we also have a bunch of subplots—Costa's strained relationship with Storm, Moashi's mentor relationship with Halvery, the highland curbs' search for lost kin, antagonism between the highland curbs and the creasia, Wisteria and Ilsa's den council, Carmine's promotion, the fate of Roup's clutter, tension in Arcove and Roup's relationship precipitated by events following Dazzle's attack, Nadine's illness and desire to pass gracefully, etc.

Plenty of subplots, which will all be addressed. But Halvery and Roup are the main characters, and the problems they are trying to solve are the two central problems of the book. The solutions to these problems do not interlock in the way that I usually interlock such solutions. However, these problems are related emotionally. Ilsa's upcoming litter gives Roup and Halvery a very personal stake in the situation with Sedaron, who intends to target cubs of this age.

Part II, Chapter 3

I've been slowly fleshing out the members of the little fight club from *Distraction*. We got to know Moashi, then Ilsa, now Costa. She was the youngest, the equivalent of about 8-10 years old during *Distraction*. Now she's 13 or 14 in human years. She makes a safe confidante for Halvery and allows him to say things that he's unlikely to say to a peer.

I had considered having him talk about his brother to Roup. But Roup probably already knows. It probably got mentioned early in their acquaintance—not as a sad story, but as a one-sentence fact about why Halvery doesn't like ferryshaft. In *Hunters,* he describes them as "nasty animals who eat cubs," but we don't get a story about it—no victim with a face.

Roup would already know about Halvery's brother, but Roup would have gotten that information at a point in time when he thought of himself as more-or-less a ferryshaft. At 5 years old, Roup would have processed this information as a threat and a reason not to trust Halvery. Roup and Arcove were traumatized youngsters themselves, and they did not have the emotional bandwidth to process Halvery's trauma or to appreciate how that early loss affected his ability to bond with others, particularly with male companions in his clutter.

Halvery was also rejected by his father in a fairly ugly fashion (that story comes out later). His mother ends up being the only "safe" person to love from that period in his life. This is one of the reasons he bonded with his female mates so powerfully and at such an early age. Many young male creasia form close bonds with their male clutter-mates during their bachelor years, but Halvery didn't.

There were some deleted paragraphs about this in that last scene in *Hunters* where Halvery is talking to Roup. If I remember correctly, I decided that it was a little too frank of a conversation about Arcove and Roup's relationship to work for young readers. I wanted 10-year-olds to be able to enjoy that book, so I cut the frankest portion of their conversation.

Halvery also likes cubs a lot, and you see a little of this in *Hunters*. Halvery is absolutely hostile towards Storm until he meets Teek and sees them interact. From that point on, his attitude towards Storm begins to soften. Halvery is the one who grabs Teek during the avalanche and keeps him from getting crushed. This tendency of Halvery's to shield cubs, even those unrelated to him, is one reason that Arcove likes him and quickly promotes him. It's not a universal trait in alpha creasia, but it's one that Halvery shares with Arcove.

Big picture: I really tried to keep *Bright Side* from sprawling. Sticking to Halvery's point-of-view helps with that. However, I did make the decision to begin Part II in Roup's, which means we know the moral quandary that he and Arcove are wrestling with.

Halvery, meanwhile, is in the dark. I did this on purpose. I think it's easy to empathize with Arcove and Roup, but a bit more difficult to empathize with Halvery. Jealousy is, after all, the least attractive emotion. I think it can be especially difficult to empathize with the way he feels excluded by their closeness and secretiveness. I wanted to give the reader a good look at what it feels like to be on the outside of that dynamic.

If Arcove was the marginal protagonist of *Lullaby* and Roup was the protagonist of *Distraction,* then Halvery is the (marginal) protagonist of *Bright Side.* I'm trying to stick to his point-of-view as much as possible, but I do think it's a more interesting story if we know what Arcove and Roup aren't telling him.

This whole book would be bigger and have a different flavor if I was showing Dazzle's point-of-view and developing the cats around him. That would make it interesting in a different way, because Dazzle has his own "damned if I do, damned if I don't" situation going on. But I'm trying to keep this tight, so we stick with limited points-of-view.

Part II, Chapter 8

Halvery and Arcove both have tempers. They have this in common. But Halvery's temper flares up hot and fast and then burns out quickly. His temper sometimes causes him to make mistakes, although he has gotten pretty good, over the course of his life, at withholding decisions and conversations until he calms down.

Arcove's temper is cold and slow. It can smolder for years. He's quite good at holding a grudge, and hurting Roup is the easiest way to get on his shit list. Time has no effect upon Arcove's anger, but actions, events, and new information do have an effect. It's not that he's incapable of forgiving serious slights; it's just that his forgiveness requires more than the passage of time.

Roup would like Arcove to say that he will show mercy to Dazzle under the right circumstances. Arcove is refusing to say any such thing. This is causing Roup a lot of mental anguish. He feels trapped by his promise to let Arcove handle the situation, which was given before this treacherous bargain with Thistle. The reason this fight between Arcove and Roup turns so ugly so fast is that they *haven't* been arguing. They've just gotten really passive-aggressive with each other, and so the tension has built and built.

Regarding Roup's game of tag immediately after the fight: Roup has always made Arcove play. He's the only person who does this, and it is a significant element in their friendship. You see this in the very first scene between Roup and Arcove in *Hunters Unlucky*. Roup wakes him up from a Keesha-induced nightmare. They have a serious conversation, and then Roup coaxes him to play by the end of that scene. In *Bright Side,* you see Roup doing the same thing, only this time he is including Halvery in the game.

Part II, Chapter 9

I wasn't actually planning to talk about Coden so much in this book, but the last time Arcove and Roup were up here was with him. So of course they're going to think about him. Of course they're going to talk about him. He's not just their friend who died. He's a symbol of lost innocence.

While they're not saying it aloud in this scene, there are parallels between the situation with Coden and the situation with Dazzle. Roup discusses some of these parallels with Halvery in Part I. Roup thought he could talk Coden out of mistakes, and he couldn't. He thought he could talk Dazzle out of mistakes, and he couldn't. Arcove had to kill Coden (or something close to it), producing a lot of regret and poorly-healed wounds. Now it feels like something similar is happening again, but neither of them can think of a way to stop it.

Part II, Chapter 12

Well, I got these guys together. Book's over! (Kidding.)

If you've been reading my books for a while, you know that I'm trying several new things here. I've never written an M/M/M scene, and I've never written a poly V. I've always been uncomfortable with poly Vs. They look too much like a love triangle, which I abhor. They also look a lot like old-school polygamy, which always seems monstrously unfair to me.

In old-school polygamy, the person (always a man) at the point of the V is getting 2x (or 3x or 100x) as much love and intimacy as he would have gotten in a monogamous relationship. And the people at the ends of the V (always women) were getting half or a quarter or a 100th of the love and intimacy that they would have gotten in a monogamous relationship.

So I have an instinctive negative reaction to poly Vs. I've always written some degree of sexual interaction between even the less attracted members of a triad. But I don't actually think that all Vs are negative. And I really can't imagine any other structure for these three characters. Halvery and Arcove are not interested in interacting sexually with each other. They are interested in some degree of intimacy for sure. Halvery has an enormous platonic crush on Arcove. But they're not interested in sex with each other.

Roup, at the point of the V, is getting the most sexual attention. In spite of this, it would be ludicrous to say that Arcove and Halvery are somehow being short-changed in the sex department. They both have large dens full of female mates. Roup has the fewest other partners, but that is entirely his own choice. None of these guys are hurting for physical connection. This particular encounter is extra for all of them.

Finally, let us pause to observe men doing emotional work for each other. I feel like, in a more conventional story structure, these guys would unload these sad tales on Lyndi or Velta or Caraca or Nadine or Costa or Wisteria or Ilsa (look, I do have plenty of ladies in the story!). In a conventional structure, they might even direct these stories at Roup because he has some feminine traits and might be perceived as an appropriate character with whom to process emotional material.

Instead, I've got Arcove and Halvery talking to each other. And Roup isn't even awake! The trauma they're sharing is uniquely male in their society, and it makes so much more sense for them to talk about it to each other. They could get sympathy from female characters or from Roup, but the true empathy and absolution they're getting from each other is special in a different way.

If you're getting a sugar headache, you'll be relieved to hear that the rest of the book is mostly run, run, run, fight, fight, fight, double-double cross. An actual encounter with Dazzle coming up in 3...2...1...

Part II, Chapter 20

I've been looking forward to writing these chapters since I started the book. The scene on the ice where Costa is dodging the creasia closely mirrors Storm's first escape from a raid. I intentionally used some of the same language. Then, of course, the tactic with the bear is similar to leading Halvery's clutter into Eyal's pack. However, the real twist comes when Halvery jumps onto the branch to break it on purpose. Now he and Storm are both in the water. Again.

Part II, Chapter 21

So there's the 2nd half of that chase reprised. This is quite a lengthy conversation between Storm and Halvery. The limited point-of-view is part of the reason it goes on so long. If we'd had Storm's point-of-view this whole time, I wouldn't have to explain his state of mind. He'd still have to explain it to Halvery, but I would probably take some short-cuts.

Additionally, I'm having Halvery recap to Storm what is going on with Dazzle. I could have just skipped some time there: "Halvery briefly outlined what had happened." Instead, I recapped it in detail because I feel like some readers may need a review or clarification. I didn't originally intend for the reversals to get quite this complicated.

Part II, Chapter 24

This chapter has a lot of heavy lifting to do in terms of catching us up on events that occurred out of sight of our point-of-view characters. Some people will probably feel cheated that Sedaron died off-screen, since he was such an unpleasant villain in "Lullaby." I had originally intended to have Sedaron at the sham conference and then kill him shortly thereafter. Our heroes were supposed to narrowly escape the same fate as Sedaron, because Dazzle switches sides at the eleventh hour. Alternatively, I considered putting Sedaron and Arcove (weirdly and unhappily) on the same side versus Thistle and Macex.

But it seemed like any of those set-ups would weaken the novel and add needless complexity. Having three villains seemed likely to dilute all of them. And if I tried to redeem Sedaron or build any sympathy for him, that would dilute what I was trying to do with Dazzle.

Finally, I feel like Sedaron doesn't exactly deserve a nasty on-screen ending. I've made the reader love Arcove, Roup, and Halvery, so it's probably difficult to see Sedaron's point-of-view. But the fact is that he really did live through some ugly stuff involving these creasia, Arcove particularly. It is entirely understandable that Sedaron couldn't forgive them. Not everyone can be Charder.

Sedaron's inability to forgive Arcove or wish him well is not what makes Sedaron a villain. The thing that makes him a villain is his willingness to provoke new violence. That is where he crosses a line. But his vitriol towards our heroes is understandable. In a sense, his firm belief that future violence is inevitable and he needs to strike first is even understandable. Macex has far fewer excuses for his behavior. Thistle is somewhere in between.

Part II, Chapter 33
And that is the action climax of the story! Obviously lots of stuff here is intended to mirror the violence in Dazzle's cave at the end of *Distraction*. Thistle echoes some of Dazzle's sentiments from that meeting. Dazzle responds with Roup's words.

Roup and Halvery pull Dazzle out of the hole in the ice together, which is intended to recall Halvery's struggle to pull Roup out of the cave. It also represents Halvery's change of heart, since he refused to help Dazzle up the embankment the night before. Now he is willing to help him.

Made in the USA
Columbia, SC
06 March 2024

32287164R00274